Bipolar WINTER

Bipolar WINTER

Volume 1

Samuel David Steiner

Published by Tablo

Table of Contents

Prologue

Mansfeld, Germany
January 1491

The candle's soft light flickered off the rough stone walls as Margarethe moved quietly down the hall. Her thin slippers and linen shift did little to keep the bitter night air at bay, but she didn't mind. The chill kept her thoughts focused on something other than what dawn would bring.

I should feel honored. She reminded herself her sins would be forgiven—all she had to do was give up what meant most to her in the world. Redemption through sacrifice, as the Church put it. And by complying, she assured her family's place in Heaven, along with safety here on Earth. Wasn't that enough?

Still, warm tears slipped down her cheeks. She quickly brushed them away with her fingertips, and then took a deep breath and silently opened the door to her son's room. Candlelight pushed against the darkness, falling on her son's angelic face as she stepped over the threshold. Seeing he had kicked off his blankets, she smiled and set her candle on the small table beside his bed to tuck him in again. But her hands stilled as fresh tears flooded her eyes. Would she never see his sleeping face again? Never see him smile or hear him laugh?

Why, God? Why do you demand my son?

He stirred, his eyes fluttering open. "Mama?"

"Yes, Martin?" she said softly.

His eyebrows furrowed. "Why are you crying?"

She shook her head and swallowed past the lump in her throat before answering. "I just love you so much."

He tilted his head. "So, they are happy tears?"

She bit her lip to keep the truth from escaping and forced a smile. "Yes, my son. They are happy tears."

Fully awake, Martin sat up and studied his mother. "Are you worried about today?" Stunned, she quickly looked away, trying to collect herself as she picked up discarded garments strewn across the floor. "No, of course not. I am…just a little nervous, that is all."

"Not me," he said. "It is part of God's plan after all."

She froze, and then turned toward him, his expression serious. At only seven years old, his maturity continued to amaze her, and she wondered if this quality was what the Church had seen in him. She sat beside him on the bed and kissed his forehead. "Yes, my son."

The incessant clatter of hooves broke the early morning quiet as a small carriage, accompanied by a dozen riders, rattled along the pitted dirt road toward Mansfeld, Germany. Stripped of the usual finery and ceremonial red, the procession drew little attention, just as Pope Innocent VIII had intended. "We will be arriving shortly, Your Eminence," Leonardo Battista commented as the carriage lurched from another pothole. As the pope's most trusted cardinal, he worried about his companion's health. The long trip had been taxing, and there was still the return trip to Rome once their business in Mansfeld was completed. Seated across from him in the plush compartment, the pope yawned wearily. Leonardo leaned forward and spoke just above the noise outside the carriage. "May I ask a question?"

"Hmm." A smile twitched at the corners of Leonardo's mouth, but he quickly sobered. He knew he was pushing the margins of propriety, but his curiosity had gotten the better of him. Still, he hesitated. "What is it you wish to know?" the pope asked impatiently.

"Excuse my boldness, Your Eminence, but is she really a witch?"

"Does it matter?" Pope Innocent bit out, his expression stern, his eyes piercing through Leonardo. "She associated with witches. That is enough, is it not?"

Leonardo sat back and lowered his eyes. "Yes, Your Holiness."

The pope yawned again. "Witches are heretics, and all heretics must be punished, their sins too great to be forgiven through Christ's sacrifice."

Leonardo nodded. "But she will be allowed to live?"

"By my grace, yes. And in return, she will become our willing servant. She is perfect, as is the boy."

"From what I hear, he is an outspoken hellion," Leonardo murmured.

The pope let out a loud barking laugh. "That he is. Intelligent, too, from what his instructors report."

"And that is what you seek?"

The pope smiled and a shiver zipped up Leonardo's spine. "Precisely."

It wasn't his place to question the pope's motives, but it still didn't make sense. "What makes this boy special?" Leonardo thought. He is just the son of a copper smelter. "What are your plans for him?" he asked tentatively.

The pope stared at—or rather—through him for a moment. "God's will," the pope said finally. "He will take part in Septem Montes, the Seven Hills project."

Septem Montes? That was the plan put in motion by the nephew of Pope Sixtus IV twenty years earlier. Sixtus's nephew had been a mere altar boy at the time but had an intellect far beyond anything Sixtus had seen.

"So, he will be the first," Leonardo said slowly.

The pope nodded. "Yes. It will not be easy on the lad, but then nothing worth doing ever comes easy."

Leonardo couldn't help but shudder. He crossed himself then said a silent prayer for the boy.

"Stop the carriage before we reach the Luther home," Pope Innocent VIII said. "I will need to change out of these traveling clothes. It is important I give the proper impression."

"He is here. He is here!" Martin's eyes shone bright as he raced toward the front door. "Mama, our special guest has arrived."

"I hardly think anyone could have missed it," Margarethe muttered, wiping her hands on a kitchen cloth. She straightened the few treasures Martin had collected and displayed on the mantel above the hearth—a pigeon feather, a small stone, a gnarled twig—trying to appear calm, but her heart pounded in her ears and she feared she would faint at any moment. Taking a deep breath, she peeked at her youngest, Jacob, still asleep in his cradle, and then followed in Martin's wake.

Hans wrapped an arm over his wife's shoulders and gave her a slight squeeze. "Shall we go greet the pope?" They stepped out onto the front stoop and waited as an inconspicuous carriage and entourage of cloaked riders came to a halt in front of their small stone cottage. Martin shifted anxiously from one foot to the other. Margarethe rested her hand on his small shoulder, as much to stop his fidgeting as to appear unified in front of the leaders of the Church.

"Is he coming out?" Martin asked, glancing up at her.

"When he's ready," Hans replied calmly. But truthfully, he was just as anxious as his son. He didn't believe the accusations against his wife, but his opinion had proved to be of little consequence. Even his position on the town council wouldn't have saved her from the pyre. Only by the pope's grace had she been spared.

Dust from the road had long since settled but still the carriage door remained closed. *Has he changed his mind?* Fear shot through Hans as they waited.

Margarethe stood stiff as a board, staring at the carriage, dread filling her with each passing second. *They have come to take my son.* She shook her head. *No. They have brought salvation.* Without it, her life would be forfeited, and her family destroyed. Hans would lose his position with the town council, and her children would forever be persecuted as the spawn of a witch. No amount of indulgences would be enough to buy her family's way into Heaven. She pulled her gaze away from the carriage and looked at Martin. So young, so innocent. She couldn't bear the thought of what watching her be burned alive would do to him. Yet that was to be the fate of her two friends very soon. The town had found them guilty of witchcraft, blaming them for the harsh winter and dismal harvest, and now they awaited execution while she had been pardoned. While Anna and Sophia were indeed outspoken, independent, unmarried, and intelligent—making them outcasts—Margarethe had never witnessed them practicing witchcraft. But either way, it didn't matter. The fact they didn't attend Mass was enough to convict them in the eyes of their fellow citizens. When the three of them had been brought before the town council, Margarethe feared for her life.

Everyone knew the witch trials were just a formality. No one who had been accused had ever been pardoned. Then Hans received a letter from Rome, explaining that despite her sins, she would soon be called upon by the Bishop of Rome to serve a higher purpose. She naively believed her prayers had been answered, until she learned the Church planned to take her son. But what could they possibly want with the seven-year-old son of a poor copper smelter? She doubted the pope himself would travel so far just to have Martin become an altar boy. Lost in thought, she suddenly realized Martin had left her grasp and was running toward the carriage.

Hans took off after him, but Martin had a good head start, having bolted out so quickly. "Martin, stop!" Margarethe screamed. Nothing was set in stone yet. The pope could easily change his mind should Martin do anything uncouth. One simply didn't disturb the most powerful man in the world, the Vicar of Christ, the supreme judge and lawgiver.

Her husband was doing his best to reach their son before he brought disgrace to his family, but years of toiling in mines had injured Hans's knees, making him lag behind. Ignoring his mother, Martin reached for the door handle of the carriage and opened it. Inside sat two men. One was dressed all in white, a gold sash draped around his neck. Seated across from him was a man clothed in a black robe with a red belt.

"Hello, Martin," said the man in white. "It is good to finally meet you."

•••

"You want to do what?" Margarethe asked, stunned.

"It is not your place to question His Holiness!" The thin glass of the windows rattled with Leonardo's booming voice. How dare this impudent witch do anything but grovel before Pope Innocent VIII.

The pope raised his hand. "She needs to know and agree fully. Without her consent, this plan will fail."

"Yes, Your Holiness," Leonardo replied, stepping back.

Margarethe shot a look at Leonardo, his head bowed, arms folded across his chest. "You do not approve of me."

Leonardo looked to the pontiff then, with a sneer, said, "No. All heretics need to be punished for their sins. Their only mercy should be given in death."

"But I am not a heretic. " Margarethe paled. So, they didn't believe her. Had they really only pardoned her to get their hands on Martin?

"There are tests we can do to be sure." Leonardo's smile held no comfort. Hans, who had been sitting quietly at the table listening, couldn't help the involuntary gasp at the thinly veiled threat. Those tests always resulted in death. Either the woman was determined to be a witch and burned alive, or she never survived the trial—which was the only way she would be deemed innocent.

Seeing Hans's clenched fists, Leonardo realized he had gone too far. The man was a good Christian who had just married the wrong woman. Feeling compassionate, Leonardo gentled his voice. "Of course, we have dismissed all charges against your wife. All we ask is that you allow us to train your son for the greater good of our Church and people."

Margarethe knew she should bite her tongue, but she couldn't just stand by and watch her son be used by these men. If they could so easily toy with her life, what would they do to Martin? "But how will this be for the good of the Church? You are telling us you want Martin to be trained to turn against the Church."

Pope Innocent VIII stood, stretching the kinks out of his legs. Two weeks was far too long to sit cooped up in a carriage. "That is correct," he said. "He will turn against us, with our blessing. Your son will be an important part of history. He will shape the future of our religion."

Margarethe shook her head. "I do not understand."

"I know, my child," the pontiff answered. "It is complex, but all you need to know is that you are serving your Church in the highest possible way." Then he turned and focused his piercing gaze on her. "And only this will allow you redemption for your association with those witches."

Margarethe nodded slowly. She wished with every fiber of her being to be forgiven and accepted into Paradise, where she might spend eternity with God. But was it right to subject her son to such unknowns for her own salvation?

"But why our son?" Hans asked. "We are grateful for your grace and compassion, but I just do not understand the reasoning." He had always hoped his son would become a lawyer.

The pope turned to Hans. "I understand your concerns and am allowing you to question us, but you must understand that this decision has already been made. Your son will take part in the plan laid out by my predecessors. This is bigger than any of us. It will not die with me, but will be passed along to the next pope and the next, far into the future." He walked over to the fireplace, smiling softly at the child sleeping peacefully in a cradle. "The truth is our numbers are declining. There is no vigor in our congregations, no excitement for young people considering which path they should follow. Christians are becoming complacent and lazy. They are easily tempted by the cunning words of heretics. And the problem will only get worse unless we take action now." He looked to Leonardo. "It is our job to convert every last man, woman, and child to follow our Blessed Redeemer and Glorious Lord."

Margarethe watched the pope pace around her small parlor, his crisp white robes so out of place among the simple wood furnishings.

"We need to wake up the world to the correct way of thinking before it is too late and their souls are damned to Hell for eternity," he continued excitedly. "We need a new wave of disciples—boys who can lead the charge in different areas of the world, giving people something to fight for."

"You're planning to start another Crusade?" Hans whispered, horrified.

"We need passion, Hans. Passion like our Church has not seen in centuries. Passion like Christ brought when He revolutionized the world with His message."

His question left unanswered, Hans tried again. "But what you are suggesting—"

The pope waved his hands impatiently. "Do you know your history, Hans?"

He frowned. "For the most part, yes."

"Then you remember the fate of the Waldensians."

Hans nodded slowly. Every Christian knew that story, how early in the thirteenth century, the Waldensians were persecuted for their teachings conflicting with the Church. "They were heretics, who were justly punished."

"Correct," the pope said. "We burned dozens of Waldensians at the stake. And? What was the result?"

Hans thought for a moment. "A dividing line was set, showing the people the correct path to choose for salvation."

"Our flock became more faithful, more devoted," the pope said, nodding in agreement. "We grew stronger."

Margarethe couldn't help but see the similarities between what had happened with the Waldensians and the current witch trials. Were Anna and Sophia being made an example of for the same reason? And now they demanded her son as well. Would the Church's greed never cease? "But the Waldensians were heretics," Margarethe said, trying to keep the rising panic from her "Our son is not. We are devoted followers of the only true Church and—"

Hans raised a hand and Margarethe fell silent. "I think I understand," he said. "Martin will become influential, will he not?" It wasn't the life he had planned for his son, but the alternative was far worse.

"That he will," the pope said with a knowing smile. "Your son will be known throughout time. People will follow his word and fight against us." His smile faded. "There will be bloodshed, but I will protect Martin and his future family. No harm shall come to him." Margarethe relaxed a bit, placated by the pope's oath. Yet, anxiety continued to nag at her.

The pope smiled at Leonardo then turned back to the boy's parents. "It's a small price to pay to unite this world under one church. Martin's followers will still be followers of Christ, but they will be impassioned to follow their own sect, with their own ideologies. Then later—much, much later—we will unite the seven factions we have created, and the Mother Church will collect her prodigal children home once more. Christianity will flourish."

•••

The first year was the hardest on the Luther family. Even though the Church had allowed her son to remain with his family during his initial training, Margarethe still mourned the loss of his innocence. Each day, Martin would attend school at the local chapel, and then receive hours of training from visiting monks. He slept only a few hours at night, and what little sleep he got was often restless. Having no time for anything but his studies, Martin stopped playing with his brother and friends, and all too quickly, the bright gleam of youthful innocence had faded from his eyes.

Margarethe's heart broke as she watched her energetic, imaginative son turn serious and often sullen. More nights than she could count, Martin would return home from his training with welts and bruises. But whenever Margarethe complained to Hans of their son's harsh treatment, he reminded her that it was God's will and they could not interfere.

After a few months, Martin stopped asking his mother to put salve on his wounds. Although she suspected the beatings continued, Martin couldn't stand to see her barely contained sorrow and guilt any longer. One day, when Martin was ten, he disappeared, never returning home from school. That night, Hans led men from the town in a search for him; three days later, Martin showed up on their front stoop—dirty, cold and hungry. He never did tell her what had happened, but Margarethe believed he'd had enough and ran away. Secretly, she'd hoped he would not return, though the life of a fugitive could never provide the freedom she wished for him. She often regretted her decision to allow the Church to use her son, and if given the choice, she would have gladly recanted it—if it would have meant Martin's freedom. But even if she burned for a crime she didn't commit, she knew the Church would still have its way. Martin would never be free.

From then on, Martin was different, his devotion and obedience almost frightening. The monks had succeeded in laying down the ground work for his training, imprinting on the boy the conviction that his calling was more important than anything, including physical suffering. Upon seeing this change, his mentors felt it was time to begin his true indoctrination, entrusting the eleven-year-old with the deepest secrets of the Church, things only a handful of men knew.

As part of their agreement with the Church, Hans had insisted that his son continue his regular education, so in 1501, Martin attended the University of Erfurt. Just before he graduated, a plague ravaged the town, killing several of his closest friends. The loss affected Martin deeply, and he began to question God's plan. Why had God allowed a plague to strike Erfurt? Why had his friends perished while he remained healthy? The only answer his mentors gave was that God sent the plague to punish sinners.

The experience left a deep impression on him. Martin Luther continued his training but with an uncertain heart. He wanted to remain worthy of God's approval, but he couldn't help wondering if this really was the correct path. Still in doubt, he graduated with a master's degree and decided to pursue his law degree, which was his father's fervent wish. Then, on July 2, 1505, while traveling back to Erfurt after a trip home, he was caught in a thunderstorm. A bolt of lightening struck the ground beside him, throwing him from his horse. Realizing his own mortality, Luther decided on the spot to devote himself fully to his calling. Withdrawing from law school, he sold his books and entered a monastery two weeks later.

Luther threw himself into the daily life of a monk, embracing the conviction that abandoning worldly comforts brought man closer to God. He wore the most uncomfortable garments he could find and routinely slept without covers at night. He ate only when necessary to keep his body from starving and refrained from speaking except to utter a confession or prayer. He studied every waking moment, and he was soon allowed to don the black robe of a confirmed monk.

He continued his private studies for five years, and then his mentors instructed him to go to Rome to receive his next orders directly from the pope. His pilgrimage to the Eternal City took forty days, and upon arriving, he was awe-struck by the beauty of the city of God. At the same time, he felt weary and disheartened. Hordes of pilgrims flooded the city, praying before relics for their salvation. Clergymen sold indulgences, promising the purchasers admission into Heaven regardless of their sins. The higher the price, the higher the level of forgiveness.

When Luther arrived at the Apostolic Palace, a priest led him to the pope's private apartment. A young man about Luther's age was working on a complex fresco of the imprisonment of Saint Peter when they walked in. The pope sat at one end of a long table, scrolls and letters spread out before him.

Upon seeing them enter, Pope Julius II said, "Raphael, why don't you enjoy lunch outside today?" The young man turned then bowed, laying his paintbrushes on a small worktable before leaving the room. "And you?" the pope asked, turning to face Luther. "Are you hungry?"

"No, Your Holiness," Luther replied.

The pope studied him carefully. "You should eat. Starving yourself is not God's will." Luther's mouth dropped open. "But—"

"I know," the pope said dismissively. "It is the way you have been taught. But from this moment forward, things are going to change."

Before Luther could sit down, a priest brought forth a tray laden with food, setting dish after extravagant dish on the table next to the pope. "Change? How?" Luther asked as he took a seat at the far end of the table.

"We need to prepare you for what is to come," the pope said. "It is finally time to put my plan—my Septem Montes—into action."

So, this is the man who is responsible for my life's work. Luther considered the older man's words as he studied him for a long moment. The nephew of Pope Sixtus IV, Pope Julius II, had conceived the secret plan of which Luther was now an integral part. A plan that would alter the course of Christianity. Conflicting emotions of admiration and distrust warred within him. This was a man Luther had been taught to revere his entire life. Yet with so much power and prestige, why did this man do nothing to help the pilgrims seeking salvation on his very doorstep?

Luther listened obediently to the pope's instructions, and by the time he returned home a few weeks later, his feeling of distrust had grown. The tranquility of his hometown did nothing to erase the scenes of corruption and profligacy he had witnessed in the Holy City. While he knew this was all part of the plan, that he needed to be shown such sin and debauchery to fuel his rebellion against the Church, he couldn't help feeling genuine disgust at what had become of God's Church.

As his training resumed, the monks relaxed their usual harsh and punishing methods, the need to cultivate fear of the flesh no longer necessary. Instead, they focused on nurturing the seeds of the new doctrines that had already taken root within his mind.

"You will need to lash out against us," his tutors reminded him.

"I am well aware of that," Luther said. The full impact of what he would need to do both terrified and excited him, allowing doubt to creep in once again. He would be going against the most powerful men in the world, almost all of whom knew nothing of the truth behind his actions. But the thought of sparking a fire in the hearts of the people, inciting them to take control of their own salvation, pushed him forward.

"You are destined to be part of God's plan. You can and will carry out your mission," his tutors continued. Luther nodded slowly. "And remember, we will always be watching."

•••

On All Hallows' Eve in 1517, Luther hammered his disputation, the Ninety-five Theses, to the door of the All Saints' Church of Wittenberg, which his tutors found fitting. The treatise objected to Church practices in ways that had never been dared before and resonated with the people immediately. Luther didn't have to wait long for a reaction. For a monk to speak out publicly against the Church as he did was tantamount to declaring war.

By January, the printing presses were running continuously, distributing copies of the Ninety-five Theses throughout Germany. The peasants relished the David and Goliath story, siding with their newfound hero. People started questioning the tax-like tithes the Church demanded. The belief that they could find salvation without paying for indulgences took hold and spread like wildfire.

While keeping up a front of outrage and disgust, Pope Leo X gave Martin a private blessing to start the Protestant Reformation soon after. He, like the popes before him, was well versed in Septem Montes and played his part zealously, depleting the Church's funds like no other pontiff before him. His feasts and boar hunts were infamous for their debauchery and gave Luther more fuel for his reformation, as he rallied the people against the sins of the clergy and their abuses of power and laid the foundation for his own religion.

Few men knew this was the plan all along.

•••

Outside Worms, Germany
1521

The Diet of Worms had gone just as Martin Luther had expected. During the three-day trial, Luther had repeatedly been brought to face the council, presided over by the Holy Roman Emperor, Charles V, himself. An honor to be sure, but one that would only help fuel Luther's reformation. Monarchs, whether they be kings or emperors, should have no authority over the will of God.

At first, Luther made a show of repentance, even going so far as to extend the trial by requesting time to consider his answer. But he had known the moment he was summoned to appear before the Diet what his answer would be. He refused to recant any of his writings, issuing a challenge to the council that unless it could convince him by Holy Scripture of his errors, he would recant nothing. The challenge went unmet, as the council was unable to support its accusations with scriptural evidence.

His stand against the Church had not been well received by clergy, and the faithful were divided in their support. But it mattered little. Everything was going according to plan. Perhaps too well, Luther thought as he rode back to Wittenberg, Germany. He left the town of Worms before a final edict had been issued, but he already knew what the council's decision would be. The emperor would declare Luther an outlaw, no doubt banning his writings and demanding his arrest.

Despite Luther's resolve, a shudder ran through him. He would face the very real possibility of being killed on sight. Being labeled a notorious heretic would provoke dogmatists to come after him. He couldn't help wondering if Septem Montes had planned for this as well. Making him a martyr would surely fuel the revolts that had already broken out across Germany, solidifying his reformation. With only a few in the Church aware of the plan Pope Innocent VIII had entrusted to him three decades prior, Luther would need to act carefully going forward. He knew he had Pope Leo X's blessing, despite the fact the pontiff had issued an edict excommunicating him several months before. But Luther had little fear for his eternal soul. This was God's Will, after all.

Everything he had done was in accordance with Septem Montes, the Seven Hills Project Pope Julius II had devised half a century earlier.

Lost in thought, Luther nearly missed the pounding of horse hooves behind him. He peered through the carriage's rear window, but despite the height of the May sun, the forest was dark, obscuring his view. Someone—rather, half a dozen someones—rapidly approached, a cloud of dust billowing behind them. Highwaymen? Fear compelled Luther to whip the reins, urging his horse to go faster, even though he knew there was no way a horse pulling a two-wheeled carriage could outrun a group of riders. Immediately, he regretted his decision to reject the offer of Prince Frederick III, Elector of Saxony, to secure safe passage for him to and from the trial. Yet once the emperor's decision was announced, even the prince himself would be punished for aiding Luther.

"They're not here for me," Luther told himself. How could anyone have possibly known he would be traveling this road? True, this was the most direct route to Wittenberg, but most travelers chose to go the long way, avoiding the forest entirely. Cast in shadow even at midday, the road through the dark forest was indeed disconcerting. Luther took this route for that very reason. The fewer people he encountered, the better.

The six riders continued to barrel toward him. Luther pulled his hat further over his eyes and veered his coach to one side, hoping the riders would continue past without paying him any heed. He couldn't be overtaken now, not when he still had so much work to do. His reformation had only just begun.

Within a heartbeat, the horsemen surrounded him, forcing his gig to a halt. He froze as each masked rider aimed an arrow at his chest. So they really were here to kill him. It didn't matter whether their target was his money or his soul. Dying here would end everything. For all of his training to no longer fear the flesh, his heart raced and his hands became so slick with sweat Luther could scarcely keep hold of the reins. He said a silent prayer, begging the Lord to allow him to live long enough to complete his work. His tutors had insisted that should he not fulfill his role in Septem Montes, Luther would forfeit his salvation. Eternal damnation would be all that awaited him.

He reached for the small coin purse tucked beneath his robes, hoping to barter for his life, only to hesitate when one of the men dismounted. Pulling his sword on Luther, the man climbed into the carriage. He pulled a length of rope from his pocket and tied Luther's hands together, securing them to the side of the gig. Then he retrieved a burlap sack from another pocket and after a moment's hesitation, pulled it over Luther's head. "Forgive us, Professor Luther," the man whispered.

Just as Luther feared, this wasn't a simple heist. The men were operating under someone's orders. But whose? For a moment, he worried that Pope Leo X had rescinded his promise, but Luther quickly dismissed it. Septem Montes was too important. Even if the pope were fool enough to go against the plan, others within the Church would never allow it. Still, doubt crept in—an uncertainty that had plagued him since the beginning. It didn't have to be him. If he failed, the Church would simply start again. The work was important, but not necessarily the man.

The reins cracked and the carriage lurched forward. *Where are they taking me?* Fear began to smother Luther, more suffocating than the burlap hood secured around his neck. If they were planning to kill him, why not just be done with it? What better place to make someone disappear without a trace than this dark forest?

Bereft of his sight, Luther tried focusing on his other senses—the breeze against his bound hands, the creak of the wheels as they rolled along the dirt road. He hadn't felt the coach turn around, so he doubted they were taking him back to Worms and the emperor. That meant they were continuing north, toward Wittenberg. Although it was his home, he knew Wittenberg was not safe. Nowhere in Germany would be safe for him.

Beyond Wittenberg lay Berlin. Did the emperor plan to make an example of him? Burn him at the stake like the Waldensians three centuries before? No—although he ruled the most powerful empire in the world, even the emperor was still a vassal of the pope. During the long and arduous ride, the uncertainty of whether he still had a role within Septem Montes weighed heavily on Luther. He offered up frequent and fervent prayers, yet his anxiety remained. His captors spoke little and only stopped when Luther insisted he be allowed to relieve himself. The bits of light he could see through the weave of the sack hood gradually extinguished as dusk fell, yet the men continued on their course as fast as the horses could carry them.

Luther had fallen asleep at some point, and when he opened his eyes, the carriage was stopped, and sunlight peeked through the hood. The man beside him untied Luther's hands from the side of the coach, but still he could not move. Every muscle in his body ached with the stiffness of remaining in the same position throughout the long journey. Luther felt a tug on the rope binding his hands.

"This way," the man said. Another grabbed Luther's arm, supporting him as he stepped down from the carriage. Gravel crunched beneath his feet. The only other sound came from the early morning songs of birds. No horses, squeaky wagon wheels, no children playing, no venders hawking their wares. None of the usual sounds of a bustling city.

The bird songs faded, and the gravel gave way to smooth stone as the men led him into a building, their footsteps echoing off the surrounding walls. Still, no one said a word. Finally, they sat Luther in a chair, untied the binds at his wrists and removed the burlap hood. Six men stood before him.

"Welcome to Warburg Castle, Professor Luther," one of the men said. "Forgive us for the rough treatment, but we had to cover your head, lest anyone see you and know you were brought here."

"But why...," Luther began, but the rest of the words failed him.

"His Highness, Prince Frederick III, ordered it so. He guaranteed you safe passage to and from the Diet of Worms, but when you fled, this was his solution—to make it appear as though you had been kidnapped. The prince will return from Worms in another couple of days. Until then, you are to stay here and keep out of sight. And while you are here, we will refer to you as the Knight George."

Again, Luther wanted to ask why, but he could only stare at them. "The emperor has not yet issued his final edict," another man said, "but the prince feels it will most certainly not be in your favor. As only the prince and the six of us know your identity, it would behoove us for you to pose as the Knight George and await His Highness's return."

The men each bowed, and then left the room, closing the door quietly behind them. Luther sat in silence for a long moment. When the shock finally subsided, he offered a prayer of gratitude. Prince Frederick was taking an enormous risk in harboring a notorious heretic, but with the prince's assistance, Luther would be able to complete his work. His Ninety-five Theses had been the first hammer blow, the first fissure in the great foundation of the Church, but more strikes were needed to awaken the masses, to make the people question what they had believed all their lives.

Seeing a small desk situated against a wood-paneled wall near the room's only window, Luther stood and walked to it. The men had set his meager belongings on the desk—his Bible, his theses, and his other writings. They had left a stack of blank pages, a quill, and small bottle of black ink.

Luther debated writing to his tutors and informing them of his whereabouts but quickly decided against it. If the letter were intercepted, he would not be the only one at risk. If the emperor discovered where Luther was hiding, everyone in Wartburg Castle would be punished, whether they knew his true identity or not. The days turned to weeks as Luther awaited Prince Frederick III's return and news of his punishment. Despite what the Church considered the actions of a heretic, word of his trial had spread, adding fuel to the fire of his reformation. But it was not enough. Luther needed to get the people out from under the apron of the Mother Church, or his reformation risked the same fate as the Waldensians'. He knew Christians needed to nurture their own faith, instead of blindly following their priests or bishops.

As Luther paced his small room, seeking guidance from familiar Bible passages, the truth struck him. "This," he thought as he closed the book and felt the weight of it in his hands. How blessed he was to be able to read the Word of God for himself. Not many in his country could read, but even fewer could read anything but their native language. Typically only clergy were taught Ancient Greek, the language of the Bible. To get the Word of God into the hands of the people, it needed to be translated.

Luther chose to begin with the New Testament, painstakingly translating each book from Ancient Greek into German, the people's language. He worked day and night, spending nearly every waking moment hunched over the small desk in his room. He repeatedly sent one of his six caretakers out for more paper and ink.

Translating offered Luther a fresh look at the beloved scriptures he knew so well, and as he labored, the work steeled his resolve. Luther believed earnestly in what he had written in his Ninety-five Theses and other volumes, crafting new theses as inspiration struck. His tutors would have him believe that everything he wrote about was a lie, fabricated to bring about a reformation of the Church that would return its lost children into the fold when the time was right.

No. The Church didn't need a staged reformation. It needed a real one. Using the pretext of continuing his work on Septem Montes, Luther grew his reformation under his own design. He enlisted the help of supporters like Andreas Karlstadt and Gabriel Zwilling to head a revolutionary reform agenda in Wittenberg while he remained in hiding at Wartburg. If his tutors got wind of his establishing a new church instead of the intended false branch of Catholicism, they would no doubt sanction his death.

Nearly a year after going into hiding, Luther finally completed his translation of the New Testament. He returned to Wittenberg in disguise, uncertain of the state of the reformation.

Zealots, calling themselves Zwickau prophets, had turned the social order into utter chaos. Their radical doctrines incited riots, a problem for the town council, but Luther was grateful for the religious confusion the zealots created. It paved the way for him to reestablish himself as a conservative influence within the reformation.

•••

Wittenberg, Germany
March 1522

Banishing the Zwickau prophets gained Luther the respect he'd hoped for from Wittenberg's town council. With it came the freedom to preach to the people without fear of arrest. Luther had taken his first step toward reining in his reformation, which had become like a petulant child during his absence. With the pulpit once again at his command, he hammered home his stance on bringing about change through the Word of God. But his control over events outside Wittenberg proved more tenuous.

Radicalism spread like a plague—one Luther was inclined to let fester. At first. The radicals' misconceived doctrines often provoked revolts, which further solidified Luther as a righteous authority among the rabble. However, the situation was quickly becoming unstable. As conflict broke out, Luther attempted to quell the rebelling peasant classes through his writings, yet their atrocities only increased. They destroyed religious statues and burned monasteries and libraries throughout Germany.

How dare they commit such sins in my name. Luther angrily paced back and forth across the length of his study. How many lives had been lost to their violence? How many of his Christian brothers and sisters had lost their homes or places of worship? Striding back to his desk, Luther picked up his quill and, once again, vented his outrage on the sheets of paper. He awaited news from Leonhard Koppe, a Torgau city councilman whom Luther had enlisted to aid in the escape of nuns from the Marienthron convent in Nimbschen. Their plan was simple, but Luther believed in its success, knowing few, if any, would search among barrels of herring for the missing nuns.

A sharp rap sounded at the door and he turned. "Come!" The door creaked open and a small boy poked his head in.

"Uh, this letter just came for you, Professor." He held out a folded sheet of paper, the flap sealed with a glob of red wax. Martin stood and took the letter, waiting until the door had closed once more before examining it. The insignia imprinted in the wax was one he recognized, matching a letter he had received some weeks before from the Marienthron convent nun, Katharina von Bora, when she had written to beg his assistance in helping the nuns escape the monastery.

Returning to his desk, he gently broke the seal and spread the pages of the letter out before him. The penmanship was hurried yet gentle.

Dear Sir,

I thank you for your assistance in our safe conduct to Wittenburg. My sisters and I shall be eternally in your debt.

Your man Koppe told me that you intend to ask our families to admit us once again into their homes. However, you and I both know that fear of canon law is a powerful adversary. Our defection from the Church will be viewed as no less than criminal. I ask instead that you find suitable husbands for my sisters, for they are more restless for marriage than life. As for myself, I shall marry none save you. For years, my life has been yours, my instruction within the monastery dedicated to assisting you with your most important work. Yet, my tutors have become restless of late. They know, Martin. And I fear how they will counter your reformation.

Eternally yours,

Katharina von Bora

Luther sat for a long moment, weighing his options. The foundation for his new church had already broken ground, taking root throughout Europe. Such flames would be hard to extinguish; yet, he knew the Mother Church was capable of doing just that. But would they? Would they risk crushing his reformation only to have to start back at the beginning? No, it was more likely they would find a way to turn what he had created to their benefit.

He picked up his quill and retrieved a fresh sheet of paper to pen a letter to the woman he could now count among his allies. He needed to know everything she had heard from her tutors. If her role was to help him, then he would accept, if for no other reason than to extend the Mother Church's illusion of control for a little bit longer.

•••

Vatican City, Italy
February 1524

Pope Clement VII eyed the other men seated around the large oval table. Newly elected to the papacy, he was by no means unfamiliar with workings within the Apostolic Palace. He had, after all, been the principal confidant of his cousin, Pope Leo X. Some of the faces that stared back at him were ones he knew well, yet this was his first time hearing of the Septem Montes.

Martin Luther had been a thorn in his cousin's side for most of his papacy and, now, Clement understood the truth. While Luther appeared to be in opposition to the Church, the unfolding of the Reformation was strictly controlled from behind the scenes of the Church. Until recently. Clement, however, preferred not to be involved. His hands were full with the Italian War.

"Holy Father?" one of his cardinals asked, as the assembled clergy waited for his response.

Clement sighed. "So, you do not believe he can be persuaded back onto the path?"

"We have little doubt, Your Holiness," another cardinal answered. "Let us just say, his tutors were quite…thorough in instilling hatred for the Church when he was a boy."

Cardinal Angelo, from the Kingdom of Castille, raised his hand and the pope nodded for him to speak.

"We have a saying in my country, Holy Father, that if a bull leaves the pasture, you do not let it trample your garden. If this Martin Luther will not return to the flock, then he should be put down."

"And lose half a century's worth of work?" a cardinal across the table bellowed. "What if the same thing happens again?"

"Calm yourselves," Cardinal Nicholas said. The oldest and shrewdest of his cardinals had served the Apostolic Palace longer than anyone, having ascended from the position of a humble friar. "Luther is simply the first step of seven. I have no doubt the others will branch off much more smoothly."

"Yes, but the first step is also the most important," another cardinal said. "The church Luther creates will have innumerable followers when the time comes to bring them back under our control. If we do not subjugate his church soon, we will have no guarantee of success."

Nicholas smiled and leaned forward, resting his chin on his laced fingers. "Angelo, did you not just tell me of a promising young priest from your country?"

"Sí, he has plans to attend the University of Alcalá within the year. But what—"

Nicholas held up his hand, cutting the cardinal off. "Holy Father, may I suggest a different course of action?" At the pope's nod, Nicholas continued, a sly smile on his wrinkled face.

"Since starting anew is not an option, and it seems Luther is unwilling to continue the work as outlined in Septem Montes, perhaps we should establish a new order, one that will…persuade Luther's church to fulfill its role when the time comes. This order could shepherd the other six branches as well, once they have been formed, should other unforeseen challenges arise. A society of soldiers, if you will. Christ's soldiers."

"Definitely the shrewdest," Clement thought, and the plan had merit. If anything, it would take the whole matter off his hands.

"And who do you propose we get to institute such an order?" one of the cardinals asked.

Nicholas's smile widened. "I believe Angelo's man will be just what we need."

Chapter One | Septem MONTES

Rome, Italy
February 2013

Aldo Lombardi nervously paced the large antechamber outside the pope's private quarters within the Apostolic Palace.

What on earth is going on? Am I really about to meet the pope?

Just six hours earlier, he was skiing with his parents at Speikboden on the Austrian-Italian border. Coming off a particularly challenging downhill run, he had plopped in the snow to unhook his skis when two stone-faced men in black suits approached and brusquely ordered him to come with them.

Definitely suspicious. Aldo decided it was best to ignore them. No one in their right mind would happily follow complete strangers, especially ones so impractically dressed for a day on the slopes. He scooped up his skis and turned to head back to the hotel when they blocked his path. After shoving their Pontifical Swiss Guard identification cards in his face, he quickly realized he had no choice but to comply.

Twenty minutes later, the men ushered Aldo and his hastily packed suitcase to their car. He didn't even have the chance to change out of his snow pants, let alone tell his parents he was leaving, and just like that, their surprise of a graduation trip to the Zillertal Alps ended as abruptly as it had begun. Also tried repeatedly to text his parents during the four-hour drive to Valerio Catullo Airport in Verona, but his cell reception was terrible anywhere outside Rome. For the duration of the drive, he sat crammed in the backseat of the guards' rented Fiat, feeling the most uncomfortable he'd been in his entire life.

Where are they taking me?

His anxiety increased as the guards maintained their stubborn silence, despite his demanding an explanation in both English and Italian. The hour flight from Verona to Rome was no better than the car ride. Realizing their destination was the Apostolic Palace brought only a brief moment of solace as Aldo's anxiety intensified for a whole different reason.

Did I do something wrong?

He chewed on the end of his index finger and gazed once again at the elegant interior of the antechamber. No one was escorted by the Pontifical Swiss Guard to the pope's private quarters without good reason. But only one thing came to Aldo's mind.

He continued to pace, the movement the only thing keeping his knees from trembling. *Please, Lord, don't let me throw up.* Aldo's stomach churned again violently.

Aldo barely managed to receive his Ph.D. in theological history from the Pontifical Gregorian University the previous week; his thesis and last two years of research were nearly refused by the graduation board. He couldn't fault them though. He'd known from the beginning that his topic was controversial, to say the least, but something in him refused to give up on it. And that stubbornness had nearly cost him his degree. Aldo sighed. His parents had surprised him with the ski trip to Speikboden without knowing how precariously close their son had come to not graduating.

He pulled out his iPhone to try texting them again when the door to the pope's chambers opened. Taking a deep breath, Aldo turned to see an older gentleman in the formal red robes of a cardinal, and his heart dropped into the roiling acid of his stomach.

"Buonasera, Signore," Cardinal Sebastiano Bastianelli, incumbent of the Holy See said with a slight bow. The cardinal was highly admired in the Catholic world and was something of a hero to Aldo. But under these circumstances, Aldo remained cautious.

Aldo swallowed hard, trying to collect himself. Bowing, he said, "Uh, Your Eminence...um, am I..."

"Not to worry," the cardinal chuckled, "I'm not here to pass judgment." He then gestured Aldo into the pope's chambers. Aldo forced his legs to move, and as he entered the large room, his trembling stopped and his nervousness subsided. Famous works of art adorned the walls, and the ceiling was covered with frescoes he thought he'd only ever see in textbooks. His footsteps echoed as he crossed the marble floor, his eyes glued overhead. During his time in graduate school, Aldo visited the four Raphael rooms in the Vatican Museum multiple times, but these rivaled their splendor.

"Beautiful, aren't they?" Cardinal Bastianelli commented, as if reading his mind.

"Yes." Aldo longed to study them in detail, but reluctantly dragged his gaze away and looked around. Several seating areas, with plush armchairs surrounding low tables, were spaced about the room and numerous bookshelves lined the walls. He suspected they held some of the rarest books in the world and itched to peruse them.

Finally, his eyes came to rest on Pope Benedict XVI. The elderly man stood patiently beside a massive desk, a vaguely amused expression on his face.

"Signore Lombardi," he said, in thickly accented English. "I have heard so much about you. I enjoyed reading your thesis on the division of Christianity. You have some very insightful theories."

Aldo froze as panic engulfed him. *What? The pope read my thesis?*

If his thesis had nearly resulted in his dismissal from the university, he could only imagine how upsetting it had been for the pope. Ashamed, Aldo immediately lowered his gaze. He felt so strongly about his research that he continued to pursue it, ignoring the advice of his professors. But he never meant to offend anyone.

Despite Cardinal Bastianelli's reassurance, Aldo could think of no other reason for his summons to the Apostolic Palace than his impending excommunication. He commanded his legs forward again and knelt before Pope Benedict.

"Your Holiness."

From the corner of his eye, Aldo noticed that Cardinal Bastianelli remained by the door as though quietly judging him. The pope extended his right hand. Aldo clasped it gently then bent his head to kiss the large gold ring on the pope's finger. The Ring of the Fisherman signified the pope as Saint Peter's successor and had served as a signet for sealing papal documents until the mid-1800s. Another set of artifacts he would love to study under different circumstances.

"Please, won't you join me for an espresso?" the pope asked, gesturing him to a chair.

What? Slowly rising to his feet, Aldo could only nod. He sat down in the plush armchair, his hands folded in his lap as he waited for a server to pour the dark brew into small white mugs. Then, just as silently as he'd appeared, the servant excused himself.

"I imagine you're wondering why you've been called here," Benedict said.

"Uh, yes, Your Holiness," Aldo replied, "The, uh, guards you sent were a bit vague on the details."

The pope chuckled deeply. "Yes, I suppose they were, mostly because they themselves were not informed. I simply said I wanted to see you and they brought you to me."

Aldo picked up one of the mugs of espresso and took a sip then smiled but said nothing. As the silence dragged on, he fought the urge to fidget, the tension in the room a thousand times greater than during his graduation board interview.

"Well, I can hazard a guess," Aldo offered. When the pope nodded, he continued. "It has to do with my thesis." He chanced a look at the cardinal who remained by the door.

The pope nodded again. "Yes, Signore Lombardi. Your thesis more than interested me. It concerned me."

Aldo's blood went cold as he imagined a future exiled from his faith, the primary motivation behind his chosen career. Maybe it would have been better to ignore his theories like his professors advised. He had already lost more than one friendship over his asinine ideas, and now it would cost him inclusion in the Catholic Church and his career, as well.

His thesis explored the seven main branches of Christianity, citing their commonalities over the often-debated differences. His conclusion bordered on heresy—that all of Christianity is essentially one religion with seven arms, and one major exception.

"Your paper was nearly rejected, was it not?" Pope Benedict asked.

Aldo swallowed. "Uh, yes, but somehow, at the last moment, the board decided to accept it, and I was able to graduate."

The corners of the pope's mouth lifted slightly. "Do you know why it was accepted?"

Because of the Grace of God? Aldo shook his head. "I had assumed that while the board may not have agreed with my theories, they saw the merits of my research." Aldo surmised the board recognized the value of time spent conducting scores of interviews and reading the written works of other Christian religions.

The pope chuckled softly. "No, it wasn't the board."

His mind spun. "Who then?"

"One man championed you," the pope said solemnly, his gaze piercing through Aldo.

Stunned, Aldo responded, "You, Your Holiness?"

"Yes."

So, I really did graduate by the Grace of God. But it didn't make sense. "Why?" he asked. "Uh, I mean, I'm grateful, but…"

"I didn't want to penalize you for getting too close to the truth," the pope said, shifting in his chair. "You single-handedly uncovered one of the deepest secrets kept by the Church for centuries." The pope frowned. "As such, your paper will never be published. Your research must never be made known to the public."

Aldo knew from the moment the graduation board first rejected his thesis that it would never be published. But hearing it confirmed by the pope himself still discouraged him. Not having one's research published was a virtual death sentence in his line of work. Not to mention all those years of legwork, reading, writing and revising—all for naught.

What am I supposed to do now?

"Not to fear. All is not lost," the pope said with a small grin.

How? If his research couldn't be acknowledged, it was as if he made it all up. He would be labeled a fraud, perhaps the biggest fraud since Charles Ponzi. Aldo stiffened in his chair. *Wait. Didn't he just say I'd uncovered a secret?*

"So, it's all true then?" he asked tentatively.

"Yes, Septem Montes is in full swing."

"Septem Montes?"

The pope nodded. "The Seven Hills. The true name for the connection you hinted at in your thesis. The seven distinct sects of Christianity were created intentionally, beginning with Martin Luther, just as you surmised."

Aldo slumped in his chair. *No way.* "I-I had pieces, but… There's more, isn't there?"

"Yes." The pope's expression turned thoughtful. "I'm curious. You never mentioned who created the concept of the seven sects."

"No. I wasn't sure who instigated it."

"But you must have had an inkling."

Aldo hesitated. "Yes."

"And?" the pope prodded. "What is your hypothesis?"

Aldo studied the intricate pattern of the rug beneath his feet. "I don't have enough facts to give an accurate conclusion." He could feel the pope's intense gaze, and beads of sweat formed on his brow. He knew without being told that he was quickly reaching the point of knowing too much. And not knowing what came after crossing that line truly terrified him.

"I didn't ask for facts. I'm curious about your theory," the pope said, leaning toward him.

Aldo tried to clear his throat, but the lump only grew bigger. "Well, um, Luther was obviously not the originator of the initial separation," Aldo said carefully. "It-it just never made sense, I mean, considering his background and his complete faith in the Catholic Church, even during the Reformation. It seemed like, from Luther's time 'til now, the course of Christianity was directed through the careful guidance of someone in power."

One of Benedict's eyebrows arched. Aldo couldn't blame him for being shocked. Even to his own ears it sounded like complete lunacy, not to mention treacherous.

"And who would that be?" the pope pressed.

Aldo looked up. The pope not only deserved his complete honesty, but also wouldn't accept anything less. And beating around the bush would only make matters worse. "It, uh..." Aldo coughed then tried again. "It seems to me that the originator would've been someone quite elevated in the Church, someone who had the will and desire to create offshoots of the Church." Though, to what aim, he still wasn't sure.

The pope nodded. "And? Who?"

Aldo took a deep breath. *He's really going to make me say it, isn't he?* "It had to have been a directive from your office." Even as the words left his mouth he couldn't believe he'd said them aloud. Accusing a pope of orchestrating such a plan, even if that pope had lived four centuries earlier, was treason. He stared at the rug at his feet, clenching his hands to keep them from trembling. There was no way he'd be allowed to remain a Catholic now.

The pope leaned back and graced Aldo with a gentle smile. "You look like a man awaiting the guillotine."

"Well," Aldo glanced at Cardinal Bastianelli, "excommunication is death to me."

The pope's eyebrows rose. "I am not known to excommunicate a parishioner for a simple honest answer." Then his face relaxed. "No, I have called you here for a different purpose entirely. I want to offer you a position."

"A job?" Aldo choked in disbelief.

"You have a bright mind and I need your help."

The pope needs my help? Aldo took a deep breath, trying to calm his chaotic thoughts. The day was becoming more and more surreal. He half-expected to wake up at any moment in the hospital from a skiing accident. "What sort of position?"

"We'll go over the particulars at a later date. For the time being, we need to get you up to speed with what has been happening." The pope's expression grew serious. "Our Church is in peril."

Aldo leaned forward. "What sort of peril?"

Benedict tilted his head. "You have an idea. You've been writing essays about it for the past nine months."

Aldo scanned his memory. He'd written numerous essays, mostly as a way of cataloging information he had uncovered during his thesis research but couldn't use in the final paper. But what had he uncovered that could threaten the Church?

"The Dark Internet?" Aldo asked after a moment. The pope nodded. "So, I was right," Aldo said, sitting back. His peers at the university had called his theories crazy. While he now knew he would never get the academic accreditation he'd hoped for, he still felt validated knowing he'd been right all along.

"What is the Dark Internet?" the cardinal asked, stepping away from the door to join them.

Aldo looked to the pope, who gestured for Aldo to elaborate. Turning to face the cardinal as the older man took the seat beside him, Aldo said, "The Dark Internet is a large underground network, buried on servers unreachable from the internet the rest of the world uses. It's vast, uncensored, and untraceable unless you know how to access it."

Cardinal Bastianelli nodded, yet his brow remained creased with confusion. "How does the Dark Internet relate to the World Wide Web?"

Didn't I just explain that? "Uh, well, if you think of the World Wide Web as an iceberg, the part above water would be the known or public internet, while the underwater portion is the Deep Web and Dark Internet. The Deep Web has never been indexed and can't be reached by standard search engines. Navigating it is nearly impossible unless you know what you're looking for. Below that lies the Dark Internet, comprised of computers and servers linked by an unhackable network. It's an entirely hidden internet."

"But what does this have to do with the Church?" the cardinal asked.

"When researching my thesis, I discovered that Church information has been stored on servers connected to the Dark Internet. Perhaps even portions of the

Vatican Secret Archives," Aldo said. "Whether it's accidental or intentional, I can't say, but—"

"Preposterous!" the cardinal cried out. "Why have I never heard of this?"

Pope Benedict held up his hand. "Listen, my old friend. You are not privy to all the secrets of this office." Then he nodded for Aldo to continue.

"It, uh," Aldo's voice cracked, "kind of makes sense if you think about it. The vast library of the Archives won't last forever. Some of the most holy and precious documents are held in the underground, climate-controlled vault, but it might be safer to record and store the papers electronically."

"Yes, we can't risk the information being lost to future generations," the pope said, folding his hands on his desk. "And so, putting the two riddles together, what do you surmise, Signore Lombardi?"

Aldo thought for a moment, trying to find the connection between his thesis and his essays on the Dark Internet. "Septem Montes. It's been uploaded onto the Dark Internet," he breathed.

"Yes," the pope said, concern evident on his face. "All the historical documentation of what would be viewed as the biggest conspiracy on Earth has been circulating through the Dark Internet."

Aldo shot forward on his seat. "But why would—"

"If it's uncovered," the cardinal said, "the stability of the Christian world would be shaken to its core." It would be chaos. Christians everywhere would lose faith in their leaders, but most of all, they would blame the Catholic Church. But why had the Church created Septem Montes anyway?

"The riots that would break out could bring about the apocalypse," the pope nodded. "You see why we've asked you here, Signore Lombardi. We need your help."

Why me? I'm just a historian, not a systems analyst. But he had to admit this could all be his fault. If someone had found merit in his research, had read his thesis, then…"You think someone uploaded Septem Montes onto the Dark Internet intentionally?" Aldo asked, though he already knew the answer. He just had no idea who would do so or why.

The pope nodded slightly. "That is my fear. There have been rumblings from the Seventh. I think they may already know something."

"The Seventh?" Aldo asked.

"The seventh sect created from Septem Montes." Benedict steepled his fingers, his elbows resting on the arms of his chair. "Six of the seven distinct religions created kept to the plan, staying within the original design. However, one, the Seventh, strayed and is now like a rebellious teenager, seeking to gain independence at any cost."

"More like a demon," the cardinal muttered.

"Who are they? Which religion?" Aldo's mind raced, trying to put all the pieces of the puzzle together. But he was missing something, some major clue.

Pope Benedict and Cardinal Bastianelli glanced at each other. Then the cardinal said, "Let's take this one step at a time."

So, they don't completely trust me. Considering the magnitude of what they were discussing, Aldo couldn't really blame them. "But how exactly can I help? Don't you need someone familiar with the Dark Internet?" The task of tracking down all traces of Septem Montes on an untraceable network was way outside his field of expertise.

"We'll have to discuss that another day," the pope said, "but for now, I must ask you to surrender all of your research."

The stern look on the pope's face made it clear there was more to the request than simply confiscating his life's work. It was a gag order. Aldo nodded slowly. "Of course."

"Good," Pope Benedict said, standing up. As if on cue, the same server who had brought the now cold espresso emerged from a door at the side of the room and placed Aldo's laptop bag on the pope's desk. "I'll have David bring you a new computer to use this evening. We have a lot of work ahead of us. You should rest." The pope then turned to the younger man dressed in white robes. "David, please show Signore Lombardi to his room."

What just happened? Aldo sat, trying to wrap his head around everything. When Cardinal Bastianelli rested a hand on his shoulder, Aldo glanced up in surprise. The cardinal smiled. "You thought you'd get a break from your studies, didn't you?"

"Yes, I do apologize for cutting your vacation short," the pope said. "But not to worry, Signore Lombardi. I am sure you will soon realize the invaluable nature of your position here. You will have access to documents viewed by an elite few from your generation. Only a handful of cardinals are ever permitted to see the Vatican Secret Archives."

Perusing the Secret Archives was any theological historian's greatest fantasy. But the prospect of fantasy becoming reality left Aldo feeling overwhelmed. "I'm honored," he replied softly.

Pope Benedict smiled. "I'll see you at breakfast tomorrow at eight o'clock in the southeast courtyard. Sleep well, Signore Lombardi."

Sebastiano turned to follow the two younger men, but the pope laid a hand on his arm, stopping him. The cardinal nodded almost imperceptibly and returned to his seat, waiting for the door to close. Seated once again behind his desk, the pope said, "Sebastiano, you disagree with me, don't you?"

"It isn't my place to agree or disagree, Your Holiness."

The pope chuckled. "But you do nonetheless."

The cardinal remained silent, but raised his left eyebrow slightly, the most defiance he was willing to show.

"Are you familiar with Sun-Tzu?" the pope asked.

"Of course," Sebastiano said. "It has always been required reading at the university."

"I'm just keeping Signore Lombardi close, that's all."

Sebastiano's eyes flashed. "Really?" he whispered. "You fooled me."

"The next few weeks will determine whether our young historian is indeed friend or foe," the pope said. "Either way, he's mired himself in this so deeply, we can't afford to leave him unmonitored."

David led Aldo through the maze of corridors to a small yet elegantly appointed room. Aldo never imagined he would set foot within the Apostolic Palace, let alone be invited to spend the night. The walls breathed history, like a faint perfume, intoxicating him. He longed to explore, but the residual effects of anxiety and lack of sleep were taking their toll.

When David politely excused himself, Aldo tossed his suitcase onto the twin-sized bed and popped it open. As he sluggishly fished for his toiletry bag, he realized he was still wearing his ski coat and pants. *Great.* He'd met the pope looking like a dark blue marshmallow. Not that his first meeting with the pope could have gone any worse. With a sigh, he stripped off his coat and pants and shoved them into his suitcase. Thankfully tomorrow was a new day. One with fewer surprises, he hoped.

Needing a task to distract his mind, Aldo hung up his garment bag and inspected the charcoal-colored suit within for wrinkles. As he looked for an iron, he noticed a narrow door opening to a quaint balcony. From it, he could see Saint Peter's Square sprawled out before him. The square lit up the darkness as a few stragglers milled about despite the winter cold. Lights illuminated the statues of

Christ and His apostles atop the Basilica and reflected off its dome, making it glow invitingly.

Aldo sat down in a small wrought iron chair situated in the corner of the balcony and gazed at the view. Finally able to reflect on all the events of the day, he mused at how quickly his life had been turned upside down. Just that morning, he had awakened disheartened at the prospect of never finding a job in his field after barely managing to graduate. Now, the pope himself was offering him a job. Despite the seemingly miraculous turn of events, Aldo remained uneasy.

Feeling a vibration in his pocket, he pulled out his cell phone. Seventeen unread messages from his parents greeted him, and he groaned. How in the world was he going to explain this? He certainly couldn't tell them the truth, especially after the pope's gag order. He scrolled through the messages.

"Where are you?"

"Did something happen? Please call us."

"The rescuers are combing the slopes for you right now. Please be okay."

Guilt crushed him. At twenty-six, he sometimes forgot that he was still a child in his parents' eyes. And no parent should have to experience such worry. Confirming he had enough cell reception, he dialed his mother's cell number. He heard only crackling. "Mom? Can you hear me?"

"Where... you... thought... avalanche..."

"Mom, you're breaking up. If you can hear me, I'm okay. I had to return to Rome unexpectedly." He heard a ping as a small rock landed near his feet. Puzzled, he bent down and scooped it up.

"Do... your father..."

"Mom, I can't really go into detail right now, but I just wanted to let you know I'm safe. I'm sorry it took me so long to call."

"...home..."

The crackling went silent and he looked at his screen to check the connection. "Mom?" Nothing. He sighed. Well, at least she knew he wasn't trapped under feet of snow somewhere, but she wouldn't let this go anytime soon. No doubt she would hold this over his head like a noose for at least the next decade. He sent her a text message for good measure then tossed his cell on the bed and looked at the stone still in his left hand. *Where did it come from?* He was on the second floor, and there were no rooms above him. Rolling it around in his palm, he was about to toss it off the balcony when he realized it wasn't just a stone. A bit of paper had been wrapped around it.

Seriously? How hard is it to find a trashcan?

But why would someone bother to weigh down a piece of litter with a rock only to throw it up here? Smoothing it out, he noticed a short message written on the slip of paper, but between the surrounding darkness and his poor eyesight, he couldn't make it out. Rummaging through his suitcase, he found his reading glasses and slipped them on. He could barely make out the penciled letters—Cipro station NOW!

From his years of living in Rome while attending university, he knew the Cipro metro station was some twenty minutes away by foot.

Can't be for me. No one even knows I'm here. Well, except Mom.

He dropped the slip of paper into the wastebasket and headed for the small attached bathroom. Eager to wash away the hours of sweat from skiing, planes, and Fiats, he turned on the shower. As he waited for the water to heat, he grabbed his toiletry bag. He shaved quickly, before the steam could fog up the mirror, and then stepped in and allowed the hot water to beat against his back. As much as he wanted to take his time and enjoy the warmth, his eyes were starting to droop. Wrapping the large cream-colored towel around his waist, he opened the door and stepped back into the room.

"Good evening, Mr. Lombardi."

Startled by the voice, Aldo whipped around. Standing off to the left side of his room was a man dressed in a black suit.

"Who are you?" he gasped.

Arms folded across his chest and his face devoid of any emotion, the man said nothing.

"Why are you in my room?" Aldo asked, looking him up and down.

"Didn't you get my note?" said a familiar feminine voice behind him.

Can't be. "Allison?" Aldo turned around, his gaze meeting the beautiful blue eyes that never failed to mesmerize him. Her honey-colored hair fell around her shoulders, not a strand out of place. "What—How…" Taking a deep breath, he tried again. "What are you doing here?" He had read that sleep deprivation could cause hallucinations in some people. But even after the day he'd had, he couldn't be that tired.

She laughed, the sound reminding him of wind chimes on a summer's day. "Surprised?"

Warmth flooded his cheeks as he nodded. He'd had a crush on Allison for the past six years, ever since he'd met her at a little coffee house near the university his sophomore year. In addition to her beauty, she had a quick mind, and he always enjoyed their conversations. He never could muster the nerve to ask her out though, afraid things would turn awkward and ruin their friendship. So, he settled for daydreams and sidelong glances.

"What're you doing here?" he asked again. His eyes swept the room. "How did you even get in? And how did you know I was here?" *I didn't know myself until a few hours ago.*

"You mean, what's a little Mormon girl from Utah doing in the middle of Vatican City?" She tilted her head to the right and smiled.

Damn, she's lovely. He grinned at her. "Something like that."

"You were onto something, you know," she said, waltzing past him.

"What do you mean?"

"Your research." She slid his suitcase aside and sat down on the edge of his bed.

"So I've been told," Aldo murmured. Of all the friends he'd made at university, Allison had been the only one to support his theories.

"Not just Septem Montes."

"How did you..." He fell silent, remembering his gag order.

Allison eyed him for a moment, making him feel more exposed than his bath towel. Then she reached out and invitingly patted the pile of clothes on the bed beside her.

What is she after? Aldo glanced at the man still standing in the corner of the room. He knew Allison well enough to know she wasn't the kind of girl to frequent the bedrooms of single men, which explained the escort. But breaking into the Apostolic Palace just to discuss his research was equally ridiculous.

"Your watch, Aldo," Allison said, suppressing a giggle. She picked the timepiece up off the top of the stack.

"My watch?" *What about it?* The simple silver wristwatch wasn't very valuable, but he treasured the gift from his parents.

"Surveillance," she said. "We've been monitoring your conversations."

Aldo stared at her for a long moment, finally deciding she had to be pulling his leg. "Sure you have." After the day he'd had, being involved in spy games didn't seem so far-fetched. *But with Allison?* The riskiest thing he'd ever seen her do was take a sip of his coffee. Yet, he couldn't ignore the fact she was here, trespassing inside the Apostolic Palace. "And when exactly would you have gotten the chance to bug my watch?"

Again, Allison giggled. "Made you wonder, though, didn't I?" She stood and walked back toward the open balcony door. "There are many secrets within these walls, and now that you're on the inside, we need you to be our eyes and ears." She turned back and tilted her head again, knowing just how well that look worked on him.

Like a charm. Aldo sighed. "Okay, for argument's sake, let's say I believe you," Aldo said, rubbing his temple. "I'm not a spy. I'm just a scholar, a historian."

Allison laced her hands behind her back. "And only you were able to connect more dots than anyone else has. You're close to the Bride's Day Secret."

Aldo sighed again. "But I have no proof." Up until an hour earlier, his theory that all of Christianity would one day be united again under the veil of the Catholic Church, like a bride and groom on their wedding day, had been just that – a theory. Now, with the pope's confirmation of his research, he knew he'd been on the right track, but he still needed the proof to support it. But the pope's confiscating his research made getting said proof a moot point.

"You'll get it, sooner than you realize. You're in the right place."

Relenting, Aldo dropped onto the bed. "What am I looking for?"

Allison pointed at herself. "You're asking me?" Right. She wanted his help but wasn't going to give him any hints.

Since Aldo had left the pope's private chambers, something had been tickling the back of his mind. Starting with Luther, he could pinpoint how each of the six sects had originated. What about the seventh? Pope Benedict had called the Seventh a rebellious teenager. In religion, rebelling would be in terms of doctrine. Whose doctrine had strayed most from the path? He straightened.

"The Seventh-day Adventists are the seventh sect," he muttered. They were the ones threatening to reveal Catholic secrets.

Allison nodded. "I agree. I suggest you start at the beginning with William Miller. The Vatican Archives should have what you need. But it might take some digging."

Aldo looked at her, wondering what her stake was in all of this. She had already graduated with full honors from Brigham Young University, and he assumed she'd be returning home now that her study abroad program had ended. "I never said I'd help. Even if I wanted to, you know I'll be watched every second." Allison's expression turned serious. "By more than one set of eyes."

Aldo already felt in over his head, and the weight of her words dragged him down further. He glanced again at the man in the corner. Allison's presence here left little doubt that the LDS Church was involved. Beyond just being aware of Septem Montes he wasn't sure how, but that meant at least two of the seven sects were on the move.

"No guarantees," he said hesitantly.

"Don't worry. We got your back. Just scribble a note on a piece of paper and toss it out the window if you need me." She winked then followed her escort onto the balcony. Slipping smoothly over the railing, they disappeared into the darkness below.

"Ever heard of a cell phone?" Aldo muttered with a sigh. He closed and locked the balcony door, pulled on his pajamas and dropped onto the bed, praying that things would start making sense in the morning.

Chapter Two | The SEVENTH

Low Hampton, New York
October 1844

William Miller cried as he watched the sun rise over his farm. The crisp morning air threatened to freeze the tears to his face, but he hardly noticed. For the last twenty-two years, he had devoted his life to teaching his followers, the Millerites, the truth.

It has to be the truth. It is right there, in the Bible. So why? More tears slipped down his cheeks as he choked back a sob.

"Unto two thousand and three hundred days; then shall the sanctuary be cleansed," Miller recited Daniel 8:14 again. It was clear as day. Jesus would be coming to cleanse the Earth, purifying the world of all evil. The exact date had been carefully calculated, taking into account all possible factors. He believed beyond a shadow of a doubt that the day of Christ's Second Coming would reward his followers and punish the sinners of the world.

That day was yesterday.

So why, Lord? He threw his hands into the air in frustration. There were no errors in the calculations, no misinterpretation of scripture. Christ simply did not come. The reason was beyond Miller's ability to comprehend. He knew in his heart that Christ would be coming. Soon. He felt it, believed it with every fiber of his being. But after this failed prediction, no one would listen to him any longer. He would be labeled a charlatan.

I will need to disappear, find a quiet place to live out my days.

Remorse filled him as he looked around the farm. This latest setback had not shaken his faith, but he feared the disappointment would be too great for his followers and cause many to lose their way.

Miller's gaze rose toward the ridgepole of his large red barn. Squinting into the sunrise, he could make out some of his parishioners, dressed in white robes—ascension robes—gathering along the peak of the roof.

Puzzled, he left his front porch and headed toward the barn. *Why are they still here? And still dressed in their robes?*

Then the hairs on the back of his neck stood on end and he picked up his pace. *No, they mustn't.*

Thousands of Millerites had gathered around Low Hampton the previous day, all dressed in white robes to make the transition to Heaven easier. Some had climbed onto rooftops, while others had hiked into the surrounding hills, all fully expecting the world to be engulfed in flames. But with the dawning of this new day, all their hopes and expectations had been crushed.

Just as he reached the barn, one man leapt from the roof, hitting the ground with a sickening thud. William gasped then rushed toward the crumpled form. "No!" he screamed as another jumped. One by one, bodies continued to rain down around him, shaking the earth beneath his feet with each impact. "Stop!" he begged, falling to his knees. "No! Please, God! No!"

Was this punishment for his mistake? To watch helplessly as each parishioner, each child of God, plummeted to their death?

When at last silence fell, Miller forced himself to his feet. Thirty dead bodies lay strewn across the damp grass, each with white foam oozing from the mouth. Finding a small vial still clutched in one lifeless hand, Miller picked it up and sniffed. *Bitter almond.* They had poisoned themselves to ensure they would not survive the fall.

Fresh tears filled his eyes, clouding his vision. Grief and frustration cramped his stomach and he retched into a nearby shrub. Unable to face his fallen brethren, he stumbled onto his porch and slumped into a rocking chair. Shivers racked his body as waves of sorrow washed over him. *Where did I go wrong? Why did Christ not come? Has Christ forsaken us?*

Feeling as helpless as a child, he watched as other parishioners silently gathered the bodies and carted them away for burial. Slowly, the sun warmed him as it climbed higher in the clear autumn sky, yet he remained slumped and lifeless in his chair. His stomach rumbled, the emptiness adding to his nausea.

He still had not moved when around midday a small figure dressed in white walked across the lawn toward him. Forcing his hazy vision to focus, Miller finally recognized the young woman as Ellen Harmon. He closed his eyes and said a brief prayer of gratitude that she had not taken her life like so many others. He loved Ellen as if she were his own daughter. Seeing her lifted his spirits immeasurably. She was beautiful to him, despite her disfigured face.

When she was nine, a classmate had thrown a rock at her, leaving her comatose for nearly a month and scarring her for life. When she finally awoke, she prayed incessantly, asking Jesus for guidance. Three years later, her family joined Miller's congregation.

He remembered that day as if it were yesterday. She was so innocent, so willing to turn herself over to God. And despite her youth, she was driven by fear for her immortal soul.

She reminds me so much of myself.

As she approached, William stood up from his chair, his legs aching. He waited until she was within hearing range before saying, "Hello."

"Good morning," she greeted him quietly.

"No…it is not," he choked out, trying to keep the grief from consuming him again.

She stopped at the bottom of the porch steps and peered up at him. "I am sorry. Truly, I am, but I have something to share with you."

"What is it?" he asked, fearing she brought more bad news. She seemed surprisingly calm, considering the morning's events.

"May I join you?"

He nodded, gesturing to the rocking chair next to his. "I am so glad to see you," he said, feeling guilty for taking comfort from her presence when so many had suffered due to his mistake.

"I had a vision."

He gaped at her as she climbed the steps and settled into the rocking chair. *She has been visited by God? Could she have the answer? Has God told her how I went wrong?*

He quickly returned to his seat and leaned toward her against the arm rest. "Please, tell me," he breathed. "Do not leave out any detail."

"It was while I was visiting some sisters. We were praying together just before sunrise when I felt the power of God wash over me. It was a feeling like nothing I had ever felt before—one I will never forget." She glanced up, her eyes bright with the memory. "His love and wisdom filled me, and I felt myself rising into the heavens, away from Earth. Me. Not my body, but my spirit. I was shown the Advent People. They were going to the New Jerusalem, the place of eternal joy."

William gazed at her then sighed. "I always knew you were special," he murmured, pride filling him. "You are a prophetess."

She nodded. "Yes."

Perhaps that was God's answer—that she was the one to lead the righteous, not him.

"I am so sorry," he blurted out. "Can you ever forgive me?"

"What is to forgive?"

William dropped his head into his hands. "I failed my people. I failed you."

"You did not fail anyone," she said gently.

"But so many…" He swallowed hard then tried again. "So many killed themselves."

A single tear fell from her eye, and she wiped it away with her slender fingers. "I heard. My heart breaks for them, but that was not God's plan. They were weak of mind and spirit, and I will pray for their salvation."

"But I was their leader," he choked. "It is my responsibility—"

"You did not fail your people," she repeated. "They failed you."

Startled by her statement, he straightened and looked at her. "How so?"

"They should trust you, despite what happened. You are a great man," she responded, her kind eyes studying him. Then suddenly, her brows furrowed. "You know something, do you not? God gave you vital information and you did not act on it. Why?"

William's body trembled. *How does she know that?*

She stared at him, her unrelenting eyes penetrating his. "I know because Jesus told me, during my vision. He told me that you would guide me one last time."

One last time? He had suspected he was not long for this world. And if God had deemed his time was at hand, he resolved to spend every last moment he had helping Ellen bring the truth to the people.

"It is true," he said with renewed hope. "I was given some documents, but I did not realize their importance, and only kept them hidden for fear of my family's safety. But I will share everything I know with you."

"Not now, but soon." Standing, she turned to face him. "You will come to me, at my home, in four months' time. That is when and where it will be."

William stared up at her. *How can she be so confident, so sure, when she is only sixteen years old?* At sixty-two, he often felt as feeble as a spring lamb. Especially today.

"I will visit you in February then," he said, standing.

Over the next few months, his failure to predict the second coming of Christ became heralded as The Great Disappointment. However, the public scrutiny could not shake his faith. Miller knew now that God had different plans for him, and he was determined to see them through to the best of his ability.

He prayed daily for the souls lost due to his error and continued to study the Bible voraciously. He read through the stack of hidden documents over and over again, taking notes for his upcoming meeting with Ellen, making sure to put the documents back in their hiding spot each night.

The documents had been given to him by William Morgan, a man Miller had met when visiting his second cousin, David, in Batavia, New York nearly twenty years prior. At the time, Miller was a Freemason trying to ensure David's initiation into a local lodge. David had received the apprentice degree, the lowest grade of Freemasonry, but could not advance beyond that. Disgruntled, David had met and befriended Morgan, who had been denied admission entirely.

Embittered by the rejection, Morgan decided to publish a book, exposing secret Freemasonic rituals. As a newspaper publisher, David agreed to print the book. Concerned the Freemasons might seek retribution, William Miller pleaded with his cousin to discard the project. But David was eager to embarrass the lodge that had rejected him and insisted on moving forward.

To ease his cousin's concerns, David suggested he share a meal with Morgan and his family. Over the course of the evening, Morgan expressed great interest in Miller's religious beliefs, asking many questions while offering very little in return. Feeling annoyed by the one-sided discussion, Miller excused himself from the table and went outside to get some fresh air. He wished he had declined Morgan's invitation.

Morgan joined him on the front porch soon after.

"I apologize," Morgan said from behind him.

William tensed. *Great. What other information is he going to try to pry out of me?*

"You do not like me very much, do you?"

"No," Miller replied flatly. He felt slightly guilty for being rude to the man, but he did not believe in lying either.

"I understand." Morgan stepped forward to stand beside his guest at the porch railing. "You are a Freemason and you consider me to be a traitor."

"Of course I do," Miller said through gritted teeth. "We all took an oath of secrecy when we joined the lodge. Now, you are dragging my cousin into this quagmire!"

"I never joined," Morgan said softly. He kept his gaze fixed on the dark expanse of lawn before them. "So, I never swore such an oath."

"Then how did you learn of our secrets?"

"I cannot say," Morgan replied, "but there are those within your organization who disagree with the credos of the Freemasons."

"Then they are the traitors." Feeling somewhat mollified, Miller turned to leave.

"Wait. I have something I would like to give you. I think you will need it," Morgan said.

Miller stopped in his tracks, glancing over his shoulder at Morgan. "I think not."

"You may not like me, but this meeting was not by happenstance. You need me."

William Miller barked a laugh. "More like you need money for your book!"

"Actually, your cousin is paying me a small fortune as an advance, so I am settled on that score," Morgan said with a grin. "I am not interested in your money."

Miller stared at him. *Then what exactly is he after? What game is he playing?*

Morgan sighed. "I am just giving you a gift. Will you accept it?"

Not until his conversation with Ellen nearly twenty years later did William Miller understand why he had accepted the small packet of papers from Morgan that day. It had all been part of God's plan.

When Morgan went missing right before his book, *Illustrations of Masonry*, was published, Miller suspected there might be a clue in the packet of documents and finally opened it. To Miller's surprise, the information contained in the papers had nothing to do with Morgan's book.

Morgan had been imprisoned several months prior for unpaid debts, but Miller found that suspicious, as did many others. When David Miller paid the debts, more unpaid debts surfaced, and Morgan was arrested again. This time another man paid the debts, but shortly after his release, Morgan was captured by two men and was never seen again.

Soon after, William Miller left the Freemasons, despite having achieved the high rank of Grand Master of the Morning Star Lodge in Poultney. Not only did he have suspicions about the Freemasons' involvement in Morgan's disappearance, but their beliefs conflicted with his faith, and he felt he should focus his attention on his expanding congregation and the Second Coming of Christ.

Many rumors circulated concerning Morgan's disappearance, but Miller believed he had been silenced by the Freemasons. Publishing his book had essentially signed his death warrant. The book exposed many of the Freemasons' secrets—secrets group members, himself included, had sworn to keep under penalty of death. In fact, many of the rituals practiced at each meeting centered around a particular oath to exact retribution should anyone ever reveal the secrets.

Miller shuddered to think of the torture Morgan must have endured.

He had kept Morgan's packet of papers tucked safely between the slats in the floor of his trunk at the foot of his bed. He never saw any use for them in his sermons but could not bring himself to dispose of them either. While the information contained in them was religious in nature, it did not fit with the truth he knew regarding of the Second Coming of Christ. The papers laid out the blueprint for something called *Septem Montes*, describing in great detail how seven distinct sects of Christianity would diverge from the Catholic Church.

After Ellen's visit, however, everything changed. He was positive Ellen would know how to use the papers to guide his people into the next phase of existence. He still did not understand their relevance to his role on Earth, but Miller had faith that, together with Ellen, the papers would help him execute God's will.

In February, Miller visited Ellen Harmon at her home in Maine. He brought the packet of documents with him, eager to see what she would make of them.

When she opened the door, he dropped to his knees on her front porch. Her entire body was glowing with a soft white aura.

"You have had another vision?"

She nodded. "Yes. It is now clear to me that I am to start a new church, one that will continue your legacy well beyond your lifetime and mine. But I need your help. Without you, I will not be able to create this movement of truth."

Rising to his feet, Miller pressed his hand to his heart. "I am here for you and my people. Just tell me how I may help."

"Good!" she exclaimed, ushering him into her small parlor.

Settling into a chair by the glowing fireplace, he pulled the packet of papers from his satchel. "I have brought the package."

"May I see?"

He handed the papers to her then sat forward, warming himself while she read through them.

For half the day she remained engrossed in study, not breaking, even to eat, until she had absorbed all of the information contained in the papers.

"So, our mission is now clear," she said finally, laying the papers in her lap.

"How so? How does this *Septem Montes* relate to us?"

Ellen motioned for him to sit next to her on the settee. "The Catholic Church has already formed six of the seven sects outlined here, but it is waiting to unfold the seventh much later. However, God has another plan, one the Catholic Church is not privy to."

"But *we* are," William said excitedly. "Are we going to build the seventh church?"

"Yes," Ellen said with a smile. "Your followers have disbanded, but we can easily recover many of them. They will flock to this new church, the seventh one, and we will lead them toward the truth."

Miller's excitement faded. *They disbanded because of me.* Certainly they would want nothing to do with him after his failure. "Is it wise to include me?" he asked hesitantly. "My tarnished reputation will surely be a hindrance. Perhaps I should just stay in the background."

"No," she said gently. "I need you. God needs you." She laid a hand over his. "You still have work to do. Your reputation is what you make of it. You would be surprised at how resilient people can be."

"But...can I not just advise you?"

"No. You must be next to me, by my side as we form this church."

Miller nodded reluctantly. He still feared that his reputation would deter many from the truth, but he had faith in Ellen. "Very well. What is your plan?"

"Before I tell you, I first need to know that you are committed. Will you continue to lead your people with the same passion you have always had?"

"Yes," he said, straightening. "Of course, I will."

"Good, because I do not believe you were wrong at all."

A glimmer of hope flickered inside him. "I was not wrong?" To have cost the lives of so many had been such a crushing disappointment, but if there were a chance he had been right, Miller would have a new lease on life.

"No," she said. "I believe Christ was indeed here on October 22nd, but He did not make Himself known. The event you predicted did in fact occur, just not as expected. And now we need to proceed forward."

"You saw this in a vision?"

She nodded.

"And?" Miller asked, his excitement returning. "What is the next step?"

Ellen leaned forward to look him directly in his eye. "We need to gather all our people in one place and have a conference. I also need to study all the papers you have given me in depth."

"How will we organize such a meeting?" Miller asked.

"The word has already been spread. We will meet mid-April in Albany."

He shook his head in disbelief. "You never cease to amaze me."

She smiled then stood to pace before the fireplace, the papers still clutched in her hands. "There is one question I have, though."

"Yes?"

"You actually met William Morgan, correct?"

"That is correct."

"And his wife?"

He nodded. "Yes. On the one occasion that I dined with Morgan, his wife, Lucinda, and their two children were there."

"Do you know what happened to her when Morgan died?"

Confused, Miller shook his head. "I never thought about it."

"She married Joseph Smith." She turned to face him.

Miller's eyebrows rose. "The heretic who called himself a prophet? Founder of the Mormons?"

"Yes."

"But her husband hated Smith almost as much as I did," he said in disbelief.

"It was an odd choice, I grant you," she said, shaking her head.

"I believe Joseph Smith was a Freemason, too." *Why would Morgan's widow marry a man associated with the secret society Morgan had tried to expose? It does not make sense.*

She nodded. "And a polygamist. Lucinda was his third wife."

William thought for a moment. The union seemed calculated to him, but to what end he had no idea. *What would Lucinda Morgan possibly have to gain? Or maybe, it was Smith who had something to gain.*

Ellen flipped through the pages in her hands, drawing her friend's attention. "I often wondered why Morgan chose to give me the papers instead of passing them on to his family," he said. "I do not even know how he came to possess them in the first place." Certainly the Catholic Church would not want such sensitive documents falling into the wrong hands.

"I believe he had a reason," she said, beginning to pace again. "We can assume no one knows he gave them to you, but I still think we should be cautious.

Now that I possess them, they will find new purpose and will likely attract new attention as we build our church." She stopped and turned to face him. "We will need to proceed carefully."

William Miller and Ellen Harmon presented a united front at the Albany Conference. Sixty-one people attended, but not everyone agreed with the new direction. Those who followed Miller and Harmon that day became the first members of their new church.

Having done what he was destined to do, Miller kept to himself, praying constantly in his final days. He also spent a fair amount of time studying the Bible, reporting to Ellen what he had learned during her frequent visits to his farm in Low Hampton.

A week before Christmas 1849, Ellen arrived at Miller's home for her usual visit. They sipped cups of tea in front of the fire as they shared recent discoveries and discussed the church's progress.

Ellen set down her cup and took William's hand in hers. "Your time on Earth is almost over," she said softly.

Miller felt a chill creep up his spine, and he nodded. "I sense it, too."

Rubbing his arm fondly, she said, "As time passes, I feel more secure in my safety. I do not think anyone knows I have the papers. Or if they do, they do not care."

"Keep vigilant," he said. "I am not so sure they are not watching you."

"I promise to be careful." She gave him a soft smile. "But remember, I am protected."

"That you are." He knew without a doubt that God would not call her home until her work was completed.

"I had another vision three days ago," she said, leaning into him as if sharing a secret with her best friend.

He looked at her, the excitement he felt every time she shared one of her visions with him returning. "And what was it?"

"The Lord Jesus came to me and guided me up to the heavens. There, He showed me His intentions for our church."

"What did He show you?"

"There are many details, but two I want to share with you today. One is Sabbath keeping. We must not only observe the true seventh day of the week, Saturday, as the day of rest and worship, but we must make it a purpose of our new church. Our Lord and Savior was very clear about that."

Miller nodded. "It is what the Bible states."

"Yes, and we are the messengers. It is our purpose to see God's Will done on Earth. We are the Sabbath keepers. In fact, our church name will guide our people and be a constant reminder of this doctrine. We shall be known as the Seventh-day Adventists."

Miller sighed in relief. He had feared he would not see the completion of their goal before his time came. Yet, here he was, witnessing the birth of something important in the hands of this young woman. "It is the seventh church of *Septem Montes*."

"Yes," she said. "We will need to lay out the fundamental beliefs of our church, and it will take time to form, but in the end, we will be the leader of all Christian faiths."

He nodded then took another sip of tea. "What was the other point you wanted to tell me from your vision?"

Ellen took his hands in hers. "As I said before, you were right. October 22, 1844 was a pivotal point for every man, woman, and child here on Earth. It marked the start of the Investigative Judgment in Heaven. Everything we do in this life is recorded and kept in Heaven. We will all be judged by our Lord Jesus Christ when He sees fit to judge us. On October 22nd, Jesus entered a new realm in Heaven, a most sacred and Holy Place, and the full investigation began."

Miller stared at her in awe. "The Lord told you this?"

She smiled. "Yes, He did. He also instructed me to make sure that your name goes down in history as a founder of the Advent Movement and the Seventh-day Adventist Church. You will be revered throughout the ages and have secured your place in Heaven."

Miller's hands trembled in hers as he broke into tears. "Thank you. Oh, thank you!"

Chapter Three | Church INFORMANT

Vatican City
February 2013

Aldo's eyes flew open to find a younger man standing over him. Startled, he bolted upright.

"Good morning, sir," the younger man smiled.

Aldo stared at him for a moment, trying to remember who he was. *That's right. His name's David.* The young priest had escorted him to his room within the Apostolic Palace the night before. "It can't be morning already," Aldo muttered. He'd only just fallen asleep twenty minutes ago, it seemed. Daylight streamed in through the gauze curtains draped over the balcony door. "But I see it is."

He flipped the sheets off and swung his legs over the side of the bed but made no move to stand. His mouth felt stuffed with cotton and his head still swam with everything that had happened in the last twenty-four hours. He had spent several years researching his thesis, only to find out that he had hardly scratched the surface. The pope had offered him a job, despite the fact he had barely managed to graduate. Then the only woman who had occupied his thoughts for the last six years had shown up in his room requesting he act as her spy.

Perhaps the biggest shock, though, was having his laptop confiscated. He understood the risk the Church faced if his research ended up in the wrong hands. And he couldn't help feeling like it was his fault Church secrets had been uploaded on the Dark Internet. Any number of people could have accessed his research during the years he spent collecting data.

David poured Aldo a glass of water from a pitcher on the nightstand. Like many of the art pieces Aldo had seen within the Apostolic Palace, the beautifully hand-painted clay pitcher looked authentic. But David seemed completely unfazed by the fact he was serving a potential informant water from an early Greco-Roman antique.

Smiling, David handed the glass to him. "I hope you slept well."

"Uh, thanks," Aldo said hesitantly. Then quickly draining the glass, he handed it back to David, who refilled it. "You seem to know what I need even before I do."

"That's my job," he replied. "I act as a valet for important dignitaries."

"Must be a slow week if you got stuck with me."

David chuckled and handed him the glass again. "Well, until I'm told otherwise, you're a VIP. Please let me know if there's anything you need."

Aldo drank the second glass then set it on the nightstand. Noticing a slim black device on the table near the bathroom, Aldo stood and walked over to it. Running his hand over the laptop's sleek surface, he asked, "Is this…"

"I apologize for not having it ready last night. I wanted to make sure it was equipped with the same software as your old one."

"Thank you, David."

David bowed then gestured to the corner of the room where Aldo's suit hung from a mahogany valet stand, already pressed. "I'll leave you to get dressed. When you're ready, I'll take you to the southeast courtyard for your breakfast meeting."

Aldo thanked him again and waited for the door to close before opening the laptop. He switched it on, and quickly shaved and combed his hair while it booted up. Getting dressed in record time, he slipped his reading glasses on, and then sat down at the table to peruse the programs and functions on the new machine. He found encryption coding software along with the newest cloud computing system, but none of his files had been uploaded.

They really did confiscate everything. He sighed. It was probably for the best though. His data had been password protected, but no doubt it would be much safer with the Holy See. And he couldn't be sure he would even need his research notes. Not if the pope wanted him to try to hack into the Dark Internet, but based on the setup of his new laptop, David seemed much more qualified for that task.

Aldo shut down the laptop and joined David in the hallway outside his room, following as the priest guided him back through the maze of corridors. A few moments later, they stepped out into a courtyard filled with a variety of flowers, all in full bloom despite the chilly February morning. Three gardeners were already busy coaxing nature out of her winter slumber.

"Good morning, Aldo," the pope called jovially from a small bistro table set to one side of a patio that ran the length of the courtyard. "I trust you slept well."

Sure. "Yes, Your Holiness. Thank you." Aldo pulled out the chair opposite the pope and sat down as waiting attendants filled his plate with fruits, eggs, and bite-sized pastries. His stomach grumbled and he realized he hadn't eaten since the previous morning.

The pope chuckled. "Ah, to be young."

"It all looks delicious," Aldo said, blushing. Well, at least he'd already lowered any expectations the pope had of his decorum with his wardrobe yesterday. Aldo waited for the pope to give his blessing before taking his first bite. As he ate, Pope Benedict watched him in silence, taking only a few small bites of a pastry in between sips of espresso.

Aldo held up his hand when the attendants tried to refill his plate a third time. "No more, thank you. It was delicious." After taking his plate and topping off his coffee, they excused themselves, leaving him alone with Pope Benedict.

The pope set down his espresso mug, and then leaned in. "I have a special research assignment for you," he said quietly.

Research? While relieved, Aldo had assumed removing all traces of *Septem Montes* from the Dark Internet would be the Church's top priority.

"I'm honored, Your Holiness," he said after a moment.

Pope Benedict nodded. "What do you know about the end of World War II?"

Aldo sat back in his chair and took a sip of his black coffee. "Just the basics, I'm afraid. As religion played less of a role at the end of the war than at the beginning, my study focused more on the first half."

"Fair enough," the pope said. "You're about to become an expert."

Aldo stared at him. "Really?" That was his first assignment? He had to be missing something. What did the Nazis have to do with *Septem Montes* ?

Pope Benedict nodded again and handed him a black leather portfolio.

Aldo opened it, expecting to find a stack of documents. Instead, he pulled out a boarding pass for a flight to Buenos Aires, Argentina, leaving that afternoon. There was information about a rental car and hotel as well. And tucked into a flap on the right side was a credit card embossed with his name. "I'm leaving now?" he asked, baffled. "But I just got here."

"I do apologize," Pope Benedict said, "but you understand our urgency." He took another sip of espresso. "I had David make the arrangements last night."

So, you planned on sending me to Argentina from the beginning.

Aldo stared at the boarding pass for a long moment. His lack of sleep wasn't helping his confusion. "You want me to research World War II in Argentina?"

"Yes," the pope replied.

Still unable to think of a logical correlation, he gave up trying. Why did it seem like this was just an excuse to keep him busy? "What precisely am I looking for?"

"That's a good question," the pope said with a wry smile. "I need you to use your keen observational skills. Look around, ask questions, scrutinize, learn. Do what you do best."

"So, be your eyes and ears," Aldo replied, using Allison's words from the night before. He was beginning to feel like the rope in a game of tug-o-war.

"To put it simply, yes."

Aldo tucked the travel documents back into the portfolio. It made sense. He'd very likely had a hand in unintentionally exposing secrets the Church didn't want made public. And while they'd confiscated his research, what better way to keep him from picking up where he left off than to distract him with a new topic? This assignment was along the same vein as his thesis, though, so keeping him in the dark couldn't be their goal.

"No hints then?"

The pope shook his head. "I don't want to feed you information that could be biased. I have theories, but I need you to approach this with a clean slate."

"I understand," Aldo said slowly. "May I ask how this assignment relates to *Septem Montes*?"

The pope thought for a moment then nodded. "I believe there is a correlation to the Seventh," he replied vaguely.

Aldo knew that the Seventh-day Adventist Church had regional offices in Argentina, but he was still missing what connected the church to the events at the end of World War II. "The Seventh-day Adventists, right?" Aldo confirmed.

Pope Benedict smiled. "I see you've already put that piece into place."

"Yes. Last night actually."

"We didn't form that sect," the pope said. "Somehow they found the blueprints for *Septem Montes* and built their religion following their own design. They keep growing in number, and we can no longer ignore the power and influence of their organization. However, I believe they could still serve the original purpose intended by my predecessors. They will be a challenge, though. They fight us at every turn, vehemently disagreeing with every nuance of the Mother Church." He stared somewhere past Aldo's left shoulder. "They insist on keeping the Sabbath on Saturday." He shook his head.

While Aldo still hadn't confirmed his theory as to why the Church had created *Septem Montes* to begin with, he believed there was only one logical reason behind it: to unify and strengthen the faith of all Christians. "Absence makes the heart grow fonder," Aldo quoted.

Pope Benedict met Aldo's eyes. "I agree, and the seven have been away far too long." His gaze drifted off into the distance again, but only for a moment. "Since you already figured out that piece of the puzzle, I can give you one tip. You'll be researching the Seventh's involvement with the Nazis."

Aldo stared at the pope. "What involvement?"

Pope Benedict shook his head. "If I tell you anything else, your judgment may become clouded. You must research for yourself, view all the information without prejudice, and form your own conclusions."

"In other words, you want the truth." *However harsh it may be* .

The pope nodded then looked at his watch. "You should be on your way soon, if you're to catch your flight."

"Right, I still need to pack," Aldo said, pushing his chair back to stand up.

"No need," David said from behind him. Aldo turned to find the young priest holding his suitcase and laptop bag. "Are you ready, sir?" David asked.

"As I'll ever be," Aldo said with a sigh. He would have liked to stay a bit longer. Turning back to the pope, he asked, "When do I return?"

"When you're finished," the pope said simply. "You'll know when that is. It might take some time."

Aldo nodded then bid the pope farewell and followed David out of the courtyard.

The cab dropped him at the airport with two hours to spare. Since he had only his laptop bag and suitcase, the check-in process went smoothly, and he was soon was sitting at the gate waiting to board. With the long flight ahead of him, he silently thanked David for booking him a seat in first class.

Once the plane reached its peak altitude and leveled out, he pulled out his laptop and started researching the history of Argentina during the 1940s. According to numerous reports, the country had been a haven for Nazis after World War II, harboring some of the worst war criminals. But he still couldn't find anything connecting these events to the Seventh-day Adventist Church.

Argentina's open-door policy for immigrants went back centuries. The only country to allow more people to cross its borders was the United States. After the war, Argentina formed a large underground network, sanctioned by Juan

Peron's government. They aided many infamous Nazi officials, offering them new identities and protection from the Allied forces. Information sourced on the internet could often be sketchy, yet it was hard to deny the number of ex-Nazi sightings in Argentina—Josef Mengele, Adolf Eichmann, and Klaus Barbie, and countless others.

Various groups hunted down and extracted the fugitive Nazis from South America and other regions around the world over the decades that followed the war. Eichmann was captured by Israelis and finally hanged in 1962. However, some war criminals were never caught, never brought to justice to pay for their crimes. Mengele was one of them. It angered Aldo that such a monster had been able to live out his days in relative peace, dying of natural causes in Brazil. No one said life was fair, but with the countless lives Mengele had mangled and destroyed at Auschwitz, Aldo couldn't accept such a gross injustice.

Focusing on his research made the long flight more bearable, though Aldo occasionally had to remove his reading glasses and rub the fatigue from his eyes. He drank cup after cup of coffee, determined to stay awake and learn as much as he could before arriving in Argentina. By the time his plane finally touched down, Aldo had filled his notebook with scribbled shorthand, a method of taking quick notes he had developed during his graduate studies.

Exhausted from fighting currents of people as they moved through the terminal, he managed to locate the rental car kiosk and picked up the compact silver sedan reserved under his name. Looking over his travel documents, he realized David had reserved him a room at the Castelar Hotel and Spa. Aldo groaned. It would take thirty minutes to get there, assuming he didn't get lost. He considered sleeping in the airport for the night but decided a real bed was worth surviving another half hour and trudged out to the rental car lot.

Even with an unintended detour, he arrived at the hotel just before one in the morning. Handing the keys for his rental to the attendant, he stumbled into the lobby. Aldo nodded vaguely when the concierge offered him a small room overlooking the Avenida de Mayo, relieved the man could speak English. His Spanish was mediocre at best, and his lack of sleep didn't encourage him to try.

Anything, so long as it has a bed. "I'm sure it's fine," Aldo said, trying not to slur his words.

"Would you like a wakeup call?" the concierge asked.

"Not on your life."

"Perhaps a *do not disturb* message on the phone then?" the man said with a small smile.

"That I'll take you up on." A few minutes later, Aldo fell onto the bed, without even bothering to remove his shoes.

He woke to the sound of morning traffic rushing past his window. He pulled the heavy curtains open, and bright sunlight poured into the room. The trees lining the Avenida de Mayo were adorned with vibrant green and burgundy leaves. *Oh, yeah. It's summer here.* He quickly showered and dressed, eager to explore.

Buenos Aires, how long will I call you home? He made his way through the hotel lobby and out to the street. He hoped it wouldn't be more than a week or two. The warmer weather was a welcome change, but he didn't want to keep giving his mom vague answers about where he was and what he was doing. Allison had been equally nosy, though not for reasons he would prefer. She texted him regularly for updates, as though already aware he was no longer in Italy. He sighed. Having been relegated to the position of friend for so long, he should be happy for some kind of development in their relationship, but espionage wasn't exactly what he had in mind.

He meandered along the sidewalk, marveling at a large colorful mural depicting the road he was on. The streets were wider than he had expected and were crowded with traffic. Pedestrians passed by at a good clip, a few nodding their heads in greeting. He stepped into a small café and ordered a cup of coffee and a pastry. As he waited for his order, conversations swirled around him in multiple languages, German and Spanish predominant.

Settling into a chair at a small bistro table outside, he pulled out his laptop. Forums were full of speculation about post World War II activities in Argentina, but the authors seemed to be mostly conspiracy theorists, ranting about unlikely possibilities and lacking any concrete proof. He found evidence of the Seventh-day Adventists' involvement with Nazi propaganda in Germany prior to the war, but nothing that linked the church to the fugitive SS officials in Argentina.

Sighing, he closed the laptop and glanced at the beautiful architecture around him as he sipped his coffee. *I need for you to use your keen observational skills. Look around, ask questions, scrutinize, learn. Do what you do best* . The pope's words echoed in his head.

Finishing his breakfast, he headed back to the hotel to drop off his laptop. As high-tech as it was, it proved to be more of a hindrance than a help. It was too easy to get sucked into the conspiracies and false information circulating the internet.

Taking only his notebook and pen, Aldo walked around the city all afternoon, eventually finding a small bookstore a few blocks south of the hotel. He picked up some travel guides and chatted for a while with the American owner. The man chuckled as he told Aldo how he had fallen in love with a beautiful Argentine woman ten years earlier and never looked back. "Love has a way of changing your life," the man said.

I don't doubt that. Allison changed his life the moment they met. Even with the mess created by his thesis, she never wavered in her support – she was the only one who believed in his work as much as he did.

On an antique table behind the counter, Aldo noticed an old Remington typewriter, a half-typed page sticking up from the top. Following his gaze, the man smiled. "My memoirs."

"I'd like to read that when you're done."

"It might be a while," he chuckled again. "In the meantime, is there anything else I can help you with?"

"Actually, I'm researching the history of Buenos Aires," Aldo said. "Do you have any books that date back to the mid 1940s?"

The man thought for a moment. "No, but there's a used bookstore just up on Avenida 9 de Julio. Turn right on Lavalle and hang a left on San Martin. You might find what you're looking for there."

"Thanks. And good luck with your manuscript."

Aldo followed the man's directions, enjoying the two-mile trek and the opportunity to walk up the widest avenue in the world. He counted a total of sixteen lanes of traffic and shook his head, glad he'd opted to leave the rental car at the hotel.

Walking through the door of the bookstore, he felt as though he'd stepped back in time. The rusty black bell above the door that announced his presence barely roused the attention of the old man behind the counter. He grunted an acknowledgment without looking up from his pile of dusty books.

Aldo quickly found the section dedicated to history and browsed through the shelves. Most of the books on war contained typical historical accounts of battles, weaponry, and famous military heroes, but oddly nothing about the Nazis. He went back to the front and waited for the man behind the counter to look up.

I'm the only patron here, old man . After a few moments, he cleared his throat.

"¿Qué?" the old man grumbled.

"Uh, I'm looking for something on war, circa 1945," Aldo said, hoping he wouldn't have to embarrass himself by butchering the man's native language. Spanish had similarities to Italian, both having evolved from Latin, a language he'd studied in university, but that did not help him here.

"The books on World War II are over there," the man muttered in heavily accented English, waving toward the section Aldo had just come from.

"Right. Thanks," Aldo said, "but I'm looking for something in particular..."

The man's eyes flicked up. "And that would be?"

Why do I feel like he's intentionally making this harder than it needs to be? With a sigh, Aldo asked, "Do you have anything about the Nazis who fled to Argentina after the war?"

The man gave Aldo a long, hard look, as though evaluating him. A bead of sweat trickled down his face despite the oscillating fan situated at the end of the counter. The old man glanced over Aldo's shoulder, his eyes scanning up and down the street through the shop's front window, and then asked in a low voice, "And why would you want to know that?"

"I'm, uh, a historian," he said carefully.

"Where did you study?"

What does that have to do with anything? "I received my Ph.D. from the Pontifical Gregorian University," Aldo said, holding the man's penetrating stare.

The man quirked an eyebrow. Finally, he said, "Come back in an hour. I may have something for you then."

Huh? Did he misplace it or something? When the man continued to stare at him, Aldo decided not to push his luck. "Great! Thanks. Well, uh, see you in an hour," he called over his shoulder as he headed out the door.

Now what? An hour wasn't enough time to make the trek back to hotel, so Aldo decided to take a walk and stumbled upon a small park. Plopping down on a wooden bench, he watched a few birds peck at the grass and pondered how his life had changed so drastically. Never would he have imagined, even just days ago, that he would be on assignment for the pope. It was an opportunity many in his field could only dream of, even if misfortune had opened the door.

Bad luck comes in threes, right? Aldo sighed. Barely graduating and inadvertently telling the world about *Septem Montes* had to count as two. Still, some good things happened as well, and for all he knew this was part of God's plan for him.

Several people strolled by, enjoying the early afternoon quiet. He chatted with one couple after their exuberant dog leapt into his lap, and then he pulled out the travel guides he'd purchased earlier. Reading through them, he made notes of places that might be worth visiting. When forty-five minutes passed, he stood and walked back toward the bookstore.

He expected a stack of books to be waiting on the counter, but the counter remained just as bare as it had been an hour earlier. He sighed inwardly and stepped over to where the shop owner still sat with his pile of books.

"Eager, are we?" The old man picked up a cane and slowly made his way around the counter. He glanced through the window to the street before beckoning for Aldo to follow him. Passing the section Aldo had searched earlier, the old man hobbled to the northern-most corner of the building. It was well hidden from the front of the shop, and Aldo hadn't even noticed it.

Aldo's eyebrows rose as he looked around. The bookshelves were filled with modern romance novels, the bright colors and lewd illustrations so out of place in this small antique shop. "Romance novels?"

"Patience, boy," the owner bit out. He picked up a worn hardcover, entitled *Carolina* , placed it on its side and pushed it forward. The shelf moved a few inches then stopped. "Damn this door anyway!" he muttered, pushing the book again. The door opened another few feet, giving them both room to squeeze through and descend several steps. At the bottom, the old man raised a shaky hand and yanked on a thin cord, turning on an overhead light to reveal a small, windowless room. Four bookshelves and an overstuffed corduroy chair that looked tan in the dim light occupied most of the space. "I'll come get you at closing time."

"What? You mean I can't get out on my own?" Aldo asked, panic creeping into his voice. He'd never been good with enclosed spaces since being trapped in a cellar when he was a child.

"Can't risk you opening the door when there's a customer out front now, can I?" The shop owner looked around the room. "I don't let just anyone in here."

Then why did you let me in? Aldo slowly nodded. "I understand. Thank you."

The owner grunted again then pulled the shelf closed behind him.

Sighing, Aldo looked around. To his relief, the room was well maintained, lacking the dampness, cobwebs and dust of typical brick basements. He could also feel a cool breeze coming from somewhere in the ceiling. He tried to reassure himself. *Just don't think about it and you'll be fine.*

Aldo glanced at his watch. Figuring hehad only about four hours until the old man returned, Aldo pulled out his reading glasses and walked over to the nearest bookcase. Scanning the shelves, he noticed that many of the spines were unmarked. Pulling the books off one by one and flipping through them, he discovered most were diaries from locals, some even written in English. Most were bound informally, the pages coming loose with age, while others were memoirs printed by large publishing houses. Without the usual index or table of contents, it was hard to tell if any of it was relevant without reading them. The ones that seemed most likely to be useful he placed in a stack to read through later.

He paged through the diary of a private tutor from the 1950s. It was fascinating, but nothing related to his research. Next, he found a book written by a young woman who had moved from Germany just after the war. She wrote mostly of a romance with an Argentine rebel. Part of him wanted to get lost in the stories, but time wasn't on his side.

A small black book on the third shelf caught his eye. The book's paper cover was wrinkled and dog-eared with stark white letters on the front that read *I was Doctor Mengele's Assistant.* The word *Mengele's* was written in a dark blood red, and a chill ran up Aldo's spine. The author was Miklos Nyiszli, a Jewish doctor who somehow survived the horrors of Auschwitz. Nyiszli warned that his purpose in writing was simply to share the facts, as terrifying as they were.

Aldo put the book on the small table beside the chair and continued to look through the shelves. Finding more books with no markings on the spine, he flipped through them, stacking the relevant ones on the table. One was a diary written by another concentration camp survivor who also recorded his experiences with Mengele. Like Nyiszli, he had been selected to aid the madman. Instead of the scribbled handwriting of Nyiszli's book, this one had been typed and bore no title on the cover. The author's name was missing as well.

Turning the book around in his hand, Aldo realized it must be one of a kind. *How on Earth did that old man come by such rare books?*

Aldo sat down to read through the stack of books, starting with the one in his hand. In it, the anonymous author detailed the various experiments Mengele performed on the Auschwitz prisoners. Referring to Mengele as the Angel of Death, a nickname Aldo had seen pop up often in his online research, the author made clear that the Nazi doctor was obsessed with twins. Any time the author found a set of twins among the incoming prisoners, he was given extra food. Just scraps, but it ensured survival for at least a few more days. The author's regret at betraying his own people rang clear through his words as he recounted the stories of all the twins he found for the young SS officer over the nineteen months he served as his assistant.

Mengele would often kill the children, dissecting their small bodies and comparing each to their twin as though searching for something. The author never stated Mengele's goal, but he seemed certain the doctor had a purpose for the experiments.

Some of the children were allowed to live for a time, even given sweets in an effort to endear them to Mengele. Chocolate was a strong lure for the starving kids, and some easily fell for the charismatic madman's ploys. The author supposed that being separated from their parents, the children may have clung to the hope that Mengele somehow cared for them. Certainly, they were singled out and treated differently, but isolated from the rest of the prisoners, the children didn't know *how* differently.

Despite his kind facade, Mengele had no problem cutting open subjects in operations, often without anesthesia. Organs were removed, the children ultimately maimed or killed during the procedures. The author's remorse for the young victims was evident in his repeated claim that Mengele's obsession with twins must have had a purpose, as though carefully cutting apart their bodies and looking for pieces to some twisted puzzle gave meaning to their deaths.

Nyiszli's diary paralleled the first book, giving Aldo more insight into the nightmares the prisoners endured. Aldo was so absorbed in Nyiszli's account, he nearly jumped out of his skin when the door creaked open.

"Closing time," the owner said, peering around the shelf.

Aldo placed a hand to his chest to still his racing heart. "Already?"

The old man barked a laugh and pointed at Aldo's wristwatch.

Aldo glanced at it, shocked to see it was just after six o'clock. He picked up the two books and handed them to the old man. "I'll take these."

"You'll not be taking anything," he said gruffly.

"But this is a bookstore, isn't it?"

"Yes. Out there, it's a bookstore. In here, it's a collection. *My* collection," the owner said.

Aldo sighed and nodded. "I see. Can I come back tomorrow?"

"Depends," the owner said then smiled. "I accept donations."

Aldo chuckled as he reached into his pocket and pulled out a green 500-peso bill, handing it to him. The man was a bit rough around the edges, but Aldo was quickly becoming fond of him.

The old man's eyes sparkled. "You may. Come before I open."

"I'll be here," Aldo said eagerly. "Thank you."

On the way back to the hotel, Aldo picked up some *sandwiches de miga* at a deli. The crustless, double-layered sandwiches were something he'd heard about from a visiting priest at the university and had wanted to try one ever since. He ordered four, knowing he'd be up for a while and would need something to tide him over.

When he got back to his room, he propped the pillows against the headboard and switched on his laptop. Reviewing the notes he'd taken at the bookshop, he filled in a few holes from memory and underlined key points. Then he searched the internet for any more information on Josef Mengele.

All over the web, he found information to support the stories he'd just read. The online versions were more vague as though they had been censored, but they still helped confirm the accounts mentioned in the journals. He also discovered testimonies that Mengele had escaped Germany after the war through ratlines established by ODESSA and eventually found his way to Buenos Aires.

Aldo sat up as a terrifying thought occurred to him. *Could members of the Seventh-day Adventist Church have been involved with ODESSA?* It seemed impossible that the Seventh would have aided in the escape of such a notorious murderer, but that was what he needed to find out.

Aldo kept reading until his eyes started to drift shut. Unable to keep them open any longer, he brushed his teeth and turned off the lamp beside his bed.

He woke a few hours later soaked in sweat, his heart racing with images from his nightmare still fresh in his mind. An operating room, his body strapped to a cold metal table, his abdomen sliced open and organs removed one by one as he watched, unable to do anything except plead for death.

Aldo dropped his head back against the headboard and took a deep breath. *Those poor children. To have gone through something like that...* Such horrors seemed like fiction to him, but for those children, it had been a terrifying reality. In moments like this, the thought of having children of his own scared him. What if his son or daughter were taken away from him? What if he weren't strong enough to keep them safe from a monster like Mengele?

He shook off the what-ifs and grabbed a bottle of water from the mini bar. After taking a few big gulps, his heart finally slowed and he settled back under the covers, praying he'd sleep peacefully.

The next morning, Aldo dressed quickly and hurried back to the bookshop. While he had found plenty of information about Mengele's life before and during the war, Aldo had not seen much about his days in Argentina, and what he did uncover was just speculation. There had to be something to connect Mengele with the Seventh, something outside their involvement with Nazi pursuits in Germany.Even if the Seventh had been part of ODESSA, their activities were concentrated in Europe. Aldo hoped the old man's collection would provide more clues.

Arriving at the darkened bookstore, Aldo looked at his watch, realizing he was an hour early. With a sigh, he walked back down the street to a café he had passed. The brightly lit shop was filled with the rich smells of espresso and freshly baked pastries. Since heavy foods like eggs and meat weren't typical breakfast fare in Argentina, he ordered an espresso and four *medialunas*. The waiter brought out the croissant-style pastries with a small dish of creamy brown spread he called *dulce de leche*. It reminded Aldo of caramel sauce and was a bit too sweet so early in the morning, so he ate the pastries plain.

When Aldo returned to the bookshop, he saw the owner leaning against the side of the building, waiting for him. After entering, the old man immediately locked the door behind them, and then led the way to the back corner. Stopping before the shelves of romance novels, he tipped his head, indicating that Aldo could do the honors. "I'll get you in four hours for lunch," he said before closing Aldo inside the room.

After a moment of deep breathing to calm his claustrophobia, Aldo dropped into the corduroy chair and picked up where he'd left off. He continued reading throughout the morning, not learning anything new. His stomach was grumbling by the time the old man came to let him out. *I'll have to find an alternative for breakfast. Pastries aren't going to cut it.*

"Thanks," Aldo said, shutting the bookshelf behind him. He walked up to the front door, noticed it was locked and glanced back at the old man.

"Closing for lunch," the owner said. "Meet back in forty-five minutes."

"Sure. Want me to pick up something for you?"

The old man shook his head and held up a crumpled lunch sack.

Aldo found a deli nearby and inhaled a sandwich. He still had twenty minutes, so he looked around for a grocer. Finding a small corner store, he purchased a bottle of water and a few protein bars, pocketing them for later.

He spent the entire afternoon in the concealed room, reading book after book. When the owner came at closing, Aldo glanced at his watch and groaned. "Six o'clock already?" He reached into his pocket and handed him another 500-peso bill. "Same time tomorrow?"

"Yes," the old man said, stuffing the money into his pants pocket.

The next two days went by just as quickly, but for all the reading he had done, Aldo barely filled a handful of pages in his notebook. On his fifth day in the room, just after lunch, Aldo found a small, leather bound book. As he flipped through it, a piece of parchment fell out. He picked it up and unfolded it, discovering a hand-drawn map. A chill ran down his spine as he studied it.

Is this what I think it is?

The map showed Frankfort, Germany toward the top, with dotted lines connecting other cities. Innsbruck, Austria was at the center and Genoa, Italy at the bottom. On the thin paper was a small illustration of a ship departing from Genoa for some unknown location across the Atlantic. No markings indicated the borders between countries, just dotted lines showing what looked to be ship routes.

As Aldo studied the book, his suspicions were confirmed. Sophia Burwitz, the author, was the daughter of a member of ODESSA and Stille Hilfe. Aldo's German was rough, but he thought *Stille Hilfe* loosely translated to *Silent Help*.

What he knew of ODESSA came from the few mentions of it he found during his research into Mengele and a film with Jon Voight from the seventies, *The Odessa File*. He wasn't convinced that ODESSA or Stille Hilfe were real, but according to this account, Burwitz had lived among members of those clandestine organizations dedicated to helping SS officers escape Germany at the end of World War II.

Burwitz detailed the long trek from Memmingen, Germany to Innsbruck, Austria where the escapees then hiked through the Brenner Pass. The route she described matched the map he held in his hands. The officers were then put on a ship bound for South America. A teenager at the time, Burwitz managed to keep her journal secret throughout the journey, hiding it among her belongings or beneath a floorboard in her cabin aboard the ship.

As he read, Aldo jotted down the names of ODESSA members in his notebook to look up later. Based on her account, though, it seemed less and less likely that the Seventh was involved. ODESSA and Stille Hilfe clearly believed in Nazi ideology, as evidenced by the stories Burwitz recounted of her parents lecturing her about their political views. But from what he knew of the Seventh-day Adventist Church, their doctrine differed greatly from Nazi principles.

Considering the Nazis' agenda, Aldo could understand why they supported Mengele's experiments during the war, but what reason would the Seventh have for helping him escape, instead of turning him over to the Nuremburg Trials?

Aldo shuttered, remembering the gruesome accounts of torture and mutilation from the diaries. He doubted such a monster would simply give up on his experiments. The man had clearly been obsessed and would most likely have found a way to continue his work once he arrived in Argentina.

But how?

Startled by the sound of the door creaking open, Aldo bolted to his feet then glanced at his watch. It was only five o'clock. He set the book aside and picked up his notebook, tucking it into his pocket. As he headed toward the open door, Allison poked her head in and grinned.

"Hi," she said cheerfully.

Stopping abruptly, Aldo took a moment to register what he was seeing. *What is she...* He shook his head. He shouldn't be surprised. *It's Allison, after all.* "Hey," he breathed. "You like to catch me off guard, don't you?"

"It's one of my things." She smiled, leaving the door cracked as she entered the room.

"How on Earth did you know where to find me?" Aldo asked. He'd been evading her text messages for the last week.

"We have a plant in the Apostolic Palace." She ran her fingers over the shelves of books as she circled the room. "I can't tell you who, but he's reliable."

"Even so, that doesn't explain how you found me *here*." He gestured at the room around them.

"Rafael," she said simply.

"Who?" Since being hijacked off the top of a mountain, he'd felt like a player in an improvisational sketch comedy, never quite knowing what was going on.

Allison stared at him. "Haven't you spent the last five days with him?"

"Oh!" Aldo smacked his forehead with the palm of his hand. *The owner* . "Rafael's his name!"

"He's an old friend."

"What a coincidence," Aldo said, unable to keep from rolling his eyes.

She chuckled. "Let's just say he and I go way back. Rafael gave me a call when you came in searching for books about the Nazis. He wanted to know if I knew anything about a young Ph.D. from Pontifical Gregorian University." She shook her head. "You weren't exactly in stealth mode, were you?"

Aldo sighed, following her out of the room. "Despite appearances, I'm not a spy."

Her bright laughter made Aldo feel refreshed after his long day of reading about war and death. He handed Rafael another bill and thanked him. "Tomorrow?" he asked.

Allison put a hand on Aldo's shoulder. "I'll come with you." She turned to Rafael. "I'll phone you when we're on our way."

Rafael nodded then kissed her on both cheeks. "Good to see you, girly girl."

Allison guided Aldo out to the street and gestured toward a parked car. Clicking the unlock button on her key fob, she said, "Hop in."

"Where are we going?" he asked, fastening his seatbelt.

"Hungry?"

He smiled. Answering his questions with one of her own was another of her habits. "Famished."

She drove out of the bustling city center and into a small residential area. Without the aid of GPS, navigating the narrow streets seemed second nature to her. By the time she pulled into the driveway of a small wooden cottage, Aldo was completely turned around.

"Where are we?"

"Pilar," she said. "It's a family home. Come on."

Itching to ask why a Mormon family from Utah would have a second home in Buenos Aires, he decided to hold his tongue and followed her into the house. The walls were all painted a matte white and sparsely decorated. She led Aldo to the kitchen, gesturing him toward one of the stools at the counter. Aside from the stainless steel appliances and colorful ceramic tile backsplash, this room was like the others, white.

He watched in silence as Allison opened the refrigerator and began pulling out ingredients. She set a pot of water to boil on the gas range and poured olive oil into a heating frying pan.

"Wine?" she asked.

"Uh, sure."

She pulled out a bottle of Torrontes from the refrigerator. Handing it to him, along with a corkscrew, she asked, "Could you open it?"

"Of course."

Using a chef's knife, she quickly peeled and chopped garlic then threw it into the hot oil. Her movements mesmerized him. Here she was cooking him a meal while he opened a bottle of wine. He grinned. *This almost feels like a date.*

"What're you smiling at?" she asked.

"Nothing," he said with a shrug. "Just thinking this is nice, that's all." He poured her a glass of wine and slid it across the counter.

"Oh, I bought it for you," she said, shaking her head.

That's right. I forgot she doesn't drink. Aldo nodded and pulled the glass back. He took a sip, savoring the flavor, then drained his glass and poured another. The combination of her intoxicating presence, his empty stomach, and the cool sweet wine immediately went to his head. Still, he knew she wouldn't hop a plane to Argentina just to wine and dine him.

"Allison, why are you here?"

"Tired of being in the dark?" she asked, throwing chopped tomatoes into the pan.

"Yes. I understand the need for secrecy, but I'll admit it's frustrating."

"I don't doubt it." She laughed as she dropped pasta into the boiling water. "Well, like you, I've been sent to research *certain* events," she said cryptically. She sprinkled fresh basil and other herbs into the simmering tomato mixture.

"World War II?"

"No, but there are connections." She glanced up at him briefly before returning her attention to the frying pan. "Have you ever heard of Project Whitecoat?"

Aldo scrunched his eyes closed, trying to remember where he'd heard that term before. "Something about US military experiments on people, right? It had something to do with testing a supposed defense against biological weapons, if memory serves me correctly."

"Yeah, it was an extensive study lasting over two decades on the effects of various treatments for a multitude of deadly viruses. Created quite a controversy when it was brought to light in the late 1960s. The experiments were conducted on army soldiers, volunteers supposedly. And get this, most were Seventh-day Adventists."

"What?" Aldo said, his eyes growing wide. "But aren't they known for their humanitarian service?"

Allison nodded as she chopped vegetables for a salad.

Aldo finished his second glass of wine then asked, "Why would they submit to that?" *It just doesn't make sense.*

Allison popped a sliver of parmesan into her mouth. "The church leaders made a deal. As you said, they're big on health and humanitarian work, but their young men couldn't avoid the draft either. So what better way to get them out of combat duty than to have them *volunteer* for medical experiments that would benefit humanity?"

Aldo gaped at her in disbelief.

"Part of the deal was that if the church supplied 2,300 young men to be human guinea pigs, in return it would be allowed to teach something called the 2,300 Days Prophecy. There was also an agreement to turn a blind eye to their teachings, specifically about how the US government was the second satanic beast mentioned in the Book of Revelation."

Aldo held his hand up, trying to fit all of the pieces together. "Okay, but wouldn't the First Amendment cover that?"

"Sort of," Allison said with a sympathetic smile. "But they wanted some added insurance that their church wouldn't be shut down or their members taken in the middle of the night for teaching doctrine that went against the US government."

"That happens? Really?"

"Of course, it does," Allison said, rolling her eyes. "It's not as free a country as you've been led to believe."

It all sounded more like a movie plot than the truth, but what reason would she have to lie? "That's crazy," Aldo muttered. If she was right, then the Seventh really had strayed as far off the path as the pope feared.

"I know. However, that wasn't their only motivation. The Seventh-day Adventists also wanted the right to observe their Sabbath by taking Saturday off from work without the fear of discrimination or persecution."

"Again, First Amendment," Aldo replied.

"It's one thing to have the right, and it's another to have the full backing of the United States government smoothing the way."

"True," Aldo said. "But that's still a heavy price to pay. I'd imagine at least a few of those test subjects died, right?"

"Believe me, it still costs the US government plenty in grant money. The Seventh-day Adventist Church made a killing off their members." She glanced up at him. "No pun intended."

Aldo shook his head. "Gruesome."

"It gets worse," Allison said, draining the pasta. "You see, there was more than one Whitecoat laboratory in existence. More than one set of experiments going on."

"You're joking." *Please tell me you're joking.*

She shook her head, and then put noodles on two plates and poured the pan sauce over the pasta. "This is where your research and mine intersect." She handed him a plate then dished up the salad.

No way. That's impossible . But if he connected everything he'd learned so far, there was only one answer. *That was how Mengele continued his experiments.*

He took a few bites of pasta, his tongue tasting nothing as he ran through the facts again and again in his mind. Hoping he'd missed some clue, he asked, "Who ran the second Project Whitecoat?" *Please tell me I'm wrong.* He'd never wanted to be more wrong in his life.

She watched him carefully before answering. "Mengele."

His fork clattered onto his plate as he dropped his forehead onto his palm.

"You okay?"

"Sorry," he muttered. "I just…I was just hoping I was wrong." How many more lives had Mengele destroyed, unaccounted for and unacknowledged by the world?

"Perhaps we should table the discussion until after dinner," Allison said, tilting her head.

"No. No, I'll be fine. It's just horrific to think he was allowed free reign for so long."

"I know."

Aldo sighed, not sure he could stomach any more, food or otherwise. But he needed to confirm his suspicions about what linked Mengele's Whitecoat to the one in the US. "Was it just a coincidence there were two Project Whitecoats?"

"Not exactly," she said. She swirled pasta onto her fork. "Why don't you eat and then we'll talk?" She smiled gently. "If you get any paler, you'll become transparent."

After finishing their meal and rinsing off the dishes, Allison beckoned for him to follow her out the back door. They stepped onto a redwood patio overlooking a beautiful grassy plain that seemed to go on for miles. Aldo could see trees in the distance, their glossy foliage reflecting light from the setting sun.

"What a beautiful place," Aldo said. "So peaceful."

"Yeah, I love this spot. Especially at magic hour. The lighting's gorgeous."

"It's an amazing piece of land. Perfect for kids," he mused, imagining them racing barefoot through the grass.

"A bunch of kids," she said, staring off into the distance. Catching herself, she looked back at him. "You look like you're ready for more answers."

Aldo rubbed the back of his neck, not sure what to ask first. "Well, why me? If you know Rafael, then you've already read all his books, right?"

"Rafael's collection wasn't pertinent until a few weeks ago," she said, settling into one of the patio chairs. "I'd just read a few books for personal interest. When I got my new assignment, I'd planned to pay him another visit." She glanced up at him. "Judging by your reaction earlier, I assume you haven't come across anything about the second Whitecoat facility."

"No, but now that I know about it, you can bet I'm going to find it if it's there," he said. "So, who gave you your assignment?" He'd assumed since her surprise visit at the Apostolic Palace that she just worked for the LDS Church, but with how far down the rabbit hole she'd taken him, that no longer seemed accurate.

"Well," she replied, tilting her head, "let's just say I'll fill you in more when I can."

An evening breeze rustled through the potted shrubs on the patio, and Aldo shivered. "You can't tell me anything else?"

"Not yet." She smiled understandingly.

He sat down in one of the patio chairs. "You said it wasn't exactly a coincidence there were two Whitecoats, but the one here couldn't have been run by the US government."

"It wasn't."

He waited a moment, expecting her to elaborate. When she didn't, he asked, "Did Mengele set it up himself? I'd think he'd have been too recognizable to conduct any kind of experiments after the manhunts."

"He had enough supporters here to keep him safe. He was also very resourceful...to say the least."

Aldo pulled his notebook out of his back pocket. "I read a book today, all about ODESSA and *Stille Hilfe*," he said. "Along with it, I found a map." He opened the notebook to the sketch he'd made of the map and handed it to her.

She looked at it carefully. "It's the ratlines, the route he took, along with all the other Nazis when they escaped Germany. This is quite a find!"

"I'll show you the original when we're at Rafael's tomorrow." He flipped back a page. "I haven't had a chance to read the memoir all the way through yet, but the author details the exodus of many Nazi officials. She never specifically mentioned Mengele, only a handful of ODESSA members, particularly her parents." He pointed to the list of names he'd written down in his notebook.

Allison stared at him blankly. "You know I can't read your shorthand. No one can." She glanced down at the open pages. "It looks like a kindergartener trying to write in hieroglyphics."

Aldo blushed. She'd teased him about his messy shorthand numerous times over their six-year friendship, yet it still stung a bit. "Right. Well, I just wondered if these ODESSA members were the ones who helped Mengele set up his experiments here."

She shook her head. "He had supporters and funding, but he established his Whitecoat laboratory on his own. He was meticulous and obsessive, and he didn't want anyone else to have a hand in how the lab operated. He wanted it set up identically to the one in the US, with a few notable exceptions."

"What exceptions?"

"Well," she sat down in the chair next to him, "first of all, he used children as well as adults."

Aldo paled. "What?"

"Toddlers," she said.

Aldo felt his dinner rumble uncomfortably in his stomach. "But how… Surely the locals would've noticed children going missing."

She nodded. "Procuring test subjects was a major roadblock. He was able to get information funneled from an informant inside Fort Detrick, Maryland, where the US experiments were being conducted. But to get his test subjects, he approached the only group willing to support his experiments. A group with its own goals and agenda. A fast-growing religion that needed funds to continue to expand into South America, as well as around the world."

"A group who'd already volunteered 2,300 men to the US-conducted Project Whitecoat?"

Allison looked at him for a moment, confirming his suspicion.

"No. Even with all of the reasons you mentioned, the Seventh-day Adventists would never support an animal like Mengele," Aldo argued. "Nothing about

Mengele's work benefits the welfare and happiness of the human species. It goes against everything the SDA Church stands for."

"Well, you're not wrong, on the surface at least," Allison said softly. "You also have to remember that it was a confusing and scary time. There were many who were deathly afraid of the Communist threat, something the Nazis offered protection from. After the war, the Nazis used that fear to worm their way into the US government through a program called Operation Paperclip. You see, top Nazi officials threatened to go to the Russians if the US wouldn't have them. Our government considered the Nazis the lesser of two evils and brought many of those high-ranking SS officers into the OSS. They took top Nazi scientists and espionage experts and wove their knowledge and skills into the fabric of our country."

"But President Truman forbade working with anyone associated with the Nazi Party. If what you say is true, how did those officers avoid prosecution in the Nuremberg Trials?"

"That's where Operation Paperclip comes in. To get around Truman's order, the records of the SS officers were altered substantially. They were basically given new identities, new paperwork."

Aldo thought for a moment. "But Mengele wasn't a part of that."

"No," Allison said. "His crimes were too great. If the Allied Forces had captured him, he would've stood trial with his comrades and then been put to death. No, he was independent, working on his own in South America. Well, not completely alone. He had support and aid from Peron and his government here, as well as many Argentine sympathizers."

Sympathizers? Who could possibly sympathize with the Angel of Death?

Aldo mulled over the information as he gazed at the darkening sky. "Do you have any idea why he wanted to experiment on children, or why he was so obsessed with twins?"

"Twins?"

Aldo nodded. "I found a diary written by Mengele's assistant. He wrote that Mengele had a particular fascination with twins."

Allison shook her head. "I only knew that he experimented on adults, the elderly in particular, as well as toddlers."

"Do you think our government knew about Mengele's experiments? If he was receiving information from Fort Detrick, couldn't he have been feeding information to his informant as well?" Aldo asked.

"No. I'm sure they didn't know. What reason would the informant have to demand quid pro quo from Mengele? Besides, the US would never condone experimenting on children. Remember how I mentioned there were several differences between the US's Project Whitecoat and Mengele's?"

Aldo nodded.

"In addition to mirroring the US's research for developing defenses against biological weapons, Mengele had other purposes." Allison leaned toward Aldo. "We believe one purpose was to look for a way to extend life," she said. "He was searching for the key to immortality."

"What?"

"I know. It sounds sci-fi, right? But we're pretty sure that's partly what he was after. I think he was trying to preserve the longevity of the Fourth Reich," she said.

Mengele wasn't the only one to believe immortality was possible. Aldo had recently read studies on aging, many of which included research on twins, in science and health journals. The researchers wanted to know what caused one twin to outlive the other when genetically they were identical. *Is that why Mengele was obsessed with twins?*

"He also wanted a way to reinstate the Aryan race..." Allison trailed off, a glazed expression on her face. "Wait, I think that may have been why he was so interested in twins. Why didn't I think of that before?" she muttered. She looked up at him, her eyes excited. "You know how God commanded the Latter-day Saints through Brigham Young to procreate after their migration west to the Utah territories?"

Aldo nodded.

"Well, it was to quickly grow His Church. What if Mengele had the same idea? I mean, if all of the women in the new postwar Lebensborn Programme could produce twins with each pregnancy—"

"New postwar Lebensborn Programme?" Aldo asked. "Didn't Lebensborn end with the war?"

Allison shook her head. "We have evidence Mengele conducted experiments to stimulate the conceiving of twins in the women of a particular Brazilian town. And get this, most were born with blond hair and light-colored eyes."

"Who's *we* ?" he asked, even though he knew she wouldn't answer this time either.

She smiled. "Can't tell you that. Not yet anyway." She thought for a moment. "But it should be okay to tell you about him," she muttered. "He did say he wanted to talk with you soon."

"Who?"

Relenting, she said, "A man by the name of Samuel P. Summers. He's a survivor from the toddler experiments."

What? "When can I talk to him?" Aldo asked.

"Soon."

"Where is he?"

Allison sighed. "We don't know precisely where he is. It would be too dangerous for him if we did. He's been in hiding for decades."

If he's in hiding, then... "How do you communicate with him?"

Allison stood up and stretched. "He emails me using a secure decentralized communication platform on the Dark Internet."

"You have access to the Dark Internet?" Aldo asked. The thought that she might have been the one who uploaded his thesis onto the Dark Internet popped into his head, but he quickly dismissed it. During the two years he conducted his research, Allison had the most opportunity, but no motive. Not to mention he trusted her more than anyone else in his life outside his parents and the pope.

She looked down at him and grinned. "Jealous?"

"Only mildly," he grumbled.

"I'll see if I can get you a date," she said with a laugh.

With the moon high in the sky, the temperature had dropped significantly. Aldo shivered again, and then stood to pace the patio, hoping the movement would warm him. "Why did he contact you?"

Allison shrugged. "Wasn't really me, per say. I'm just his most recent contact. He's been in communication with my higher-ups since he first went into hiding, though he's been emailing me frequently the last week or so. Somehow he caught wind of the research you're doing and wants to help. He said he'd like the truth to come out."

Did he read my thesis? While the offer of help was reassuring, a fresh wave of guilt washed through him. He couldn't help feeling his thesis was growing out of control like a cancer.

Allison's cell phone rang. Her ringtone sounding like an old rotary telephone and Aldo smiled. Glancing at the screen, she said, "It's Rafael. He calls me nightly now that I'm here." She slid her thumb across the screen and held the phone to her ear. *"Hola, abuelito."* A moment later, her smile vanished, and the blood left her face. "No," she breathed. *"Are you okay?"*

"What's going on?" Aldo asked, panic creeping into his voice.

"Get someplace safe and call me back when you can... Rafael? Rafael?!" she cried into the phone. She stared at the screen then dropped her arm to her side. "The bookstore's on fire. Rafael managed to get out, but..."

"His collection?" Aldo asked.

"Gone."

Chapter Four | Monarch PROGRAMMING

Argentina
February 2013

Allison Gillespie's mind raced. *Please, Lord. Please let him be okay.* The loss of Rafael's collection and livelihood made her feel sick to her stomach, but if her dear friend hadn't escaped the building in time… She shuddered and shook her head to clear away the thought. As rare as some of the books in his collection may have been, they couldn't compare to his life.

This was too much of a coincidence. *First, Aldo shows up at Rafael's, and not five days later the whole shop goes up in flames?* Someone clearly didn't want him snooping around.

Allison glanced up at Aldo, his face ashen with shock. *Well, at least we know we're on the right track* . But it also meant someone was watching him. Closely. She would have to be more cautious from now on. She couldn't let anyone else get hurt, especially Aldo.

She had grown rather fond of him over the years. Her colleagues had their doubts about whether he was up to the task of ferreting out the truth, but she knew firsthand how tenacious he could be, a trait she found oddly charming. His task would be that much harder now that Rafael's collection was destroyed, but Aldo had never been one to shy away from a challenge. Well, except when it came to asking her out.

For now, she had to make sure Rafael was safe, and that he stayed that way. Then she would focus on finding who destroyed his bookstore.

"And Rafael's okay?" Aldo asked, seeing the concern on her face. He felt like someone had taken a jackhammer to the ground at his feet. He had known the man less than a week, but to Allison, the bookstore owner was like family, as irreplaceable as some of his books.

"He made it out alive. That's all I know," Allison said, heading toward the door.

"Is the fire department on the way? Does he need an ambulance?" Aldo followed her back through the house.

Allison grabbed her purse off the table by the front door. "I don't know. The call got cut off before he could tell me anything else." She yanked the front door open. "I'll be back after I find out what happened and make sure he's okay."

Aldo grabbed her arm. "Let me get this straight. You want me to stay here while you rush off to a burning building?"

"Look, I'll be fine. I'm not all sugar and spice, you know." She gave him a stiff smile.

He put his hand on her cheek, forcing her to look at him. "You are to me, and I'm coming with you." When she stared up at him, he blushed and dropped his hand. "We both want to make sure Rafael is safe."

"Fine. Get in the car." Allison yanked the door shut behind them and hurried to the sedan without bothering to lock up. He'd barely fastened his seatbelt before she threw the car into gear and barreled down the quiet streets leading out of the neighborhood.

Aldo watched her for a moment. "This wasn't an accident, was it?"

She shot him a look. "You want the truth?"

"Always," he said quietly.

She sighed heavily and raked a hand through her hair. "The timing seems too coincidental. Just as we're getting close to an answer this happens? That's why I want to check it out." She skidded around another corner, slamming Aldo into the door panel and narrowly missing an oncoming car. Unfazed, she gripped the steering wheel and pushed the small 4-cylinder engine to go faster.

When they were safely out of the curves, Aldo released his death-grip on the door handle. "This is all my fault, isn't it?" he muttered.

"Why would you say that?" Allison's eyes met Aldo's briefly before returning to the road.

"Well, as you put it, I wasn't exactly in stealth mode."

"No, you weren't. But if they found you, it was because they were watching Rafael."

"And you're not worried the people who set the fire might still be there?"

"All the more reason to get there as soon as possible," Allison said. Approaching the heart of the city, she weaved through late night traffic like an Olympic skier taking on the slalom. As they turned onto Avenida 9 de Julio, traffic slowed to a standstill, with officers already diverting cars onto side streets. People were gathered around the police barricades to watch the blaze, mesmerized by the bright flames shooting through the busted windows and illuminating the night sky.

Allison parked in an abandoned lot several blocks away, and they hurried toward the crowd, getting as close to the barricades as possible. With the building beyond saving, firefighters focused all their efforts on keeping the blaze from spreading to the neighboring stores.

Aldo scanned the crowd, but Rafael was nowhere in sight. He looked over at Allison, who seemed to be scrutinizing each of the bystanders. "Have you been able to get through to his phone yet?"

She shook her head and walked toward a tall police officer. Aldo followed. "Excuse me," she said, tapping the policeman on the shoulder.

The man turned around, revealing the oddest shade of light, light blue eyes Aldo had ever seen. So out of place amongst the dark-eyed Argentines, it was almost like someone had replaced his irises with larimar stones. *An ex-patriot?* He wondered.

"Can you tell me what happened?" Allison asked.

"We're not sure yet. We just got on the scene," the cop said in heavily accented English.

"Were you able to save anything?"

The officer's brows pulled together as he studied her carefully. "Do you have an interest in the store?"

Allison tilted her head then flipped her hair over her shoulder. "It's my favorite used bookstore," she said. "The romance section's amazing. They always seem to carry books by my favorite authors." She looked wistfully at the burning building. "I just hope it won't be completely destroyed."

The man shrugged. "The firefighters are doing their best, ma'am."

"Thank you," she said, giving the officer one more flirty smile before moving away. As she walked around the ever-growing crowd, Aldo trailed behind her, darting glances back at the officer. Something about the man didn't feel right, and the fact his eyes never left Allison made Aldo feel even uneasier.

"I don't think you fooled him," he whispered.

"Guess I need to work on my acting skills."

"Yeah, you do," Aldo said with a grin. They stopped at the outer edge of the crowd, keeping the officer in their line of sight. "Hey, did you notice anything weird about that officer?"

"What do you mean?"

"Well, his eyes were strange."

Allison glanced back at the cop. "Yeah, they were."

Based on the man's accent, he was definitely a local. "Probably just contacts," Aldo muttered.

"I doubt it."

He stared at her. "What makes you say that?"

Instead of answering, she pulled out her phone and began taking pictures. At first he thought she was snapping pictures of the burning building, but peering over her shoulder he saw she was really photographing the bystanders.

"Find Rafael yet?" Aldo asked.

"No, but that could be a good thing."

"I hope you're right."

She aimed her phone to snap another picture. Aldo glanced at her subject—the tall officer. Two men had joined him, their height identical to his. The trio towered over the rest of the spectators in the crowd. When Allison's cell phone camera flashed, the officer pointed at her. The other two men nodded then moved toward Allison, pushing their way through the crowd.

Aldo grabbed Allison's arm. "I think we should—"

"Run!" she cried. They raced down the road, back toward the car, dodging onlookers.

Aldo risked a glance over his shoulder. *Crap! They're gaining on us.* Aldo was more of a long-distance runner, and sprinting had never been his strong suit. He could already feel his body lagging while Allison was strides ahead of him. With another several blocks to go, he mustered his strength, forcing his legs to move faster.

They were almost to the car when Aldo felt a shove from behind. He stumbled, lost his balance, and hit the pavement hard. Ignoring the sharp pain in his knees and elbows, Aldo scrambled to his feet, only to have Allison fall into him, landing on top of him in a heap.

One of the men pulled Allison upright, shoving a gun into her ribs. "Get up," he grunted at Aldo, his accent strikingly similar to the officer's.

Aldo complied slowly, instinctively raising his hands above his head. The other man pulled lengths of ropes from his pocket and tied Allison's hands behind her back. He then did the same to Aldo.

"Where are your car keys?" the first man asked.

For a moment Aldo thought Allison wasn't going to answer. Then finally, she said, "My purse."

Keeping the gun jammed against Allison's side, the man nodded to his partner, who retrieved her tan bag and fished out the keys. As soon as his partner had the car door open, the man pushed Aldo and Allison into the back seat.

"You drive," the man said to his partner. He climbed into the passenger side and immediately turned around to aim the gun at Allison.

"Did you start the fire?" Allison asked.

"What do you think?" the man grunted.

That would be a big, fat yes.

As they headed away from the burning building, Aldo twisted his wrists back and forth, desperate to free his hands. He continued, even when his skin began to sting, but still the knots refused to loosen. He looked over at Allison. She was staring straight ahead, her face a mask of calm.

"Where are you taking us?" she asked smoothly.

How does she do that? It's as if we're out for a Sunday drive given her level of concern. Meanwhile, I may throw up at any moment. Aldo couldn't help feeling like their roles had been reversed. Wasn't he the one who was supposed to stay calm and collected in the face of danger?

"You'll see soon enough," the man smirked.

She looked thoughtful for a moment then asked, "What do I call you?"

"Hans."

Aldo cringed at the man's confidence. His disinterest in their seeing his face or knowing his name was unnerving.

She tipped her head toward the driver. "And your friend?"

"I don't see how it's going to matter," Hans replied. "Knowing our names won't help you."

Allison shrugged. "You're right. It doesn't matter. All of you look the same."

They drove another thirty minutes before pulling up to what looked like an abandoned elementary school. The moment the car stopped, Aldo's door snapped open and his arm was nearly yanked out of its socket by the nameless man. At the same time, Hans retrieved Allison, jamming his gun into her ribs once again. Before Aldo could get his feet under him, Hans' partner dragged him through the main entrance and along a dark corridor. At the end of the hallway, the man pushed Aldo into a large empty room, probably the old gymnasium or cafeteria. Cleared of any remnants of its former use, the open space trapped their echoing voices.

"There's no point in screaming," Hans said, pushing Allison into the room, "but you're welcome to try."

"I think I'll save my energy," she replied coolly.

"Good idea," Hans smirked. "You'll need it."

"When do we start?" the nameless man grunted.

"Soon. Be patient." Hans nudged them toward the far side of the room until they stood before a large metal door. Shiny and new, the door had clearly been installed recently. They waited in silence for what felt like an eternity until a series of beeps sounded and the door slid open.

Are there more of them? Aldo glanced around, expecting to see more men with guns waiting on the other side of the door or hiding in the shadows, but all he saw were two cameras mounted high on the wall.

Bright light flooded through the doorway and Aldo's eyes adjusted slowly. Various devices and high-tech machines lined the walls of the small room, and Aldo had no idea what many of them were. Five reclining metal chairs sat in the center of the room, a computer terminal mounted behind each. When Aldo noticed the foot and wrist straps attached to each chair, he took a step back.

"Oh no, my friend," Hans said with a chuckle as he grabbed Aldo's arm. "We reserved a chair just for you."

Aldo's stomach rolled, his feet rooting to the spot. Allison breezed past them, walking briskly into the room, her expression almost bored.

"Are you looking forward to this then?" Hans asked her as he tugged Aldo toward the chairs.

She stopped and stared up at him for a long moment before muttering, *"El chiflado."*

Hans ignored her and turned back to Aldo. "Let's not be difficult now," he murmured, getting right into Aldo's face. "You wouldn't want to embarrass yourself in front of the lady."

Aldo forced himself to meet the man's eyes then gasped. His irises were exact duplicates of the police officer's—that odd, pale, watercolor blue. *How is that possible?* Aldo looked at the other man. Same eyes. Both men were tall and blond as well. Obviously brothers, perhaps twins. Perfect examples of Hitler's Aryan race. Aldo's gaze flickered between the two men. "Are you two..."

Hans chuckled. "Brothers, yes."

"That's one word for it," Allison said, meeting Hans' hard gaze.

Hans' partner walked over to the terminals mounted behind the chairs and started punching buttons. The chairs began to move ominously, yet only Aldo seemed concerned.

Hans untied Aldo's hands and pointed to the chair closest to him. "Sit."

"Uh, that's okay. You first."

Hans looked over at his brother then back at Aldo. "Cute." He pushed down on Aldo's shoulders, forcing him backward into the chair.

Terror gripped him. Aldo's instinct to fight warred with the reality that he'd never win in a brawl against someone as big as Hans. Aldo's arms and legs were strapped to the chair before he could even think of what to do.

Oh, God. Bile rose in his throat. He gulped, swallowing it back down. "Why are you doing this?" he asked, panicking. "We really don't know anything. We only ran because you started chasing us. I mean, I don't even know what you think we might say or to whom. Right?" He looked to Allison, but she only shrugged.

"You can say you underwent Monarch Programming," Hans said, securing Allison to the chair next to him.

Monarch Programming? Aldo's eyes flashed to the small wheeled tables beside each chair, lined with medical instruments and syringes full of questionable liquids. "That doesn't sound good," he muttered.

"It isn't," Allison said.

Aldo wasn't sure whether to believe her, but the disinterested look on her face belied the weight of her words.

"Don't worry," Hans smirked, walking around behind them to join his brother. "You won't remember any of it."

Well, that's comforting.

It was clear from his attitude that Hans was enjoying the torment and was also completely unconcerned with the possibility of failure. Strangely, Allison seemed just as confident.

Stuck in the middle, Aldo wasn't sure what to believe. Fear made him question her confidence. He trusted her, but what if her mask of indifference was just a defense mechanism? What if she was really just as scared as he was?

Come on, Aldo. Calm down and think. He pulled against the wrist straps. He could see no way out of this. No one even knew they were here. If Allison really did have a plan, what could he do to help? He glanced at her again. Her eyes surveyed the room, as if she were trying to memorize every detail.

Monitors beeped rhythmically behind him as the captors tapped away at the keyboards.

Trusting her, Aldo took a deep breath. If all he could do was buy her some time, then…"What's Monarch Programming?"

Hans chuckled. "You might know it as MK Ultra."

Aldo's entire body tensed. *What?* He thought MK Ultra was just a rumor, a conspiracy theory concocted by people with fantastical imaginations—and too much time on their hands. "But, but that's just a conspiracy theory, right? To make people question their government."

"Oh, it's real, all right. The CIA stole Herr Mengele's research and called it their own."

Aldo's skin chilled against the cold metal chair as images from his nightmare flashed through his mind, surging bile back into his throat. If the CIA had been dabbling in Mengele's sandbox, then the rumors might have even been understated. MK Ultra was designed to manipulate people's minds, using a combination of drugs, pain, and hypnosis. According to reports he'd read online, the sadistic psychiatric tool traumatized the subjects so badly they couldn't even remember what had happened.

And these two Aryans are going to do that to a couple of researchers?

"What do you want from us?" Aldo whispered.

"Information," Hans replied, staring down at Aldo. "And your pledge of loyalty." A sickening smile slowly spread across his face.

"Unlikely," Allison said, holding his gaze for a moment before glancing at the door.

Hans chuckled again. "I'm going to enjoy breaking you, woman." He looked past them to his brother standing at the terminals. "Are you ready yet?"

"Not quite."

"Well then, let's start with something easy while we wait," Hans said. He crossed his arms over his chest and stood like a statue in front of Aldo. "What do you know about Project Luz?"

Luz. Luz. Why does that sound so familiar? "Luz is Hebrew for almond." The words were out of his mouth before he even realized he was thinking aloud.

"I'm not looking for an etymology lesson," Hans said.

"Besides, you got it wrong," Allison added, her voice the same cool tone she always used when they discussed religion or history over coffee and hot cocoa. "*Luz* is Hebrew for almond tree." She shook her head. "You two freaks of nature are part of Project Luz, aren't you?"

"You may see us as freaks, but like it or not, we're the future of humanity," Hans replied.

"I don't understand." Aldo said with desperation as he tried to overcome the feeling of suffocation consuming him. Allison sighed, and a little of the tension eased from Aldo's muscles.

Hans rolled his eyes and muttered something under his breath. Then he said, "Luz is another name for the resurrection bone because it's the *nut* of the spinal column."

"What's the resurrection bone?" Logic told him it was most likely a bone believed to enable resurrection, but Aldo figured there was more to it than that.

"Everyone has the bone in their spine. It's indestructible. Water can't dissolve it. Fire doesn't burn it, nor can it be pulverized. It lives beyond death." Hans turned to Allison. "Care to add anything?"

Allison shrugged. "You forgot to mention that Mengele started Project Luz under Hitler's direction during World War II. He was looking for a way to extend life. His life." She calmly gave Hans a once-over then said, "So, if you two are part of Project Luz, who are you supposed to be?"

"Who do you think?"

"I'd prefer not to guess," Allison replied, but Aldo could hear the suppressed shudder in her voice.

The rhythmic beeping ceased, and Hans smiled. "Sounds like our question and answer session is over." He looked past them at his brother. "Ready?"

"Yeah."

I'm not! Aldo tried to twist out of his restraints again, but the leather only rubbed his skin raw. He looked over at Allison, but her gaze was fixed on the door.

"Anytime now!" she shouted.

With Allison's words still echoing through the room, the door blew off its frame and half a dozen men dressed in black rushed in, guns drawn. Several low pops sounded, and Hans' brother dropped to the floor with a thud.

"No!" Hans yelled, his eyes widening. "You do know where he is, don't you? The Thirteenth Child." Hans reached for something as a flurry of bullets hit his chest. His body jerked back and forth violently before falling to the floor like a downed tree.

"Took you long enough," Allison scolded, as one of men released her from the chair.

Another came around to free Aldo. "Are you okay, sir?"

Aldo swallowed. All he could manage was a nod.

The man beside Allison signaled his men and turned to them. "Let's go. We need to get you out of here quickly."

"What about their command center?" Allison asked.

"Taken care of."

The men led the way back through the abandoned building. Outside, bright spotlights flooding the courtyard and a high-pitched whirring noise drew Aldo's attention overhead. A fleet of small aerial drones hovered above them, illuminating numerous dead bodies strewn about the grounds.

Oh, God. What the hell is going on here? He caught only a glimpse as the group hurried him toward a waiting van, but each dead body appeared to be male, with the same white-blond hair as Hans and his brother.

One by one, the drones dropped, each landing in a different location, and the surrounding darkness closed in. Before Aldo's eyes could adjust, he was half thrown, half pushed through the van's open door onto a row of seats, and then everyone else piled in behind him. The door slammed shut and the van squealed away, throwing Aldo against the far side.

They were barely out of the complex when several massive explosions sounded in succession behind them. Aldo looked back to see an inferno engulf the old school building.

"Another Fifth Reich camp cleansed," the driver called back over his shoulder. "Thanks for helping us locate it."

"I'd say *anytime* , but let's not do that again," Allison said, picking herself off the floor. She took a seat next to Aldo.

"Of course," the driver replied. "Normally we prefer to not get civilians involved, but what can we do when they go looking for trouble?"

"I know, I know. My bad." Turning to Aldo, she asked, "You okay?"

Uh, no. "Sure," he muttered.

She smiled sympathetically. "I wanted to tell you everything would be all right, but I couldn't. I needed Hans to believe he'd succeed."

"Right." Aldo glanced around the van. Every pair of eyes was focused on him, even the driver who seemed to be watching him through the rearview mirror. "You knew they would come for us. How?"

Allison held out her left arm. "I have a sub-dermal microchip implanted in my arm."

He stared down at her arm, expecting to see some kind of hideous circuitry or, at the very least a scar, but only saw smooth pale skin. "Like an RFID tag?"

"No. That technology's pretty limited. This type allows someone to actually track you with a simple handheld GPS device."

"Human tagging," Aldo said, amazed. "Like in Revelation?" The Bible stated that in the last days the beast would mark everyone on their right hand or forehead.

"And no one shall buy or sell without it," Allison recited, tucking her arm at her side. "I know."

"What are *you* doing with one?"

Her lip twitched. "It's not in my right hand or forehead."

"I think it still counts." The mark of the beast signified an association with Satan, not something one should take lightly.

She sighed. "Look, I'm not a proponent of universal tagging, but you have to admit, in this particular case it came in handy."

"Yeah, I'll give you that," Aldo said, shaking his head. "That's why you were so calm the whole time."

"Is that how it seemed to you?" Allison asked with a tilt of her head.

"You looked like you were waiting to catch a bus, not about to be tortured."

Allison smiled. "Thanks."

"I'm not sure that was a compliment," Aldo replied. She laughed, the sound calming his racing mind a bit as he began to process everything that had happened. The fire, the strange policeman, the chase and their subsequent capture. "Did you allow yourself to get caught?"

Allison shifted in her seat and glanced out the window at the passing scenery. "Yes," she said quietly.

"But…why?"

"Because she's headstrong and doesn't listen to orders," the driver interjected.

"That's not true, Tony. I was just…I was pissed, okay?" She crossed her arms over her chest. "Those jerks burned down Rafael's shop. What was I supposed to do?"

"So, you think that justifies endangering Mr. Lombardi?" Tony said then sighed. "Let us handle it. That's why we're here. We've already blown up several Fifth Reich facilities all over Argentina, and we were close to tracking down this latest one. You just had to be patient."

"I didn't anticipate..." her words trailed off as she looked at Aldo. "That's why I wanted you to stay at the house."

"What? So you could've gone through that hell by yourself?" Aldo demanded, his voice rising.

"Okay, okay. Enough. Sorry I said anything," Tony said. "Let's count this as a win and move on. We were able to track down the camp thanks to Allison's chip, and Mr. Lombardi got a firsthand look at the Monarch chairs and clones."

Aldo froze. *What did he say?* "Hold on." Aldo rubbed small circles into his temples. "Go back a step. What did I see?"

Allison quirked an eyebrow. "The Monarch chairs and clones," she replied slowly, as though talking to a foreigner.

"Seriously?" Aldo laughed nervously. *Weren't the Aryans just twins?* "I mean, I know cloning is possible. Dolly proved that, but human cloning is not only unethical, it's illegal."

Allison tilted her head. "You think that's going to stop them?"

Aldo shrugged, but he knew she was right. Just because something was illegal didn't mean it wasn't practiced. There would always be those who would push the boundaries of right and wrong, out of simple curiosity or a morbid sense of power. But the thought of some madman playing God scared him more than the Monarch chairs had.

"There's more of them," she replied quietly. "Many more. Exact copies, all cloned from DNA extracted from the resurrection bones of a few select people. That's what Hans was talking about. Project Luz."

"Who are they clones of?" Aldo wasn't sure he wanted to know the answer.

Allison leaned back in her seat, laying her head against the headrest. "We don't know for sure. Eichmann probably. Maybe Rauff."

"You're telling me someone's making clones of the most sadistic men of the last century?"

Allison nodded. "That's why I'm here. Why we're here." She gestured around the van. "We're trying to keep the Fifth Reich from continuing Mengele's work. And protect those who've been affected by it."

Aldo nodded slowly. He just wanted to pretend this was all a bad dream. But to his dismay, he knew there was no backing out now. And he wasn't about to leave Allison, even if he could, now that he knew the kind of danger she was putting herself in. "Who exactly are the Fifth Reich? There were mentions of it when I was researching Mengele online. Some sites called it the Fifth Reich. Others referred to it as the Fourth Reich Expansion Phase."

Allison nodded. "Yeah, the Fourth Reich, also called the Fourth Reich Birthing Phase, was formed right after World War II. It consisted of surviving Nazis and their new followers, thousands of men living here in South America, and was led by Mengele. The Reich included a closed order within the Seventh-day Adventist Church." She paused then said, "I believe that's what the pope sent you here to uncover. We know they were part of Perón's sanctioned underground network, but the rest is all speculation. I have an insider who's filled us in on all the details, but until we have proof, we can't do anything."

Aldo pulled his notebook out of his pocket. "What details?"

Allison smiled. "You always were a good student." Aldo looked at her out of the corner of his eye, and she chuckled. "Well, the order's mission was to use the church's worldwide connections, their wealth, and medical and education systems to ensure Mengele's success in bringing about the resurrection of Hitler and those in the Fourth Reich – Mengele included."

"Was that why Mengele never got caught? He could stay hidden because he had the order to do the legwork for him?"

Allison smiled. "Not much gets past you, does it?"

"I could say the same about you," Aldo replied as he scribbled notes into his notebook.

"Mengele was the brains behind everything while a network of administrators and engineers put the designs together and used the loyalty and massive organization of the Fourth Reich to get the work done. While they were not all active in the church, most of this inner circle were born into and educated by the SDA Church."

Aldo reviewed what he had just written. "So, when Mengele died on February 7th, 1979, the Fourth Reich became the Fifth Reich?"

She nodded. "The Reich fell out of Nazi hands. Well, Nazis who were out in the open, anyway. Some believe the Fourth Reich still exists today. There are even some in different parts of U.S. and South America who want to become head of the so called Fourth Reich." She waved her hand. "Anyway, it was his protégés, the clones, who gave birth to the Fifth Reich."

Images of clone armies, thousands deep, standing at attention and marching across open plains flashed through Aldo's mind. It all seemed so sci-fi, but as Tony had pointed out, Aldo had just witnessed the reality of it firsthand.

"Is the church still involved?" he asked.

"Yeah. The order's smaller now, but they're smarter. They've done a darn good job of covering their tracks, too. Not even the church's members know about them." Allison patted Aldo's hand on the seat. "You've got your work cut out for you."

"Thanks," he muttered.

Allison smiled. "Why don't you get some rest?" She glanced around the van. "Looks like we could all use some."

"We have a few more hours before we get to our destination," Tony said.

Aldo nodded, then laid his head against the cool leather seat, and his eyes drifted shut. His body quickly relaxed and his breathing slowed, but despite his efforts to clear his thoughts, Aldo's mind kept replaying what had happened at the camp.

He recalled the terror and helplessness he had felt, and a chill ran through his body, prickling his skin. *They're dead. They can't come after you again* . But no matter how hard he tried, he couldn't erase the sight of Hans' chest riddled with bullets, his body grotesquely jerking back and forth, and the horrible thud of his dead weight hitting the floor.

Aldo's eyes popped open, and he slowly sat up.

"You okay?" Allison asked.

"Who's the *thirteenth child* ?" he asked. When Allison just stared at him, he continued. "Hans yelled something about a *thirteenth child* right before he died. I think when he saw your men storm into the room."

Allison sighed. "I was going to get into that tomorrow, but…" She waved her hand, around the interior of the van. "You have the Thirteenth Child to thank for our rescue."

"What do you mean?" Aldo glanced around the van, expecting Allison to point to one of the six men. "Who is it?"

"A man named Samuel Summers," Tony offered.

Samuel Summers? He looked at Allison. "You mean the survivor of the toddler program? The man in hiding?"

"Well, he's not really hiding," Allison said. "We're protecting him. He's been helping us locate Fifth Reich camps all over South America, along with identifying members and their support teams. Not to mention tracking down their funding sources. Trust me, there are a lot of people out there who'd love to know where he is."

Aldo pinched the bridge of his nose. *Okay, so Mr. Summers is helping Allison with her mission, but how? Even if he did extensive research on the Dark Internet, I doubt he could pinpoint each camp or identify its members.* Aldo glanced around the van. *And then there's these guys. How exactly do they fit into all this?* "Who did you say you worked for again?" Aldo asked Tony.

"I didn't, but we're part of the NSA."

Aldo cocked an eyebrow at Allison. "You're with the NSA?"

"No, I'm independent."

Aldo shook his head. "I feel like every time I learn something new, it just creates more questions."

"Keep asking," Allison said, patting his knee. "It's the only way to get answers."

Her hand left his leg too soon, and he bit back a sigh. *Focus.* If the last few hours were any indication of how this job was going to go, Aldo needed to arm himself with as much knowledge as possible. "Why is Mr. Summers referred to as the Thirteenth Child?"

"He was the thirteenth and last toddler admitted into Mengele's science experiment," Allison replied. "Well, the North American branch of it. The South American location had a much larger pool of subjects – about four hundred elderly men and women and around three hundred children. The SDA church shut down the North American location after Mr. Summers for fear of the public catching wind of it."

"What happened to the other twelve?"

"They all survived," she said, "though none were the same afterwards. Part of the agreement was that their families were given the chance to promote their most promising child to a position of power within the Seventh-day Adventist Church."

They were buying success for one child by sacrificing another? "So, even if one child ended up mentally or physically disfigured, it didn't matter?" Aldo tried to imagine what those kids must have gone through, their own parents willingly handing them over to be turned into guinea pigs. He shook his head. "What kind of parent would do that?"

Allison sighed. "Unfortunately, power in one of the wealthiest Christian movements in the world is a strong lure."

That's the second time she's mentioned the church's wealth. Is it really that wealthy?

"Mr. Summers' father had been a guinea pig himself in Germany during World War II and was one of the recruiters for Project Whitecoat in the US," she continued. "He believed it was his sworn duty to sacrifice his son, just as Abraham had, if asked by his church."

"That's crazy!" Aldo cried.

"In case you haven't caught on, sanity had little to do with it," Tony said. "The point is these atrocities really happened, and now we're trying to clean up the mess."

"Right." Aldo took a deep breath, trying to calm his rising emotions. "Did they use MK Ultra on those kids?" he asked softly.

Allison nodded. "We think so. Most of them. Not the Thirteenth, though. We know he was spared, along with two others. The church leaders planned to make each of them president of the General Conference one day."

Why? Why hand over your own kid to be subjected to unthinkable experiments, when you have such high hopes for their future? Then it dawned on him. Those children would become adults who would make perfect puppets for the executive committee to control.

"What happened to the other two?" Aldo asked.

"One of the boys was the son of the church's treasurer. He wasn't treasurer at the time his son was part of the Toddler Program, but there's been talk he acquired the post as compensation for his *sacrifice*," Allison said, making quotation marks in the air with her fingers. "And like father like son, the boy followed in daddy's footsteps and eventually became treasurer as well. Apparently, he wasn't really president material, and it's rumored his accounting skills are just as questionable. The other boy is now in office. His focus so far has been ecumenism and preparing the congregation for the end of the world." She rolled her eyes before continuing. "Their founder, Ellen White, made several End Days prophecies in her book, *The Great Controversy*, and with everything that's been going on in the Middle East, they're convinced the end will be here before we know it."

Aldo had read the book several years earlier and made a note to review it again, along with White's other works. If the Seventh-day Adventist Church was as intimately tied to this as the pope seemed to fear, Aldo was going to need a deeper understanding of its teachings. "And the last one?" he asked. "Did the thirteenth toddler get what was promised?"

"Well, he was considered special right from the start, and as the Toddler Program progressed, the plan for him changed. Members of the Seventh-day Adventist Church love the health message, right?" When he nodded, she continued. "Well, he was to take advantage of that and encourage the members to use emerging technologies developed by Loma Linda and other medical arms of the church to research life extension. Not just resurrection, but eradicating all forms of disease, including aging."

Aldo shook his head. He could certainly understand the desire to live a long, healthy life, to want to cure loved ones afflicted with a life-threatening disease, but how could people who called themselves Christians be okay with playing God to that extent? How could they aid and harbor a monster like Mengele just to conduct life extension research? But the evidence for the Seventh-day Adventists' involvement with Mengele and programs like Project Whitecoat was mounting.

The van hit a pothole, tossing Allison into Aldo's side. But instead of scooting back, she stayed tucked next to him.

"Sorry about that," Tony called back.

"Keep your eyes on the road, would ya?" the man in the passenger seat scolded.

Allison shifted to face Aldo. "You see, when he was born, Mr. Summers was delivered by Dr. McCluran, the lead physician for the North American branch of the experiment. So, Summers was essentially handpicked for the program. And here's an interesting little tidbit. McCluran's father was one of the original Freemasons assigned by William Miller to assist Ellen White in founding the Seventh-day Adventist Church."

So, between his father and his physician, Mr. Summers was pretty much guaranteed to be chosen for the experiments. "If Mr. Summers' new role was to encourage further research into life extension, was he also offered a high-level position within the church?" Aldo asked.

"Yes," she replied. "But as he grew older, he wanted no part in the corrupt church and left."

I don't blame him. "I imagine that didn't go over well."

Allison shook her head. "No. Elder Frogburger, the General Conference president at that time, used the full influence and financial backing of the church to put Mr. Summers behind bars."

"What? What were the allegations?"

"A white collar crime. Frogburger used his position to *encourage* the bookkeeper to forge a second set of accounting books for the company Mr. Summers managed."

Aldo's mouth fell open. *Seriously? He was betrayed by his own father and then wrongfully accused of a crime just because he wanted nothing to do with the church?* "How long was he in prison?"

"The federal judge sentenced him to forty-seven months," Allison said. "Frogburger claimed he was just following orders from his father-in-law though. But guess who his father-in-law was."

Aldo shrugged.

"The treasurer."

"You mean the one whose son was part of the Toddler Program?"

"Yeah.   There's   evidence he rigged the General Conference presidential election to get his son-in-law into office, so I'm inclined to believe he was probably behind the false allegations as well. Since he was due the right of ascension, but neither of his natural sons were as malleable, he violated the agreement of the Toddler Program to force the church leaders to elevate his son-in-law to the office of president."

Tony shook his head and chuckled softly. "To this day, I doubt Frogburger even knows how or why he got the promotion."

"Plus, his checkered past made him the perfect puppet for the job," Allison added. "And in the end, he became the first president of the Seventh-day Adventist Church to be thrown out of office."

"For what?" Aldo asked.

"Well, the members were told he resigned for personal reasons, but the truth is he was involved in a multi-billion dollar investment fraud of church funds."

Aldo gaped at her. "Multi-*billion* dollar?"

"Uh-huh. Much bigger than the little land deals mentioned in the media." Allison reached above her head, stretching her arms, then dropped them back into her lap with a yawn. "Mr. Summers helped bring that about. After reading the   first   defense   document   Mr.   Summers   prepared,   the   original federal prosecutor quit the case so he could conduct a secret investigation into Frogburger and the heads of the church. It's the largest scandal in the history of the Seventh-day Adventist Church, yet its members are still mostly in the dark."

"That whole group is still being watched today," Tony said.

"Well," Allison said with another yawn as she laid her head on Aldo's shoulder, "get some sleep while you can, 'cuz you probably won't get much once we get there."

•••

Aldo woke each time the van hit a bump in the road, but quickly drifted off again, exhausted and content to have Allison beside him, her soft hair tickling his neck. When low voices overtook the soothing rumble of the engine, he slowly cracked his eyes open. Pale early morning light had begun to creep in through the front and rear windows, towering trees the only thing visible through the windshield.

"Where are we?" Aldo asked quietly.

"Sierra de la Ventana," Tony replied, glancing back over his shoulder. At some point during the night, he had switched places with the driver. "It's a mountain range about six hundred kilometers south of where we picked you up." He turned back to the driver. "It's just off here," he said, pointing out the side window.

"Finally." The driver steered the van onto a narrow gravel road. "I've had to pee for the last three hours."

"Thanks for that," Allison groaned.

The driver smiled and pulled the van up to a small cabin set back in a grove of evergreens, and then killed the engine. "Everybody out," he yelled as he jumped down and slammed the driver's door shut behind him. The side door slid open and they slowly climbed out, everyone taking a moment to stretch the aches from their limbs.

As Aldo glanced around, he realized it was not the peaceful retreat it had first seemed. Tucked back behind the cabin were several more buildings, much larger and painted to blend into the surrounding foliage. Men in camouflage were perched in the treetops, as well as on the ground, while drones similar to the ones he had seen at the Fifth Reich camp zipped about between the trees.

Other tank-like drones, small and compact, crawled across the open spaces, as if they too were patrolling the area.

"Sleep well?" Allison asked, coming up beside him.

Warmth flooded his cheeks as he remembered the feel of her head on his shoulder. "I'll live. Though I'm not sure I'll ever sleep well again."

She smiled. "I'm sure you'll get used to it eventually."

"How long did it take you?"

Before she could answer, Tony hooked an arm around each of their shoulders. "Come on. Let's get some breakfast." He led them toward one of the larger buildings and into a deserted dining hall. A buffet line, filled with piping hot eggs, meats, and freshly baked pastries, awaited them, the delicious smells drawing them forward.

"Oh, God bless you, Benny," Allison breathed, scooping up a plate. "I'm starved."

"I called ahead," Tony said with an exaggerated pout. "Do I get any credit?"

She flashed him a grin then gave him a quick hug. "Always."

Trying to ignore their playful banter, Aldo started filling his plate with eggs and ham. He knew he had no right to be jealous. But the realization that he was no more special to her than a colleague hit harder than he'd expected.

"You okay there?" Allison asked.

"Huh? Oh, yeah."

"You sure? 'Cuz your face says you're not."

He took a deep breath and relaxed his facial muscles. "I'm sure. It's just been a long night."

Allison heaped her plate with food until bits of scrambled egg tried to roll off the edge. "Gonna be a long day, too. We have a lot more to discuss. But first, let's eat."

Aldo followed her to a long table and sat down across from her. They ate in silence, Allison making quick work of the mound on her plate. As Aldo returned to the table with a second helping, he noticed a tall man with short gray hair enter through a door at the far end of the room. Immediately, chairs scraped the floor as the men around him shot to attention, their arms glued to their sides.

"At ease," the tall man said, his deep voice booming through the cavernous space. "Continue with your breakfast." As the men returned to their seats, the man slid into the chair next to Aldo. "Hello," he said, extending his hand. "I'm Commander Jenkins. I'm in charge of this facility."

Aldo swallowed his mouthful of cinnamon roll then quickly wiped his hand on a napkin before taking Commander Jenkins' hand. "Nice to meet you, sir."

He smiled. "*Mr. Jenkins* is fine. After you've finished, I have an important communiqué from your boss."

Aldo stared at him blankly for a moment. *My boss?* Then his eyes widened. "You mean…"

Jenkins nodded.

Aldo pushed his plate forward and stood up. "I'm done."

"Good, then follow me. Oh, and you'll need this while you're here." He handed Aldo an ID card, complete with photo.

Aldo stared at it. The shirt in the photo was the same one he was currently wearing. *When the heck did they take this?*

"I'll catch up to you later," Allison said, a fresh mound of food on her plate.

Jenkins glanced down at her. "You're coming, too."

"Yes, sir," she sighed. Aldo smiled as she looked longingly at the discarded food before she stood and joined them.

They followed Jenkins out of the dining hall and down a narrow corridor. At the end of the corridor, Jenkins swiped his own ID card through a slot then typed a sixteen-digit code into a keypad beside a metal door with the words *Authorized Personnel Only* in large red letters. He paused as he gripped the door's handle. A moment later, a light above the door blinked and a soft click sounded. Jenkins pushed the door open.

Why the need for such high security? To require passcodes, chips, and fingerprints, they were definitely trying to keep someone out. But who? They were in the middle of nowhere in Argentina.

Jenkins led them down ten flights of stairs to another corridor lined with offices. Each room they passed was windowless, and the cool, damp air confirmed they were well below ground. Gesturing toward one of the offices, Jenkins said, "We can speak freely here."

"What's the message?" Aldo asked, as Jenkins closed the door behind them.

"The pope has resigned."

"What?" Aldo stared at him, certain he'd heard wrong. *Impossible.*

Unfazed, Jenkins pulled out a chair from the long conference table and sat down, gesturing for Aldo and Allison to join him. "He announced his resignation publicly today but had a private message for you delivered across the Dark Internet to our office."

Aldo remained where he was. "You're working with the pope?"

"Yes."

The NSA working with the Vatican? "Why?"

"We have the same goal," Jenkins said, glancing up at him. "To stop the Fifth Reich at all costs."

Aldo looked at Allison then back at Jenkins. Both of them were clearly not as concerned about this new development as he was. "But why did Pope Benedict resign?"

"He didn't say, but he did say he wants you to continue your research."

Aldo nodded. He knew that much. His assignment was too important to abandon part way. "Did he say anything else?"

"He said not to worry about the Saint Malachy Prophecy or the Final Pope."

"What's that?" Allison asked.

Aldo staggered backwards until he dropped into a chair. "Only the end of the world."

Chapter Five | Peter the ROMAN

Argentina
February 2013

Aldo leaned back in the chair, his eyes staring but seeing nothing. *The pope resigned?* He had seen Benedict in Rome just a week earlier. Had the pope already been planning to resign then? If so, why hadn't he said anything? *Such a decision probably isn't something you discuss with a mere historian.*

The damp air of the basement conference room sent a shiver across Aldo's skin. A pope's term was traditionally, and expected to be, until death. Since the very first pope, only a small handful had resigned, and the last one to do so was nearly six centuries ago. Whatever Benedict's reason, it had to be an extremely good one.

"What do you mean *the end of the world?*"

Aldo glanced up to see Allison staring at him, her face ashen with shock. "Right. Sorry," he said, straightening in his chair. He gestured for her to sit and she reluctantly complied, never taking her eyes off him. Appearing unfazed, Jenkins was already seated at the other end of the table. "The, uh, *Prophecy of the Popes* is basically a slew of phrases published by the Benedictine monk Arnold de Wyon back in 1595. He credited the prophecy to Saint Malachy, who was an archbishop in Ireland in the twelfth century," said Aldo.

A bit of the tension left Allison's face and she leaned back, crossing her arms over her chest. "What did the phrases say?"

"They're descriptions of all the popes who were to be from that time on."

Allison's brow furrowed. "How could he possibly know how many there were going to be? No one knows that."

"Well, that's the rub," Aldo said. "The story is that Malachy had a vision while in Rome, visiting Pope Innocent II. He documented the vision in cryptic phrases, which were stored in the Vatican Secret Archives until being rediscovered and published by Wyon." The prophecy was controversial, and many believed it was simply a hoax created to promote the selection of Cardinal Simoncelli as pope in 1590. As a historian, Aldo didn't believe there were enough facts to support Wyon's claim, but the accuracy of the prophecy to date was hard to refute.

"Okay, but what does it have to do with the end of the world?"

"He predicted there would be only one hundred and twelve popes total."

"How many have we had?"

Aldo ran his fingers through his hair. "A hundred and eleven."

Allison stared at him. "What happens when we run out of popes?"

"That's the million dollar question, now, isn't it?" Jenkins said, his hands folded on the table in front of him. His slight frown gave Aldo the impression he didn't put much stock in the prophecy. Aldo cleared his throat. "Well, the prophecy states that the last pope will bring about the destruction of Rome."

"But what do you think?" Allison leaned forward eagerly.

"I, uh, don't want to say."

"Oh, come on, Aldo!" she groaned.

"Look, I honestly don't know. Some people think it means the end of days. Others take it as the sign of Christ's return and his final judgment."

"But that's not what *you* think, right?" Allison asked.

Aldo thought for a moment, unsure of how to answer. He didn't fully believe the last pope signaled the end of the world, but he didn't fully doubt it either.

"You do believe it," she said, sounding incredulous.

"Look, it doesn't matter whether I do or not. There are numerous ways of interpreting it, but I don't necessarily think it means we're facing the Apocalypse."

"Not *necessarily*," she muttered sarcastically. Sighing, she softened her voice. "Okay, so who's the last pope in the prophecy?"

While all the phrases were cryptic, the last one was even more so. "All it said was Peter the Roman, a.k.a. The False Prophet."

"That's it? A bit vague, don't you think?"

"I didn't write it," Aldo said, crossing his arms over his chest.

"What was Benedict's pseudonym?"

Aldo sighed. "Glory of the Olive."

"Huh?"

"It was *Glory of the Olive,* " he repeated.

She opened her mouth, as though she meant to say something, but closed it again. After a few moments, she said, "He chose the name *Benedict* after the founder of the Benedictine Order. The Olivetans were a part of that order, right?"

"Impressive," Aldo said. "The other interpretation is that his focus was peace and the olive branch is a strong symbol for that."

"It's still vague."

"Sure, but out of the one hundred and eleven phrases, each one was found to correlate to a pope. Though some connections were stronger than others."

Jenkins' phone vibrated. He snatched it off the table, quickly checking the screen before slipping it into his pocket. "Looks like we're ready. Aldo, would you follow me?" he asked, standing up. "Samuel Summers has some things he'd like to discuss with you."

"The Thirteenth Child?" Aldo whispered.

Jenkins coughed softly. "Yes, but we don't call him that. It reminds him of a painful period in his life."

"Ah, yes. I would imagine," Aldo said. "What should I call him?"

"Mr. Summers is fine."

"May I come, too?" Allison asked, already on her feet.

Jenkins nodded. "He specifically requested your presence."

"Really? I'm honored."

They followed Jenkins down a series of corridors until they came to another door with a restricted access warning.

"I need you two to stand over there," Jenkins said, pointing to a rectangle marked on the cement floor.

Allison immediately complied, tugging Aldo with her when he glanced around looking confused. She tipped her head toward the ceiling, indicating a security camera. "He has to clear us as guests since we're not chipped," she whispered.

"But you said you had a chip."

She shook her head. "It's really only for tracking."

Stepping up to the door, Jenkins waved his hand past the wall on his left and a tiny light within the opaque glass surface blinked green. Then he opened a panel beside the door, revealing a small screen, keypad, and what looked like a camera lens. When the screen flashed the word *Ready* , he leaned forward and said, "Hopscotch." He held his face before the lens, and a pale blue light briefly illuminated the area around his left eye. Then a *click* sounded and the door slid open. He closed the panel, and then waved Aldo and Allison forward.

"Hopscotch?" Allison asked with a smirk.

"My daughter's favorite game," Jenkins answered as he sealed the door shut behind them.

The room was much smaller than Aldo had expected, considering the high level of security to enter. Three white concrete walls surrounded a small table with a computer terminal and a single chair. Looking up, he noticed even the ceiling was concrete, with no visible air vents.

He took a deep breath, then another. *It's just a room . Just focus on your job and don't think about it.*

"We can speak with Mr. Summers here," Jenkins said, gesturing toward the table. "It's connected to the Dark Internet, and this room's been NSTISSAM Level One certified against Van Eck Phreaking and other means of spying."

Aldo eyed the computer terminal. "What's NSTISSAM?"

Jenkins smiled. "Also known as Tempest. The terminal's been outfitted with Red/Black separation as well. It's the most secure communication line available." He bent over the keyboard, clicking away until white noise could be heard through the speakers. "We're not going to use video for this call—too risky—so you won't be able to see him."

Aldo nodded and sat down. *Why does Mr. Summers want to talk to me?*

Allison stepped up behind him and gently placed her hand on his shoulder. His heart pounded in his chest as he waited for the connection to go through. A moment later, the computer's screen went black. Then the white noise faded into the background as a deep voice resonated through the speakers.

"Hello, Aldo."

"H-hello, sir."

"It's good to finally talk to you. I've been following your career for some time."

What? For a moment, Aldo's voice caught in his throat. "You have?"

Mr. Summers chuckled—a deep, rich sound that helped ease the tension knotting Aldo's neck. "Yes."

But why?

Before Aldo could get the words to leave his mouth, Mr. Summers continued. "I knew you would play an important role in all this. You see, I'm sometimes gifted with foresight and clairvoyance, as well as the ability to detect lies or malicious intent."

Aldo looked back over his shoulder at Allison who nodded her head. *Seriously? She actually believes in this kind of thing?* He didn't want to outright doubt the man, but he was always skeptical when it came to prescience or other paranormal abilities. He preferred to work with facts.

"You're an honest man," Mr. Summers said. "You don't wish to imply that you believe something is true when you've yet to be convinced. So, you remain silent. I appreciate that."

Aldo stared at the speakers. He hadn't thought out loud again, had he?

"All I ask is that you keep an open mind and consider the possibility that I may be able to foretell the future once in a while," Mr. Summers said.

Aldo coughed to clear his throat. "Okay."

"Good! And it might help to know that my abilities didn't come to me naturally. They aren't something I was born with or given due to some kind of miracle. They're a side effect from a drug I was given as part of the testing done on me as a child."

What kind of drug would cause side effects like that?

"A drug called Transpose," Mr. Summers continued. "The development of that drug was the whole reason for the Toddler Program."

"Were all the children given that drug?" Aldo asked.

"Twelve of the thirteen were. The one who wasn't was the son of the former Seventh-day Adventist General Conference treasurer."

Aldo thought for a moment, recalling his conversation with Tony in the van. "The one who rigged the election to get his son-in-law elected as president?"

"Yes," Mr. Summers said. "He didn't want his son to be given Transpose. Probably feared it would make his son unfit for the position he was promised within the church. But in the end, it didn't matter and he had to resort to getting his son-in-law elected."

"Was the drug that dangerous?" Aldo asked.

"Well, no drug is without risks or pain. Transpose even more so. In fact, my body has been going through a sort of transformation for some time now."

A drug administered in adolescence still affects the body decades later? Unbelievable. "Do you know all the effects of the drug?" Aldo asked.

"No. No one does. But I was watched and studied for some time. Various doctors and medical scientists have visited me over the years, looking for signs of change. I'm still observed by at least one doctor every week."

So, from the beginning, they knew the effects would last years. "What was the drug supposed to do?"

"Increase longevity."

Aldo blinked. "Come again?"

"Transpose is thought to extend life," Mr. Summers said calmly. "Mengele was obsessed with the idea of living longer. He was researching different theories on how to get the body to defy aging."

"How much longer?"

"Hmm, it's hard to say. If I had to guess, thirty or forty years maybe. But knowing Mengele, his plans were to make it indefinite."

Remembering something Tony had mentioned, Aldo asked, "Were the Seventh-day Adventists aware of this?" Through the speaker, Aldo could hear Mr. Summers draw in a deep breath, almost as though he had been anticipating that question.

"Oh, yes. Most certainly. There are those in the upper echelons of the church's organization who are desperate to find keys to longevity. They thought Transpose was an answer to their prayers."

Aldo shook his head. "It's still hard to believe they were willing to give up so much for this experiment."

"It's a driving force for many," Mr. Summers said. "To live as many years as possible while keeping a decent quality of life is something people have sought for thousands of years. And now, they may have finally found the answer. Theoretically, Transpose slows down the aging process, perhaps even reversing it for a few years."

"A fountain of youth," Aldo murmured. "If that's true—if it really works, it'll be sought after by not just the Seventh-day Adventists."

"It already is. Many different groups have been looking for a way to extend life. Have you ever heard of Calico? It's a recent venture started by the CEO of Google, with the sole purpose of tackling aging. Then there's Peter Thiel, co-founder of PayPal. He's been on a mission for years to find a cure for death. There are top gerontologists and inventors, like Dr. Aubrey de Grey and Ray Kurzweil, who've said we have the technology right now to live a thousand years or longer." Mr. Summers sighed. "Needless to say, some groups would love to find the remaining participants of the mirror Whitecoat experiment."

"Do you know who they are?"

"Only three of the nine from the North American branch are still alive," Jenkins answered, "but we're working on locating the rest of them, so we can protect them. Tracking down the ninety or so surviving members from South America is posing more of a challenge."

"Yes," Mr. Summers said. "The theory is that when the subjects hit their mid-fifties, they undergo the process known as Transpose, for which the drug is named. However, the process might not hit until the subject's mid-sixties. Depending on if and when this takes place, it could make tracking down the subjects more difficult."

Aldo thought for a moment. "Have you hit this transitional phase?"

"Not yet," Mr. Summers replied. "I'm sixty, though, so it could happen any time. And when it does—if it does—there are plenty of people who would like to do experiments on me to try to duplicate the results."

"Think you'll lose your ability to see into the future when it happens?" Aldo asked. "Or maybe it could give you fair warning of when it will start."

Mr. Summers chuckled. "It isn't something I can control, and it doesn't happen with any regularity. I just get premonitions, usually centered on a specific subject."

"Still, that's impressive." Aldo felt the warmth from Allison's hand on his shoulder. *Wonder what he could tell me about my future.*

"It's not what you're thinking," Mr. Summers said, "like a fortune-teller or superhero. And I'm certainly not a prophet. I know the side effect wasn't intentional."

"Do you know if any of the other subjects were affected by similar side effects?"

There was a long pause—long enough Aldo feared the connection had been lost. He glanced at Jenkins leaning against the wall, but the commander only yawned.

"Honestly," Mr. Summers finally said, "I've been wondering that myself. As Jenkins mentioned, we only have tabs on three of the nine surviving participants of the Toddler Program. But there are some…indications that the current president of the General Conference of the Seventh-day Adventist Church has been experiencing some of the same effects and has been using them to navigate his way through an attempted takeover of the church's political side by a left wing cabal."

Silence filled the room for a long moment until Aldo managed to summon the courage to ask the question that had plagued him since the start of their conversation.

"How do you use your ability?"

"That's a good question. One that someone with an ethical mind would ask," Mr. Summers replied softly. "There's a lot of suffering in the world. Wars, famine, disease. But in First World nations, it's of a different nature, which stems from people's basic fear of change. My ability has made me aware of how this suffering can be eased and avoided. I've foreseen that someone with a specific voice will come along who will be able to speak to every culture, persuasion, philosophy, and religion. To every political or general viewpoint. That person will bring peace and harmony, along with a sudden balance, teaching the entire world to tame their minds and stop the raging which is driving humanity toward a dangerous precipice."

Aldo whistled. That was a tall order. But still, he could feel Mr. Summers' passion and conviction. The man truly believed it was his mission to help and perhaps save humanity.

"I've given you a lot to think about," Mr. Summers said. "Please, do what you do best and mull it over. Talk to the others there and ask questions. We'll talk again in a few days. In the meantime, I'll consider what your role is in this as well. So far, all I've foreseen is that you're instrumental to our plans."

Aldo's mouth dropped open. "Wait. What?"

Mr. Summers chuckled. "No more hiding behind desks and history books, Aldo. You're entwined in this farther than you realize. And now that I've spoken to you, perhaps I can figure out more specifically what your role will be. I just need time to digest everything. Allison?"

"I'm here." She leaned closer to the mic, her hair sweeping across the back of Aldo's neck.

"Thank you for bringing him up to speed. I'll talk to you soon and ask that you continue to help him in any way you can."

"Of course."

The screen went to standby as white noise once again filled the room, but Aldo continued to stare at the monitor for a long moment.

"Sorry I couldn't tell you earlier," Allison said, walking around to stand next to him.

He turned to look up at her. "You knew?"

"Yes," she said softly. "Mr. Summers approached a few key people about two and a half years ago, asking that we keep an eye out for you. He wanted you to be protected, safeguarded."

Aldo's head began to swim. "That day…when I met you at the coffee house, you were keeping tabs on me?"

She shrugged. "I've never been much of a coffee drinker."

"So, I was an assignment," he said flatly. *God, I feel so stupid. Of course. She'd never be interested in someone like me without a reason.*

She caressed his arm with her fingertips and a shiver coursed through him. "At the beginning, maybe," she said, "but now, you're more than that." Her normally guarded expression was gone, her face filled with a pain he couldn't quite identify.

While he longed to ask what she meant, at the same time he feared her answer. That her 'more than that' just meant he'd been upgraded from *assignment* to *friend* . But even if he'd found the courage, one look at the smirk on Jenkins' face shut him up for good. The last thing he wanted to be was an object of amusement.

"We have one more call to make," Jenkins said, stepping away from the wall. "Are you ready? Or do you need a bit more time?"

Aldo's body tensed. "Who is it?" He wanted time to at least catch his breath and try to make sense of everything he'd learned from Mr. Summers, but he knew anyone using this secure communication system wouldn't be someone to keep waiting.

"Pope Benedict," Jenkins said.

"Really? But he resigned. I assumed he'd be resting."

"The announcement's been made, but technically, he's still the current pope."

"When's the conclave set to be held?"

"Soon. The Vatican's promising to elect a new pope before Easter," Jenkins said.

"I wonder what Benedict's new title will be?"

It wasn't until Allison answered that Aldo realized he'd said it aloud. "Pope Emeritus." He smiled at her. Intelligence certainly was sexy, especially on her.

"So, you ready?" Jenkins asked again.

Aldo blew out a breath. "Give me just a moment." He stood up, stretching his legs. While he was doing his best to keep his claustrophobia in check, the knowledge of being underground, in a small concrete box with no windows was taking its toll.

"Take all the time you need," Jenkins said with a touch of impatience.

Aldo stiffened then whipped around to face Jenkins.

"Wait. Don't tell me Pope Benedict is actually waiting for my call."

"It's not like he's on hold," Jenkins said, gesturing absently with his hand, "but, yes, he's waiting."

Aldo dropped back into his seat. Taking a deep breath, he said, "Okay, I'm ready." Even after sharing breakfast with His Holiness, he still couldn't get over the waves of nervousness that gripped him every time he spoke with the pope.

Jenkins clicked a few keys on the keyboard and almost immediately, the computer's screen flashed to reveal the pope's face. Behind him, Aldo recognized the interior of his office within the Apostolic Palace.

"How are you, my son?"

The pope's familiar face and voice instantly soothed him, and he relaxed into the chair. "I'm fine, Your Holiness. But how are you? I've been so worried."

Benedict chuckled low. "I exaggerated my weakness. Don't worry about me. I'm as healthy as I ever was."

"Then…why did you resign?"

"It was time. It's been part of the plan since the beginning that I step down."

That still doesn't tell me why . But he knew that if the pope wanted him to know the reasons behind his decision, His Holiness would tell him. And as much as his curiosity was strangling him, Aldo wasn't about to push the issue. "Do you know who will take your place?" he asked instead.

Benedict shook his head. "No one knows. However, there has been a lot of supposition, especially from the Seventh, that the next pope will be a Jesuit."

"Really?" Confused, he asked, "But aren't those who are part of the Society of Jesus all bound by oath not to take on a position of authority within the Church?"

"It will be a surprise for many, if it comes to pass, but as I said, we won't know for sure until the College of Cardinals meets."

But Easter feels so long from now.

"Do you know what you'll do when the new pope is elected? Do you think you'll stay in Vatican City?"

"I was born the son of a policeman," the pope said. "Did you know that?"

"Yes," Aldo replied sheepishly. He had always admired Pope Benedict and had researched his early life while studying his papal career in college. Still, it was embarrassing to admit that to the person in question.

Benedict chuckled again. "I would expect no less from you, my boy. Then you also know that during World War II, I was forced to join the Hitler Youth Movement. At the time, I was afraid. My family and I resented the Nazis, particularly when they murdered my cousin for having Down Syndrome." There was a long pause before the pope continued. "But later, it proved a blessing. I could establish myself as a radical pope, one who took a harsh stance on certain subjects, and people attributed that to my time in the Nazi army and as a prisoner of war. But even from the age of five, I knew I wanted to join the priesthood."

"Yes," Aldo said. "You and your brother were ordained by Cardinal von Faulhaber in 1951." *But what does all this have to do with his plans for the future?*

"Did you see my paper on the collaboration of men and women that came out last year?" the pope asked.

Aldo nodded. "It was quite controversial."

"Yes, and part of the reason I've been deemed the Grand Inquisitor by my enemies," Benedict chuckled again. "It's all part of the design, the plan, to bring about the final stages of *Septem Montes* . I need to set up an undercover inquisition to clean up the Church, as well as the Seventh, while the new pope is brought in. He'll be the one to bring back the major protestant churches into the fold."

"You mean you'll create the discipline while the new pope reunites everyone under one church again?" Aldo asked.

"That's right."

"Do you think the new pope will be in agreement with the plan?"

"Of course."

"But he hasn't even been chosen yet."

"Not officially," the pope said, a hint of humor in his voice.

"So, you *do* know who he is!" The suspense was getting to him but he knew he'd have to wait, along with the rest of the world, until it was announced at the close of the conclave.

"There is always a greater plan, my son. Larger than any one of us."

Yes, but from where Aldo stood, it seemed like an impossible undertaking, particularly when it came to the Seventh. "What will you do about the Seventh?" Aldo asked.

"Ah, that is where you come in," Pope Benedict said.

"Me?" He could already feel the weight of Mr. Summers' expectations pressing down on him, and he feared another boulder was about to drop.

"Of course. We need you to go undercover and become a part of the Seventh."

"What?" Aldo bolted upright, nearly toppling his chair, and stared at the monitor. "I keep trying to tell everyone I'm not a spy!"

"Which is why you are perfect," the pope said with a smile. That hint of humor was back, but it only served to escalate Aldo's anxiety.

Mentally counting backwards from one hundred to calm himself, Aldo slowly took his seat again. *I'm screwed. I'd do anything for my pope, and he knows it.* Shaking his head, he said, "How could I possibly infiltrate such an organization?"

"Simple. By becoming someone so sought after, they will come to you."

"No one would be that interested in a religious historian, particularly one fresh out of college." Aldo looked around the room. Both Allison and Jenkins had sympathetic looks on their faces, confirming his fear that there was no way he was getting out of this one.

Great.

"Perhaps not at the moment, but you're about to go through a radical transformation." The pope grinned.

He's enjoying this . Aldo sighed, resigned to accept whatever scheme the pope had in store for him. He was just about to tell Benedict that when images of drastic facial reconstruction surgeries, from movies like *Mission Impossible* and *Face/Off* , flashed through his mind. Would the pope really alter his appearance? He snuck a glance back at Allison, trying to recall if she was a Tom Cruise fan.

Idiot. That's not the point here. As much as he didn't want to go through something so terrifying or permanent, Aldo had pledged his loyalty to the pope and the Church, and he had meant every word. "I'm here to serve," he finally said in a low voice.

"Don't look so glum," the pope chuckled. "We're just doing a little surgery on your profile, that's all. Nothing painful."

"Really?" Aldo blew out the breath he'd been holding. "Thank you."

"Don't thank me yet. You're about to gain a new uncle."

"Excuse me?"

"We're going to doctor your files," Jenkins explained, "give you new familial ties. You're about to become very attractive to the Seventh-day Adventists."

"But—"

"We need someone on the inside," the pope said, cutting off his objection, "to track their movements, their plans, so we can counter their attacks more fluidly. Right now, they're a mystery. We expect them to come out against the Jesuits with a new fervor, but it would help to know when and how. I fear it might get bloody before long."

"Bloody?" Aldo asked. Would the Seventh-day Adventists really start a war against the Catholic Church?

"The Seventh is more powerful than you realize," Jenkins said. "It has become a force unequaled by any other religion on the planet, besides the Catholic Church. They have money and power and use both to continue their own version of Project Whitecoat."

"Wait. They've continued experimenting?" Aldo asked, searching Jenkins' face. Aldo assumed their involvement had died with the Toddler Program.

"Well, they haven't begun any new experiments that we know of," Jenkins said. "However, we do know they're keeping careful tabs on all the children who were part of the Toddler Program. Their various hospitals and research facilities are monitoring and researching possible outcomes using the samples they've collected from the participants they've been able to locate."

"They are obsessed with their earthly bodies," the pope said. "They wish to stay alive as long as possible."

"And it seems to be working. Lately, their followers have been showing a tendency toward longevity," Jenkins said. "It's hard to ignore the correlation."

A sinking feeling grew in the pit of his stomach as Aldo put the pieces together. "Who's going to be my alleged uncle?" he asked slowly. Also was pretty sure he already knew the answer but still hoped he was wrong.

The pope was silent for a moment. "I'll let Jenkins answer that question. We'll be in touch soon. God bless you, my son."

The screen flashed back to standby and once again static crackled through the speakers.

Aldo silently looked up at Jenkins. The sympathetic look was back on the older man's face.

Jenkins glanced at Allison, and then turned back to Aldo. "Your files will state that you're the estranged nephew of Mr. Summers."

Aldo let out a long groan. *Dammit! Why did I have to be right about this?* One of the most sought-after and hunted men in the world, a man who had chosen to lay low and accept protection from the NSA, would be his new uncle. Aldo shook his head. He was about to become very popular, and not in a good way.

"We'll be right there with you," Allison said softly.

"Uh, not really," Aldo muttered. "Or are you suddenly going to become my sister or something?"

"No." Her smile fell. "It would be too conspicuous if two estranged relatives suddenly showed up. But we wouldn't put you in this position unless we felt we were able to protect you."

Aldo nodded, feeling childish. He'd already agreed to do it, so he had no right to get angry now. Besides, none of this was Allison's fault. He glanced between her and Jenkins. Everyone on this team was putting their lives at risk to bring down terrorists like the Fifth Reich. And all they were asking of him was to learn about the Seventh-day Adventist Church and report his findings to the pope.

Jenkins' phone vibrated, the sound echoing off the room's thick, bare walls. He glanced at the display, and then at Aldo. "Mr. Summers is ready to speak with you again."

That was fast. Didn't he say he needed a couple of days? I sure as hell do . Aldo nodded. "Does he know about the plan? That I'm about to become his nephew?"

"Yes," Jenkins said with a smile. "He and Pope Benedict worked that out before talking to you."

Wow. That's not a partnership I would've put together.

Aldo had just enough time to stretch the kinks from his back before the monitor went black and Mr. Summers's voice filled the room once more.

"Aldo, I just had a premonition, a very strong one, and felt the need to talk to you right away."

"Yes. I just got off the phone with Pope Benedict," Aldo said. "He told me the plan."

"Good! Are you on board with it?"

"Yes," Aldo replied reluctantly.

"Thank you. I know we're asking a lot, but it's imperative that our plan succeed."

Great. Don't pile on the pressure or anything. However, it was nice of Mr. Summers to actually care about his opinion while everyone else just seemed to expect him to follow orders.

"What was your premonition?" Aldo asked.

"I didn't think you believed in such things," Mr. Summers said playfully.

"Oh, I'm still skeptical," Aldo replied, "but I'm also curious."

"That's good enough for me. First, I need to give you some background information. Allison's gotten you up to speed on Mengele's work in Argentina, correct?"

"For the most part, yes," Allison said before Aldo had a chance to reply.

"Good. Well, during his time there, it was important that the world believe he was a broken man, old and beaten by the war. Too tired to continue with his work. However, the opposite was true."

"The world wasn't ready to face that," Aldo said.

"No. The public couldn't handle the thought that a monster like Mengele was living out his days peacefully. And Mengele fed right into their need for his disappearance and created Project Deflection. Set up by the same Seventh-day Adventist order that helped carry out his experiments there, the project was dedicated to creating a daily paper-trail, portraying Mengele as a cripple who couldn't take care of himself."

"And people bought it?"

"Hook, line, and sinker, I'm afraid," Mr. Summers said. "Evil is hard to look in the face."

"What about his friends and family?"

"Well, his first wife refused to follow him to Argentina, so they divorced. But he later married his sister-in-law. She and her son were ordered to live quietly, avoiding any public notice, including the many reporters who came to interview them. Mengele knew there were those who could read a person's body language, detect when they were telling lies, so he made sure his relations remained off camera and out of the media. But even if they had been interviewed, I believe he hid the truth from them. They probably didn't know anything about what Mengele was actually doing. Probably just assumed his frequent trips into Paraguay and Brazil were for his job selling farm equipment."

"You said they stayed off camera, but what about phone interviews or traced calls? There are experts who can detect lies in someone's voice pattern, right?"

"True, but the order had that covered, too. They never allowed his family members to have their voices recorded, in the event they were questioned about him." Mr. Summers sighed. "So far, Project Deflection has lived up to its name. Anyone researching this will only find accounts of how Mengele was a broken old man during his remaining years."

"Instead of the head of the mirror Whitecoat project," Aldo mused.

"Exactly," Mr. Summers said. "There's another thing that might not sit well with you..." He fell silent for a long moment, the white noise in the background the only sound in the room. "There's emerging evidence that Hitler didn't really commit suicide in that bunker in 1945."

"What?" Aldo gasped. How was that possible? "But...they found his body, along with Eva Braun's. It's true they were burned beyond recognition, but they made a positive I.D. using the dental work from his lower jaw."

"The Soviets found the bodies when they captured Berlin and almost immediately had them transported to Russia," Jenkins said, cutting in. "The dental identification wasn't done until the 1970s. But do you know how many times those bodies were buried and exhumed before that? Who knows if they even had the right one by the time they did the identification. I hate to say it, but it's looking more and more likely that his suicide was faked."

"I know it's a lot to take in," Mr. Summers said, "and perhaps I shouldn't have mentioned it, but I think you need to consider the possibility when researching Project Deflection. I'm sorry if I'm overwhelming you."

This is bordering on ridiculous. Aldo knew his history. If there was anything he prided himself in, it was that. He had read Trevor-Roper's report and Hitler's biography by Kershaw.

"Aldo?" Mr. Summers asked quietly.

Aldo had always thought it strange that Hitler and Braun would marry when they knew they only had hours left together. With their double suicide, marriage wouldn't change anything regarding Hitler's Last Will and Testament. As far as Aldo knew, they never had any children.

"Aldo?"

Aldo continued thinking. Why would Hitler's officers bother to specifically place their bodies in a shell crater and burn them? The Soviets were mere days away from capturing the city, with their planes constantly raining down bombs. Wouldn't the resulting fire and destruction be sufficient to render the bodies unrecognizable? Aldo also couldn't ignore the fact that Hugh Trevor-Roper, the man chosen to investigate Hitler's death, was no homicide detective. *It would have been like asking me to research it.*

A warm hand slid to his shoulder and he jerked his head to see Allison staring down at him, her face worried. "You all right?"

He nodded slowly, and then looked back at the blank monitor. "For the sake of argument, let's say I believe you. If he didn't die in Germany, then where did he go?"

"You have to understand," Mr. Summers said, "that while we're uncovering more and more evidence, the more research we do, it's still all speculation right now. But I strongly believe he was never too far away from Mengele. He was eager for Mengele to complete his work. After all, he wanted to live forever."

"Are you telling me he's still alive?" *How many damn shoes are going to drop today?*

"No," Mr. Summers said, "but there were Hitler sightings in various places throughout the Americas after the war. It's possible quite a few of them were attempts to deflect anyone from discovering his true whereabouts. We know the sightings in the U.S. were fabricated, obviously. But more and more evidence is proving he lived out his last days quietly in Argentina."

"When did he die?" Aldo asked.

"The current theory is 1965, while visiting his good friends, Walter and Ida Eichhorn, at the Eden Hotel in La Falda."

"But…the jaw bone. Even if the Soviets mixed up the bodies as Jenkins said, wouldn't the dental record still prove it was his?"

"In order to pull off this scale of a deception, they had to plant several key pieces of evidence—"

"So, you're saying he ripped out his own jawbone to leave for the Red Army to find?" Aldo scoffed.

Mr. Summers sighed over the speaker. "Perhaps we should pick this up another time."

"No. I'm sorry. It's just…it all seems so implausible."

"That's exactly why so many chose to ignore the evidence and believe the official report, especially back then. Stalin tried to convince the world that Hitler had escaped to the West at the start of the Cold War in an attempt to make the U.S. look bad. That in turn put pressure on the U.S. government to contradict the claims and reinforce the public belief that Hitler really had committed suicide in 1945. But getting back to your question, the jawbone belonged to a skull found at the bunker, that's true. And even if the technology had been there to make an accurate dental identification, Berlin had been completely sacked by the Soviets. What's the likelihood any medical records would have survived the bombings? But in 2009, the skull was tested again and found to be from a woman in her forties. It couldn't possibly have been Hitler's and was even too old to have been Eva Braun's. Of course that discovery was never broadly publicized."

"So, he and Mengele lived happily-ever-after in Argentina."

"Well, I don't know about that," Mr. Summers chuckled, "but they did live to be old men. Mengele's mission, his purpose, was to keep Hitler alive in South America for as long as possible. And if that failed, to resurrect the Fuhrer after his death. Since he couldn't experiment on Hitler, he developed Transpose and tested it on toddlers. Concurrently, he was conducting research on the resurrection bone. It wasn't so much a fallback as the ultimate goal, since Mengele knew he would eventually die even if Transpose worked. But Transpose proved the priority. What better way to ensure you have all the time you need to research resurrection than to make yourself live longer."

"But he did die, as did Hitler," Aldo said. While he was still skeptical, he was finding it a bit easier to go along with the theories Mr. Summers kept presenting to him. And as much as he didn't want to admit it, even to himself, it was extremely fascinating.

"Exactly. Which is why the Seventh-day Adventists took over as leaders of the project. And why the Fifth Reich is still alive and kicking, trying to gain power in Buenos Aires."

All that just to bring one man back from the dead? No, that's not the ultimate goal anymore. The Seventh-day Adventists were after longevity and resurrection, but not for the sake of seeing Hitler return to power. And from what Allison had told him about the Fifth Reich, they seemed more interested in cloning their own brand of superior human. But what did all that have to do with his job of helping the pope bring the Seventh back into the fold? Mr. Summers seemed to know more than he was letting on, but—

"Your premonition. You never told me what it was," Aldo said.

"Yes. Thank you for reminding me. My vision took place at the last camp you blew up. Allison?"

"Yes, sir?" she replied, stepping closer, her shoulder bumping into Aldo's as she bent down.

"I'll need you and Aldo to return there, alone. Aldo will need your help to find something crucial to our project."

Wait. We have to go back there?

"Can you tell me anything else?" she asked.

"No, I'm afraid not. All I know is that we're running short on time. Have your team accompany you to the camp, but they'll need to wait outside the walls. Only you and Aldo should conduct the search."

"What are we looking for?" Aldo asked.

"Something small," Mr. Summers said vaguely.

Small? Well, that really narrows it down. Aldo suppressed the urge to ask if it was bigger than a breadbox. Sighing, he said, "You really can't tell us anything else?"

"Aldo," Mr. Summers said quietly, "I realize you have no reason to trust me, but I trust you. I know you'll find what you need to find without incident. If I say anymore, it will influence your actions. You must find what you find on your own."

Allison and Aldo looked at each other.

"So, I'm the one to find this item?" Aldo asked.

"Yes," Mr. Summers said, "but it's important that Allison be there with you."

"We'll leave first thing tomorrow morning," Allison said, laying a firm hand on Aldo's shoulder.

Does she think I'm going to try to escape? Or is that supposed to be reassuring?

She squeezed.

"Right," Aldo said, taking the hint. "First thing."

"Thank you," Mr. Summers sighed with obvious relief.

Aldo sighed as well, but in resignation. The man's alliance with the pope should be enough to gain Aldo's trust, but he still wasn't convinced about the whole supernatural aspect.

"Don't worry. We'll find whatever it is you need us to find," Aldo said, trying to reassure both Mr. Summers and himself.

"I know you will." Then, with a chuckle, Mr. Summers added, "Nephew."

Chapter Six | The BOX

Argentina
February 2013

This is insane. Aldo shook his head as he stepped through the warped metal gate of the destroyed Fifth Reich camp. If the explosion had been powerful enough to bend wrought iron, what made Mr. Summers think they'd find anything among the rubble? And still in one piece no less? Yet here they were, returning to the place where Aldo had nearly met his maker the day before.

Aldo shuddered at the memory and forced one foot in front of the other. The high mountain rain wasn't helping matters, stirring up the stench of burnt wood and cloth—a mix of smells he wasn't likely to forget for a long time.

Something crumbled in the distance, the sound making him jump. Aldo froze, and pointing his flashlight into the darkness, expected to see Hans's zombified corpse stumbling toward him.

Wait. If this place was a Fifth Reich compound, that means they were making clones, right? He groaned inwardly. *Oh God. I really hope we don't come across a bunch of bodies.*

"You okay?" Allison asked.

He glanced over at her. She had stopped a few feet ahead of him, her long blond hair plastered to the sides of her face from the rain. "Yeah, sure. Peachy."

Allison laughed, the sound emphasizing the emptiness of their surroundings. "Could've fooled me. You're not alone, you know. I'm scared, too."

"Whatever," he muttered. "Why would this scare you," he gestured to the destruction around them, "when you seemed perfectly fine with being strapped to that Monarch chair?"

"Well, if I hadn't known Tony's team was keeping tabs on us, I would've been terrified. Besides," she said in a low voice, her eyes glued to her feet, "I've never been one for dark places." She glanced up at him quickly. "But don't tell anyone, okay?"

Really? She suffers from nyctophobia? He never would have guessed that. And despite her obvious embarrassment, he thought it was adorable. He gave her a soft smile. "You got it."

Debris lay scattered across the expansive courtyard and they picked their way through it, moving closer to what was left of the main structure. Aldo silently inspected the surroundings as they went, but all he saw were twisted strands of metal poking up from crumbling hunks of concrete.

"What exactly are we looking for?" Aldo whispered.

Allison shrugged. "You know as much as I do."

"Really?" *I doubt that.*

"Well, about this at least."

"Great. Then we're both clueless."

Coming to the end of the building, Aldo hesitated and offered a silent prayer. *Please don't let there be any disembodied hands or glass jars full of fetuses.* There was a reason his Ph.D. was in history and not human anatomy.

Taking a deep breath and holding it, he rounded the corner then let it out in a rush of relief. *Just more rubble.*

"What's wrong?" Allison asked.

"Huh? Oh, nothing. I just didn't know what we'd find. *Who* we'd find," he clarified.

"Oh. Tony's team already cleaned up everything after the explosion, so we won't have to worry about any, uh, subject matter."

Aldo stared at her for a moment then looked around. She was right. It was the cleanest explosion he'd ever seen. No yellow crime scene tape, no glass shards everywhere. Even the rubble seemed like it had been gathered into neat little clusters. "The local police let you clean up their crime scene before they even launched an investigation?"

"The police never came. Officially, this place doesn't exist, so the explosion won't make it into the media either."

"How's that even possible?"

Allison smiled. "We have powerful friends."

Aldo swallowed back a snort. "That's a bit of an understatement."

"It was actually pretty easy. This elementary school's off the beaten path, which is why the Fifth Reich chose it. Plus, it's been abandoned for some time, so it wasn't too hard to keep it off the public radar."

He shook his head in amazement. He'd always assumed government cover-ups and spy games were Hollywood fantasy. Well, until those two Pontifical Swiss guards showed up in Speikboden.

Aiming his flashlight, he bent down to turn over stray pieces of brick. "If Tony and his team already cleaned everything up, is there even anything left for us to find?"

"I assume it's something they missed when they came to retrieve all of the files and documentation that survived the blast."

"Hmm," he murmured. *Still, it'd sure be nice to know what I'm looking for.* He turned over another brick, and then another. *What does something that seems insignificant at first even look like?*

"Go with your instincts," Allison said.

"Right," he said, rubbing his eyes. *Did he even have any?* "You sound like Yoda. Sorry, but I flunked Jedi training."

She giggled. "I just mean you should trust yourself. So far, Mr. Summers has never been wrong in a prediction."

"How many has he made?"

"Hmm. Not many, but still, I trust him."

"Yeah, but you've known him longer. And don't forget, your input is equally important here," Aldo said, pointing at her with a brick.

She shook her head. "Nope. I'm just a guide."

He tossed the brick back onto the pile. "Why would I need a guide in a place like this? It's not like I can get lost."

Allison crossed her arms over her chest, her expression strangely serious. "Not that kind of guide. Besides, even if Mr. Summers requested I be here, you're the one he actually saw in his premonition. And not just one vision either—several."

Sighing, Aldo straightened. "Okay, but I still don't get why he insisted it be just you and me. Wouldn't it be faster if the others helped?"

"You saying you don't like being alone with me?"

"Uh, no." He could already feel his face heating and just hoped it was dark enough she wouldn't notice. "That's not what I mea—"

Allison shook her head at him again, laughing. "I know what you meant. Look at it this way. You'll find the object, but without me, you might have trouble."

"Oh."

"Every hero needs a guide, right? Especially at the beginning of their journey. They don't believe they're special, so the guide not only provides information but encouragement also." She tilted her head at him, a sly smile playing on her lips. "Didn't Luke have Yoda?"

Aldo grinned and shook his head. "If I'm a hero, you've got your work cut out for you."

"You never did give yourself much credit." She looked past him then slowly began to turn around in a circle, as though scanning the piles of debris.

"Do you see something?" Aldo asked, watching her.

"No. I'm just a guide, remember? You're supposed to follow my lead."

"But you're not going anywhere," Aldo chuckled.

She threw him a stern look over her shoulder but continued to spin. "Were you always this obstinate?"

"Probably."

She stopped spinning and sighed heavily. "Come on, just try it. We're not going to get anywhere sifting through all these piles of rubble. Just try to focus on this place. These trees. These ruins. *The here and now,* " she added mystically.

"Right," Aldo muttered. "Easier said than done."

Allison gave him a piercing stare. "Do you want to be out here any longer than necessary? 'Cuz I sure don't." She held her hands out, as if to catch the rain, emphasizing her point.

Sighing, he spun around, feeling like an ostrich in ballet class. Completing a single rotation, he looked back at Allison with a cocked eyebrow.

"Slower," she huffed. "It isn't a race."

"Fine," he said, not caring that he sounded like a petulant child. Taking a deep breath, he closed his eyes, trying to block everything out. All the horrible memories of his experience here. All the things he'd learned in the last twenty-four hours. *Man, my life's done a complete one-eighty.* Sighing in frustration, he took another deep breath and tried again. *Focus.* He let the breath out slowly, counting to ten before taking another. He mentally pulled up the aerial photo Tony had shown him of the compound, and then he overlaid what he'd seen of the destruction, creating a map of sorts.

Upon opening his eyes, Aldo was surprised to discover he could see how each mangled chunk of concrete fit together to form the walls. *Over there was a classroom.* He crosschecked what he was seeing against his mental map. He swept his flashlight across the landscape as he spun. *And there the room with the Monarch chairs.* Aldo saw splintered tree limbs, the remnants of wooden school desks, broken glass and bits of plastic—probably from the drones—he hadn't noticed before. They didn't do as good a job cleaning up as he'd first thought. The scattered and torn pages of books, probably old textbooks. Even a red plastic lunchbox with the faded image of a superhero on the front. "I wish I knew what I was looking for," he said as he completed another turn.

"It'll hit you. Just give it time."

"I'm pretty sure that's something we don't have," Aldo muttered. *Otherwise, we'd be doing this in the light of day instead of in the middle of a rainstorm.* Seeing the white of more paper flash beneath the beam of his light, he wondered if maybe the *something that will seem insignificant at first* wasn't an object at all, but information. Moving closer, he bent to pick up a page, but whatever had once been written on it was now completely blurred by the rain.

"Find something?" Allison asked, joining him.

"No." He let the soggy page drop to the ground again, feeling strangely like a litterbug. *No helping that. This whole place is a garbage dump now.*

Walking back to his spot to resume his spinning, Aldo suddenly stopped and cocked his head to the right. His light had glinted off something metallic hidden beneath a pile of rubble. "Over there," he said, pointing to the pile.

"Where?" Allison asked excitedly.

"There." He hurried toward it, Allison jogging to keep up with him.

"What do you see?"

"Can't you see it?"

"No," she said.

He stopped and blinked, but the glint of metal was gone. He swept his flashlight over the debris. Nothing. "Damn. I thought I saw a box, but now I don't see it."

They walked to the mound, canvassing the entire surface with their flashlights. Mangled rebar, aluminum window casings, and dismembered chair legs—but no metal box.

Aldo heaved a sigh. "Must've been a trick of the light."

"No...I don't think it was," Allison said slowly. "It was a box, right?"

"I think so. I only saw it for a split second."

"Tell me exactly where you saw it."

Aldo studied the mound in front of him. "I'm pretty sure it was around here." Moving to where he had pointed, Allison began to pull chunks of concrete and bricks off the pile, throwing them behind her. Reluctantly, Aldo joined her. "Do you really think there's something here?" he asked.

"Well, it's worth exploring at least," she said. "Besides, we have to start somewhere." She tipped her head to smile up at him. "And you never know, we may get lucky."

While luck had never really been on his side, somehow she made him feel like the odds might be in their favor this time. But after nearly an hour of toiling in the rain, they had only managed to move most of the pile from one spot to another.

"There's nothing here," Aldo said, standing up. He dropped the piece of rebar in his hand back onto the pile then bent backwards to relieve the ache in his lower back. "I was wrong. It's as simple as that."

Allison brushed wet hair away from her face with the back of her hand then kept digging. "We're nearly to the ground. Let's just finish this pile."

Then what? I go back to spinning around like an idiot? Aldo shrugged. "I guess it can't hurt." *Well, anymore than it already does.* Stretching his back one last time, he bent down to retrieve more debris, trying not to think about the fact they should both be wearing gloves for this.

"Exactly," Allison said. "I've learned to follow my hunches. I can't tell you how many times I've second-guessed myself, switching gears and wasting a bunch of time. But every time I went back to my original thought, I found the answer was right there the whole time." She sat back on her heels, holding her muddy hands out in front of her.

Most of the girls he knew in college would have been complaining about their nails for the last hour. Or the rain. Or the cold. Or they would have simply refused to dig through dirty and possibly dangerous debris to begin with. But not Allison. Even his mom usually left the hard work to his dad.

Aldo froze. *Mom and Dad. Dammit! I completely forgot.* He groaned then threw the piece of rebar onto the new pile.

"What's wrong?"

"I forgot to call my parents. Knowing my mom, she probably has a missing persons ad in every newspaper across the U.S. by now." He dropped to his knees and pulled more chunks off the pile, heaving them behind him in frustration. He shook his head. *She's gonna be livid.*

"Didn't I tell you?" Allison asked, her face confused.

"Tell me what?"

"I called them before meeting you at Rafael's. Told them I'd gotten you an interview with my company but you had to come immediately or risk losing out on the opportunity. And since the interview process is pretty involved, you'd be staying with me in Utah until it was over." She flashed him one of her brilliant smiles. "Your mom was more than happy to let you off the hook."

"Are you serious?"

"Yup," Allison said, clearly pleased with herself.

He sighed. *Out of the frying pan and into the fire.* Instead of panicking about her son's whereabouts for the last few days, his mom was no doubt joyfully planning his wedding instead.

"What?"

"Nothing. Let's just get this done so we can get out of here." He had a phone call to make.

They worked in silence, the only sounds the rain pattering on the ground around them and the crack of each chunk of debris as it landed on a new pile. As Aldo picked up another piece, his fingers scraped along something sharp and he sucked in a breath. He tossed the chunk of concrete aside, and then grabbed his flashlight to inspect the damage. Blood oozed from a long gash down his middle finger, mixing with the mud coating his hands. *What the...* Aiming his flashlight where the chunk had been, he saw the corner of a metal box peeking out of the rubble.

"Oh, you're hurt!" Allison cried, hurrying to his side.

"Yeah, but look." He pointed down at the box.

"Is that the box you saw?"

"I think so." Shifting the flashlight to his right hand, he used his left to clear away the rest of the debris and pull the box from its tomb. It was about the size of a cash box with no visible markings. He handed it to Allison. How in the world had he seen it under all that debris?

"The lid's been crushed."

"Hang on. Maybe we can..." He stood up and moved over to the new pile, pulling out a piece of rebar.

"Good idea!" she exclaimed. "Let me see that." Setting the box on the ground, she grabbed the rebar from him and worked the end of it under the edge of the lid. After a moment of prying, it creaked open. Inside was a ring of keys, a USB stick and a slip of paper. On the paper, written in black ink, were *April, 37 th and Fillmore,* and *2,300.* Aldo figured the number was a reference to the 2,300 days prophecy, but he couldn't figure out why it was written on a piece of paper and stored in a lock box.

"What do you think these keys go to?" Allison asked, picking them up.

"Knowing our luck, probably here." He gestured to the destruction around them.

"Good point. And I doubt we'll get much off this USB stick." She held it up, showing him the damaged connector.

Why would a group technologically advanced enough to mass-produce humans still be storing vital information on thumb drives?

"Well," Allison continued, shoving the ring of keys and the USB into her pocket, "I'll have Jenkins check them both out. Who knows? Maybe we'll get lucky."

Aldo took the piece of paper from the box, and then tossed the box back onto the pile of rubble. "What about the note?"

Allison glanced at it then shrugged. "Probably nothing, but we should mention it to Mr. Summers when we talk to him."

Back at the compound, they were once again ushered into the small sealed room with the computer terminal, treasures in hand.

"Keys and a thumb drive, huh?" Mr. Summers asked over the speaker. "Doesn't seem quite right. What do you think, Commander?"

"I haven't had my analysts evaluate them yet," Jenkins replied, stepping closer to the terminal, "but I think Aldo may be right about the keys. They probably opened the different rooms of that compound. And we might be able to extract any remaining data from the USB but it'll be a challenge."

There was a pause, and then Mr. Summers said, "I see. And you didn't find anything else?"

Aldo pulled the damp note from his pocket, but before he could reply, Allison said, "No. I'm sorry. Should we go back and try again?"

"Wait. What about the piece of paper?" Aldo held it out.

"A piece of paper?" Mr. Summers asked.

"I still don't see how it's of any significance," Allison scoffed.

"I don't know. I think—"

"What does it say?" Mr. Summers asked, cutting him off. Aldo could hear a note of excitement mixed with impatience in Mr. Summers' voice.

"Uh, it just says *April, 37* *th* *and Fillmore,* and the number *2,300.* I'm not sure about the twenty-three hundred reference, but I think the rest of it implies something is going to happen in April at this location."

"But what?" Allison asked.

"How am I supposed to know?"

"No, I think it's worth looking into," Mr. Summers said. "Commander?"

Jenkins leaned forward. "Yeah, I'll check it out. See if we can at least pinpoint the location."

"Thank you," Mr. Summers replied. "Aldo, I would like you to jot those details down in your notebook so you have them with you."

"Me?" Aldo looked down at the slip of paper in his hand. His finger had been cleaned and bandaged by someone Tony referred to as Buster, but it still throbbed. "Wasn't I supposed to find it for *you*?" he asked.

"Not necessarily," Mr. Summers said. "Most of my premonitions have been connected to you, so it wouldn't hurt to keep the information with you. For now, tell me what happened while you were out there."

Aldo gave him a brief rundown of the events, with Allison jumping in on occasion to supplement the narrative from her perspective.

"And you saw the box from that distance?" Mr. Summers asked.

"Well, no. I thought I saw something that looked like a box, but when I got closer, it wasn't there."

"You're not giving yourself enough credit again," Allison said, leaning against the desk. "You thought you saw a box, so we checked it out, and lo and behold, what do we find? A box. I mean, what are the odds? It was buried under a ton of rubble, so there's no way you could have actually seen it. Yet you pinpointed its exact location and what it was."

"Wait," Aldo said, waving his hands in front of him. "You're making it sound like I had a vision or something. It really wasn't like that. It was just a trick of the light, and with it being nighttime and the shadows…" He sighed. "I just got lucky."

Mr. Summers was silent for a moment then said, "Perhaps you're right."

"You don't believe that, do you?" Aldo muttered.

"I believe you have an ability to see things, spot important details, where others would pass them by."

"So I'm observant."

"Yes, but more so than you realize," Mr. Summers said. "Just remember to trust yourself, and know that if nothing else, I believe in you."

"Right," Aldo said hesitantly. Even with the success of finding the box, he didn't feel remotely confident. The last week had felt like just a big game of follow-the-leader.

•••

A week later, Aldo sat in the passenger seat of a black sedan on his way to the airport, nervousness wringing out his stomach like a dishcloth. Up until the moment his luggage was dropped into the trunk and Jenkins climbed behind the wheel, Aldo had hoped it was all just a mistake. That they didn't really expect him to pull this off—to pretend to be Mr. Summers' nephew and infiltrate one of the biggest hubs of the Seventh-day Adventist Church: Loma Linda, California.

Yet, here he was, on his way to the Ezeiza International Airport. And this time there would be no team of men in black to bail him out. *Just take it one step at a time.* Thanks to an intensive cram session, he was well versed in the Seventh's religious practices, beliefs, and hierarchy. And while he was confident in his study skills, his acting…not so much. "The first step is to make contact," Aldo muttered.

"Yes, but remember, let them find you," Jenkins said. "You'll be on their radar after all the data we put on the Dark Web this week."

"Okay, but how do I get noticed? Won't I have to put myself out there for them to realize I'm in town?"

"You just have to follow the plan, Aldo. Don't be too obvious or eager, and let them find you. They will be alerted to your travel plans the moment you check in at the airport."

That's a scary thought. Did they monitor everyone's movements or was he just special?

"Won't they be a tad suspicious that they'd never heard of me prior to this week?" Aldo knew from his long conversations over coffee and hot cocoa with Allison that Mormons kept meticulous genealogical records, so who was to say the Seventh didn't as well?

Jenkins flashed him a grin. "Their greed will override any concerns they may have. Even if they suspect you're a fake, they wouldn't want to take the chance of letting you slip through their fingers. They're desperate for any information connected to the Thirteenth Child. When he went into hiding, they scoured the world for him, but couldn't find a trace. Now they'll think all their hard work has paid off—that after all their searching, they finally found his nephew. Trust me, they'll eat it up."

Aldo fidgeted with the seatbelt strap across his chest. "But why his nephew? Why not pose as his son? Wouldn't that be more enticing?"

"Yeah, but also more suspicious. Think about it. They know Mr. Summers doesn't want to be found, so why would he suddenly let his son fall into their laps?"

Aldo glanced out the side window. The forest had given way to the concrete jungle as they drove through Buenos Aires toward the airport. "Just seems risky," Aldo muttered. Not just for him, but for Mr. Summers and their mission. *If the Seventh realizes I'm an imposter, it could tip them off.*

"I know, but we're confident it will work. Mostly because you can just be yourself. You don't need to memorize anything or have any acting skills."

"Don't I need to know all about my new uncle?" Aldo asked.

"Nope. You're estranged, remember? He and his brother haven't spoken for years, in large part due to the experiments. Something the church is also aware of. So, you know next to nothing about him and have no idea where he is."

"Shouldn't I know all about the experiments then?" Aldo asked. "I mean, wouldn't his brother, uh, my father have told me something about why they're no longer speaking?"

"Don't worry. We've got it covered," Jenkins said gently. "Just because you're his nephew, it doesn't mean you'd necessarily know all the details." He paused for a minute then said, "And it's not like we concocted this plan last week."

Really? "How long has this been in the works?"

"Around six months or so."

Six months? They knew about this while I was still scrambling to finish my thesis? Aldo hit the button to lower his window. He suddenly needed some air. "After one of Mr. Summers' premonitions?" he asked after a moment.

Jenkins nodded. "You first made an appearance in Mr. Summers' visions over six years ago. It's only been six months since we finally knew what your role in all this was and we could begin planting data on the Deep Web hinting at the possibility of a viable relative."

Taking a deep breath, Aldo decided worrying wouldn't do him any good. He would just have to trust them. Besides, with that much time to prepare, they would likely have covered all the bases.

Still feeling uneasy, Aldo reminded himself that even if he did get caught, there wasn't much the Seventh could do about it. It wasn't like he was breaking any laws. *It'd be embarrassing, but what's the worst that could happen?*

When they arrived at the airport, Aldo resisted the urge to ask the dozens of questions that had popped into his head in the previous five minutes—convinced by the serious look on Jenkins' face that he was starting to get annoyed. As he climbed out and retrieved his suitcase from the trunk, Aldo had the sick feeling that Allison's sentiment of just *winging it* was going to become his reality.

The flight from Argentina to California was just as long and tiring as his trip down there two weeks prior. Unable to take his mind off his mission long enough to get any sleep, Aldo took the opportunity to transcribe his notes and upload the file onto the Vatican's secure cloud system. He spent the remaining hours doing more research. In his mind, knowledge was power, and the more he had, the better he would feel about the whole situation. He refreshed his memory of the Seventh's beliefs and practices and also delved into its history. He had studied it briefly in college, focusing mainly on the church's early years and the life of its founder, Ellen G. White. This time he concentrated his search on the church's current hierarchy and events. He also looked up anything he could find on his destination.

Loma Linda, California did not disappoint. It was exactly the intellectual community near San Bernardino the internet said it would be, with the main points of interest being the university and hospital. If there were at least some tourist attractions, then he could get out there and *let them find him* , but at this rate... Aldo shook his head as he drove his rental car through town.

Circling the university and hospital a second time, Aldo noticed the library. Maybe he could spend his time there and kill two birds with one stone. He also made a mental note to check with the front desk at his hotel for other possibilities. As much as he was dreading this mission, the sooner the Seventh found him, the sooner it would be over.

Jenkins had booked him a reservation at the Loma Linda Inn, a small hotel situated close to the university. He parked his rental in the back lot, and then hauled his suitcase into the lobby. When he asked the clerk at the front desk for places to visit, she handed him a single sheet of paper, listing all the churches, medical facilities, family attractions, and local parks in the area. This definitely wasn't the kind of place a single guy, fresh out of college, would choose to go on vacation. *I'm going to need a convincing reason for being here.*

He thanked the clerk then headed for his room. *I could say I came to tour the campus*, he thought as he hoisted his suitcase onto the bed. *No. Why tour a university when I already have a Ph.D.?* Seeing the hospital in the distance from his hotel room window, he tried to think of an illness he could suddenly contract that would warrant a doctor visit, but nothing came to mind. Well, nothing that wouldn't require a battery of tests he wasn't willing to subject himself to.

I'm probably just over-thinking this.

Even after an entire day of travel, sleep eluded him. He propped himself up in bed and turned on the TV, hoping a marathon of old movies would induce sleep, but the sun came up all too soon. Reluctantly, he took a shower, and then headed to a café that boasted the best French toast in town.

With all the time in the world to kill, Aldo walked around town, visiting the university and all the local parks, but even that didn't take most of the day. At the university's library, he found copies of Ellen G. White's *The Great Controversy* and other works. Figuring the library only allowed books to be checked out by students—and wanting to remain as inconspicuous as possible—he read as much as he could until the library closed, adding any pertinent information to his notebook.

Feeling like he'd already exhausted all possible locations in Loma Linda, Aldo spent part of the following day at the San Bernardino County Museum. Other than a nice elderly couple who told him about the fetus and skeleton collection at the Alfred Shryock Museum of Embryology, no one approached him. Still, he couldn't resist the urge to glance over his shoulder every five minutes.

Back at his hotel, Aldo searched for information online about the museum the elderly couple had mentioned. Located on the university's campus, the Alfred Shryock Museum of Embryology housed one of the largest collections of human embryos and fetuses. Shryock had apparently been dean of the School of Medicine from 1914 to 1915, and then the chairman of the Department of Anatomy. He died in 1950, leaving behind his legacy—his research and the aborted fetuses and embryos doctors had sent him from around the world.

Quite the hobby. Aldo's stomach turned.

According to the museum's website, Shryock's purpose for the collection was to show the development of a baby in the womb from three weeks to birth. But Aldo couldn't help wondering if there might have been other reasons behind Shryock's fascination. Could he have been conducting research similar to Mengele's?

Aldo called to set an appointment for a guided tour, only to discover the museum had been closed for relocation. *No wonder I didn't see it when I was at the campus yesterday.* Researching further, he found out it wasn't scheduled to reopen until the fall. Normally, he would have just left it at that, but something about the nature of this exhibit made the closure seem significant.

Early the next day, Aldo found Shryock Hall, a two story cream-colored structure. Not sure what he expected to accomplish, Aldo meandered around the building and soon found the deserted rooms that previously housed the exhibit.

Aldo stopped a passing student and asked where he might go to learn more about the exhibit.

The young man pointed down the hallway. "Professor Applebee can help you," he said. "His office is just over there."

"Thanks." Locating the door with the professor's name, Aldo knocked, waited a moment then knocked again. No answer. *What am I even doing here?* He sighed. Even if he managed to track down the professor, he doubted they would grant him access to the museum.

Turning to leave, he bumped into a short, white-haired man. "Oh, I'm sorry."

"Quite all right," the older man said. "Is there something I can help you with?"

"Oh, I was just looking for Professor Applebee."

"Well, you found him," the professor chuckled. "And you are?"

Aldo froze for a moment, trying to remember who he was supposed to be, before realizing he was just himself. "Aldo Lombardi," he answered finally.

"Are you sure about that?" Professor Applebee replied, a smile creasing the lines around his mouth.

"Yes," Aldo said sheepishly. "Sorry. I guess I'm still a bit jetlagged."

"Ah, where are you coming from?"

"Um, Italy." *By way of Argentina.*

"Really?" The professor pulled a key from his coat pocket and opened his office door. "Whereabouts in Italy?"

"I just received my Ph.D. from the Pontifical Gregorian University."

The professor's eyebrows shot up. "That's quite an accomplishment. In what field?" He stood back and gestured for Aldo to proceed him into the room.

Aldo nodded his thanks and walked into the small office. It was clean and orderly, without a single trace of dust on the many bookshelves that lined the walls. "Uh, history." *I should probably leave out the fact my focus was religion.*

"So, then what brings you to our university?" Professor Applebee asked, closing the door behind them.

You mean, what's a Catholic historian doing trolling the halls of a Seventh-day Adventist medical school? "I'm just passing through," Aldo replied, taking a seat in one of the chairs facing the desk. "Was headed to Colorado on vacation, a graduation trip of sorts, but I decided to stop off for a few days. This is an amazing campus you have here." He glanced around the room. "When I was visiting the San Bernardino Museum, someone told me about the embryo exhibit. I understand it's amazing. But when I called for a tour, I learned it's currently closed to the public."

"Yes," Professor Applebee said. "It's being settled into its new home."

"The Centennial Complex, right?"

"That's correct."

"Would you happen to know who the curator is? I was hoping I could persuade them to let me have a glimpse before I have to leave town."

Professor Applebee smiled. "I am, along with a few other professors."

"Really?" *Man, how lucky can I get?*

"It's a shame about your timing," the professor continued. "The collection's definitely not one to be missed."

Aldo slumped in his chair. "I was really hoping to see it, but... is there anything you can tell me about it?"

The professor was silent for a moment then, resting his elbows on the desk, he said, "I'm curious. What interests you most about the exhibit?"

Other than its possible connection to Mengele's research, Aldo had no interest in it whatsoever. But he couldn't exactly tell Applebee that. Staring at the surface of the professor's desk, racking his brain for a believable excuse, he noticed the university's crest on sheets of letterhead. "Honestly," Aldo said, "I was drawn here by the university's motto: *To Make Man Whole.* I don't know much about the field of medicine, but still, I admire all that you do here to help mankind through medical research. The advancements you've made, the things exhibits like this one can teach the students here, they may one day help me or someone I care about." The words rolled off his tongue with sickening fluency. While it wasn't entirely a lie, it was enough to make him feel disgusted. No one could benefit from research done on innocent children.

Applebee nodded, the grin on his face assuring Aldo that he'd given the professor the answer he wanted to hear. Then he tugged back the sleeve of his suit coat and glanced down at his wristwatch. "I have a lecture in twenty minutes, but if you can meet me back here in two hours, I'll see what I can do."

"Really? Thank you very much! I really appreciate this."

Aldo excused himself then headed to the library to kill time. Pulling books on human anatomy and fetal development off the shelves, he settled at one of the tables to read, all the while feeling like he was being watched. But every time he glanced up from his research, he only saw more students, their noses buried in their own stack of books.

The two hours flew by, and Aldo began to make his way back to the professor's office. As he got closer, he noticed a tall man with short blond hair walking down the corridor toward him, his gaze hard and inquisitive.

Instinctively, Aldo froze. Since his encounter at the Fifth Reich camp, he saw Hans and his brother in every tall fair-haired man he met. Stalking the concourses of airports, lounging at parks, sipping coffee at restaurants. *Get a hold of yourself. Just because they're tall and blond, doesn't automatically make them clones. Besides, this guy's eyes are brown.*

Still, his pulse quickened.

"Mr. Lombardi?" the man asked.

"Yes?" Aldo replied hesitantly, giving the man a tentative smile.

"Professor Applebee asked me to escort you to the Centennial Complex," the man said, his gaze holding Aldo's.

Aldo nodded slowly then followed the man down the hallway and past the professor's office. As they climbed the stairs to the second floor, he took a deep breath. This whole spy business was making him jumpy. Still, he was just going to see an exhibit. What was the worst that could happen?

Chapter Seven | Comradeship of the THREE WOES

Loma Linda, California
February 2013

As Aldo followed the blond man down another corridor, he couldn't help feeling like a death row inmate taking his final walk. Aldo knew he was being silly—paranoid even—to be so nervous. Yet with each step he took, he couldn't shake the feeling something was not right.

Students rushed past, no doubt on their way to classes, and for a moment he envied them. Just a few weeks ago he had been in their shoes, blissfully unaware of the world's secret history.

True, he could have chosen to stay cooped up in his hotel room, but he had never been very good at waiting around or letting things go—hence the jolt of fear he felt every time he saw someone who resembled Hans.

He stared at the blond man's back and shuddered involuntarily. *Geez, calm down. It's not like they've got a Monarch chair stashed away somewhere in the school.* He took a deep breath and quickened his pace to keep up with the man's long strides.

When the man suddenly stopped before a set of double doors, Aldo nearly collided with him. Stumbling back, he mumbled an apology, but the man only glanced down at him, seemingly unfazed.

This part of the school was completely deserted, and Aldo had the feeling very few people ever came here. He reminded himself the exhibit wasn't yet open to the public. Still, why would the entire wing be unoccupied?

The blond man pulled open the right door, and then stood back and gestured for Aldo to enter. Stepping into the spacious room was like stepping into a mad scientist's laboratory. Every surface was lined with jar after jar of fetuses, their amber liquid glowing sickeningly in the afternoon sunlight streaming through the large bank of windows on the opposite side of the room. Aldo knew most of them probably would not have made it to full term if given the chance, but the lost lives displayed like trophies disturbed him nonetheless.

"Hello, Aldo. Welcome to the magnificent exhibit of Alfred Shryock!"

Doing his best to mask his disgust, Aldo turned to see Professor Applebee standing off to the side, his arms extended. Unable to form words, Aldo just nodded. Behind him, the blond man closed the door, the unmistakable click of the lock sending a fresh wave of anxiety through Aldo. Then the man turned, positioning himself before the doors like a stone-faced sentry.

"Is everything okay, Aldo? You look a little pale."

"Huh?" He turned back to the professor. "Oh, yes. Just a bit tired. But this is amazing." He took several more steps into the room, noticing for the first time the fully articulated skeletons interspersed among the shelves of jars along the walls. He could understand why such a collection would be beneficial to the medical community, but it still felt wrong. Judging from the proud grin on the professor's face, he didn't share Aldo's view.

"It's always interesting to see the effect this exhibit has on people," Applebee said. "Forgive me, but that's why I had you escorted here, so I could witness your reaction first hand."

So all that was for his entertainment? Wanting to kick himself for feeling so anxious, Aldo chuckled. "Well, I'm glad I didn't disappoint then."

Applebee beamed. "To date, no one ever has. It's an incredible collection, unlike anything ever assembled before. Many other institutions have sought to own it, offering tidy sums of money, but we'll never give it up." He glanced around the room, his eyes full of pride and adoration. "It's just too valuable as an educational tool."

"I can see why. I read online you also have wax models of fetuses at various stages."

"That's right," the professor said. "Made by wax artist Friedrich Ziegler. He and his father were known for making representations that were used worldwide by students and researchers. Their models are perfect for showing the various organs and illustrating how the cardiovascular and nervous systems develop. We keep a few on display, but nothing compares to seeing real tissue." He walked over to a partition lined with more jars, beckoning for Aldo to follow. "See here? Shryock subjected these specimens to a chemical that turned them transparent."

"Wow," Aldo whispered. The effect was startling, as though a tiny alien species of jellyfish instead of human embryos were suspended in the fluid. It enthralled the scholar in him, enough that his disgust was temporarily forgotten.

"And over here, he stained the calcium deposits of these with Alizarin Red to show how the skeletal structure develops."

Aldo stared into the jars. The dye had turned the fetuses' bones a deep magenta. The connective tissue and skin remained an opaque ivory, making the tiny bodies look like they were molded from plastic.

Straightening, Aldo followed his enthusiastic guide around the rest of the room. If nothing else, Shryock had certainly been thorough. Based on the size of his collection, it seemed like he had acquired every embryo and fetus available at the time. But Aldo still wasn't convinced the doctor had humanity's best interest at heart when he put this collection together. Was it really necessary to go to such lengths to study human development? Perhaps Aldo's recent research into Mengele's work was clouding his judgment, but Shryock's collection seemed more obsession than educational tool.

"Which is the oldest?" Aldo asked softly, trying to keep his voice from cracking.

"In terms of development? This one over here." Applebee pointed at a single jar on a shelf along the south wall as he led Aldo to it. "It was aborted at twenty-four weeks gestation."

Of all the specimens he had seen, this one looked the most like a baby. He could make out facial features and each tiny toe. Unable to look any longer, he turned back to the professor. "How did Shryock obtain all of these?"

"Alfred was a popular professor here," Applebee answered, his voice full of pride. "It's said that he's the only member of the faculty to have touched the lives of every single student, either directly or through this collection. As a result, he developed an incredible network of physicians all over the United States who would send him aborted fetuses at different stages of development."

Aldo nodded, trying to think of what else to say when all he really wanted to do was leave. "Well, they're, uh, incredibly well preserved."

"Yes," Applebee said, "and you'll notice the variety he received. The most popular with the public are the malformed specimens."

"Malformed?"

"Oh, yes!" Applebee exclaimed, already hurrying toward another corner of the room. "They're the perfect example of just how badly things can go wrong. It's truly miraculous most of us turn out the way we do."

Aldo stood silently in front of a table holding a dozen specimens. One jar contained a fetus with a small protrusion sticking out from its skull. Several had major deformations of the skull, their faces nearly indistinguishable. Another appeared to have an extra leg growing from its pelvis, like the beginnings of a Siamese twin.

Twins.

Aldo straightened, realizing that was the one thing he hadn't seen among the specimens. In the early stages of development, you wouldn't be able to tell if the fetuses were twins, not unless they were preserved together in the same jar. Yet each jar only contained a single specimen. He glanced around the large room. *Seriously? In a collection this size, there isn't a single pair of twins?* "Are there any twins in the collection?" he asked.

"What?"

At the tightness in Applebee's tone, Aldo looked back at the professor. *Did I say something wrong?* It seemed an innocent enough question to him, yet Applebee's reaction made him think otherwise. The older man's smile had faded to a harsh frown, instantly aging him. Why would asking about twins upset him? Unless he knew about Mengele's work. Or had Shryock really been conducting his own experiments?

Deciding he'd better tread carefully, Aldo squatted down in front of the specimen with the extra leg and pointed at it. Then looking up at the professor, he said, "This one looks like it was beginning to form into Siamese twins, so it made me wonder if there were other twins in the collection."

Applebee scrutinized him for a long moment, each second that ticked by increasing Aldo's anxiety. Finally, the professor nodded. "Actually, yes. We have a few, but they're not ready for display yet. In order to keep the specimens well preserved, we periodically have to refresh their solution."

"I see." *How convenient that only the twins are out for restoration right now.*

"Would you like to see them?" Applebee asked, his friendly smile back in place.

While Aldo didn't think he could stomach seeing any more canned humans, something told him he shouldn't decline. For one thing, it would blow a huge hole in his cover story. Not only had he asked for special permission to see the exhibit when it wasn't open to the public, but he had specifically asked about twins as well. To decline now would be way too suspicious.

"May I?" Aldo asked with forced enthusiasm.

Applebee held his gaze, his smile twisting slightly. "Of course."

When the professor continued to stare at him, unmoving, Aldo gestured toward the exit. "Lead the way—"

Wait! Where'd Blondie go? Aldo whipped around to find the tall blond man standing right behind him, a syringe in his right hand. "What the—What's going on?" he demanded, his arms shooting out to keep the man at bay.

"I had expected a relative of the Thirteenth Child to be smarter," Applebee said with a sigh, "yet you fell right into our lap."

"Whose lap? What are you talking about?" Aldo backed away, not taking his eyes off the syringe.

"You can drop the pretense. We already know all about you."

Aldo took another step back, losing his balance as his feet bumped into something. He fell backward, landing on his back with a hard thud. Before he could react, the tall man pinned him to the floor and Professor Applebee jammed the needle into his thigh.

•••

"Mr. Lombardi's been successfully kidnapped, sir," said the voice over the speakerphone.

Successfully? Allison silently questioned the choice of words. She sat across from Jenkins in his office, listening to the report on Aldo's current status and barely managing to hold her tongue.

"Perfect," Jenkins replied. "Inform me immediately once you've confirmed where he's being taken."

The moment Jenkins hit the button to disconnect the call, Allison leaned forward, resting her forearms on his desk. "How is this perfect? You wanted him to make contact with them, not get himself kidnapped."

"A serendipitous turn of events actually. If we're really lucky, they'll take him directly to their headquarters."

"Don't you care about what could happen to him?" Her hand clenched into a fist and she slammed it against the desk's surface, knocking over a picture frame.

"You mean, like you did when you got him strapped to a Monarch chair?" Jenkins sighed as he righted the picture. "Look, Allison. I know Aldo's your friend, but this is bigger than any one of us."

Her friend? Lately she'd been feeling like there was more to their relationship. When they were about to be tortured at the Fifth Reich camp, it had taken everything she had not to spill their plan so she could ease Aldo's fears. And the look of hurt in his eyes when he learned she had approached him under false pretenses when they first met had nearly broken her.

She had known for a long time how he felt about her—the poor guy was adorably obvious. But she couldn't seem to straighten out her own feelings.

"We're going to need to trust in Aldo's abilities," Jenkins continued. "The moment there's any sign of danger, I'll have the team pull him out."

She snapped to her feet, her eyes burning into his. "And how is getting kidnapped not a sign of danger? They're obviously intending something malicious. Otherwise there'd be no need to kidnap him."

Jenkins remained seated but held her gaze. "Perhaps you're not giving him enough credit. The pope, Mr. Summers, and I all believe he can pull this off. Even your superiors are on board. So why are you doubting him?"

She slumped back into her chair. "I'm not doubting, just... What am I going to tell his mom?"

Jenkins gave her a sympathetic look. "Is that really what you're concerned about?"

•••

The darkness slowly faded as intense pain tore through Aldo's skull like a baseball bat hitting a watermelon. He creaked his eyes open and groaned as light pierced through lace curtains hung from the window of a small, unfamiliar room.

Where am I?

Then it all came back to him. Professor Applebee. The fetus exhibit. The blond man and the syringe.

Aldo bolted upright, only to be hit by a flood of nausea as his head throbbed uncontrollably. He fell back against the pillows, his hand on his mouth to quell the need to hurl. *Bastards.* If they would go this far to intimidate a relative, Mr. Summers' need to remain in hiding seemed completely rational.

But now that they had him, what did they plan to do with him? He wouldn't be of any use to them experimentally. Even if they believed the information Jenkins put on the Dark Web, his *blood tie* to Mr. Summers wouldn't have been affected by the Transpose experiments.

It could only be one of two things. Either they knew he was a spy or they planned to interrogate him for information about his supposed uncle. Neither possibility boded well for him.

Aldo sighed. *I told them I wasn't cut out for this.*

When the nausea finally subsided, he rolled over gingerly and glanced around the room. The walnut furniture looked to be Colonial, specifically Queen Anne style, while the large floral rug was more modern. Small landscape paintings adorned the eggshell-colored walls, giving the room a feel reminiscent of a bed and breakfast.

Where in the world am I? Taking a deep breath, he slowly eased into a sitting position, and then propped his back against the large headboard. Aldo's skin grew clammy as another wave of nausea struck, and he closed his eyes, resting his head against the scrollwork along the top of the bed. *What the heck did they inject me with?*

Hearing the door squeak as it slowly opened, Aldo stiffened. A petite woman with somber features poked her head into the room. She wore a starched cotton dress, with her grayish-brown hair swept back into a tight bun. Keeping her eyes down, she carried a tray of tea and small pastries across the room.

"I'm sure you must be hungry," she said, her voice barely above a whisper. "I brought you an herbal tea, which will help relieve your headache. And the muffins should ease your nausea."

"How did..." Aldo tried, but his voice broke as more pain crackled behind his eyes.

"It's the usual side effects," she said softly as she set the tray on the bedside table.

"Usual?" he bit out. "Do you make a habit of drugging and kidnapping people?"

Her hands trembled as she poured him a cup of the tea, and Aldo instantly regretted his harshness. *Wait. I'm the victim here. I shouldn't be feeling guilty.*

"I'm truly sorry. I'll leave you to shower and change," she gushed before hastily making her retreat. "You'll find everything you need in the bathroom."

"Wait. Tell me where I am."

But the door was already closing quietly behind her.

He sat there brooding for a moment, and then leaned over, lifted the teacup and sniffed its contents. The pale green brew smelled of fresh herbs. The thought that she could have poisoned the tea crossed Aldo's mind, but he quickly dismissed it. What reason would she have to drug him again? And even if she had, poisoning couldn't feel any worse than his current condition. It might actually bring welcome relief.

Aldo took a sip, the warm liquid instantly calming his stomach. Leaning back against the headboard, he closed his eyes. After a few minutes, he took another sip and then another until the pounding in his head eased enough that he could function again. Aldo set the empty cup back on the tray and eyed the muffins. As tempting as they looked, he didn't think his stomach could handle anything solid at the moment.

Only when he hung his legs over the side of the bed did he realize he was wearing a kind of nightgown. *Did I get lost in time or something?* Between the antique furnishings, the woman with her out-of-date clothing and hairstyle, and his linen nightgown, Aldo feared he had somehow ended up in the 1700s. Half-expecting to find a washbasin and pitcher in the bathroom, he sighed in relief at the sight of the small pedestal sink and tile shower.

His suitcase had been propped on a cabinet next to the toilet. Aldo's appreciation for his personal effects notwithstanding, the sight of his belongings was still disconcerting. His kidnappers knew enough about him to know which hotel he'd been staying at, even which room number.

Aldo pulled off the nightgown, and then stepped into the shower, standing under the cool water for several minutes before he reached for the soap. The shower calmed the feverishness of his skin, making him feel human again.

After dressing, Aldo slowly carried his suitcase into the bedroom, fearful the slightest movement would revive his migraine. But the tea seemed to be working as promised. Aldo set the suitcase on the bed and found his wallet and watch in the front zipper pocket. He put on his watch then flipped through his wallet, verifying nothing had been removed. He didn't think they had taken anything, since theft wasn't their objective, but he was relieved nonetheless to see all his cards and identification exactly as he had left them.

My laptop!

Looking around the room, he realized both his laptop and cell phone were missing. *Great.* He groaned, but he wasn't really surprised. They would be stupid to leave them in his custody. At least he had the forethought to upload all of his data onto the Vatican's cloud server. Digging through his suitcase to see if any other items had been taken, he discovered they had left his notebook. *But why?* Considering the condemning information written inside, he figured they must have just overlooked it. He slipped it into his back pocket, and then tucked his suitcase under the bed.

Nothing in the room gave any hint of his whereabouts. There were no personal items, nothing to indicate he was being held in someone's home, but it didn't have the frequently used feel of a hotel room either. He moved to the small window, brushing the lace curtains aside with his hand. Lush grass stretched to meet a line of shade trees several stories below, an arbor and benches set strategically around the perimeter. Either the owner was a master gardener or this really was some kind of inn.

Aldo walked to the door and tentatively pressed the handle, expecting it to be locked. When it turned in his hand, he let out a small sigh of relief, and then slowly pulled it open, cringing as the hinges squeaked. The hallway outside was empty. He slipped out and shut the door behind him.

Across the hall was a railing, leading to a wide circular staircase. Glancing over the edge, Aldo could see the banister bordering the second floor below him and where the staircase ended at ground level. It reminded him of an early twentieth-century mansion-turned-museum, from the warm wood moldings and wainscoting to the intricate crystal chandler dangling from a thick chain just beyond the railing.

He was almost certain most houses from this era had a back servant staircase but figured he would waste valuable time searching for it. He also didn't want to chance running into Professor Applebee or his accomplice in the process. His best bet was to get down the main staircase and out the front door as quickly and silently as possible.

Aldo crept down the hall toward the top of the stairs. Hearing movement on the floor below, he froze, only beginning again once all was quiet. Each hardwood tread groaned with age as he clumsily made his descent to the second floor. *I'm really no good at this kind of thing.* He'd never even tried to sneak out of the house back in high school.

Just as he reached the second floor landing, a door opened to his right and a woman stepped out. Not the same one who'd brought him the tea—this woman had a lavender scarf covering her hair and neck, leaving only her face visible. The same was true for her dress. Only her hands, a warm brown against the stark black and white fabric, remained uncovered. Seeing him, she smiled and stepped closer. "I'm glad to see you're feeling better, Mr. Lombardi. Please follow me."

Without giving him a chance to protest, she walked down the next flight of stairs to the main floor, waiting at the bottom for him to join her.

So much for sneaking out. The only way he would make it out the front door without her sounding the alarm would be to shut her up somehow—something he wasn't about to consider doing. *Now, Blondie on the other hand...* His hands clenched at his sides.

Chagrinned, Aldo followed the woman to the foyer. Nooks and crannies in the walls held small statuettes and elegant vases of fresh white flowers. He even passed an impressive stained glass window, marveling for a brief moment at its intricacy.

"This way," the woman said, gesturing to a set of double doors on the opposite side of the foyer.

Before she could open them, Aldo held up a hand. "Wait. Wait a minute. Look, I don't even know where I am or who you're taking me to see. And I only have a vague idea of how I even got here."

She smiled again. "I'm sure Dr. Knight will explain everything. You're in good hands here, Mr. Lombardi." She pulled the door open, holding it for Aldo to enter ahead of her.

Who?

He stepped into a large library. Bookshelves stretched to the second floor ceiling with a balcony running along the perimeter and a spiral staircase at the back of the room. An older man with salt-and-pepper hair sat in a burgundy leather chair with a thick book open in his lap. When he saw Aldo, his face brightened and he stood, setting the book on a small table beside the chair. The tall and slender man crossed the room with the clumsy grace of a giraffe.

"Mr. Lombardi," he said, "I'm so glad to see you up and about." Putting his hands on Aldo's shoulders, he gently squeezed. Aldo assumed the gesture was meant to be reassuring, friendly even, but it felt awkward coming from a complete stranger. Looking past Aldo, the man said, "Thank you, Aaminah. Can you tell Agnes that Mr. Lombardi is feeling better now?"

"Of course." With that, she quietly closed the door, sealing them inside.

"Please, come and have a seat, Mr. Lombardi." The man headed back to his chair, but Aldo remained standing by the door.

What the heck's wrong with these people? Did they really think all would be forgiven that easily? "I was told you could tell me where I am," Aldo said, trying to keep the contempt from his voice.

"Oh! Yes. Where are my manners? My name's Andrew Knight and this is my home." He spread his arms, encompassing the room. "You're most welcome here, Mr. Lombardi."

"Thanks," Aldo said coolly, "but I can't stay."

Dr. Knight's smile fell, but he nodded. "I understand, but would you at least stay until we're sure there are no lingering effects from the drug you were given? I'm afraid my associate, Professor Applebee, can be a bit overzealous at times."

An understatement if I ever heard one . "If I overstepped in requesting to see the Shryock exhibit then I apologize, but drugging and kidnapping me is a bit excessive, don't you think?"

Knight sighed as he eased down into his leather chair. "As I said, he can be a bit overzealous. And he's extremely protective of Shryock's collection."

Aldo cocked an eyebrow. "Enough to commit a felony?"

"Pardon me for saying so, but can you really blame him, Mr. Lombardi? A stranger suddenly shows up, asking questions about the exhibit when he already knows it's closed to the public. Not only that, but he's a young man, fresh out of college, whose major has nothing to do with medicine. You have to admit it was suspicious."

Aldo sighed. *Mr. Jenkins probably wants to strangle me about now.*

"Still," Knight continued, "that doesn't excuse his behavior, and I would like to make it up to you however possible, Mr. Lombardi."

"*Aldo's* fine," Aldo said as he stepped further into the room. While it wasn't the way Jenkins would have preferred, he had definitely made contact. The least he could do was make the most of the opportunity to gather information.

The smile returned to Knight's face. "*Aldo* then." He gestured to the matching leather chair opposite him and Aldo sat down. "While you're recovering, please feel free to use my library as you wish."

"Really?" Aldo glanced around the room, drinking in the majesty of it. Every inch of space on the two story floor-to-ceiling bookshelves was occupied. More books, some still open with ribbons hanging from their spines, spilled onto low tables around the room. Before the large bay window overlooking the garden stood several pedestals, thick volumes displayed on top like crown jewels.

Among the books Aldo noticed numerous antique hand-carved wooden masks and statues with intricate designs and vibrant earth tones that suggested an affinity for African artifacts. Aldo pointed to the nearest one. "Your collection of African tribal pieces is amazing."

"Thank you. Most are from Brother Pierson. Knowing I'm an avid collector, he would usually bring me a souvenir or two whenever he visited the Southern African Division." Knight's expression turned wistful. "I haven't added anything new for some time now."

"Brother Pierson? You mean President Robert Pierson?"

"Yes. He was a good friend of mine."

If Aldo remembered correctly, Robert Pierson had been president of the General Conference back in the late 1960s and 70s. One of the things that stuck with Aldo when he read about Pierson's career was that the man had been called an architect of "the decade of obscurantism". The article didn't go into detail about what exactly Pierson was trying to *obscure* , just that it was an attempt at controlling biblical studies among church members. Was it just coincidence that Pierson's "decade of obscurantism" began just as information about Project Whitecoat was going public?

Interesting . But how do I get Knight to tell me more about it without screwing up like last time? Deciding to bait him, Aldo said, "I'm sorry for your loss. My uncle told me stories about what a great man he was."

"Did your uncle know him?" Knight asked, his hopeful tone encouraging Aldo to continue.

"I think Brother Pierson's sister was his nanny, or tutor...or something." He shrugged for effect.

Knight nodded but didn't offer anything further and the conversation seemed over before it could really begin.

Unable to think of anything to say that would spur his host on, Aldo glanced out the large bay window, noticing the same arbor and benches he'd seen from the window in his room. Tipping his head toward the garden, he asked, "Who's the one with the green thumb?"

This time Knight's smile held genuine warmth. "My wife, Agnes."

"She's quite talented. The garden's beautiful. Did she grow the herbs for the tea she gave me as well?"

"Yes. She makes a variety of home remedies, mostly for the brothers and sisters in our church. They tend to come by whenever they have a cold or some other minor ailment."

"Even with the university and hospital close by?"

Knight nodded. "They prefer a more traditional approach, as do we."

So, I'm still in Loma Linda. That was reassuring. It would make it easier for Jenkins' team to find him once he managed to escape.

Knight picked up his book from the side table, resting it in his lap but leaving it closed. "Are you familiar with the history of the university?"

Aldo shook his head. "Not really, I'm afraid. Nothing more than what was in the brochures I picked up at the visitors center." Truthfully, he'd learned quite a bit about the school's history while at the library, but since Knight seemed to want to tell him all about it, Aldo wasn't about to stop him.

"Did you know Ellen White was instrumental in establishing the original Loma Linda Sanitarium?"

"Really? But wasn't it established toward the end of her life?"

Knight nodded. "She saw it in a vision." His reply held a kind of reverence.

Even after his experiences with Mr. Summers, Aldo still wasn't convinced things like visions and premonitions could be trusted—God didn't speak directly to just anyone—but voicing any disbelief now wasn't going to get him anywhere. "What did she foresee?"

"That the land where the university now stands would be offered to the church for much less than its value. She described seeing a property in Southern California where people were being treated outside under large trees. She was very specific."

"Did she foresee the school, too?"

"Yes. The property was originally purchased by another group, but when they failed in their endeavor, it was put back on the market. When no interested parties stepped forward, the price continued to drop like a stone. It wasn't long before the asking price was a third of the original—only forty thousand dollars. John Burden purchased the property under Ellen White's direction. Even the money he needed for the purchase arrived through divine guidance," Knight said with pride.

"But the school wasn't established until after the sanitarium, right?" Aldo asked, leaning forward to rest his elbows on his knees.

"Yes, a year later, in fact. And Alfred Shryock didn't arrive until 1910." Knight smiled. "I understand it took some convincing to get him to leave his somewhat cushy life and become a teacher at a newly founded school, but his devotion was to the church."

"But it sounds like it was his calling. He came to be truly loved and respected by the students from what I understand, even those he never taught."

Knight nodded. "And many went on to be successful physicians. Numerous lives have been touched because of his dedication to human wellness." He met Aldo's gaze, holding it for a long moment. "Applebee isn't alone in his admiration."

"No, I suppose he isn't," Aldo muttered.

Knight rested his hands, one on top of the other, over the book in his lap. "So, tell me. What was your reason for wanting to see the collection so badly? You mentioned to Applebee that you were inspired by the university's motto, but I still find it hard to believe a historian and recent graduate of the Pontifical Georgian University would be so interested in a medical exhibit."

Shifting uncomfortably, Aldo leaned back in his chair. The conversation was moving onto dangerous ground. If he didn't answer correctly, it could ruin everything. Not to mention they might just drug him again. *No pressure.* "What I told him was true," he began slowly. "I honestly believe collections like Shryock's can help many people..."

"But?" Knight prompted.

"But I wondered at what cost, and I wanted to see for myself." Perhaps it was risky sticking so close to the truth, but that was where Aldo felt most comfortable. "The professor showed me some of the tests Shryock had done on the specimens. Do you think he might have been conducting other tests as well?"

"Such as?"

"Well..." *Man, I wish they had cue cards for this kind of thing.* "...when I'd first learned about Shryock's collection, it reminded me of experiments the Germans did at Auschwitz."

Knight cocked his head to the side. "But all the specimens in Shryock's collection were deceased before he ever received them."

So, he's at least somewhat familiar with Mengele's work. That's a start. "Yes," Aldo chuckled softly. "After seeing the exhibit, I really couldn't find any similarities. That's why I asked about twins. If Shryock had been conducting experiments on twins, there would at least be some kind of correlation."

"What made you think there would've been a correlation to begin with?"

"Oh, I didn't," Aldo said, "other than the experiments were being conducted around the same time. Human experimentation isn't heard of very often, especially in modern times, so when I was told about this exhibit, it reminded me of those at Auschwitz since they were the only other ones I knew of."

"I see."

Aldo could sense Knight pulling away. Was it guilt or had Aldo inadvertently insulted the man by comparing his beloved Professor Shryock to the Angel of Death? Was he probing into territory where Knight didn't want him trespassing? Or did he simply not share Aldo's view on the matter? Going for broke, Aldo said, "My uncle used to tell me stories about things like this."

Knight straightened. "Your uncle?"

"Yes. He was always babbling about conspiracies, most of them connected with Josef Mengele."

"Really? What sort of conspiracies?" Knight asked.

"I don't remember most of them now. It's been so long since I've even seen him...but it was his stories that made me curious about history." That wasn't too far from the truth, but if Aldo was going to get anything out of this guy, he was going to have to pull off a few whoppers. When Knight just nodded, Aldo sighed inwardly. *Man, this guy's a tough nut to crack.* "I do remember one story though, probably because it always seemed so outlandish."

"What's that?"

"Well, he used to talk about how the Seventh-day Adventists helped Mengele continue his experiments in Argentina," Aldo said tentatively. He wasn't sure that admitting he knew anything about the connection between Mengele and the SDA Church was a good idea, but it was the last straw he could grasp.

Knight grimaced, and then quickly propped his chin in his hand, no doubt trying to appear undaunted.

Gotcha!

"That does sound rather far-fetched," Knight said thoughtfully. "Why did he think that?"

"Who knows," Aldo said flippantly. "He had some crazy notion that there was a secret group of men from the church loyal to Hitler and Mengele. That they created false identities for them and everything."

Knight's brows furrowed. "Why would they do that?"

"I don't really remember the specifics. Something about," Aldo gestured with his hand, the movement helping him organize his thoughts, "hiding from the Nazi manhunts and allowing Mengele to continue his research." He tried to keep his responses vague, still concerned about what Knight and Applebee would do if they realized how much he really knew.

"But why did your uncle think Seventh-day Adventists were involved?" Knight asked.

Aldo sighed for emphasis. "You've got to remember these were all the ramblings of a crazy old man. We always found his stories entertaining, but we never believed any of it." He swallowed back the guilt he felt for slandering Mr. Summers, telling himself he'd apologize later.

"Yes, well, I admit I find it rather interesting myself." Knight smiled, and then gestured for Aldo to continue.

"Well, I think it had to do with Hitler's rise to power. According to my uncle, Seventh-day Adventists were instrumental in garnering support for Hitler by passing out pamphlets and other propaganda."

"Yes," Knight said, his expression suddenly sad. "The German Seventh-day Adventists had to make tough decisions back then."

"True. If they showed their support, they could avoid being banned like all the other small denominational churches at the time. But why go so far as to actively promote a fascist dictator?"

"Fear mostly," Knight replied. "They were driven by it and eventually became obsessed with surviving above all else. They were willing to sacrifice so much for Germany, for their corporal existence, but they forgot what it was to be a Seventh-day Adventist in the process."

"Or a member of the human race," Aldo muttered.

"Yes, and while I hate to admit it, I can kind of understand why. Hitler was very persuasive. Not only that, but he shared some of the same beliefs."

"You mean like not drinking caffeine or alcohol?" Aldo said, remembering his research into the Seventh-day Adventist Church on the plane from Argentina.

"Exactly. He also didn't eat meat. And when the government mandated that all children needed to attend school on the Sabbath, the Adventist kids were permitted to study their Bibles while in class, which was a huge concession."

"So, that's why, after the war, they didn't renounce the Nazi party and continued to support and aid Nazi fugitives," Aldo said thoughtfully, as if understanding it for the first time. He leaned back into the plush leather of the chair and crossed his arms over his chest. "I guess I can kind of understand how my uncle got some of his crazy ideas, but still... being so adamant about Hitler surviving the war and Mengele doing everything he could to ensure Hitler ruled forever..." He shook his head. "He used to say that Mengele had a contingency plan in place if he failed to keep Hitler alive."

"What kind of plan?"

For having supposedly never heard any of this before, he sure is taking it all in stride . "See, that's where the secret group of men came into play. I think they had a special name or something, too. Master Comrades, or Comradeship... I can't remember exactly, but they were to continue Mengele's work in secret through a project embedded in the medical arm of the church."

Knight gasped. "What?"

Nice touch, but it's obvious you know something.

Mr. Summers had told him all about the Comradeship of the Three Woes during his week-long cram session—how a few of the members, known as Master Comrades of the Seven Times, became liaisons for the medical research being conducted in Argentina and the United States. They were also charged with keeping Mengele and Hitler alive as long as possible, giving them all the assistance they needed and providing protection during Mengele's frequent trips into Brazil.

"I know. Crazy, right?" Aldo replied smoothly. "One of the many reasons why he and my father no longer speak."

"Then you have no idea what he's up to now?"

I bet you've been dying to ask that. "No, I haven't seen or heard from him since his feud with Elder Frogburger."

"Yes, I've heard about that."

"If you ask me, he just has a persecution complex. He really believed Frogburger was ordering fellow members to prosecute him," Aldo said with a sigh. That was the worst part of this whole spying business—trying to stomach all the lies and act like it didn't affect him.

"What made him think so?"

"I'm not really sure. I just remember overhearing my dad complain about it. I was pretty young when it happened," Aldo said, remembering Tony had told him it took place sometime in the mid-1980s.

Knight nodded. "It kind of became an internal war between top members of the church and your uncle."

"So I've heard. But Dad wanted no part of it. Practically disowned my uncle because of it."

"Well, at the time, not many were aware of what Frogburger had been doing behind the members' backs with his fraudulent investment deals. But when he finally fell, he brought down at least eighteen other doctors and ministers with him—all those who had helped him along the way. They lost their licenses, reputations...some even their marriages."

"But he still managed to escape prison, right? I'd heard that the church arranged for Frogburger to sell computer equipment while continuing to serve in the church as a minister. Granted, it allowed him to pay off a small part of the damages which the church would have had to eat otherwise, but still..."

"Yes, well, it's all in the past now."

No, it isn't. Mr. Summers is still trying to put his life back together after getting thoroughly screwed over by your church . Aldo wanted to scream.

Knight stood up, stretching his legs. "How about a walk through the gardens? I bet you could use some fresh air."

Aldo stood as well, breathing a small sigh of relief. "I could. Thanks." He wasn't sure if their conversation had confirmed Knight's suspicions about him, but at least now he was sure about one thing. He and Applebee knew, and were likely members, of the secret group behind the Toddler Program. Like it or not, Aldo was exactly where the pope wanted him to be.

Strolling through the garden in silence, Aldo soon found he couldn't keep from yawning.

"You must be tired," Knight said. "You're here to recover and all I've done is talk your ear off. I'm sorry."

He makes it sound like I had the flu. "I am a bit tired," Aldo said. "I think I'll head back to my room for a bit." He could feel the effects of the tea beginning to wear off and preferred to be lying down before the watermelon smashing began again.

Knight nodded. "I understand. Here. Let me help you." He offered his hand, but Aldo waved him off.

"I'll be fine," Aldo muttered. "Just need a good night's rest." He stumbled on the patio steps and nearly went down, Knight catching his arm before he could hit the pavers.

"Let me help you," Knight repeated. "I am a medical doctor. So you're in good hands."

Deciding he'd get to his room faster if he cooperated, Aldo held his tongue as Knight called into the house for Aaminah, giving her instructions before steering him through the library and back up to the third floor. Each step seemed to wake up the beast in his head more and more until it was raging. Aldo managed to keep his composure, repeatedly assuring Knight that he didn't need an examination.

Only after he was tucked in and finally alone did he let out a groan of pain. While he had managed to learn a bit from his conversation with Dr. Knight, Aldo felt like his day was ending as it had begun.

Chapter Eight | The PAWN

Loma Linda, California
March 2013

"What kind of drug did they give him?" a low feminine voice asked.

Is that Allison? The voice sounded near, yet at the same time far away, as though filtered through a vaporous swamp. Aldo struggled to focus.

"I have no idea," a man replied, "but I intend to find out. What did Applebee tell you when you called him?"

"He wasn't very responsive. All he said was that the chemical had been injected."

"Which means it was probably very concentrated..." The man's voice faded. Afraid it would disappear altogether, leaving him alone in the darkness, Aldo listened intently. "...forbade him from using drugs not fully tested...do an inspection of his laboratory in Argentina..."

An oppressive silence filled Aldo's ears until he was sure they had vanished. Then the man's voice filtered through the thick blackness again. "We'll need to keep an eye on him over the next few days and watch for any additional side effects."

"You think it was the drug's concentration that caused him to lapse into unconsciousness again?"

"Most likely... Keep hounding Applebee until he gives you some answers."

"Yes, Doctor. What would you like me to do if Mr. Lombardi insists on leaving when he wakes up?"

At first Aldo wasn't sure he'd heard her right.

"Whatever it takes. Just keep him here."

Who are these people? Keep me where?

As Aldo's confusion and panic grew, the voices wavered, moving further away until they were almost indistinguishable.

"...think he can hear us...?"

"I doubt it, but...continue...in my library."

Once again, the darkness swallowed him.

•••

Slowly, Aldo's consciousness returned, as though switches were being flipped on all over his body. Sporadic twitches sent tingling sensations up legs that felt like lead weights and arms that seemed to be covered in buzzing bees. Aldo sluggishly flexed his fingers, trying to shake them awake. His whole body felt weak, like he had been dead for a while.

Managing to pry the rusted hinges of his eyelids open, he found himself surrounded by vaguely familiar white walls topped with turn-of-the-century crown molding stained in a rich coffee tone. The linen nightshirt tugging at his throat as he tried to sit up sparked a feeling of *déjà vu* and he remembered the older woman with the tight bun. The herbal tea. The house and gardens.

So it hadn't been a dream. He really had been drugged. Had the conversation he'd heard been real, too? They were holding him captive under the pretense of helping him recover from an experimental drug of their own making? *Bastards.* No way would he hang around playing lab rat. But as his head fogged and stomach turned, Aldo realized he wouldn't be going anywhere in his current state. And he did not want to jeopardize the plan the pope and Mr. Jenkins had carefully constructed over the last six months. Not to mention Allison and Mr. Summers were counting on his success.

Aldo clenched his fist. *Screw the mission.* No one said anything about risking his life. He was there to learn, not be their guinea pig. What if the drug they had given him had lasting effects like Transpose? Just like Mr. Summers, he'd had no say in what they had done to his body.

Why me, Lord? Until a few weeks earlier, his life had consisted of graduating with his Ph.D. by the skin of his teeth and trying to muster the courage to ask Allison out on a date. And he was sure failure in either one would mean his life was ruined. Now, here he was, his life *actually at risk* and forever altered by decisions he had no control over.

Aldo sighed and leaned back against the headboard. He felt groggy, as though his entire head and mouth had been stuffed with cotton, while his stomach felt painfully hollow. But thankfully, the cranial bat bashing he had received the day before was only a haunting memory.

As he rubbed the crustiness from his eyes, something rough brushed his face. He pulled his hand away, only to see a thin clear plastic tube taped to the back of his hand. The tube ran to an IV hook standing at the foot of the bed. Beneath his linen nightshirt, electrodes clung to his chest, the wires running to the heart rate monitor mounted to the IV stand.

Just how long was I out?

He glanced around the room for a clock or calendar, anything that would tell him how much time had passed. Sunlight streamed in through the lace curtains at a low angle. He knew from his brief tour of the gardens with Dr. Knight that his window faced east, so that meant it had to be just after dawn. The following morning? The day after? No, the empty feeling in his gut told him more time had passed.

He noticed a cup and pitcher on the table beside his bed, drops of condensation running down the sides. Snapping up the cup, he filled it with cool water, gulped it down, and then quickly refilled it and drained it again.

Setting the cup back on the table, he maneuvered his legs over the edge of the bed, trying to stretch the stiff weakness from his muscles. He planted his feet on the floor, and then stood up slowly. Wobbling, he grabbed the bedpost for support until he felt steady enough to let go and then walked around the bed to the IV hook. The attached bag gave a list of various lipids, amino acids, vitamins, minerals, and glucose. The port for additional injections branching off the tube concerned him much more.

Aldo peeled off each electrode and tape, and then gently pulled the tube from the vein in his hand, holding a tissue over the hole until the bleeding stopped. *Bastards.* He had no way of knowing if they had drugged him again. Even if they had, it was too late now, but he wasn't about to give them another opportunity. He was getting the hell out of there.

Wait, my cell phone.

Aldo started digging through his suitcase when he remembered they had confiscated his cell phone along with his laptop. *Dammit!* Considering the GPS tracking function would be able to pinpoint his exact location, and they would have to get through the lock screen and log into his cloud account to disable it, his phone likely wasn't even on the premises. No doubt they had it and his laptop in a secure place where they could try to extract any usable information.

Thank God he had uploaded his research to the Vatican's cloud server and wiped his laptop's hard drive clean each time he used it. He sighed. Cell phones and laptops were replaceable, but he didn't even want to imagine the chaos that would ensue if they got their hands on his research. Not to mention what his captors would do to him if they learned he was a fake.

Checking to ensure his notebook was still with him, Aldo shuffled into the bathroom, glancing at his left arm as he lifted the toilet seat. Mr. Jenkins had offered to implant a tracking device beneath the skin at his wrist, like the one Allison wore. While the reassurance that they would always know his whereabouts had been tempting, he couldn't bring himself to consent to it. Left arm or not, it was too close to the Mark of the Beast mentioned in the Book of Revelation. Though Aldo had to admit, after what he had endured since meeting Applebee, he might consent to it if Mr. Jenkins offered a second time.

He shook his head. No, that kind of mindset drives people to give into temptation. He just had to trust in the pope. That and not ever agree to do anything like this again.

When he finished relieving himself, Aldo moved to the sink to wash. Glancing at his reflection in the small oval mirror, he froze. A week's worth of beard growth had sprouted in scraggly clumps along his chin and cheeks. While his father, being of Mediterranean decent, could compete with a poodle for volume of body hair, Aldo had thankfully inherited his maternal grandfather's Native American complexion and hair growth pattern. What little facial hair he had grew in sparsely, with bare patches along his jaw line. Aside from the few months during his freshman year of college he'd attempted to grow a goatee, he had always kept himself clean-shaven.

Disturbed by the sight, Aldo immediately retrieved the bag of toiletries from his suitcase. After slathering on shaving cream, he made quick work of removing the Brillo pads from his jaw. As he picked up a small white towel to pat his face dry, he heard a knock at the bedroom door. "Yes?" he answered hoarsely, shuffling back into the bedroom.

"Mr. Lombardi? Oh, good. You're awake. How are you feeling?" a woman called through the door. The same voice he'd heard in that hazy dream.

Checking on your test subject? Aldo pulled the door open.

The Middle Eastern woman he met earlier stood in the hallway, a stack of papers clutched in her hands. Preoccupied with leaving the last time he saw her, Aldo had not noticed much more than her ethnicity. Again, only her face was visible, surrounded by a wine colored scarf. She seemed older than he, though not as old as the other woman. But he had always been a horrible judge of age.

Forcing a smile, he said, "Better now that I'm back on my feet again."

She returned a smile. "I'm glad. We were really worried. Doctor Knight's been up for the last thirty-six hours watching over you. I finally convinced him to get some sleep, but he'll be upset if I don't tell him you're finally awake."

"Thirty-six hours?" Aldo gaped at her. "How long was I out before that?"

"I'll let Doctor Knight explain. Do you think you can make it down to his library?"

"I think so. Just give me a few minutes to finish putting myself back together."

"Take all the time you need." She smiled again, the whiteness of her teeth contrasting against the warm tone of her skin.

Wanting to make sure he committed his guard's name to memory, he said, "Thanks, uh...um. I'm sorry, I forgot your name." He gave her a sheepish smile for good measure. If he was going to tough it out until he could escape or be rescued, he was getting every scrap of information he could in the meantime.

"Aaminah."

"Thanks, Aaminah."

"Would you like me to have Agnes brew you some tea?"

"Oh, no, thank you. Something to eat would be good though. I'm starving." Just as the words left his mouth his stomach rumbled loudly. Moving his arm to cover his stomach in embarrassment, he intentionally knocked the stack of papers from her hands and they fluttered to the floor. "Oh, I'm sorry. I guess I'm still a bit shaky." Quickly, he stooped to gather them for her, muttering repeated apologizes as he scanned the documents for any useful information.

"Please, Mr. Lombardi, I'll get them. You should take it easy. You're still recovering." Snatching the papers from his hand, she hurriedly scooped up the remaining pieces. Then nodding her thanks, she left in a hasty retreat down the hallway.

So she's not just a nurse . Aldo closed the door and returned to the bathroom. Plagued with frequent dizzy spells brought on by hunger, Aldo took his time showering. As he washed, he mulled over the glimpses of information he had gleaned from Aaminah's documents, but none of it really made sense. Several pages seemed to detail Muslim customs and theology, while others covered Seventh-day Adventist doctrines. One term, in particular, had caught his attention: the Three Woes.

An end of days prophecy from the Book of Revelation, the Three Woes were the final signs before Christ's Second Coming. Like the Ten Plagues of the

Old Testament, each woe would bring anguish and destruction, though on a global scale, with the third woe literally being the end of the world. But Muslims didn't believe in Bible prophecy. So, why were the Three Woes mentioned in documents about Islam?

Man, I could really use my laptop right now . Aldo gritted his teeth.

Aldo found the library empty when he walked downstairs twenty minutes later. Assuming his host would be joining him shortly, he slowly walked the circumference of the room, his eyes scanning the volumes lining the lower shelves of the towering bookcases. Since Dr. Knight had graciously given him free access, he made a mental list of the books he would read first. A majority were popular Seventh-day Adventist books, many of them ones he had seen at the university's library.

The desk at the center of the room sat bare, save for a couple of books stacked at one corner. He was sure he had seen a laptop there the other day...or whenever it was. Not that he would have been able to use it even if Dr. Knight were trusting enough to leave it there. It was most likely password protected and Aldo was not foolish or brave enough to attempt hacking into it. Considering how Aaminah had reacted at his room earlier, Aldo had the impression Knight was rather protective of information.

So, why the free access to his personal library? Aldo had yet to see any titles that couldn't be found in any public or university library, but a good deal of Knight's were first editions. The shelves felt more like a museum collection than sources of knowledge. That meant the information Aldo was really after wouldn't be easily obtained. Still, he planned to learn all he could while he recovered.

An elaborately illustrated Bible sat on a carved wooden pedestal in an alcove with a soft spotlight illuminating it like a piece of art. Was it coincidence that it was opened to chapter nine in the Book of Revelation?

Keeping his finger between the pages to mark the place, Aldo discreetly flipped to the inside of the front cover. As he'd suspected, a family tree spread across the pages. He assumed Dr. Knight descended from famous names within the SDA Church, but none of the names listed rang any bells. However, Aldo knew only the few names that had come up in his research. Still, he made note of some to look up when he got the chance. It would be nice to know who exactly this man was. Allison would be a great help with that. With her connections inside the Mormon Church, she could probably have Knight's entire genealogy mapped out in a matter of hours.

On a twin pedestal sat a leather-bound 1911 edition of *The Great Controversy* , Ellen White's most famous book. Her portrait hung just above it, as though she were being canonized. Having read the book in its entirety while at the university's library, Aldo just skimmed through the pages, looking for any highlighted passages or notes scribbled in the margins. He found nothing, not surprising considering the book was a first edition and Knight had it displayed like a religious relic.

Aldo walked to a second alcove displaying Uriah Smith's book *Daniel and the Revelation* , 1912 edition. As with many religious books, the Bible included, both of these volumes had been repeatedly edited over the years, to ensure their content fit with current social views. The fact that Knight kept these early versions in his home, proudly displayed, seemed like a possible point of contention between him and his church.

Hadn't Knight mentioned something like that during their previous conversation? Something about preferring to do things in a more traditional way? So, then why the interest in Mr. Summers? The experiments done on Mr. Summers while he was in the Toddler Program could hardly be called *traditional* . Likewise, nothing about Aldo's current situation could be considered traditional.

Aldo began to sense that Dr. Knight was not on good terms with his church. There was also his connection with Applebee. From the conversation Aldo had overheard in his room, Knight gave the impression he disapproved of Applebee's take on the medical field. Not only that, but despite his show of care and concern, Knight seemed to be the one who wanted Aldo in his home. *But this place has to be better than wherever Applebee could've taken me.*

Aldo glanced around the room. Could this all be a front? Portraying the humble doctor to the outside world while searching for Mr. Summers and any information on life extension? But didn't the SDA church have the same goal? So, why the charade of contention? Did he think it would gain him Aldo's sympathy?

Aldo shook his head. There was another possibility—one that seemed the most likely and most terrifying. Based on everything that had happened to him since meeting Applebee at the university, Aldo was convinced the professor had to be involved with the secret group Mr. Summers had told him about. Applebee's obsession with Shryock's collection and research. The Hans look-alike assistant. The experimental drug. All the pieces were there, except for how Knight fit into the puzzle.

Aldo knew enough about Knight to know the man wasn't what he seemed. The fact he could orchestrate Aldo's kidnapping, eliminating evidence of his stay in Loma Linda, proved he had resources. It only made sense those resources would be the members of the Comradeship of the Three Woes, a secret society tucked so deeply into the fabric of the SDA Church only a very few even knew it existed. If so, then playing a simple doctor with traditional roots, even if it went against the general beliefs of the church, would be a good way to throw people off his trail.

Hearing the door creak open behind him, Aldo brought his attention back to the book open in his hands, a compilation of all four volumes of Ellen G. White's *Spiritual Gifts*. Pretending to be so absorbed in reading as to not notice Knight's presence, Aldo scanned the contents to discover the very sentiment that had caused such controversy between the church and the outside world.

But if there was one sin above another, which called for the destruction of the race by the flood, it was the base crime of amalgamation of man and beast, which defaced the image of God and caused confusion everywhere .

Aldo's skin crawled at the blatant racism. Everyone was entitled to his own opinion, but to think some races came from man procreating with animals was ludicrous. It highlighted how different things were back then. He flipped forward to the following chapter.

Every species of animal that God had created was preserved in the ark. The confused species which God did not create, which were the result of amalgamation, were destroyed by the flood. Since the flood, there has been amalgamation of man and beast, as may be seen in the almost endless varieties of species of animals and in certain races of men.

"You must be familiar with this book to have flipped through to this page so quickly," Knight said from behind him.

Aldo nodded, closing the book with a reverence he didn't feel as he turned to face the tall older man. "I'm a historian, so I'm familiar with many religions and their texts. I studied Ellen G. White's writings about the crime of amalgamation extensively in college." Only a partial lie. While he had been introduced to White's writings in college, it wasn't until his visit to Loma Linda University's library that he'd read this particular book cover to cover.

"She's very clear on her thoughts about mixing God's species, isn't she?"

"Yes," Aldo said, putting the book back in its place. As if thinking aloud, he continued, "After all, if God had intended for races to be mixed, he wouldn't have bothered to create different ones." Aimed at probing for Knight's viewpoint on the matter, his statement nonetheless made him feel ill, as with any lie he'd told since childhood. Lying always invoked the memory of the taste of Dial soap. His mom had been old school in her forms of punishment. To this day, he couldn't even stand the smell. He sighed inwardly. Another reason he wasn't cut out to be a spy.

Knight touched his shoulder. "There aren't many in the Catholic world who would agree with you. It must have been lonely."

Aldo gave him a tight smile. "I'll admit I've never heard anyone voice a similar opinion, especially in Rome where I went to college."

"You were in Rome until just a few weeks ago, right? Did you get caught up in any of the recent political unrest there?"

The eagerness in Knight's tone seemed odd. "About the new Prime Minister election?

Andrew nodded.

"No. There were a few groups protesting, but as far as I know nothing came of it. Although I saw on the news recently that a tourist was held at knifepoint."

"I see."

And that ends that discussion. Aldo inwardly sighed. *I see* was becoming Knight's standard reply whenever he didn't feel like discussing something further. But why the sudden interest in Rome?

The silence dragged on until Aldo finally walked over and dropped into one of the burgundy armchairs, too exhausted and dizzy to continue standing. "Any chance you could tell me how long I was unconscious?"

Almost reluctantly, Dr. Knight followed, his lanky gait making Aldo wonder how tall he was exactly. That kind of height had to be annoying.

"Six days."

"Six—what? Are you serious?" He'd been dead to the world for an entire week? *And at the complete mercy of my host.* His stomach churned at the thought. He just hoped Allison was keeping his mom pacified. The last time he had missed his weekly call home, his mom had gone ballistic, and he was already in hot water after disappearing from the ski slopes.

Aldo briefly thought about using that as an excuse to request making a phone call home, but he knew the line would likely not be secure, and he wasn't willing to risk being overheard. Not only that, but without his cell phone, he wouldn't know what to dial. He hadn't thought to memorize Allison's or Mr. Jenkins's numbers.

Aldo studied Knight for a moment. He had already resigned himself to enduring his confinement until he recovered, but what would they do if he did try to leave? Just how far would they go to keep him there? Deciding to test the waters, Aldo stood up. "Thank you for your care, but I'm feeling better now, so I really should be going."

Dr. Knight's expression remained calm. "There's no telling if you might lapse into unconsciousness again, Aldo. I would prefer it if you stayed until I'm sure there are no lingering side effects."

Heading toward the door, Aldo glanced over his shoulder. "I'll check myself into a hospital if anything crops up."

"I'm afraid I can't allow that, Aldo."

Before he reached the door, it opened and Aaminah entered, carrying a tray with two bowls of oatmeal, two smaller bowls of what looked like applesauce, two mugs and a stainless steel carafe. She handed the tray to Aldo. "If there's anything else I can get you, please let me know." Looking past him, she said, "Doctor?"

"Thank you, Aaminah. That's all for now."

She excused herself, the sound of her locking the door from the outside nearly making Aldo laugh at the audacity.

Aldo carried the tray over to Knight and set it down on the low table positioned between the armchairs. "And if I refuse?"

"Couldn't you just consider yourself our guest?"

Aldo laughed humorlessly. "A guest would be allowed to leave."

"True, but I am allowing you free reign of the house and the library. You can go anywhere you like, so long as it's on the premises."

"And this is all just to ensure my health, is it?"

"Of course."

Reluctantly, Aldo took his seat.

"Good. Now, let's eat. I'm sure you must be famished. Would you like some tea?"

Unbelievable. Aldo realized Dr. Knight was accustomed to getting his way. People who could coerce others into doing what they wanted were usually in positions of management. But this man was supposedly a simple doctor?

Too tired to argue any further, Aldo threw his arm out in a gesture of submission. "Sure. Why not."

Knight handed him a mug of herbal tea then a bowl of oatmeal. "It's hot, so you'll need to eat slowly. And your stomach has shrunk, so you'll be on softer foods for the next few days."

And whose fault is that?

"Once you've had your fill, how about some fresh air?" Knight asked with a cheerfulness that made Aldo want to throw something at him.

Aldo wanted to decline just to spite him, but then changed his mind. A walk would give him the opportunity to assess the rest of the grounds. "I suppose some fresh air would be good. I have been bedridden for a week, after all," Aldo said with barely concealed bitterness.

Knight continued, "If you get tired, we have a lovely spot with a bench where you can sit and relax." Aldo wondered if the doctor was oblivious or simply choosing to ignore his comment,

Despite his hunger, Aldo managed to eat only about half the applesauce and a few bites of the oatmeal before he set the dishes aside. He then stepped out onto the patio and took a deep breath of the cool early morning air.

"Beautiful day, isn't it?" Knight observed.

Aldo didn't bother replying. Every day in Southern California was beautiful.

They had barely reached the bottom of the patio steps when Agnes appeared at a door down the side of the house. "Excuse me, dear, but you have a phone call."

"Thanks. Do you mind escorting our guest over to the perennial garden? I'd like him to take it easy, and the fresh air will do him good."

"Certainly." She crossed the patio, carrying a tray with a pitcher of water and a glass, as Knight headed back into the house.

Before closing the door behind him, the doctor turned back to Aldo. "Oh, I should let you know that we have another guest staying with us as well. She's still settling in, but you may see her about. Agnes can fill you in on the details."

A guest or another prisoner?

"She's not really a guest," said Aldo's guide as she led him to a bench tucked beneath huge shade trees and surrounded by a variety of flowering plants, most of which Aldo had never seen before. "She's more like our charge. We're looking after her for a while...possibly indefinitely."

"What happened?"

"She's had a difficult time," she said vaguely after a long pause.

Aldo nodded. "Mind if I ask what you mean by *a difficult time*? I would hate to inadvertently do something that might upset her."

Agnes let out a long sigh and sat down next to him on the bench. She seemed uncomfortable discussing it, and her hesitation provided all the more reason for Aldo to understand the situation. "Her father was...abusive to her. So we're taking custody of her while he's on probation."

Aldo's hands clenched at his sides. "What did he do?"

"I'm sorry, Mr. Lombardi. I don't think Robyn would want me to go into the details with you," she said, shaking her head, "but I will tell you that it's been ongoing. It's made her reclusive and distrustful of others, particularly men. Andrew's the only one she's been willing to talk to about this, but then we've known the child since she was born. Her father's a good friend of Andrew's...*was* a good friend." She stood to leave. "So please don't take it to heart if she avoids you."

"Right. Thank you for telling me."

She gave him a warm smile. "Please, relax and enjoy our little piece of nature."

Alone in the garden, Aldo tipped his head back, watching the sunlight sparkle through the leaves overhead for a long moment. The day had begun to warm and the breeze ruffling his hair offered a welcome relief.

His sense of justice demanded he do something to help the poor girl, but what could he really do? He was an outsider in all this. All he could really do was offer her friendship. Considering the circumstances, that might be just what she needed—to know that there were still men in the world who would treat her with kindness and respect.

Well, nothing's going to get resolved with me just sitting here . Aldo decided to ask Dr. Knight if he could bring one of the books from his library outside. As he stood up, a twig snapped behind him and he turned to see a small figure unsuccessfully attempting to hide behind the trunk of a tree. Perhaps she thought her mass of curly brown hair would be camouflaged against the bark.

Unsure of whether to pretend he hadn't seen her or to greet her and try to convince her he was not a threat, Aldo finally decided to test the waters. The longer he avoided her, the more difficult it would be to encourage her to open up to him.

"Hello there," he said, taking a few careful steps forward. When the girl's shoulders tensed, he stopped. "Are you a guest here, too? I've been a bit sick lately, so this is my first time outside in a week." When she didn't so much as move, he tried again. "Was this your bench? I'm heading back inside now, so please feel free." Still nothing. Sighing, Aldo picked up the tray with the water pitcher and headed across the lawn to the house.

When he returned with a book ten minutes later, the girl was seated on the bench, her face turned toward the sky. Her clothes were baggy and much too thin for the weather.

Assuming announcing his presence would be better than approaching quietly, Aldo called to her from across the lawn. "Hello again." She jumped in surprise and instantly dropped her head, her long hair falling forward to shield her face. *Bastard* . Aldo's thoughts turned to anger as he witnessed the effects of her father's abuse. The poor thing couldn't be more than fifteen, still a child by anyone's standards.

"The garden's beautiful, isn't it?" he continued as cheerfully as he could. "Mrs. Knight has done an amazing job." Afraid the girl might bolt for the house at any moment, Aldo remained close to the edge of the flowerbeds as he walked, giving her a wide berth should she feel the need to escape.

She said nothing, her gaze fixed on the hands in her lap. He stopped a few feet from the bench and waited, but she remained silent.

"Would it be all right if I joined you? I found this book on botany in Dr. Knight's library and thought I'd see if I could figure out what kinds of plants these are."

His answer came several moments later when she scooted to the far edge of the bench, nearly pressing herself against the wrought iron armrest. *Well, at least she didn't run away crying.* He sat down, making sure to give her as much space as he could, and then quietly started thumbing through the book.

Aldo hadn't lied about his interest in the plants. In his Colorado hometown, most things would still be covered in snow this time of year, but Mrs. Knight had managed to grow a lush garden in the dry, cool southern California climate. He hadn't seen any kind of sprinkler system on his trek to and from the house either. She didn't water all this by hand, did she? There had to be at least three acres of land.

As Aldo flipped through the book, scrutinizing each illustration and cross-checking it against the plant in front of him, he noticed the girl's shoulders soften, but still she refused to raise her head. Though it saddened him, she had every right to do whatever made her feel comfortable. He just hoped she wouldn't stay cowed forever. And since he was sequestered for at least a few more days, he had the time to be patient.

When he stood up too suddenly, eager to take a closer look at one of the plants tucked along the back edge of the flower bed, she bolted to her feet. "Oh, sorry," he said, cursing himself. "I, uh, just wanted a better look at that plant." He pointed to a large succulent with a single flowering stock that rose from its center and drooped over like a fuzzy candy cane. All interest in it lost, Aldo walked toward it anyway. Crouching down, he examined the spiny leaves as though completely fascinated, but all his attention was on the spooked creature behind him.

She took a step forward, and then hesitated.

Aldo heard a door slam at the house, and he turned to see Mrs. Knight crossing the lawn with a tray in her hands. "I thought you might be hungry again, Aldo dear, since you weren't able to eat much at breakfast."

Dear? Since when were they close enough for her to use terms of endearment? Then it struck him. She was trying to help. If she seemed to be on familiar terms with him, it could help ease Robyn's fear.

"I also brought some cookies, fresh from the oven, for you, Robyn. And some milk. If you'd like something else, just let me know." She set the tray on the bench as Aldo climbed out of the flowerbed.

"Sorry I went traipsing through your flower bed, but I wanted to see that plant. Is it a variety of agave?"

She beamed. "Yes. That's very good, dear."

"Ah, well, I had help." He held up the botany book in his hands.

"Still, there are those who wouldn't have bothered." She touched her hand to her face as though she'd forgotten something. "Robyn, honey, this is Aldo Lombardi. He's the one I mentioned to you before. He will be staying with us while he recovers."

Finally, bravely, she peeked up at him. She had a large bruise on her right cheek, which seemed to make opening her eye difficult. The left side of her jaw was also discolored. The bruises looked horribly painful and he didn't want to imagine what other injuries her baggy clothes were hiding. *Who would do that to a defenseless little girl?* As an only child, he didn't know the feeling of having a sister, but he imagined it was akin to the fierce protectiveness he already felt for Robyn.

"Hello," Robyn said, her voice barely audible.

Agnes turned to Aldo. "Now, Aldo dear, I want you to take it easy. Don't overexert yourself. I'll have lunch ready for you in your room in about an hour."

"Even though you're feeding me now?"

"Small, frequent meals. Doctor's orders." She beamed at him again then turned toward the house, plucking weeds from the flowerbeds as she went.

"Well, should we dive in, Robyn? Those cookies look incredible. My favorite, too." The moist oatmeal raisin cookies with milk were much more tempting than the square of red Jell-O, bowl of cottage cheese, and glass of... something greenish-brown.

Hesitantly, she sat down again and lifted a cookie from the plate, nibbling at it like a small animal.

Thank you, Mrs. Knight . He was sure Robyn had been ready to go back into hiding before their hostess came and gave him another chance.

Careful not to make any more sudden movements, Aldo slowly ate his Jell-O and most of his cottage cheese. The greenish-brown liquid turned out to be a blend of carrot and spinach juice, which was surprisingly tasty. They ate silently, neither saying a word even after they both finished their snack.

Finally, Aldo rose. "I think I'll head back inside for a nap. I'm still pretty exhausted." Gesturing to the tray, he asked, "Are you finished?" When she nodded ever so slightly, he lifted the tray from the bench then eyed the botany book. Throughout their meal, he had noticed her occasionally glancing at it. "Can I leave that with you, since my hands are full? You can just hand it to Dr. Knight when you come inside."

This time her nod was more apparent.

He smiled. If plants were a means to get her to open up and forget about what she had been through, then he would learn as much as he could while they were together at the house. "Thanks. Hopefully, I'll see you tomorrow." He turned toward the house. The energy he had felt earlier was completely gone, so more botany books would have wait until after a nap.

The next few days whizzed by at a surprising pace. Aldo spent most of his time either sleeping or reading in the library. When he noticed Robyn in the garden beyond the large bay window, he joined her if his energy level permitted. His recovery was taking longer than he had expected, frustrating him to no end. Dr. Knight kept telling him to give it time, but Aldo's patience was growing short. The election of the new pope would happen any day, if it hadn't already, and being disconnected from the world was causing Aldo more anxiety.

Aldo felt virtually the same as he did when he woke up from his week-long coma. Strangely, he typically felt better in the morning but progressively worse as the day wore on. He didn't know much about human anatomy, but he figured seven days was plenty of time to purge the body of toxins. So why did he still feel like crap?

He sat on the bench in the garden, sipping the carrot and spinach concoction Mr. Knight always included with his lunch as he stared up at the sky. Aldo couldn't help feeling they were somehow prolonging his recovery. As caring as the Knights had been, he still didn't trust them, particularly Dr. Knight. The man was hiding too many secrets. But if so, how and why? The wound on his hand from the IV had healed nicely and he hadn't seen any new injection sites during his morning showers. Was he just being paranoid?

No. He had definitely heard Dr. Knight order Aaminah to keep him here by whatever means necessary. What better way to do that than to keep him physically incapacitated? He lifted his glass to take another sip when realization struck. *Dammit! The food.* He peered down at the greenish-brown sludge and nearly gagged, wanting to fling the glass across the lawn. Instead, his grip tightened. Conscious that anyone could be watching from the house, he discreetly poured the remaining contents into the flower bed beside the bench.

Pulling out his notebook, he wrote down his suspicions and any physical effects he could remember experiencing over the previous week. He had no idea which foods they had poisoned, but logically he could start by eliminating anything processed. He would have to do it without their realizing though. Who knew what they would try next.

Absorbed in his thoughts, Aldo didn't hear Robyn approach. "Mr. Lombardi?"

"Oh, Robyn. Good morning." He glanced down at his watch. "Well, I guess it's afternoon now. I've been sleeping so much my days are all mixed up."

"Are you feeling any better?" she asked, concerned.

He shook his head. "Not really, but don't worry. I'll be fine."

She sat down on the bench beside him. "How do you know Andrew and Agnes?" she asked softly.

Normally that question would come up just after meeting someone, not over a week later, but then this was the first time she had engaged in an actual conversation rather than broken bits of chatter that always felt one-sided. Still, he would have preferred her first question not be that one. "Well, Dr. Knight's, uh, an acquaintance of a professor I know. When I got sick, he brought me here so Dr. Knight could treat me."

"So, you're not a member of the church then."

"Uh, no, I'm not. Does that bother you?"

She shook her head. "I kind of figured you weren't. You seem to eat chicken and fish regularly, but many Seventh-day Adventists are vegetarians."

"Ah, right." He remembered reading in White's book *Counsels on Diets and Foods* that *meat-eating,* as she called it, was to be done away with for those awaiting the Second Coming. She also mentioned that eating animal flesh numbed the brain and affected one's morality. So far, he had only seen a few studies on the health risks related to the consumption of meat, most pertaining to the consumption of red meat. Still, giving up meat entirely wasn't something he was ready to do just yet. "Are you okay with my being Catholic?"

She nodded. "It doesn't matter to me, but my father—" She broke off, a shadow swallowing her expression. The bruises on her face may have faded over the past week but the wounds on her heart were still fresh.

"Oh, I forgot to tell you," Aldo said cheerfully, sensing now was a good time to change the subject. "Mrs. Knight agreed to let me have a small plot of land in her vegetable garden to plant something and I thought I'd ask you to help me. My energy's still pretty low, but it's a good excuse to get outside, right?" He gave her a big smile. "You get so much sun here, I bet watermelon would be good. What do you think?"

"I love watermelon," she replied softly.

With each passing day, Aldo felt more and more like himself. He continued to accept whatever food he was served but found creative ways of disposing of what he thought might be contaminated. He watered different areas of the garden with the carrot and spinach juice each day while muffins and pastries were flushed. Since he didn't know if the drug was a powder or a liquid, he couldn't be sure the vegetables and meats he was served hadn't been sprinkled with *extra seasoning* , but he had to take his chances. Eating nothing would make him just as weak as the drug did.

As his energy slowly increased, he spent more and more of his waking hours in the library. He carefully set aside any books he thought might interest Robyn to share with her the following day. Two weeks into his confinement, he had exhausted the books lining the first floor shelves, yet he still hadn't found anything to link Knight to the Comradeship of the Three Woes.

Unable to sleep one night, Aldo slipped quietly through the second floor entrance of the library. Knight's collection had the organization of a second-hand clothing store, with no rhyme or reason to the shelving of the books. Not that Aldo could blame him. Keeping such a vast number of books organized would be a full-time job.

Aldo walked along the narrow balcony, scanning the titles, when he noticed one missing its spine. The pages were hand-stitched together and seemed to be missing a front cover as well. He pulled it from its resting place to flip through it. Each page contained entries handwritten by an anonymous author. The dates at the top of each entry caught his attention—spanning from 1919 to 1931. Turning back to the first page, he skimmed through the entries, surprised to find they read more like meeting minutes than a journal. The author seemed to be documenting discussions, but Aldo could sense a kind of fear in the words, as though the conversations weren't supposed to be transcribed.

Feeling like he had stumbled upon the 1920s equivalent of the Watergate Tapes, Aldo tucked the book under his arm, and then turned to leave when he heard voices coming from below. Carefully leaning over the railing, he peered down to see Dr. Knight walking toward his desk with Robyn trailing behind him.

"The church still has him on probation, but I'd advise you not to press charges against him. Arresting your father would only bring unwelcome attention to the church."

Her response was too quiet for Aldo to hear.

"Why didn't you tell me his drinking had gotten so bad? We might have been able to prevent all this."

Jerk. This is not her fault

"I suppose if I had been part of the Toddler Program, I'd drown myself in wine, too," Knight mused. "Now, don't cry, my dear. It's not your fault. Unfortunately, your father's abusive nature is something that's all too common among the upper echelons of the church. And not just ours, either. And there's the fact that he's old enough to be your grandfather." Knight sighed as Robyn began to sob softly. Sitting in one of the leather armchairs, Knight gripped her shoulders. "You have to be strong now, my dear. There's still work for you to do. I'll worry about your father. You just keep your mind on the task at hand."

Robyn rubbed the tears from her eyes, and then nodded.

"Very good. Now, go get some rest. It's late and you have a visitor coming to see you tomorrow."

Instead of heading toward the double doors that opened to the foyer, she crossed the room and started up the spiral staircase, less than three feet from where Aldo stood. Glancing around wildly for a place to hide, Aldo noticed a narrow alcove at the other end of the balcony. He scrambled and ducked into the shadows just as her head cleared the top step.

"Are you all right, my dear? I thought I heard a noise," Knight called from the first floor.

"It's nothing," Robyn replied. "I just stumbled a bit." Her gaze fixed on Aldo's location for a moment before she hurried out the door to her room.

The next morning, tired from reading most of the night, Aldo trudged back to the library. He had promised to find books on starfish for Robyn, a promise he'd all but forgotten after discovering the handwritten book. If the author's accounts of what transpired in those meetings were true, Aldo had found a major clue.

Excitement coursed through him until he remembered he had no one to tell. *But that's what my notebook's for.* He flexed his fingers, which still ached from transcribing the book's contents into shorthand. He would have liked to show Allison and Mr. Summers the original book, but his notes would have to do. He had more work to do, but he still had to play the role of a recovering patient.

Not wanting to disclose that he was familiar with entering the library through the second floor, Aldo took the usual route down the main staircase and across the foyer. As was his habit, he knocked first, and then opened the door, only to stop dead in his tracks.

Professor Applebee sat in the burgundy armchair Dr. Knight usually occupied. "Well, good morning, Mr. Lombardi. I trust your stay has been a pleasant one."

Instinctively, Aldo glanced over his shoulder to check for Hans look-alikes, but the foyer was empty.

"Please, come in and have a seat. I'd like to apologize for the way I behaved last time."

Liar. Every last one of you is a liar. Aldo flung the door shut behind him then walked across the room, dropping into the chair opposite him. "Well?"

"Well...to be honest with you, I knew who you were the moment you stepped foot into my office."

Of course he did. What other reason would they have to keep him confined? Still, Aldo played his part, feigning confusion as he straightened in his chair. "What do you mean?"

"We'd been looking for you," Applebee continued. "So, you can imagine my surprise when you delivered yourself right into our hands."

"I don't understand. What do you mean by you know who I am?" Aldo asked.

Applebee eyed him pityingly as though he were a failing student. "You're the nephew of the Thirteenth Child, the closest blood relative we've been able to get our hands on."

Aldo gave him a perplexed look. "Are you talking about my uncle? Why are you calling him the Thirteenth Child? And what does it even have to do with me? My father and I haven't spoken to him in years."

"Yes, I know," Applebee said. "But that was by your father's choice, was it not?"

Aldo shrugged. "I believe the decision was mutual. I certainly had nothing against the guy. To me he was just a crazy old man who told outlandish stories."

Applebee relaxed in his chair and steepled his fingers. "I believe your uncle might share your sentiment. While it's true he may have no desire to see your father again, a long lost nephew is an entirely different matter."

So, what? I'm bait now? Or was he trying to persuade Aldo to go looking for Mr. Summers? So Applebee could follow the breadcrumbs, no doubt. Still, Applebee answered at least one question plaguing Aldo since his arrival. Conducting experiments on him and interrogating him for information weren't the only reasons they had kidnapped him. They also planned to use him as a tool to lure Mr. Summers out of hiding.

Nice try . Aldo held up his hand. "So, let me get this straight. You kidnapped me and have been holding me prisoner here for nearly a month because you're concerned about my relationship with my uncle. I don't see how that's any of your business."

"Oh, trust me, it is."

"Really? How so?"

Applebee leaned forward, resting his elbows on his knees. "No need to get so testy, my boy. I just came to visit and chat, that's all. And apologize for overdoing it. We don't normally drug people and kidnap them. It got a bit out of hand."

"What do you normally do then?" Aldo bit out. "Drug people but let them go free while you watch for the fallout?" *Oh, shit.* Why did he always let Applebee goad him into giving up information?

Applebee smiled as he rose from his seat. "I'll be back to check on you in a few days. In the meantime, is there anything I can do for you while you're here?" he asked.

"You can give me my cell phone and laptop back."

"Nice try, boy. You know I can't do that," Applebee walked toward the door then turned around. "If you ever need to talk to me, for any reason, just send word through Andrew and I'll come as quickly as possible."

Don't hold your breath.

Aldo watched Applebee leave, and then sat there for a moment, trying to collect his thoughts. As much as he was pissed at himself for playing into Applebee's hand, at least he now knew their objective. But if what he had overheard last night was true, they had a child from the Toddler Program in custody already—Robyn's father. So why continue to go after Mr. Summers? His designation as the Thirteenth Child seemed significant in some way, though Aldo wasn't sure how, other than Mr. Summers had been the thirteenth and last child accepted into the program.

As Aldo stood and walked toward the spiral staircase to resume his search for books on starfish, he noticed Applebee cross the lawn outside. Seeing the professor approach Robyn, he started to rush to her rescue, but she didn't seem disturbed by Applebee's presence.

Was Applebee the visitor Knight had mentioned last night? Aldo watched through the large bay window as Applebee spread her eyelids open with his fingers then tipped her chin up as though examining the faded bruising along her jaw line. Why would Applebee be monitoring her health when there was a doctor living in the same house?

Taking his selection of books on echinoderms outside, he found the young girl in the vegetable garden, tending the small watermelon sprouts they had planted together. To cut down on the growing time, Agnes had purchased starts from a local nursery, but Aldo wondered he would still be here when they were finally ready to eat.

Seeing him, Robyn waved him over excitedly. "Look! Look! They've begun to blossom already," she said.

Aldo tucked the books under his arm, and then crouched down beside her. "Hey, you're right. I didn't expect them to flower so early."

She looked up at him, beaming. "I know. I can't wait." Her smile faded as she continued to stare at him.

"What is it?" he chuckled. "Do I have something on my face?"

She reached up and brushed her palm along his cheek. While the resulting zap of static made him flinch, she seemed unfazed, keeping her hand on his face as she studied him. "You didn't shave this morning," she said.

"Ah, yeah. I was a little preoccupied."

To Aldo's surprise, she didn't move her hand. They had touched a few times before—when he would hand her the tray with her lunch or when they sat next to each other on the bench to pour over the books he had brought. He was always careful, afraid even the slightest touch would make her feel uncomfortable. But this was the first time she had touched him deliberately. Was she getting over her fear of men? Or was she getting too attached to him? The idea of a surrogate little sister sounded nice, but with her current family situation and his job with the Holy See, Also was not confident he could be the big brother she needed.

"It, uh, completely slipped my mind," he continued. "Makes me look weird, huh? Allison thinks so, too."

Her hand dropped away. "Who's Allison? You've mentioned her before."

Had he? His legs tired from crouching, Aldo plopped onto the grass beside the vegetable garden. "She's a good friend of mine."

"Just a friend?" she asked, one eyebrow cocked skeptically.

He chuckled. "Well, I'd like her to be my girlfriend but...I don't think she can see me that way."

"Why not?"

He sighed, not sure how to explain the complexities of adult relationships to a fifteen-year-old. "Well, there's a big difference between *like* and *love*. While you may like someone, that doesn't mean you want to spend the rest of your life with them."

She thought for a moment. "And you would? You'd like to spend the rest of your life with her?"

"Yes," he answered immediately. He had never put it into words before, never thought about what he wanted out of a relationship with Allison past dating, but there was no hesitation. "Yes, I would."

"If you get married, could I come stay with you? I could babysit your kids."

Embarrassed at the thought of Allison and him with a house full of kids, he ruffled Robyn's hair. "Hold on, now. I think you're jumping the gun a bit. I've got to ask her out on a date first."

"What are you waiting for then?"

•••

"What are you smirking at?" Allison whispered.

Mr. Jenkins waved her off and continued recording the transmissions coming from the listening equipment they had set up all around Dr. Knight's estate. While Aldo's confession caused her heart to race, she felt guilty for eavesdropping on his private conversation. The poor guy had been put through the wringer and now he'd practically proposed without even knowing it. She smiled. Of course, as far as his mom was concerned, they were already engaged.

Two weeks had passed since she and Mr. Jenkins had joined his team at their base of operations in Loma Linda, California. While she was still acclimating to the cooler climate, Allison was relieved to be down the street from Aldo rather than in another hemisphere.

When the speakers went quiet, Mr. Jenkins said, "I'm invited to the wedding, right?"

"Oh, knock it off, will you? Saying that kind of stuff to me is one thing, but you know Aldo's going to be mortified when he finds out just how much of an open book his life's been for the last several years."

"And I'll leave you the task of breaking that to him."

She rolled her eyes. "So anyway, when are we going to get him out of there? It's been a month already."

Mr. Jenkins gave her an apologetic look. "We can't. Not yet anyway. We're still not sure who exactly this Dr. Andrew Knight is. The security around his estate is ridiculous for a simple private residence. Took my team longer than it should've to set up their eavesdropping equipment without being detected. Learn anything new from Mr. Summers?"

She shrugged. "Only that Knight's part of a secret group within the church—likely the group's regional leader—but Mr. Summers hasn't been able to confirm which one."

"Not a Master Comrade of the Seven Times?"

"No, of that he was pretty sure." Allison tugged at the camisole beneath her t-shirt. She was covered in sweat from being cooped up in a small apartment with five NSA agents, and the silky fabric clung to her like a second skin. "It might be one we haven't even heard of yet."

Jenkins nodded. "The team tailing the professor hasn't turned up anything either. But at least now we know what their objective is."

"Yeah." Allison was relieved to hear Applebee trying to taunt Aldo into being bait for Mr. Summers. When Aldo was kidnapped, she had worried Dr. Knight was going to perform a lobotomy on Aldo before sending him back. Still, knowing the kidnappers wanted to use Aldo as bait and letting them actually do it were two separate matters. Aldo was still stuck in a house with only one person who had no ill intentions towards him— a fifteen-year-old girl.

"Did you tell Mr. Summers about Robyn's father?" Jenkins asked. "If it's the guy I think it is, he's a pretty powerful church official."

"Yeah, he seemed to think so, too. He said Elder Albrecht came over from Germany as a child after World War II and grew up in Argentina where he was part of the Toddler Program."

"Good. See what else you can dig up on him."

She smiled and jumped to her feet. "On it." Sitting in a spacious library beat being stuck in a cramped apartment any day.

•••

Aldo found Robyn on the bench in the perennial garden, her shoulders slumped and her hair shielding her face just as it had the first time they met. "Hey there. Are you okay?" he asked quietly, still worried he'd spook her.

When she glanced up, he saw streaks of tears staining her face.

Sitting down next to her, he reached over and wrapped his arm across her shoulders, giving them a gentle squeeze. "Same nightmare again?"

She nodded, wiping her face with her sleeve.

"Feel like telling me about it?"

"It's just," she sniffed, "I see my dad. Like normal, you know. But then he suddenly comes after me, chasing me with glowing red eyes... I don't know what he'll do if he ever catches me—" Her voice broke on a sob.

"Oh, it's okay. It was just a dream, remember? Your father can't get to you. I won't let him. And Agnes won't either. Have you seen her arsenal of rolling pins?" His attempt at humor earned him a half smile.

"I know, but...I just wish I could go somewhere where he'd never find me."

"If you did that then you'd be all alone." Aldo wanted to say he thought that would be scarier, but he had no idea what kind of real-life nightmare she had been living, the fear and betrayal she must have felt at the hands of her own father. Was it like the fear he'd felt being strapped to the Monarch chair? At the mercy of someone bigger and stronger than you while they did whatever they felt like with your body? He shuddered.

"Not if it was a big city. I wouldn't be alone if I was surrounded by millions of people," she said hopefully.

"True, but you can still feel alone, even if you're in a crowd." He ruffled her hair, a gesture that was becoming a habit. "It's better to be around people who know you and care about you."

"And you'll be around?"

Aldo thought for a moment. He didn't want to make promises he wasn't sure he could keep, but didn't want to let her down either. He nodded slowly. "For as long as I can."

Chapter Nine | The Advent RITE

Silver Spring, Maryland
December 1919

Isaac Andrews sat at the back of the large meeting room, his mouth gaping in disbelief. *Did Brother Prescott really just say that?* The leaders were going to start phasing out one of the Seventh-day Adventist Church's founding principles, replacing it with doctrine in direct opposition? He glanced around at the other Bible conference attendees, all members of the Shmita Advent Rite of Freemasonry—all of them seemingly undaunted by the news.

This decision isn't as sudden as they would have me believe.

He was initiated into the Rite just a few months prior, but already Isaac had come to understand it wasn't the concordant noble brotherhood he was led to believe. This secret society of prominent leaders within the Seventh-day Adventist Church followed its own set of beliefs and practices—rituals with deep-seated origins he still knew almost nothing about.

And now this talk of introducing doctrine on a Holy Trinity? He wanted to shake his head, to doubt Brother Prescott's words, but he remained frozen on the slat-back chair. What else have they not been telling him?

The Seventh-day Adventist Church had been founded on anti-trinitarian principles. To disregard those principles would make the church just like all of the other Christian churches that had sprung up across the country over the last half-century. Why would they intentionally eliminate the very doctrine that set the Seventh-day Adventists apart as the one true church?

Sister White, the church's prophetess, had been very clear on that particular principle. After his initiation, Isaac was granted access to additional writings of hers—writings the members of the Rite had kept in secret. Sister White's teachings didn't conform to the Arian beliefs of the church's other founders, whose views on the nature of God aligned with traditional Protestant orthodoxy. White likened God to a candle—the first candle that lit all other candles. His light—His breath—she believed, came to them through His only Begotten Son, Jesus Christ. There was no Trinity. There was no third entity—no disembodied soul—in the councils of Heaven. There was only God, the Father, and to worship some made-up ghost was a direct violation of the first Commandment.

Did the church leaders not consider themselves Christians who believed in the world's first and purest religion? Being Advent Muslims like him, did they not follow the same religion that Adam and Eve brought out of the Garden of Eden? Did they really want to start preaching against the truth of One God? To disregard Scripture and knowingly tell falsehoods to their followers, turning the Seventh-day Adventist Church into some off-shoot of Roman Catholicism? What of their creed: *The Bible, and the Bible alone* ?

The urge to challenge the noble brotherhood's declaration burned in the pit of Isaac's stomach, yet he hesitated. While he couldn't in good conscience let the leaders distort the doctrines God had given them through Sister White's visions, he feared this was much bigger than they were letting on, as if something was at work beneath the surface. Something a simple 22 year-old clerk wouldn't be able to stop on his own.

Isaac's mind raced at the possible repercussions this decision could have on the future of the church, a church he had been raised in and believed with every fiber of his being. If they began teaching of a Holy Trinity, wouldn't that mean they would need to eliminate teachings on Investigative Judgment and the 2300 Day Prophecy as well? He stifled a gasp. Those teachings were cornerstones of the Adventist faith. What reason could the leaders possibly have for changing the church's beliefs so drastically?

Isaac's palms grew sweaty as he continued listening to Brother Prescott's address. Wiping his hands on his trousers, Isaac picked up his pencil and resumed transcribing the meeting's discussion, but the words appearing before his eyes only increased his alarm.

"…we are doing both in our teachings," Brother Prescott continued, "but we need to choose our battles carefully if we are to survive as an organization." The thump of his heavy boots echoed about the room as he paced across the hardwood floor. When the sound abruptly stopped, Isaac glanced up to see Brother Prescott pointing to an elderly gentleman seated in the front row. "Yes, Noble Brother Wilson? You have a question?"

Isaac watched the old man stand, and then slowly bend down to set his black bowler hat on his chair before straightening again. "It is not only our monotheistic belief that conflicts with the principle of a Holy Trinity," Brother

Wilson said, his voice hoarse with age. "Some of our other founding doctrines do as well. What is to become of them?"

A knowing smile spread across Brother Prescott's face. "All of those teachings will be phased out eventually. Investigative Judgment, the 2300 Day Prophecy, the Third Woe. All of them—"

Suddenly, Brother McDaniels stood, effectively cutting off Brother Prescott's explanation. "Before you continue, I must ask that all transcription of this discussion be ceased." The General Conference president then turned toward Isaac. "Noble Brother Andrews?"

Isaac stiffened. Were they going to kick him out again, isolating him from the discussion? He had been given the responsibility of being the Rite's official scrivener soon after his initiation, a task he would have relished if it weren't for their habit of always sequestering him. In his opinion, the scrivener should be present for the duration of every meeting, yet it seemed whenever something important was about to be discussed, the president would have him wait in the foyer. Since he had taken on the role, Isaac's lodge book was filled with holes left by missing information. The bits of discussion he was allowed to transcribe contradicted others until none of his notes seemed to make sense.

The bitter frustration of their constantly hindering his task, a task which they themselves had assigned him, seethed through him, and he made no move to leave. Had he not been *stepped up to*—found worthy—just like the rest of them? Had they not conferred the 32 degrees upon him during his initiation, bestowing him with the honor of being called a noble brother? Did they not trust him to keep his oath of silence? If so, then why did they appoint him to the task when Brother Sadler could have continued as scrivener?

But then, Brother Sadler was an enigma himself. Since his initiation, Isaac had yet to meet the man as he was always mysteriously absent from lodge meetings. More and more, Isaac was confident the Shmita Advent Rite of Freemasonry was desperate to keep secret whatever was said in the off-the-record discussions—and not just from the public, but most especially from the church's followers.

With all eyes on him, Isaac tucked his pencil into his lodge book and closed it. When Brother Alcott didn't move from his position guarding the door to take the book and escort him out, Isaac set the book on the chair beside him. If they were actually going to allow him to stay this time, he wasn't about to argue.

Surprisingly, Brother McDaniels gave him a nod before turning back to Brother Prescott, who also nodded. Then the General Conference president took his seat again, turning the floor back over to Brother Prescott.

Gesturing to encompass the assembled group of men, Brother Prescott said, "As you all know, we cannot have our followers questioning what they are being taught. Therefore, these other teachings must also be phased out. However, we will not fade them out immediately. It will take some time. We may not even see the completion of this goal within our lifetimes, but we must move forward for the sake of the church's image."

What does he mean, "the church's image"? Shouldn't they be more concerned with truth?

The thumping resumed as Brother Prescott began pacing the room again. "We will curtail teachings of the Third Woe first," he continued. "Our aim is to have that particular doctrine completely silenced within the next 50 years."

"Which brings me to my next question," Brother Wilson interjected. "What does this have to do with Islam?"

Isaac had been wondering the same thing. The Seventh-day Adventist Church had not been shy in its prejudice against Catholicism since the beginning, but a fear of the Tribes of Ishmael had begun to creep into the Rite's discussions of late. Considering Islam had been quiet for nearly three centuries, Isaac thought the fear unfounded.

"Well, as I'm sure you are all aware, Sister White," he bowed toward the East in respect for the Rite's Sovereign Grand Advent Inspector General, "made numerous prophecies throughout her lifetime. Among those prophecies, she warned of the rise of Islam." He walked over and tapped the original copy of Sister White's 1850 Prophecy Chart mounted in an elaborate gold-leafed frame on the wall. "Here, in the Prophecy of the Three Woes. She also describes a vision in her writings where she saw angels restraining the four winds, which appeared as an angry horse. And that when this horse was loosed upon the Earth, it would bring devastation and destruction in its wake. This *horse* would bring about a holy war with Rome."

Isaac remembered reading that passage in the Rite's secret collection of Sister White's writings. It had stuck with him, as the next few lines seemed like a call for followers to stand up for their beliefs: "*Shall we sleep on the very verge of the eternal world? Shall we be dull and cold and dead? Oh, that we might have in our churches the Spirit and breath of God breathed into His people, that they might stand upon their feet and live. "*

"What makes you so sure her vision or the Prophecy of the Three Woes refers to Islam?" Brother Wilson asked. "Could her vision not have been about the Great War? Surely the four winds she spoke of referred to the Central Powers of Germany, Bulgaria, Austria, and Turkey."

Brother Prescott nodded, a smirk spreading across his face, as though he enjoyed the rhetorical challenge. "We know without doubt that her vision *and* the Prophecy of the Three Woes," he tapped the chart again, "refer to Islam because her husband told us so." He walked over to the pulpit, shuffled through a stack of papers and held up a folded letter, the red wax seal already broken. "If you will remember, he stated as such in this letter. Noble Brother White wanted to ensure that we, his noble brethren, knew just how strongly Sister White believed in Islam's role in the Prophecy of the Three Woes. He wanted to ensure we were prepared."

Brother Prescott stepped from behind the pulpit to pace the floor again. "While the Great War did certainly bring devastation to the Continent, we must remember, Noble Brothers, that the fight was political. Not religious. Not only that, but war had already been raging on the Continent for over a year when Sister White succumbed to her soul sleep. If, as you asked," he gestured to Brother Wilson, "the Great War was what she had seen in her vision, she would have certainly said as much." He shook his head. "No, this war, this *angry horse* has yet to be loosed. And when it is, it will engulf the whole earth. Even now, angels in Heaven are holding it back, giving us time to prepare for its stampede." He held up the letter again. "Just as Noble Brother White instructed, we must be ready. In a holy war between Christianity and Islam, as we are now, we will be viewed as an enemy by both sides. Our monotheistic teachings have already been condemned by many in this country as heterodox." Abruptly stopping in his path across the room, Brother Prescott slammed his hand against the pulpit, causing Isaac to jump. "No. If we as a church are to survive this Third Woe, if we are to see the Second Coming of Christ, we must align ourselves with one side or the other."

Is he suggesting we have to choose between becoming Catholic or following Islam? The thought terrified Isaac. He glanced around, feeling Brother Alcott's piercing stare boring into him. He stiffened. Having the Rite's warden watching him so closely only added to Isaac's trepidation. Carefully wiping any trace of shock or fear from his expression, Isaac turned his attention back to Brother Prescott.

"So, what then?" a man in the front row demanded. "Are we supposed to just abandon our faith?"

A chair scraped across the wooden floor as Brother Mills stood. Brother Mills, a doctor and owner of a nearby sanitarium, was one of the more prominent members of the Rite. His sanitarium had become famous in recent years, touted as a haven that could cure all manner of ailments. He was also responsible for many of the health programs that had been established within the church. Isaac found him to be shady and exploiting, a man more interested in his pocketbook than his patients.

"Noble Brothers," Brother Mills said as he stepped toward the pulpit. "We are not suggesting that we abandon our faith. Far from it, in fact. The intention is to do what we can now so that we may preserve our church into the future. By phasing out Sister White's teachings of One God and adopting the doctrine of a Holy Trinity, it will allow us freedoms we would otherwise be denied. In this predominantly Protestant country, we are viewed as brothers for our anti-Catholic viewpoint. Yet, at the same time we are branded as a cult for what they call our heterodox doctrines. By altering our monotheistic teaching, we will gain the support of our Protestant brethren, and we can align ourselves more closely with Rome."

"Why would we want to be closer to Rome?" the same man from the front row asked. "We're not Catholics. We are Seventh-day Adventists."

Murmurs erupted around the room. Many of the attendees, including Isaac, seemed to share the man's sentiment, while others demanded that the doctor be heard.

Brother Mills stood next to the pulpit, patiently waiting for the room to quiet. When it finally did, he calmly said, "For appearances. In the eyes of the Catholic Church, we will *appear* to be closing the gap between our faiths, yet all our followers will see is a re-affirming of our anti-Catholic principles. We will gain the Vatican's sympathy should the need for their support arise in the future *without* losing any of our followers."

Playing both sides. Isaac was disgusted with the thought. It was just what he'd expect from the cunning businessman.

Stepping away from the pulpit, Brother Mills slowly walked the length of the room, his eyes meeting each member's in turn. "However, the biggest reason to support adopting the teaching of the Holy Trinity is that the Mother of Testimonies predicted it. Sister White called this prophecy the Alpha of Apostasy. Only through it will we be prepared to embrace the Omega of Apostasy, which she prophesied would quickly follow. By doing everything we can to ensure that her prophecies come true, the world will come to view the Seventh-day Adventist Church as the only true church."

By teaching false doctrines? Isaac could scarcely believe what he was hearing.

"But doesn't Sister White's prophecy warn of what altering this teaching will mean for the church?" Brother Wilson asked. "Didn't she fear that adopting the teaching of the Trinity would bring us to the attention of Islam? If this holy war is coming as you say, won't Islam see us as an enemy as well?"

"Which is why we must start doing what we can *now* to prepare the church for what is to come," Brother Prescott interjected. "Sister White did not leave us with an outcome for the Prophecy of the Third Woe. We do not know who the victor of this coming holy war will be— only that it will happen." Brother Prescott tapped his finger against the top of the pulpit, as though thinking for a moment. Then he said, "A Chinese military general once said, '*Know your enemy and know yourself, and you will be victorious.*' By adopting the principle of the Holy Trinity, we will close the gap with Rome and, as Noble Brother Mills said, count them as allies should the need arise. In addition, we will slowly phase out all teachings of The Third Woe and Islam's role in it, removing ourselves from Islam's view and safeguarding us from their anger."

Brother McDaniels stood, and then and walked over to join Brother Mills and Brother Prescott at the pulpit, creating the appearance of a united front. "We must study the Quran more vigorously than ever, Noble Brothers," the general conference president said. "We must learn all we can about this coming storm."

The room fell silent for a long moment until finally Brother Wilson said, "Shall we put this decision to a vote?"

"That won't be necessary," Brother Mills said. He glanced at Brother McDaniels, who nodded his consent for Brother Mills to continue. "I have already met with envoys from the Vatican. In exchange for agreeing to weave in teachings of the Holy Trinity over the next two generations, I asked that the Catholic Church ignore our other teachings, in particular those pertaining to Bible prophecy. However, in time, we will eliminate our teachings on the Mark of the Beast from the Book of Revelation as well."

This is ludicrous. Isaac could not believe his ears. The church he had been raised in was slowly going to become a mere shell of what Sister White had intended. And the frightening part was that she had known this would happen. She had written about her true doctrines being ignored, of how blinded men would lead the church astray. And how future generations of followers would never question what they were being taught, nor realize how thoroughly and completely they had been deceived by the very leadership they trusted.

And here he was, watching her predictions come true before his very eyes. But what could he do? The men in this room were at the helm of the church. To speak out against them would mean more than excommunication. His thoughts turned again to his predecessor, Brother Sadler, and he shivered.

"This has already been put into motion?" Clearly outraged, Brother Wilson stumbled to his feet and his cane clattered to the floor.

Brother Mills nodded calmly. "Some of the local conferences have been teaching about the Holy Trinity since the early 1890s. The purpose of this meeting was really only to initiate the adoption of the Holy Trinity across all conferences."

Isaac clenched his fist in his lap, the only outward display of frustration that he dared. He had felt Brother Alcott's gaze on him throughout the meeting and he wasn't about to give the man cause to throw him out. Yet, he couldn't help feeling shocked and helpless. Just as Sister White predicted, heresies—what she had referred to as the Omega of Deadly Heresies—had cleverly made their way into the church's teachings, even before she had succumbed to her soul sleep. If something wasn't done to stop the church's leaders, Isaac had no doubt even more changes would be made. Some teachings could become altered to the point of being almost unrecognizable. And millions of God's people would unwittingly be led astray.

While the church leaders viewed Sister White's prophecies as needing to be fulfilled at all costs, even at the expense of their followers' salvation, Isaac knew they were warnings. Warnings of what would become of the church if the leaders had their way—if God's people ignored His Spirit and Breath.

Hopelessness consumed him. What could one man, barely into adulthood, possibly do to oppose the entire leadership of the church? Who would even believe him?

Murmuring around him brought his attention back to the front of the room where Brother Prescott stood behind the pulpit, flanked by Brother Mills and

Brother McDaniels. "As I said before," Brother Prescott said, "we are going to have to make some sacrifices if our church is to survive the coming war. While the doctrines of the world church will be changed and altered to meet that end, we," he gestured around the room, "will continue to uphold the rituals and traditions of this noble brotherhood. The Lord bless us and keep us."

On cue, every man in the room stood and turned to face east.

"The Lord make His face to shine upon us and be gracious unto us!" Brother Prescott continued, calling the meeting to a close. "The Lord lift upon us the light of His countenance and give us peace! Amen!"

In unison, the assembled group of men all said, "So mote it be! So mote it be!" Then they bent at the waist, bowing and rising, bowing and rising, until they had completed the ritual seven times. Isaac went through the motions with them, grateful when he straightened after the last bow and could finally escape.

Chairs scraped across the wooden floor as the men gathered their coats and hats, preparing to leave. Isaac scooped up his lodge book, shoved his gloves into his coat pockets and discreetly headed toward the door, terrified one of the men would intercept him and start a conversation. *They'll know.* He feared one look at his face would betray the depth of his alarm.

Desperately searching through the pile of overshoes left in the foyer, Isaac finally located his own tattered pair and was pulling them on when a dark shadow fell over him. He looked up slowly to see Brother Alcott silently holding out his hand. Isaac forced a smile, and then surrendered his lodge book into the taller man's custody. The Rite still didn't trust him enough to allow him to take the book, but after tonight, he no longer wanted the responsibility. Having the book in his possession would only increase the Rite's watchfulness over his every action.

After quickly flipping through the pages of the lodge book, Brother Alcott nodded his approval, and then stepped to the side. Isaac bowed his head, bidding him goodnight before heading toward the door. Once outside, he took a few deep, cleansing breaths, trying to calm his anxiety. How was he ever going to sit through another one of those meetings?

The night was moonless and cold, with the smell of snow on the air. Taking the main road out of town, Isaac walked slowly, terrified the brotherhood had sent someone to follow him. Was this how Brother Sadler had felt? After what Isaac had heard in the meeting, the previous scrivener's disappearance seemed even more suspicious.

Had Brother Sadler found the courage to expose the truth about the Shmita Advent Rite of Freemasonry? Was he then silenced? Isaac prayed he wasn't next.

The winter chill clawed at his fear, prodding him to quicken his pace. As soon as the warm glow of the streetlamps was swallowed by the encroaching darkness at the edge of town, he made a mad dash for home. His mind raced along with his legs, desperately searching for something solid, something stable to grasp. He knew there was little chance his fellow brothers and sisters of the church would listen to him, not when it was his word against the leadership. But he resolved to find a way. God's people had the right to know the truth.

Isaac knew he would likely not live long enough to see his work completed, but he prayed God would not abandon His people. And he prayed that God would one day send someone to awaken the Laodicean members of the church asleep in their ignorance. Someone who, like the voice of Wisdom in the book of Proverbs, would cry out among God's people and bring Sister White's true doctrines back into the light.

Safely inside his small one room cottage, Isaac bolted the door, and then pulled the drapes closed. Lighting a single oil lamp, he carried it to his desk in the corner and gathered sheets of paper, his pen, and ink well. Then he sat down and meticulously recorded every detail he could remember from the meeting.

By the time he finished, the oil in the lamp was nearly empty and dawn's light was beginning to peek through the drapes. His hand hurt from holding his pen and tears stung his eyes. If only he could do more to protect his beloved remnant church. But this was the only way. For now.

He looked down at the pages full of secrets on his desk, knowing his life would be over if the Rite ever found them. He carefully gathered the documents, and then glanced around his small home. A prickling of fear resurfaced as his eyes swept over the wood stove. If he just burned them... He took a step forward, and then stopped, clutching the pages to his chest.

No. This is bigger than just me. This was worth any sacrifice he had to make.

He gripped the back of his chair and pulled it to the wardrobe. Climbing up, he tucked the pages safely on top, making sure none was visible. He would have to find a better hiding place soon.

Chapter Ten | The JUDGE

Loma Linda, California
April 2013

"What do you mean, we're leaving?" Allison asked. The tiny apartment had been buzzing with activity from the moment she walked in. Routers, servers, monitors, and other computer equipment littered the cramped kitchen counters. Cables trailed along the linoleum floor to laser-based listening devices propped in one of the two small windows of the living room, while thermal cameras occupied the other. Every flat surface seemed to be cluttered with a piece of surveillance or cryptographic equipment.

"Don't worry. Jackson and Lawrence will stay and keep an eye on things here. Aldo will be fine." Mr. Jenkins continued stuffing documents and files into his already-overloaded briefcase. When she didn't move, he glanced up at her. "Well, don't just stand there. We have to catch the next flight to D.C."

Folding her arms over her chest, Allison leaned against the wall near the front door, the only place out of the path of rushing NSA agents. "First, tell me what's so urgent that we have to fly all the way across the country."

"We just got word from CTU that bio-weapons are on the move." Without looking up, Jenkins tossed a stack of satellite images at her, and then slammed his briefcase shut. "Those are pictures of two bio-labs along the border of Argentina and Uruguay. The first lab is a bio-safety level three and the second is level four, working with exotic and highly dangerous strains of microbes." He pinched the bridge of his nose in apparent frustration, and then pointed to what looked like ants in a line at a picnic, marching away from a grayish rectangle she assumed was one of the labs. "Our eyes on the ground confirmed that each one of those trucks is carrying a Class III biological safety cabinet loaded with CBWs."

Allison's skin turned cold. Something big was about to happen if they were transporting that many chemical and biological weapons. She straightened, pushing away from the wall to study the images more carefully. The time stamp in the corner of each image revealed they had been taken earlier that morning. "Do you know where they're heading?"

"New York, though it hasn't been confirmed yet."

She swallowed against the lump in her throat, but managed to ask, "To be released or sold?" Neither option was good, but if the bio-weapons were changing hands as opposed to being prepared for dispersion, they might have more time. Maybe only days, but every extra second increased their opportunity to intercept the weapons and prevent a potential terrorist attack. Or possibly all-out war.

"Sold," Mr. Jenkins answered as he dumped small handheld devices haphazardly into a black duffle bag.

Allison released the breath she'd been holding. "And the buyer?"

"That also needs to be confirmed. And that's where you come in." He zipped the bag, hauled it off the sofa, and shoved it into her arms. "As the liaison between the NSA and Mr. Summers, I need you to find out what he might know about this. But we need to get our asses to D.C. stat before we can confirm anything."

The next eight hours whizzed by as Allison hurried after Mr. Jenkins, bypassing security as they rushed through the San Bernardino airport to their terminal. Their government identification secured priority seating on the next flight to Washington, D.C. and allowed them to keep their luggage with them. Not being held up at baggage claim upon arrival would save them precious minutes.

During the flight, Mr. Jenkins briefed her on what he knew of the situation. The NSA, with cooperation from several other government bureaus, had been watching both bio-labs since the 1950s. Because the labs were in South America, monitoring them was really the only thing they could do. They couldn't shut down the facilities without probable cause, and until that morning, no CBWs had been reported leaving either location.

"Were these labs also set up by Mengele?" Allison asked.

Mr. Jenkins shook his head. "Mengele's focus was on human experimentation, in its numerous forms. The brains behind these labs is an Argentine cartel. They've been damn good at covering their tracks, too. We're still trying to get evidence to prove a connection with the Argentine government, but so far we've come up empty."

"What makes you think there even is a connection?"

"Well, that's the dilemma," he sighed. "Their operation's too covert to be run by a band of mere riff-raff. So, that suggests the involvement of some larger, more powerful organization, but without evidence we just don't know who we're dealing with." He leaned in close, his voice low so none of the other first-class passengers could hear. "This shipment alone has the capability of killing one-third of the earth's population."

Allison choked on her ice water, coughing until she could breathe normally again. Nearly three billion people? That was equivalent to the populations of China and India combined. "But who…who would want to murder that many people?" she asked, trying to keep her voice from rising. *Other than the Nazis* . If those bio-weapons made it to New York, the Nazis brutality during World War II would look like child's play. "And why?"

Mr. Jenkins shrugged. "We'll learn more once we land. Holt's meeting us at the White House, and it sounds like he's been on the phone with the CIA all morning."

Allison had only met Mr. Jenkins's boss, Paul Holt, once, the introduction consisting of a quick greeting and handshake. She got the impression the director of the Counter Terrorism Unit (CTU) preferred his agents to be older and male. That, or he had an issue with her personally. "What do they need from us?"

"Not sure, other than we'll need you to contact Mr. Summers. My suspicion is that this has something to do with the mess your boyfriend's in."

Allison rolled her eyes, already used to his teasing. "What makes you say that?"

Jenkins tilted his head and smiled. "Not denying it anymore, huh?"

"I just got tired of you not listening."

"What? I like Aldo. You should give the guy a chance."

"I do, too," she said, exasperated. "But it's not like I've had the time to do anything about it." Several heads turned in her direction and her face heated with embarrassment. Lowering her voice, she whispered, "And you trying to play matchmaker isn't helping, all right?"

He held up his hands in surrender. "Fine. Just don't drag things out for too long."

She sighed. Six years was already too long, much longer than most guys would wait anyway. She had expected Aldo to get over his crush long ago since her job forbade her from reciprocating. But with each passing year his feelings seemed to grow stronger, dragging hers along with him. His disclosure to Robyn had only served to confuse Allison more. So many things stood in their way—their jobs, their religions, and now this new terrorist threat—that she feared there was no room in God's plan for them to be together.

She watched Jenkins take a sip of his coffee, waiting for him to explain what bio-weapons from South America had to do with Aldo's being held captive in California. When he didn't, she prompted him. "So?"

"Oh, right. Well—now, this is just speculation, mind you—but what if our buyer is a certain religious organization? Or a group within one." Before she could recover from her shock, he held up an index finger. "As I said, speculation. Remember that note Aldo found at the Fifth Reich camp?" When she nodded slowly, he continued. "Well, my analysts confirmed it's a pier in Brooklyn, New York. It wasn't until the satellite images showed movement around the bio-labs that we thought there might be a connection."

"But-but—"

He held up a hand. "We won't know more until we're briefed at the White House. But even if I did know more, this isn't exactly the right venue to discuss classified information." He nodded his head slightly at the other passengers in the first-class cabin.

Reluctantly, she nodded. She was desperate to ask why some of the most powerful leaders within the Seventh-day Adventist Church might be secretly planning to bring about Armageddon. *They wouldn't, would they?* She didn't want to think so, but after Aldo's experience in Loma Linda, she wasn't so sure anymore.

•••

Paul Holt sat in the waiting area outside the White House Situation Room, impatiently tapping his foot. Jenkins had texted to let him know they'd landed at ReaganNational Airport over an hour earlier. So, what was taking them so damn long? If there was anyone you didn't want to keep waiting, it was the President.

No doubt it's that woman's fault. The agitated Holt questioned why Allison was even involved in this matter. Women always seemed to complicate situations and he already had enough to deal with.

At the end of the hall, a door opened, and then footsteps echoed across the floor. Holt suppressed a groan at the unmistakable click of high heels on marble, the ornate rug doing little to soften the noise. He never had understood the purpose behind women cramming their feet into those impractical shoes. *You can't chase down suspects in them.* Hell, they could barely walk in them most of the time.

A White House staff member turned the corner and ushered Jenkins and the woman into the waiting area. Holt stood to greet them. "About time you got here." He gripped Jenkins's hand, giving him a firm handshake.

"You do realize it's rush hour, right?" Jenkins asked. "But it's good to see you, too."

Holt turned and extended his hand. "Ms. Gillespie."

"Please, call me Allison." She gave him a warm smile, which only proved to agitate him more.

His one attempt at marriage had ended after only a few years with his realization that he preferred capturing terrorists to dealing with the fairer sex. Now happily single and approaching retirement, he looked forward to spending his days fishing for striped bass along the banks of the Potomac.

"What's the current situation?" Jenkins asked.

Holt sighed. "I have to brief the President before I can fill you in, but first, I need you to contact Samuel Summers so I can confirm your suspicions. But seeing as how Ms. Gillespie is the only one who knows how to get in touch with him, I had to wait till you got here."

"Sorry about that, but with everything he's been through, it was hard enough just getting her superiors to agree to let her work with us." Jenkins gave him a tight smile. "Is there somewhere we can make a secure call?"

Holt nodded, and then hailed the staff member still hovering at the edge of the waiting area. "Jerry, can you get us a secure phone line? And let the President know I'll be ready to brief him in five."

"Yes, sir. Follow me." Jerry led them down the hallway to a small room. Fragile-looking vases overflowing with bouquets of fresh flowers sat precariously atop petite side tables throughout the room. Holt tucked his hands into the pockets of his slacks before he could bump into anything and embarrass himself.

After gesturing to a corded phone on a table beneath the only window, Jerry excused himself.

"How do we know with certainty it's secure?" Allison asked.

Holt flipped the unit over to show her the specifications. "It's a secure communications interoperability protocol standard device, SCIP for short, equipped with FIREFLY." When she gave him a puzzled look, he glanced at Jenkins for help.

Jenkins chuckled. "Don't worry. The NSA developed these encryption systems. It'll be fine." Picking up the receiver, he said, "We just have to enter a key code so the system can set up an encrypted connection with the other end." He dialed, and after a few moments, handed the phone to Allison.

She entered a series of numbers and greeted the person on the other end of the line. "Will it be all right if I put you on speaker? Okay, just a moment." She pressed the speaker button then set the receiver on the table.

"I've been expecting your call," a deep voice said through the phone's small speaker.

"I have Mr. Jenkins and his boss, Mr. Holt, with me." The young woman stepped aside and gestured Holt forward.

"Yes, I know," Summers said. "This is regarding co-weaponized organisms heading out of South America, right?"

"How do you know that?" Holt asked. When the voice on the line remained silent, he looked at Jenkins and Allison.

The young woman shrugged. "He, uh, has his ways."

"I can't really explain, not without taking up too much of your time," Mr. Summers said. "Which is something we don't have much of right now. To put it simply, I had a dream."

Dumbfounded, Holt glanced at Jenkins, the only other person in the room he knew to be sane. Jenkins waved him off, gesturing for him to continue.

Before he could, Allison asked, "What do you mean by co-weaponized?"

Holt sighed. "I was going to get into that when I briefed you later, but it basically means someone out there has a God complex." When Allison stared at him blankly, Holt cleared his throat and tried again. "They joined two strains to create their bio-weapons, in essence creating a super strain."

"Is there no way we can create some kind of antibiotic or vaccine to counteract it?" Allison asked.

"Even if we could, it would only be for the two strains we know were used. There's no way to predict how the new hybrid has evolved or mutated. It'd be like trying to create a vaccine for every possible strain of influenza in the next twenty-four hours. Our best bet is to stop the bio-weapons before they reach the buyer." Holt turned to face the phone again. "Mr. Summers, Jenkins has reason to believe the bio-weapons are headed for New York, purchased by individuals within the Seventh-day Adventist Church."

"To be specific, members of the Comradeship of the Three Woes," Summers interjected.

"What's that?" Holt asked. "Some special club or something?"

"It's a secret organization within the SDA Church, comprised of prominent members," Summers explained. "They have their own rituals and secrets, and unfortunately, they operate off their own set of rules as well."

"Were you able to confirm if that's the same group Dr. Knight is involved with?" Allison asked.

"Unfortunately, Dr. Knight has proved rather elusive. However, his connection to Professor Applebee could be all the evidence we need. It's pretty clear the professor has ties to the Fifth Reich, confirming his involvement with the Comradeship of the Three Woes." Summers sighed. "As such, I'm concerned about the safety of our historian friend."

Noticing Allison clench her fist, Holt suspected there was more to that, but now wasn't the time. "If this Comradeship as you call it is connected to the Fifth Reich, then the note found at their camp in Argentina would suggest the hand-off is indeed in Brooklyn. However, there hasn't been any definitive evidence to prove this group is the buyer."

After a pause, Summers said, "Until this morning."

Holt stared at the phone. How could he know that?

"What happened this morning?" Jenkins asked.

Holt rubbed his temple to ease the headache growing behind his eyes. "About the same time our satellites were taking pictures of the bio-weapons leaving the labs in Argentina, one-point-four billion in Euros was transferred from several off-shore accounts registered to the Roger Frogburger Enterprise." He glanced at Jenkins. "I had my team watching the church's movements after you told me about your suspicions." He turned his attention back to the phone. "Mr. Summers, what can you tell me about Roger Frogburger?"

"Well, he was the man behind my current predicament. Unfortunately, there's not much more I can tell you, except that the enterprise is now run by a board, all members of the church hand-picked by Frogburger's father-in-law. Frogburger was mostly just a puppet, both as president of the world church and as chairman of the enterprise."

"Any idea how an enterprise, established by a simple computer salesman and church leader, came into such a large sum of money?" Holt asked.

"He's been skimming money off the top of church accounts for years, beginning during his presidency," Allison answered. "We know that several billion came from six church-owned hospital retirement trust funds in South America, which he funneled through other church agencies and off-shore corporations to eliminate any paper trail. All this came out after Mr. Summers's trial."

Jenkins nodded. "The federal judge who presided over Mr. Summers's trial conducted an extensive investigation, beginning in the pretrial discovery phase back in the early 1990s. Probably be a good idea to get him in on this. His name is Lewis Jason."

"Right," Holt said, glancing at his watch. "Track him down and have him patched through to the Situation Room. I'm already late for my meeting with the President."

•••

Needing a break from transcribing the anonymous journal he'd found in Dr. Knight's library, Aldo joined Robyn in the garden where she was tending to the blossoming watermelon plants. He set down the stack of books he'd brought then plopped onto the grass beside her. She didn't even look up.

She had grown more distant with each passing day. At first, Aldo worried her nightmares were getting worse, but her withdrawal only seemed to involve him. To everyone else, she was her usual self—cheerful, yet shy—even to Applebee, whom Aldo avoided whenever he came around to conduct the girl's weekly check-ups.

However, Aldo had to admit he hadn't been as attentive to Robyn as the others were. While he no longer needed to sleep off the effects of the drug, he kept up the appearance of frequent naps, using the time instead to transcribe information into his notebook. He had a feeling Agnes might be catching on though, considering his inexplicable need to use the bathroom every time she served baked goods.

Feeling like he was losing his only ally at Knight's estate, Aldo reached out to ruffle Robyn's hair, only to have her flinch and scoot away. His hand hovered awkwardly in the air for a moment before he tucked it at his side. "I, uh, brought you a new stack of books on embryophytes." When she silently continued to pull non-existent weeds from around one small watermelon sprout, he tried again. "I found the one on mosses to be particularly interesting."

Still nothing.

He sighed. He couldn't really blame her. What teenage girl would want to spend the afternoon discussing non-vascular plants with a man almost twice her age? He honestly didn't really care what they discussed. He just didn't like that she was treating him as an enemy when he had no idea what he could have done wrong.

Perhaps this is for the best. Concerned about leaving Robyn alone in the house, surrounded by deceitful men, he had put off any thought of escaping. With his body finally feeling normal again, Aldo shifted his focus to gathering as much information as he could from Dr. Knight's library. He still had no idea how to free himself, let alone with a teenage girl in tow, but leaving without Robyn felt wrong. But her recent behavior suggested she would be much happier without him there.

I'd be much happier if I weren't here either. Aldo missed his parents and Allison terribly, and being disconnected from the world heightened the feeling. World War III could have broken out for all he knew. He felt like he was living in a dream or a walking coma. He wasn't even sure exactly how much time had passed since he first arrived at the Knights' house. He kept a tally in his notebook but wondered how many days he lost drifting in and out of wakefulness.

Unfortunately, he had yet to really learn anything new, other than bits of information he pieced together from the books in Knight's library. He tried shadowing Knight's assistant, Aaminah, but the Saudi woman always managed to give him the slip. It didn't help that he was horrible at hiding. Even as a kid, Aldo was always the first one found when playing hide-and-seek. The few things he had discovered about the elusive doctor seemed trivial and unimportant. He doubted the NSA or the pope would care about Knight's taking lessons on Islam from his assistant, particularly the verbally-transmitted record of teachings, deeds, and sayings of the Prophet Muhammad.

While it did seem odd to Aldo that a staunch member of the Seventh-day Adventist Church would want to learn so much about the Muslim religion, who was he to judge? After all, hadn't he learned all he could about the Church of Jesus Christ of Latter-day Saints after meeting Allison, despite being a devout Catholic? He still had no idea how they would solve the problem of their religions if he ever managed to ask her out, but he would worry about that later. He had to escape his captivity first.

Aldo continued to sit in the grass beside Robyn for a minute or two longer, to enjoy the cool spring air. A breeze rustled the leaves in the trees overhead, and he could almost hear their melody. Spring had always been one of his favorite times of year, one of fresh starts and new beginnings. Of course, spring in California was just an extension of summer, not at all the dramatic reawakening he had experienced growing up in Colorado.

Aldo looked forward to these quiet moments in the garden, but reluctantly, he admitted defeat and stood to return to his room. "Well, let me know if you want to talk about it." He glanced at the stack of books beside her but hoped she would open up to him about anything other than bryophytes. "I'll see you at dinner, okay?"

Silence. He couldn't even get her to look at him anymore.

Dejected, Aldo trudged across the lawn toward the house. Just as he reached the kitchen door, he heard someone step out onto the patio. Peering around the edge of the house, he watched Dr. Knight bypass the cushioned wrought iron chairs and continue down the steps and onto the lawn toward the vegetable patch.

Dr. Knight never goes into the garden. The only thing Aldo had ever seen the doctor do outside was eat breakfast or perhaps chat with the professor on the patio. The garden seemed to be strictly Mrs. Knight's domain, one of the reasons he assumed Robyn preferred it.

Suspicious, Aldo slid along the side of the house until he could drop behind the boxwood hedge that bordered the north side of the property. He crept along behind the row of shrubs until he was within earshot of the vegetable garden. Knight was crouched beside Robyn, shuffling through the stack of books.

"Are you still keeping your distance?" Knight asked, so softly Aldo could barely hear him.

Aldo edged closer.

When Robyn nodded, the doctor sighed. "Didn't I tell you that suddenly changing your behavior would only make him suspicious? I need you to use your gift to find out who he really is. Why do you think I've kept you here?"

"I know, but…I don't like this," she muttered. "What if he…" Her voice faded.

Knight sighed again and tapped his finger on the stack of books. "Do you really think someone who cares more about teaching you botany than he does about escaping could be that dangerous?"

"I know he's not dangerous. He's only ever been nice to me." Sitting cross-legged on the lawn, she tore out a fistful of blades and let them float back down onto her lap.

"You're worried about betraying him?"

She glanced up at the doctor, but he shook his head.

"You have to remember that he betrayed you first, my dear. Didn't your dream tell you that he's lying, that he's been lying this entire time, pretending to be someone he's not?"

Aldo sucked in a breath. *Her dream told her?* Could Robyn be like Mr. Summers? Aldo hadn't believed precognitive dreams were even real before talking to Mr. Summers. Now, he seemed immersed in a world of the unexplained, and he had been given the impossible task of trying to explain it. Could Robyn have inherited her ability from her father, who was also in the Toddler Program? Aldo wasn't sure such things could be passed onto offspring, but who knew what kind of DNA manipulation they may have done to her father as a child.

"You also said that he's hiding something," Knight continued. "You need to find out what that is." The doctor leaned closer and brushed his hand down her long curly hair. "I know you're trying your best, but we're running out of time."

Out of time for what? And more importantly, what did that mean for him? If they knew he wasn't who they'd been led to believe he was, what would they do with him once they found out the truth? Discovering a spy for the pope had been living under their roof for weeks would no doubt put him in even greater danger.

When Robyn slowly nodded, the doctor abruptly dropped his hand and stood up straight beside her. "Good. Now, come inside and get cleaned up. The professor will be here shortly for your checkup. Don't forget to tell him about any side effects you're experiencing." Without another word, Knight stalked back across the lawn to his library.

Well, that explains a lot. No wonder they'd been so relaxed around him lately. They were using her to get to him, hoping he'd lower his guard. Much to his chagrin, Aldo realized it had almost worked, too. He couldn't fault Robyn, though. Surrounded by people who watched her every move, she probably had no choice but to comply.

Aldo crept back along the hedgerow toward the house. After befriending Robyn, he had hoped to one day introduce her the world outside her church. To nurture her independence and show her there was life beyond her father's cruelty and her church leaders' lies. Even if he wasn't able to take her with him when he escaped, Aldo had planned to return and free her from Dr. Knight's control. He even imagined Allison taking Robyn under her wing like a big sister. But now, Aldo wasn't sure any of that was possible. Despite the fact it was necessary, Aldo had lied to her. He doubted there was any way she would ever believe him.

Glancing back toward the garden to make sure Robyn didn't see him emerge from behind the hedge, Aldo stood and walked straight into a concrete column. Stumbling, he fell backwards into the grass, and then looked up to find Hans towering over him. Aldo stared in horror. *No, that can't be him. I saw Hans…in Argentina.* His stomach turned at the memory.

"What do we have here?"

Aldo cringed as Professor Applebee stepped into view.

"Didn't anyone ever tell you it's rude to eavesdrop?" Applebee asked, sneering down at him.

Slowly, Aldo climbed to his feet. "But kidnapping's okay? Or how about drugging someone? And let's not forget using a teenage girl against her will."

Applebee shook his head. "Robyn's been more than happy to help us. Haven't you, *schatzi* ?"

Aldo watched her walk past him without making eye contact, only to hide behind the professor. His heart sank as he realized how truly alone he was.

"But it seems we now have to change tactics," Applebee continued. He nodded to the tall, blond man, and then turned and walked back to the house, Robyn trailing behind him.

"What do you mean?" Aldo yelled after him. "What're you gonna do?"

The blond man leaned down and grabbed a fistful of Aldo's oxford shirt. Tugging Aldo onto his tiptoes, he dragged him toward the house, following Applebee up the three flights of stairs to Aldo's room. Two more Hans-lookalikes waited inside.

"Search it," Applebee demanded.

Watching the men dump his few belongings onto the bed and pull books from their shelves, Aldo's anger rose. "What are you doing? Stop it." He tried to twist out of the man's grasp but only succeeded in popping the shoulder seam of his shirt. The blond man released his grip on Aldo's collar only to clamp his hands around Aldo's arms instead, pressing him against the wall.

"Check the bathroom, too," Applebee said.

"But professor..." Robyn stepped forward to stand in front of him. "The doctor wouldn't—"

"Andrew wants answers as much as we do," the professor snapped.

Her gaze immediately dropped to the floor. "But you don't even know what you're looking for," she whispered.

Aldo could see the girl shaking, elevating his anger. "Hey, leave her alone."

Ignoring Aldo, Applebee kept his hard gaze on Robyn. "Only because you haven't done your job. All you had to do was read him, yet you couldn't even do that. Useless." He shoved her to the side, returning his attention to the rampaging clones.

What exactly did they expect to find? They had already taken his laptop and cell phone. The only things of value they let him keep were his watch and his wallet, both of which he always kept on him. That and his notebook...

Damn it, the journal. He quickly wiped the surprise from his face, hoping no one had noticed. He had not finished transcribing it and hastily stashed it under the area rug in case Agnes came in to clean while he was outside. Finding that journal in his possession would be all the proof they needed to confirm he was a fraud.

Still suspended in the blond man's grasp, Aldo tried again to wriggle free. With his feet barely touching the floor, he swung his legs, hoping the momentum would propel him away from the wall. The man staggered but recovered quickly and pinned Aldo's legs with his own.

Robyn walked over, placing her hand on the side of Aldo's face and he froze. "Why are you helping them?" he whispered. "You don't know what this could mean."

For the first time in over a week, she met his gaze. "I have to." Blondie tightened his grip on Aldo's arms, locking him in place, as she closed her eyes.

What is she doing? Aldo winced from the pain in his arms but kept his gaze on Robyn. It wasn't until her eyelids fluttered that he realized this was probably what Applebee meant by *reading him* . Unable to do anything else, Aldo tried to empty his mind, to think of anything other than his research. He thought about his mother and father, about Allison and how much he wanted to see them all again soon. He pictured his friends from the university and what they might be doing now that they had graduated. Would he see them all at the commencement ceremony, assuming he could get out of this place in one piece?

A moment later, Robyn opened her eyes and stepped back. "The carpet. There's something hidden under the carpet."

Damn it!

"See? Was that so hard, *schatzi* ?" Applebee bent down and flipped the carpet aside, revealing the journal sealed in a large zip-top bag. Pulling the coverless book from its plastic sheath, he thumbed through the pages then slowly stood. The professor glared at Aldo for a moment, and then snapped his fingers. The crashing in the bathroom ceased as the other Hans-lookalikes returned to the bedroom and surrounded him. One grabbed his legs while the other rolled up his sleeve.

Aldo panicked. "Wait. What are you doing?"

"I'm afraid you've overstayed your welcome, Mr. Lombardi," Applebee hissed.

"What? Hold on. Let me explain."

Robyn shrank into a corner of the room as the three clones held him in place, his struggles no match for their strength.

"Oh, don't worry," Applebee said as he pulled a syringe from the pocket of his suit coat. He tapped the air from the tip before handing the syringe to the clone holding Aldo's arm. "There'll be plenty of time for you to explain *everything* later."

•••

Holt hurried down the hallway toward the Situation Room with Jenkins and Allison trailing after him. "Let me know the minute you get Judge Jason on the line." The situation was getting more and more disastrous by the second. He only hoped what the judge had to say would help shed some light on things.

Jenkins's cell phone buzzed, and Holt stopped in his tracks, gesturing for him to answer it quickly. Holt was still waiting for an update from the team in Argentina, but he trusted the team's leader, Tony, not to let the shipment of bio-weapons out of his sight. When he pulled Jenkins to cover the historian in Loma Linda, he put Tony in charge of taking out the remaining Fifth Reich camps. Now, thanks to this latest cluster, that task would have to wait.

"What do you mean?!" Jenkins yelled into his cell. "Where are they taking him?!" He paced up and down the hallway.

No . He's stomping. Holt couldn't remember the last time he had seen his subordinate so pissed. That didn't bode well for their current situation.

"Well, find out, damn it!" Jenkins shoved his cell back into his pocket, and then glanced up at Allison and cursed under his breath.

"I heard that," she muttered, her arms crossed over her chest. Holt was amazed at how calm she sounded. Most women would've been nervous after witnessing that little tantrum. "It's Aldo, isn't it? What happened?"

Jenkins sighed. "His cover's been blown. Apparently, they were using the little bird to get to him. Jackson didn't say what they were holding over her though, but that's probably why security's been so lax the last few weeks." He ran a hand through his hair, which seemed thinner now that Allison really looked at him. "Somehow they found something to prove he's not really Mr. Summers's nephew." Jenkins tried to walk past her to join Holt where he waited outside the Situation Room, but she grabbed his arm, stopping him.

"And? What happened to Aldo?"

Holt noticed the tightness in Jenkins's jaw.

"They drugged him again and hauled him off. With only the two of them still in Loma Linda, they didn't have enough men to raid the place." Jenkins laid a hand on her shoulder. "But they're tailing them as we speak and have orders to intercept him the first chance they get. We'll get him back. Don't worry."

She lifted her chin. "Fine, but don't expect me to just sit here and do nothing." She turned on her heels to march back down the hallway when Jenkins grabbed her arm.

That does it. Holt walked toward them. "What the hell is going on?" he demanded. "You two do realize we have a national security issue to deal with right now, and you're arguing like this is some kind of lovers' quarrel."

Jenkins let go of her arm. "I'm sorry, sir. Allison's a good friend of Mr. Lombardi and my team failed to keep him safe. It's understandable she'd be upset."

"Friend, huh? Seems like more than that if you ask me," he muttered. Her mouth opened to protest, but he held up a hand, cutting her off. "But what exactly do you expect to do about it now? You think racing off to California after him is gonna do any good?"

Before she could answer, Jenkins's cell buzzed again.

What is it this time? Holt's foot started tapping out his annoyance. *Damn it. I don't have time for this.*

Jenkins held out the phone to him. "It's Tony."

"About damn time." He grabbed the phone and held it to his ear. "What do ya got?"

"The trucks are still heading north, sir. We're not sure exactly what their destination is yet, but it looks like they might be planning to take the shipment across the border into Paraguay. They've been avoiding the main roads, probably to bypass any checkpoints at the border, but they'll have to cross the Paraná River at some point."

"Good. I'm heading in to brief the President now, so contact Jenkins the moment you learn anything new. We've got two satellites monitoring them as well, but I need your team to keep on them in case there's a chance to intercept. Don't let those trucks out of your sight."

"Yes, sir."

Holt tossed the phone back to Jenkins. "Keep on top of the situation in California and update me on any changes." He pointed a finger at Allison. "Take her with you. She's only going to cause trouble if she stays here, twiddling her thumbs."

"Sir, I—"

He turned on her. "If you want to get your boyfriend back, then make yourself useful. You're not going to help anyone running around like a headless chicken."

She stared up at him for a moment with her eyebrow quirked high on her forehead. He expected her to burst into tears, but to his surprise, she only smiled. "Yes, sir."

"Good." Maybe this woman had some sense in that head of hers after all. He turned back toward the situation room. "And get that judge on the line a-sap."

•••

Tony Garrera dropped his cell into the pocket of his black cargo pants, and then eased the Jeep back onto the road. The night was moonless and dark, but he kept the headlights off and his speed slow as he followed the line of trucks north. From the passenger seat, Buster checked the GPS, the glowing green map showing they were still in Argentina, traveling along the sliver of land bordered by Paraguay, Brazil, and Uruguay.

"What'd the big man say?" Jones asked from the back seat.

"To keep on keeping on."

"I still think we should intercept the trucks now while we have the chance." Seated beside Jones, Davis drummed his fingers against the window frame.

"There's only eight of us." Garrera glanced in the rearview mirror to ensure the other Jeep still followed.

"Normally, that's all we'd need to take down a convoy like that," Buster muttered.

"But this ain't normal." Garrera tapped his brakes to signal the other Jeep of a steep grade ahead. "One mistake and that cargo gets loose…" He shook his head. "Let's just say this would no longer be a stealth operation."

Buster only grunted.

"We could call in the rest of the team. They're only monitoring the remaining camps anyway," Davis interjected.

"Think about it, dumbass." Jones smacked Davis's shoulder then stretched his arms behind his head again as he leaned back against the seat. "All kinds of shit could go down without us knowing if we pull Benny's team off surveillance." He yawned then said, "Having some lunatic wipe out a few billion people with those bio-weapons would suck, but I don't want the world overrun by clones either."

"Not even if they wore armored suits like the ones in *Star Wars* ? That'd be pretty badass, having a whole army of soldiers genetically programmed to do your bidding." Davis leaned forward, as if trying to engage Tony and Buster in the conversation.

"Why not just use robots then?" Buster asked without turning around.

Damn it . Garrera shook his head. *Don't encourage him* .

Davis rolled his eyes. "Cuz they'd be expensive to manufacture."

"And clones aren't?"

"Okay, guys. Enough. Can we get back to reality now?" Garrera asked. Normally, he'd let their banter slide, but this topic was hitting too close to the truth. It hadn't happened yet, but Mr. Summers had warned that it would. It was only a matter of time. Now, his team was doing everything they could to stop the Fifth Reich from making their legions of armored soldiers a reality.

A beep sounded and a message from the other Jeep flashed across the screen on Buster's lap.

"What'd he say?" Garrera asked, maneuvering around a pothole.

"To get your head out of your ass and pay attention." Buster pointed out of the windshield. "Convoy's caboose is changing course."

"Shit." Garrera jerked the wheel, veering into the brush along the side of the dirt road, and slowed to a stop, trying to kick up as little dust as possible. "Are they heading this way?"

Already standing on the back seat, Davis leaned over the Jeep's roll bar and pressed a night-vision scope to his right eye. "That's affirmative."

"Shit," Garrera muttered again. He knew they should have used a civilian vehicle. Dressed in street clothes, they might have been able to pass themselves off as a group of lost tourists trying to find their way back to Buenos Aires. As it was, their black jeep and black clothing screamed incognito. They couldn't get caught. "Is it just the one vehicle?"

"Yup. Rest of the convoy's maintaining their course," Davis said.

Garrera breathed a small sigh of relief. One car wouldn't be able to follow them both if they split up. He turned to Buster in the passenger seat. "Tell Maynard to scatter and continue radio silence. We'll catch up with them at the rendezvous point."

A moment later, he watched through the rearview mirror as the other Jeep headed back up the road the way they had come. Instead of following, he turned the wheel and plowed through the dry brush, forging his own path away from the main road. Davis held onto the roll bar, keeping the night-vision scope trained on their pursuer.

Buster switched the image on the screen back to the GPS map and informed Garrera of a side road about a quarter-mile ahead. Garrera accelerated, swerving around tree stumps and boulders. Their route through the underbrush would be easily noticed, so the sooner they got back onto the road the better. But they couldn't deviate from their course too much. If they lost track of that shipment, there would be more at stake than just the lives of his team.

•••

Holt stared up at the wrinkled face on the video monitor. Judge Lewis Jason was older than he had expected and did not sound like a man in good health. The retired federal judge coughed incessantly, each time making Holt feel guilty for forcing him onto a video conference from his hospital room. But his information could help them stop a potential catastrophe.

"I understand why the Roger Frogburger Enterprise is suspected of being involved in the purchase of these bio-weapons," the President said, "but what does this situation have to do with the Summers trial? You tried that case nearly two decades ago, right? Back in 1996."

"Yes," the judge answered with another cough.

Feeling the need to help the old man out, Holt interjected, "That's when Frogburger accumulated most of the money used in this transaction, Mr. President."

"Yes," Judge Jason wheezed as he waved to someone out of view. "If you would, Agent Larson is part of the team helping me investigate Frogburger and other world leaders in the Seventh-day Adventist Church." A barking sound echoed through the speakers as the judge coughed again and Holt cringed. "I ask that she answer your questions in my stead."

"Understood," the President said.

A woman stepped into view on the monitor and sat down beside the judge's hospital bed. Despite her feminine suit, her posture held the confidence and hardness of a seasoned field agent. "Mr. President, I am Special Agent Amelia Larson." She tipped her head in greeting, and then listened as the judge whispered something in her ear. She nodded and turned her gaze to the monitor. "Most of what we know about certain elite members of the Seventh-day Adventist Church came to light during the Summers trial when Frogburger and his cohorts used their considerable influence to have Mr. Summers brought up on charges for a white-collar crime that never happened."

"So, he was their scapegoat," the President replied.

Agent Larson nodded. "Yes, they needed a way to keep public and civil eyes off their shady land dealings. But there were other reasons why they chose Mr. Summers specifically to take the fall, such as issues within the church they believed would be resolved with Summers behind bars. You see, Mr. Summers was supposed to reveal certain things to church members." She flipped through the stack of documents in her lap. "Things like the Seven Sacred Sciences, but he left the church before completing his role. He said he chose to leave because he didn't feel he could support the changes the leaders were making to the church's original teachings. Needless to say, the church leaders weren't exactly pleased with his decision."

"Judge Jason, if you knew he was innocent," Holt asked, "why did you still sentence him?" That particular point had been bothering him since reading through Summers's case file.

Judge Jason thought for a moment, and then muttered something to Agent Larson, giving Holt the impression both were still deeply invested in this case.

"He felt it was for the best," Agent Larson replied. "If he walked Mr. Summers through the system, it would allow us to conduct an investigation into the SDA Church, and Frogburger, without them being aware of it. So, just as they had done, he used Mr. Summers as a diversion." She leaned toward the judge as he muttered again and returned her gaze to the monitor. "Not to mention it also allowed us to investigate the FBI special agent who was managing the U.S. versus Summers case. Judge Jason had his suspicions about the agent from the beginning. This same FBI agent had been involved with issues surrounding the SDA Church on more than one occasion in the past—helping them resolve certain situations that were causing the church some embarrassment."

The judge cleared phlegm from his throat. "Seemed like more than a coincidence that the agent was involved yet again." He reached for the glass of water on his bedside table, Agent Larson helping him. After taking a few sips, he nodded for her to continue.

"We learned through our investigation that this agent had been involved in the church's plan to destroy Mr. Summers's reputation from the beginning. When Mr. Summers chose to walk away from the church, the world leaders considered it a betrayal and used the FBI agent to exact their revenge." She fell silent as a knock sounded in the background. After dismissing the nurse, the judge again nodded for Larson to continue. "Judge Jason sentenced Mr. Summers to forty-seven months, with thirty-six months' probation and limited lifetime contact as a way to let everyone know that while we were going to continue to watch him, we were watching those who set him up as well."

"Wasn't there another defendant in the trial?" Holt asked. Another name had come up in the file several times, but very little information had been included about the man.

Agent Larson nodded, strands of brown hair falling loose of her tight bun. She tucked them behind her ear then said, "Yes, John H. Fielding. Our team interviewed him during the investigation. His statement corroborated the FD-302 reports of the interviews conducted with Mr. Summers during his pretrial. Mr. Fielding also informed us that the FBI agent had tried to convince him to lie on the stand, telling him he'd get a lighter sentence. With only the falsified set of books as evidence of the crime Mr. Summers had been accused of, the agent was hoping to use Mr. Fielding's testimony as proof. But Mr. Fielding refused to lie and ended up spending over two years in prison and was on probation for another three. He also has a million-dollar judgment against him, which he'll have to make payments toward for the rest of his life. Not to mention the man will forever be labeled a federally-convicted felon."

"Knowing the truth," the judge interjected, "I really wish I could have given him a lighter sentence, but it was out of my hands due to federal sentencing guidelines. The only good thing that came of it was that his sacrifice helped pave the way for our investigation." He glanced at the stack of papers in Agent Larson's lap. "You received the additional documents Amelia faxed over, correct?"

"Yes," Holt answered, holding up his copy for the judge to see.

"Good. Those pages detail the truth behind this case—the truth I would have exposed had I not felt it necessary to protect Mr. Summers. I've already instructed Amelia to make these documents public in time, but for now, it's enough that you know the truth."

Looking through the documents the special agent had faxed to the Situation Room over a secure line, the President asked, "You continued your investigation even after Frogburger resigned?"

"Yes," Agent Larson replied. "While Frogburger was forced to resign and pay back a small portion of the money he'd," she waved her hand through the air as though searching for the right word, "*obtained* through questionable means, we knew there was more to the church's involvement. This wasn't just Frogburger's personal vendetta against Mr. Summers as the church would have us believe. We're dealing with a religious organization which, while relatively small in terms of membership, is one of the wealthiest organizations in the world."

"As such, I've urged my team to continue to watch the church closely, and not just their shady business dealings." Judge Jason took another sip of water and carefully returned the glass to the bedside table. He looked tired and life-weary, the graininess of the monitor not helping his appearance. "You see, many of the church's doctrines are based on prophecies, and those prophecies seem to be a driving force behind many of their actions."

"Meaning?" the President asked.

"The leaders are doing whatever they can to make those prophecies come true, even if that means being involved in illegal activities," the judge replied.

He leaned his head back against the headboard. "The current situation in South America is a perfect example. What better way to bring about the End Times and fulfill a prophecy than by dispersing CBWs? Discreetly, of course. The church is extremely sensitive about its public image."

Holt gritted his teeth. *Humanitarians, my ass* . The SDA Church had hospitals and medical research centers across the globe, researching ways to extend human life, yet they could so easily wipe out billions of people from the planet?

Coughing again, the judge turned the discussion back over to Agent Larson. "Mr. President, you've heard the claims that their founder, Ellen G. White, made a prophecy in 1904 about the events that took place on September 11th, 2001, correct?" When the President nodded, she continued. "That prophecy, which you'll find in volume 9, page 11 of the *Testimonies for the Church*," she flipped through more documents, "tells of how *tall towers* and *an entire city block of buildings* would be destroyed. Many members believe that if Building Seven had not fallen to the ground that day then Ellen White's prophecy wouldn't have been completely fulfilled. There's speculation that the building was brought down intentionally, just to make her prophecy come true."

Holt nodded. "Yes, the Counter Terrorism Unit looked into that. The investigation NIST conducted after Building Seven collapsed stated that a single column caused the structural failure. Yet, numerous engineers and architects have come forward, saying that isn't possible. The way the building was designed, it couldn't have collapsed from a single column giving way. There's also the fact that the columns were constructed of thick steel, which only melts at extremely high temperatures. But the NIST report states the failed column had melted through, even though the fire inside the building only reached temperatures of about nine-hundred degrees, even with the fuel from the airplane. We haven't made it public yet, but we believe the building was brought down by something other than the plane crash…likely strategically-placed high explosives."

On the video monitor, the agent nodded. "Yes, that was our conclusion as well. Mr. President, just as with the events of September eleventh, we believe the church may be trying to bring about the fulfillment of another prophecy through the purchase of these CBWs."

"How so?" the President asked.

"Their End Times prophecies state that, first, Islam would attack the United States in what the church calls the beginning of the Third Woe. Most Muslims refer to it as the Third Jihad. And later, Islam will attack our financial structure then the rest of the world. Many believe this is exactly what we're seeing happen right now."

Holt discreetly glanced at his watch again, his anxiety escalating. He hadn't heard anything from Jenkins or Garrera in over thirty minutes, and in these kinds of situations, no news was generally not good.

"Nine-eleven is believed to be the first attack, and the market crash of 2008 was their strike against our financial structure," Agent Larson said.

"So, you think the purchase of these CBWs could very well be the beginning of their third and final attack?" the President asked.

"Yes. The church's leaders believe in their founder's prophecies so blindly, they seem willing to do everything they can to make sure those prophecies come true. Without their members discovering the truth, of course." She tapped her finger against the pages on her lap. "Because of this prophecy, they believe a war is coming—one that will attempt to destroy every descendant of Abraham."

"And instead of waiting for the inevitable, they plan to instigate it?" the President asked.

Holt nodded. "It's more likely the group intends to sell the weapons to a third party, sir." Holt glanced up at Agent Larson for confirmation.

"Agreed," she said. "As much as they want to make their founder's prophecy come true, they won't do it at the risk of their public image. It's more plausible that they will instigate their buyer into setting off their desired chain of events."

"Do we know who their buyer might be?" the President asked.

"Not as of yet, sir," Holt answered. "There's speculation it will be one of the radical groups of Islam."

"Yes, I would have to agree, Mr. President," Agent Larson said. "Our investigation turned up evidence of an agreement Frogburger's father-in-law, Kevin Emery, made with a terror organization in Syria before his death," Agent Larson said. "The transaction took place back in the early 1990s but was never finalized due to our investigation into the church, which began in late 1993. This most recent transaction could be the fulfillment of that agreement."

"Why would they wait so long?" the President asked.

"They were forced to put their actions on hold until they were sure they weren't being watched," Agent Larson replied then held up a file. "I also faxed you a copy of the Stuttering Brief. Most of our initial information about the church came from this brief, which was the first defense document Mr. Summers submitted at the start of his pretrial. Due to the extent of information in this brief, his pretrial was extended to four years. In it, Mr. Summers describes how Frogburger's criminal activities were all for the sake of creating offshore accounts in order to funnel money. Money paid to his father-in-law for items procured from South America, like the bio-weapons, purchases Frogburger apparently knew nothing about. The brief was so shocking in its detail the lead prosecutor for the case quit the same night it was submitted and started working with FBI agents to determine the brief's level of competency. Those same agents eventually became part of our investigation team."

"If you knew all this then, why did no one stop it?" the President asked.

"Simple lack of evidence, sir," Holt explained. "It was mostly speculation until the money finally changed hands this morning at the same time our satellites were taking images of the trucks loaded with bio-weapons leaving the labs in South America. We had nothing solid to present to their government to request a search of the premises. We also had to consider how dangerous things could've become. Not only was the SDA Church directly involved in government projects like Project Whitecoat and Project Paperclip, but they were also involved with CIA run mind-control experiments like MK Ultra—and still are." Holt leaned forward, resting his elbows on his knees. "My point is that if they're willing to be part of these experiments in exchange for religious freedoms and large grants, it makes you wonder what else the church is involved in."

"Which is why my team has continued to investigate them," Judge Jason interjected.

"We know that they're currently helping to develop global covert hacking programs, advanced human tagging RFID transponders, and cyber weapons—using their largest hospitals as laboratories and research centers," Agent Larson offered. "They even have connections here in D.C. to help push bills through legislation, and if things go according to their plan, human tagging will likely become standard across the country by the end of the decade. We're already seeing people signing up to be implanted, as well as people on social media doing DIY implanting." She tucked more loose strains of hair behind her ears. "There are other secret projects run by members of the SDA Church which we're still investigating, but so far everything Mr. Summers has told us has been accurate. What worries me is that he says there are more prophecies being kept secret by the church—prophecies our team has yet to get its hands on. The leaders fear their church would lose credibility if they were to reveal the prophecies before they happen."

"Better to say, '*See? I told you so*', after the fact, huh?" Holt said.

Agent Larson nodded. "But thanks to Mr. Summers, we do know that one of the prophecies predicts that church members will become aware of their leaders' lies. We just don't know when or how."

Holt glanced at his watch. "Judge Jason, just a few more questions. I noticed in the file on the U.S. versus Summers case that Mr. Summers also told you about a sealed document."

"Ah, yes. You're referring to the parallel mind-control research program in the CIA called MK Orion," the judge replied.

"Yes. When MK Ultra was shut down, seven boxes containing documents and evidence survived. They're known as the seven limited hangout boxes because small amounts of information from them has been released periodically over the intervening years, likely to keep the more disturbing information secret. While the public has, for the most part, been made aware of MK Ultra, MK Orion is still a mystery. It's a self-contained program and was never closed down, even after the mess caused by MK Ultra and other related projects. But how exactly does this pertain to Mr. Summers's trial or, more importantly, to the bio-weapons in South America?"

The judge nodded to Agent Larson who answered for him. "Our team suspects that MK Orion is under the administration of federal agents who have influence within the Seventh-day Adventist Church. We're still trying to gather concrete evidence, but their research seems to tie into the End Times prophecies I mentioned earlier."

"They certainly have their fingers in a lot of pies," Holt muttered.

Judge Jason nodded. "It's hard to believe, isn't it?" The older man sighed. "I had always believed that this church was one of care and concern. That's the message they project at least, and their humanitarian works have done tremendous good in the world. But these secrets within the church are like a darkness hidden behind their mask of righteousness, a darkness which has led to some of the most evil things in the world. They may claim their deeds are to benefit humanity, but how does harboring a known mass-murderer like Mengele benefit humanity? How does purchasing bio-weapons, capable of killing nearly three billion people, benefit humanity? Even their wealth was obtained through tainted means, by selling their young men and children into experimental programs like Project Whitecoat."

Holt straightened in his seat. "Yes, and if the church manages to carry out the transaction Kevin Emery started nearly two decades ago, it stands to gain over two billion dollars from the sale of these bio-weapons."

•••

You've got to be shitting me. Garrera looked in disbelief at the message on the screen in Buster's lap. Even after he read it a second and third time, the words didn't change. He groaned inwardly, trying to figure out how he was going to deal with this latest SNAFU.

He and his men were hunkered down in the Jeep, waiting for the all-clear from Davis, who was acting as lookout in a nearby tree. The convoy's scout vehicle had passed by about twenty minutes earlier, and he suspected it wouldn't be long before it circled back.

With all that, Garrera now had to try and patch a secure call through to Jenkins and inform him that Mr. Lombardi had been sighted about thirty miles south, near an active Fifth Reich facility. What the hell the historian was doing back in Argentina Garrera had no idea. They were lucky Benny's team happened to be in the area doing surveillance.

Damn it. Allison's gonna shit bricks when she finds out. Sighing, he pulled the small monitor off Buster's lap as he caught up on much-needed sleep.

"Keep eyes on him," Garrera typed in reply. "Split up your team if you have to but don't lose him."

"It'll spread us pretty thin," came Benny's response a moment later.

Tony sighed. Nothing he could do about that. They still had to meet up with Maynard's team at the rendezvous point, and then catch up with the convoy. He briefly considered asking Holt to send him more men but doubted they would get there in time to be of much help. He'd just have to make do.

Hearing a twitter from Davis in the tree above them, Garrera clicked the screen off and ducked down just as a car drove by. Their Jeep was hidden among the underbrush some fifty feet from the dirt road. Thank God it was the dead of night. Trying to hide a black Jeep in the sparse underbrush in the middle of the day would have been impossible.

When the coast was clear, Garrera pulled the monitor back onto his lap and clicked the screen back on. "Do the best you can," he typed back to Benny. "If you see an opportunity to get Lombardi out safely, take it. And see what you can find out about how he ended up there in the first place. I'll get you extra men if I can, but don't hold your breath."

"Roger," came the simple reply.

Now Garrera had a phone call to make.

Chapter Eleven | The GUARDIAN

Washington D.C.
April 2013

How many times am I gonna have to fly across the country today? Allison stood in the security checkpoint line at Reagan National exasperated at the situation. She had landed in D.C. twelve hours earlier, and now she was about to board a flight back to California. Not that she was going to argue. She had wanted to jump on a plane the moment she heard Aldo had been taken from the Knight estate. She was now getting her wish, but for a different reason.

After learning of Aldo's situation, Allison's superiors immediately ordered her back to California. They assumed responsibility for keeping Mr. Summers hidden when he was released from prison in the late 1990s, and his safety was the agency's top priority. Now, with Aldo's cover blown, Allison's superiors feared his captors planned to extract information from him, and Mr. Summers' location could be compromised. Considering Aldo knew next to nothing of Mr. Summers' whereabouts, Allison was more concerned about Aldo's immediate wellbeing.

Jenkins promised to update her as soon as he received news from his team based in Loma Linda, but she couldn't shake the fear she might never see Aldo again. Allison had been in her fair share of sticky situations since joining the agency and had dragged Aldo into a few along with her, but this was the first time she ever felt so terrified. A piece of her would die if something happened to him.

Isn't that your answer then? If she could no longer imagine her life without him in it, wasn't that proof she was in love with him? She missed seeing his face flush at the slightest touch. She missed spending hours talking with him about nothing. He was a serious and careful guy, and when he did laugh, it was deep and honest and had a way of making her skin tingle. He was the person she missed most when she was alone, even more than her parents and siblings.

She sighed. *I'm done for.* She had suspected for a while that she was in love with him but chose to ignore her feelings since she could do nothing about them. But now, with the real possibility of never seeing him again, she had to acknowledge the truth.

The line moved forward slowly. Too slowly. But without Jenkins' NSA clearance, she had to wait just like everyone else. She slipped off her heels and set them in the plastic bin. Then she dumped her purse, cell phone, keys, and laptop bag in another bin and rolled them forward on the conveyor belt. She hadn't been able to pack much else when they left San Bernardino in a rush to catch a red eye that morning. But despite her exhaustion, she felt relief knowing she was headed closer to Aldo.

Allison's priority was ensuring Mr. Summers' safety, but after that... She shook her head. No, getting involved with Aldo could make matters worse. She would jeopardize her safety and that of many others if the men behind Aldo's kidnapping got their hands on her. She had to trust Jenkins' men. They had rescued Aldo and her from the Fifth Reich camp with deadly efficiency. And Tony and his team were currently moving heaven and earth to stop a convoy of bio-warfare agents. She looked at her beige heels in the bin on the conveyor belt, grudgingly admitting that Jackson and Lawrence were much better equipped to save Aldo than she was.

Stepping forward, she raised her arms as instructed, allowing the x-ray booth to scan her body. She'd only been questioned once about the subcutaneous chip in her left arm but carried an information card in her purse just in case. Given the all clear, she collected her belongings, slipped into her heels then hurried through the terminal to her gate.

Arriving just as final boarding was being called, she lined up with the coach passengers and smiled at the inquisitive toddler peering over her father's shoulder in front of her. The mother cradled a sleeping infant in her arms, and Allison felt her heart squeeze at the quintessential image of family. That was what she wanted. The sleepless nights, the stinky diapers, the stains, cuddles, tears, laughter, all of it. And she couldn't picture anyone other than Aldo sharing it with her.

How did I let this happen? Aldo was supposed to be an assignment and nothing more. Somehow the stubborn historian had won her over. She dropped into her seat next to the window, and a grin spread uncontrollably across her face as she remembered his clumsiness and naïve honesty, two things she'd found charming about him from the day they'd first met.

Then her smile faded. *He'd better be okay.* Checking her cell phone one more time for any word from Jenkins, she sighed, switched it to airplane mode, and tucked it back into her purse. As the flight attendants began demonstrating the emergency procedures, she said a silent prayer for Aldo's safe return.

•••

Aldo could feel the effects of the drug finally relinquishing control of his body, but he remained as flaccid as possible. Heavy nylon straps bound him to a wheelchair, so any movements he made would be severely restricted. Still, he remained motionless to conceal his regained consciousness from his captors.

He remembered being drugged in his room at Dr. Knight's house, along with various flashes of sounds and images, but he had no idea how much time had passed. A security checkpoint, muffled voices, the feeling of weightlessness—each memory followed by the feeling of a dark, heavy blanket shrouding his senses. Now that the shroud was lifting, he couldn't afford to be injected again.

With no idea where he was or how long he had been unconscious, Aldo could only listen and occasionally peek through cracks in his eyelids. Secured in the back of a van, his wheelchair faced the windowless rear doors. A man sat beside him, his features familiar, but Aldo couldn't place him. Blonde hair... a bulky build...*He's one of the men who drugged me.* Where were they taking him?

"Can't you drive any faster?" a familiar voice scolded over the drone of the van's engine. The floor jumped as the van hit a dip in the road, shifting Aldo's wheelchair, and his limp body pushed against the restraints at his wrists and ankles.

"This road's more treacherous at night," a voice replied in heavily accented English. "But we'll be there soon. Besides, it's not like he's going anywhere."

Something slammed and the man beside Aldo stiffened.

"I'm not worried about him escaping, *der schwachkopf,*" Applebee snapped. "I need you to hurry so I can to get him to my lab before the effects wear off. I can't give him another dose without the risk of killing him. You think I went through the trouble of forging medical documents and transporting him all the way down here so he could end up a cadaver?"

"No, sir."

Aldo heard someone give a heavy sigh, then Applebee said, "By Allah, I swear I'm surrounded by idiots. If that stupid girl had just done as she was told to begin with…" his voice trailed off. The van hit another pothole and Aldo's head flopped to his opposite shoulder. "And then Andrew, totally unconcerned that our secrets might be exposed. Doesn't he realize what's at stake?"

Aldo felt hands grip the sides of his head and move it back to its previous position.

"How's the patient doing?" Applebee asked.

"Heart rate's steady, sir," the man beside him replied stiffly.

"Check his responses."

Aldo felt something brush his arm, then a click sounded and the pressure on his right wrist vanished. His shoulder rotated as the man raised his arm, letting it fall limply into his lap.

"He's still out."

"Good," Applebee replied. "I'll need to do blood work on him the moment we get there to see if the drug he was given last month has started to take effect."

Aldo bit back a gasp. *Damn it!* Applebee just confirmed his worst fear. He'd hoped Applebee and Agnes had only been giving him sedatives to keep him in Loma Linda, but the nagging fear that they had experimented on him while he was unconscious never left his mind. *Monsters.* Experimenting on volunteers like the 2,300 men in Project Whitecoat was one thing, but doing it on unsuspecting civilians and children was unforgivable.

"Then you boys can wake him up and find out what he knows," Applebee continued.

Thoughts of truth serums and torturous interrogations flashed through Aldo's mind and he forced his body not to tense. If they found out what he knew, a great number of people would be at risk. Allison, Mr. Summers, the pope, Jenkins, and all of the men on his team working to destroy the Fifth Reich camps. *No, I can't let that happen. I know too much.* All of the evidence Aldo had collected in his notebook could be used against them if…

Oh, Lord. My notebook. Unable to feel much of anything, he couldn't tell if his notebook was still where he last remembered it, in his back pocket. Had they already read through it? No, if they did, why would they need to find out what he knows? Were they still trying to find Mr. Summers through him, even knowing he wasn't really Mr. Summers' nephew?

As the van continued over the rough road, Aldo desperately tried to think of a way out. He focused on the sounds around him, waiting until he was sure the man beside him had his attention elsewhere. Then he creaked his eyes open, scanning the van's floor beneath his wheelchair for anything he could use. To his surprise, the guard had left his right arm loose, lying across his lap, and Aldo prayed the man wouldn't realize his error. The rest of the interior was hard to make out in the darkness, and Aldo noticed only black piles gathered on the opposite side of the van.

By the time the van finally came to a stop, dread moistened Aldo's skin and pricked his fingers. He frantically tried to come up with a plan, but all he could think about was getting away as quickly as possible. Cool air rushed against his face as the rear doors burst open. Another door slammed, and Aldo heard Applebee barking orders, his voice quickly fading into the distance. Then his wheelchair shifted as the man beside him climbed out.

"Leave him," the driver said with a heavy accent. "We need to get this equipment inside and set up first."

"And I need him out of the way in order to do that," the other man snapped. "Don't see why the professor's so concerned about this dead weight anyway. Just another one of the flawed race." He continued to mutter to himself inaudibly as he wheeled Aldo out of the van. A moment later, the wheelchair stopped, and Aldo listened as the crunch of footsteps on gravel moved away from him.

Aldo listened intently for any other sounds, daring only to peek through half-closed eyelids when the bustling around him temporarily quieted. On the opposite side of an expansive gravel lot stood an imposing structure. Nowhere was the camouflage of the NSA's complex; instead, the massive gray building clashed with the surrounding trees and rock, ominously lit against the looming darkness. Aldo quickly scanned the perimeter but didn't immediately see any guards or surveillance cameras. Either the security was top of the line and well integrated into the environment, or Applebee never had visitors.

Hoping for the latter, Aldo slowly moved his right arm over to unhook the strap at his left wrist. Hearing movement behind him, he returned to his previous slouched position. More footsteps crunched across the gravel drive as the men returned to the van for more gear.

"Just grab the case of vials for now. The rest of that we can deal with later." The doors of the van slammed shut and Aldo's heart pounded as the men's footsteps drew closer.

"How much longer until we can call it a night?"

"Hard to say. You know how the professor gets when he's in work mode."

"Yeah, I almost feel sorry for this poor schmuck."

Aldo's wheelchair rocked as one of the men kicked it, and instinctively he held his breath. When the rocking stopped and the footsteps moved away, he let his breath out in a rush. Peeking through his eyelids again, he removed the heart rate monitor from his left index finger. Then he bent forward to release his ankles, keeping his eyes on the building across from him. With his legs free, Aldo gripped the wheels and slowly pushed, forcing the chair backwards. His limbs still weak from the drug, he summoned all of his strength to wheel the chair to the edge of the gravel lot where it met the road. It sloped away from the compound, descending into the night, the grade too steep for him to attempt to move the wheelchair safely. *Without the chair then* . It would be slow going with his legs still mostly numb, but the surrounding forest offered better odds.

With the wheels teetering at the edge of the slope, Aldo looked back at the building one last time before pushing himself off the chair. He stumbled over to the side of the road, slumping behind a tree as the chair rolled down the slope and disappeared into the darkness at the bottom of the hill. A moment later, he heard a faint crash as it collided with a tree. Afraid the noise had roused their attention, Aldo remained still, the tree's rough bark painful against his awakening skin.

Taking deep breaths, he opened and closed his fingers then flexed his feet, trying to work blood and sensation back into his limbs. He moved his right hand down to massage his leg, his hand brushing along the back of his pants. His back pocket was empty.

Damn it! They did take my notebook.

"Where is he?!" Applebee yelled.

"He was right here a second ago."

"Well, he's not now, is he?" Applebee hissed. "Do you have any idea what will happen if he gets away?" Gravel crunched as the men moved across the lot. "No, of course you don't, you expendable fool."

Hearing a pop then a thud, Aldo slowly peered around the tree's trunk. The group of men, seven or eight of them, stood on the other side of the van. Through the gap beneath the vehicle's undercarriage, Aldo could see another man—his guard—lying on the ground with a bright red hole in his forehead.

Oh, God! They have guns? Aldo shrank into himself, desperate to shroud his body in darkness. *Please, God. Don't let them find me.*

"Find him," Applebee ordered. "He couldn't have gone far."

Multiple beams of light slashed across the darkened forest as the men started down the road. Aldo listened for their footsteps to fade before he crawled through the underbrush in the opposite direction. His mostly numb body quickly tired and his arms and feet caught on tree roots, making his progress slow.

Finally reaching the side of the van, Aldo kept his eyes on the dead man to ensure they were alone. Seeing no other feet, he dragged his body forward on his elbows, and then reached up to grab the van's side mirror. He pulled himself up, working his feet under him until he could lever his body up into a standing position supported by the side of the van. Easing the driver's side door open, he climbed in, shutting it softly behind him as he bent forward to keep his upper body out of view. He felt along the steering column for the ignition only to find it empty. Checking the sun visor, under the floor mat, and the center console proved useless as well.

Reluctant to check the pockets of the dead man for the van's keys, Aldo realized he had no other option. Never had he needed or wanted to know how to jumpstart a car until right now. Turning to open the driver's door, he froze. A pair of eyes shrouded in black stared back at him through the window.

•••

When the convoy's scout vehicle passed by again, Tony and his team were ready. With the Jeep concealed behind a row of trees, Buster sat in the passenger seat holding the control monitor while Tony manned the RFV unit mounted to the back of the vehicle. Jones lay on his stomach in the underbrush, propped on his elbows with his gun in hand, while Davis maintained his position in a tree on the opposite side of the road. Timing was everything. Their RFV had a range of about fifty meters, so they had only one shot.

As the gray sedan barreled toward them, Tony tracked its silhouette against the dark landscape with the RFV's dish, waiting until it got as close as possible. Then, silently bringing his arm down, he signaled Buster to activate it. The RFV's multi-frequency radio waves instantly stalled the sedan's engine, and it coasted gently to a stop. Silence fell, and then a moment later the ignition whined as the confused driver tried repeatedly to restart the vehicle. Without hesitating, Tony signaled with a shrill whistle, and Davis dropped from the tree beside the car, pulling the driver's door open as Jones immobilized the passenger.

"Nighty-night," Davis chirped as he injected the driver, and then tossed the gun back to Jones. Tony hopped down from the Jeep as Davis and Jones secured their sleeping prey with rope. They hauled the men to the side of the road then searched their pockets for communication and surveillance devices. Davis grabbed an old iPhone from the driver's shirt pocket and looked it over before handing it to Buster. "Damn, it's a first edition. Might actually be worth something to antique dealers."

Buster rolled his eyes. "Probably don't need to worry about it containing anything vital, but keep it in case they try to contact their scouts." He tossed the phone to Tony who then slipped it into his pocket.

"Well, time to play catch up," Tony said. Davis handed him the keys to the sedan, and Tony popped the car's trunk open as Buster switched off the RFV. Davis and Jones dumped the two unconscious men into the trunk. "Buster, you and Jones meet up with Maynard at the rendezvous point. Davis and I'll take their car and catch up with the convoy. Signal me once you're in position."

Buster gave a nod while Jones just yawned. Tony shook his head. His team definitely had its quirks, but they always had his back. His trust in them was the only reason he believed they might actually be able to pull this off.

Without the interference from the RFV, the scout vehicle started immediately. Tony gunned the engine and barreled down the dirt road, punishing the car's shocks with every dip and rise. They had to catch up to the convoy before it could reach the border of Paraguay. Continuing their pursuit into another country would only add to the bureaucracy and paperwork Holt already had to deal with.

"Smells like toe jam and corn chips in here," Davis complained, leaning back and propping his boots up on the dashboard.

Tony sighed. "Suck it up, buttercup." There were worse things than riding in a car that smelled like his high school days. If even one vehicle of that convoy made it to their destination, thousands of people were likely to die.

•••

Allison released the grip on her laptop bag, and it fell to the tile floor with a thud as her body swayed from shock. "What?" she whispered. She had just stepped into the entrance of her agency's headquarters in Los Angeles when Jenkins called. "How?"

"We're not sure, but Benny's positive it was Aldo. Somehow they managed to fool airport security and customs to get him out of the country," Jenkins replied, his voice calm.

How? How could he be so calm knowing Aldo had been taken to Argentina? How did he expect her to be calm? How were they going to get him back? And what if that horrible man experimented on Aldo before they could reach him? She turned, leaning her shoulder against the marble walls of the foyer for support.

"Stop. I know what you're thinking," Jenkins said with a sigh. "Don't go assuming the worst before it even happens. Benny's been instructed to keep eyes on him, so I'll have more information soon. Besides, don't you think Aldo has earned our confidence in him? The kid's held up a heck of a lot better than most scholar types I know."

Kid? Aldo was no kid. He had handled everything thrown at him when most people would have curled into a corner and cried. That was what she wanted to do right now.

"He's tougher than you think," Jenkins continued.

A tear slid down her cheek. "I know… it's just…"

"Don't worry. My team and I will do everything we can to get him back. Just promise me one thing."

She swallowed, trying to clear the lump in her throat so she could speak as her eyes blinked back more tears. "What?" she asked, her voice breaking.

"Stop hesitating," he said quietly. "You regret not telling him everything, don't you? So, the next time you see him, don't worry about all the *what ifs* and just be honest." Jenkins sighed again. "You know I'm not the most religious man, but I don't see how a God as loving as you believe He is could punish you for being in love with a good man like Aldo. And if God's going to hold your religions over your heads and kick you out of Paradise or whatever, then maybe Paradise isn't for you. I personally would rather spend eternity in Hell with the love of my life than be alone in Heaven."

Allison's chuckled weakly and wiped another tear from her face. "Thanks for that, Reverend Jenkins."

"Don't give up before you even take the first step. You promise me that and I'll do everything I can to make sure you get the chance… Well, we'll do everything we can to get Aldo back whether you promise me or not, but you know what I mean."

Having already found her resolve during the long flight from DC, she said, "I promise." Her superiors would no doubt be disapproving. She might even lose her job, but she could not imagine a life without Aldo in it. She still wasn't sure how they'd work out the differences in their religions, but she had faith God would show them the path if they met Him halfway.

"Good. I'll call you the moment I hear anything."

Slipping her cell phone back into her purse, she pulled out a small mirror to check the state of her face. Not ready to have a discussion about her love life with her boss, she removed as much evidence as she could with a tissue. Then taking several deep breaths, she bent to pick up her laptop bag and headed down the long hallway toward Brother Benson's office. The marble walls and tile floor echoed with each step she took, giving the illusion of companionship. Their stark white purity had always felt inviting before, but today they seemed to enclose around her in an oppressive hardness.

Stopping before a heavy walnut door, she took another deep breath and knocked.

"Come," called Brother Benson's voice.

She pushed the door open to find Brother Benson seated behind his desk, Brother Evans in one of the chairs opposite him.

"Sister Gillespie, it's about time you arrived." Brother Benson stood to shake her hand then gestured to the other armchair positioned in front of his desk. She set her bag down and shook Brother Evans' hand before taking her seat. "Has there been any update on the situation with Mr. Lombardi?"

The news about Aldo still fresh, she bit the inside of her lip to keep her emotions in check. Nodding, she cleared her throat then said, "Yes, I just got a call from Commander Jenkins. The professor and his men have taken Mr. Lombardi to Argentina. He's not sure how they were able to get him out of the country, but his team is tracking him as we speak."

Brother Benson and Brother Evans exchanged a look, and then Brother Benson sighed. "It seems pretty clear they plan to interrogate him, using unsavory means no less." He looked up, holding Allison's gaze until she couldn't help bouncing one knee in nervousness. "Despite your assurances that Mr. Lombardi has not been privy to any information concerning Mr. Summers' whereabouts or our agency's involvement, we cannot take that chance. We'll need to be more vigilant than ever."

Allison was silent for a moment. She had always wondered why a Mormon agency would be in charge of keeping a former convict safe but never felt it was appropriate to ask. But now, with so much at stake, she couldn't keep quiet any longer. "Brother Benson, may I ask why we are responsible for Mr. Summers' safety and not protective services?"

"What do you mean?"

"Well, Mr. Summers' unique circumstances seem unrelated to the church, so I don't understand why we are even involved, other than the fact that keeping an innocent man safe is the right thing to do."

"And that's just it, isn't it?" Brother Evans answered. "It's the right thing to do, so we're doing it. Besides, the directive comes from higher up, so I see no reason to question it."

Allison nodded slowly. "I see." *So, you don't know either.* Over the last year, she had suspected as much. The more she talked to Mr. Summers and the more time she spent with Aldo, the more she realized that her superiors had no clue what was really going on. All they seemed to care about was following orders. *Well, I care.* About Mr. Summers and Aldo, about the bio-weapons headed for New York, about Septem Montes, everything. And if they weren't going to give her answers, she knew someone who could.

•••

Aldo slowly scooted backward, his eyes never leaving the face in the window, and pressed himself against the center console. Even if he managed to escape through the van's side door, his legs still weren't cooperating. Unarmed and trapped, his mind raced.

The driver's door opened, and the shrouded face peered inside. Aldo reached for the first thing he could find and chucked it at the man. The disposable cup bounced harmlessly off his arm. The man looked down where the cup lay on the floor mat, and then back up at Aldo. Slowly, he brought his hand up and held one finger to his mouth hidden under the black hood.

What? Who are you, and why do you want me to be quiet? If either of them sounded the alarm, the others would surely come running. When the man continued to hold his finger to his mask, Aldo slowly nodded.

Then he reached below his chin and lifted the mask, exposing his face up to his eyebrows. Black paint encircled brown eyes and a full auburn beard and mustache obscured his mouth. "Mr. Lombardi, I'm here to get you out," the man whispered. "Can you move?"

"W-who are you?"

"NSA. Part of Tony's team. Name's Benny." He glanced over his shoulder then back at Aldo. "I'll tell you more, but we need to move." He pulled the mask back over his face then held his hand out to Aldo.

"My legs are still numb," Aldo warned, moving back into the driver's seat. Benny nodded and helped him out of the van. While Aldo held onto his shoulders for support, Benny quietly closed the van's door then knelt down and hoisted Aldo onto his back. With careful steps, Benny walked into the surrounding darkness.

When they were about fifty yards from the compound, Benny set Aldo down, leaning him against a tree. After removing his mask, he said, "My bike's just ahead. Think you can make it?"

"I'll have to. I'm not going back there."

Benny smiled. "Can't blame you, but we'll have you back to Sierra de la Ventana before you know it. Good thing, too. I'm on breakfast duty today."

Aldo continued to flex his hands and feet, slowly regaining strength in his limbs. When Benny offered his hand again, Aldo was able to pull himself to standing, but another piggyback ride was required. While his legs could finally bear his weight again, running was a different matter. Aldo wondered if he'd ever be able to run again.

Benny stumbled on the rocks and tree roots in the darkness as they made their way down the mountain. Aldo couldn't help glancing over his shoulder occasionally to make sure no one was behind them. He hadn't seen or heard Applebee's men since they'd left the compound, but he knew they were still looking for him. Applebee made it clear he wasn't about to let Aldo escape alive. Not when he suspected what Aldo knew. The journal in his room at Dr. Knight's house was all the evidence Applebee needed to know the secrets Aldo could be hiding.

"Damn it," Aldo hissed.

Benny skidded to a stop, dirt and rocks rolling down the hillside. "What?" He looked around them as though expecting to find them surrounded.

"We need to go back," Aldo said.

Benny set him down then turned to face him. "Why? What happened?"

"They have my notebook."

Benny cocked an eyebrow at him. "Your notebook? You want to go back for your notebook."

"I know it sounds ludicrous, but I really need to get that notebook back. It's the whole reason we're in this mess."

"What do you mean?"

"The reason Commander Jenkins had me infiltrate the SDA Church was for the information in that notebook. It's contains everything I learned while I was imprisoned at Dr. Knight's estate."

"Then if they have it, they already know what you learned."

"Well, that's the thing. From what I overheard, they seem to have an *idea* of what I know, but not everything. If they already knew everything, why bother bringing me all the way to Argentina? Well, other than to experiment on me."

Benny stared at him. "Experiment?" He shook his head and sighed. "Look, the chances of the two of us going in and making it back out alive with your notebook are slim to none."

Aldo knew Benny was right, but he was also sure that returning to the pope empty-handed would render the whole mission a failure.

"Come on. We'll need to enlist the help of some friends." Benny knelt down and hoisted Aldo back up, hooking his arms under Aldo's legs to support him as they continued their trek down the hillside. "The rest of my team's keeping tabs on another Fifth Reich camp, but taking out this compound just jumped to the top of the priority list. We'll have to sit tight though. It'll take them a couple hours to get here." He weaved through the trees as though he knew exactly which direction to go. "In the meantime, we'll get you some food and water and see if we can't get those legs working."

•••

Allison took the stairs down to the basement where her office was tucked into one corner. Rarely used after she was assigned to watch Aldo six years earlier, the small room consisted of a desk and chair, the only decorations a framed picture of her family and a potted plant no one apparently bothered to water. She pulled out her laptop and set it on the desk to boot up while she connected it to the secure lines running into the room along the ceiling. While she could call Mr. Summers on her laptop from just about anywhere, she only did so when connected to a secure network, like the one in her office or at the NSA's headquarters.

After dialing, she entered her code when prompted, and then waited for the line to connect. A moment later, Mr. Summers' face came into view. "Good morning," she said, relieved to see him looking well. He seemed just as he had the last time she had seen him, his graying hair still full, his eyes bright with wisdom. "Well, I guess it's afternoon now."

"Quite all right. You've had a busy day so far."

You have no idea. Well, actually maybe you do. "Do you have some time? I need to go over some recent developments with you."

"Why don't we start with the questions you have," Mr. Summers replied. "I can see they're weighing on your mind."

Her forced smile faded. She never could get anything past him. He always seemed one step ahead of her. Soon after being assigned as his contact, she began a personal game to see if she could surprise him, but she'd had to admit defeat within the first year. "So, you know about Aldo."

On the screen, his expression turned somber, and he nodded. "Both the situation with Aldo and the bio-weapons are tenuous, but I have faith in Commander Jenkins and his team."

She nodded and smiled weakly. "Have you had any new premonitions?" she asked, hoping he'd seen Aldo safe and sound.

"Nothing specific, but I believe one of my earlier predictions will be coming true soon."

"Which one?"

"If you remember a year or so ago, I predicted that someone special would come forward and make the members of the SDA Church aware of the secret actions of their leaders. The pieces are finally falling into place, and that person will soon bring the information forward."

"What will that mean for Septem Montes?"

Mr. Summers tilted his head in thought. "Hmm, it's hard to say how people will react, particularly large groups of people, but if enough members care about the truth, much needed changes will start to happen within the SDA Church.

How those changes will affect the Catholic Church's plans, I can't say. We'll have to wait and see." He folded his hands in front of him, his gaze piercing into her through the monitor. "Now, what's on your mind?"

Allison sighed. "I'm just feeling rather lost. Like I've been working toward a goal for so long without knowing what that goal really is."

"I see. So you want to know about my involvement with your church."

She stared at him and chuckled. "I'm an open book, I see. Yes, my superiors don't seem to know or care about the circumstances, so long as they follow orders. But it seems odd to me how we would come to handle your protection instead of a government agency. I feel like the church is keeping things from me."

"Your frustration is understandable," Mr. Summers replied. "I've been there myself, in fact. So, it's not just you. The church has its own agenda, and historically it hasn't been the most forthcoming with its members. That is why the men within the LDS Church are able to join the priesthood even when they have no knowledge of counseling or ministry. The church expects them to do as they're told without question." He sighed. "That expectation has become so ingrained, it's common for people to approach members of the church and expect them to give up their possessions and volunteer their time simply because they are asked."

"But what's wrong with helping thy neighbor?"

"Nothing," Mr. Summers replied. "Giving of yourself is commendable but doing so without determining the truth behind the request is naïve. Church members also practice discrimination, choosing to avoid involvement with those they deem sinners. In that, they are similar to the Seventh-day Adventists in that way."

Allison hated to admit it, but it was true. She had seen such behavior in her own ward. A teenage girl who found herself pregnant came back to church looking for support and forgiveness, only to be met with harsh rejection. It broke Allison's heart that Christians could preach about the unconditional love of Christ yet be so prejudiced. She joined the agency hoping to help correct such hypocrisy.

"They go through the temple ceremonies," Mr. Summers continued, "and receive their ordination to the Melchizedek Priesthood and are called to positions within the church without putting any thought or effort into the reasons why."

"They aren't nurturing their own faith," Allison mused.

"Yes, true faith comes from struggling for an answer and believing even when you may not get that answer. You can't nurture faith simply by following orders."

"Why stay then? How can you trust us to keep you safe? Wouldn't a government agency be better able to protect you from the SDA Church?"

Mr. Summers sighed. "It's kind of a long story. I have…certain ties to the LDS Church. And don't get me wrong; I have nothing against the church itself. I'm still trying to get my temple recommend card reinstated, but there have been obstacles and inconsistencies." He leaned back in his chair. "As you know it all started with my trial. But to truly answer your question, I should probably explain how certain events played out."

Allison nodded. "I might be able to meet you in the next day or two." She would have to sneak out to ensure she wasn't followed, and given the situation, Brother Benson certainly would not approve her making the trip up to Northern California to Mr. Summers' home.

"What's wrong with now?" he asked puzzled.

"Are you sure you're okay discussing your past over a video call like this?" Even with the secure line, she didn't want him to feel anxious.

"Not to worry, my dear. I'd rather you stay safe."

She nodded. "If you're sure."

Mr. Summers smiled. "Of course. Now, let's see… after I left the SDA Church, I felt lost. Religion was still a big part of my life, but I could no longer believe in the church I'd been raised in. Soon after, I discovered the Church of Jesus Christ of Latter-day Saints. The genuine kindness of the people I first met drew me to the LDS Church, and I decided to join. I met my wife about that same time."

"Wait, you're married?" She'd known him for six years and visited him at his home several times over that period. How was she only now learning such an important detail?

He chuckled. "Yes, my family's been kept hidden for their protection—which is why you were not informed of their existence."

She wanted to ask about his children—how many he had and if any of them showed signs of the DNA manipulation he'd experienced during the Toddler Program. Instead, she said, "I see." Then she gestured for him to continue.

"During my wife's and my courtship, it became clear that I would be indicted for a white-collar crime I never committed."

"The bookkeeper for your company falsified your accounting records and destroyed the original sets, right?" Allison interjected.

"There were numerous others involved in the intrigue, but yes, she was bribed by the former president of the SDA World Church to frame me, though at the time I wasn't aware of their plan. I knew they weren't happy and they had been using various methods to harass me for years prior to that, but I didn't realize they would use my company."

She shook her head. "To go to such lengths just for a vendetta."

"Well, it wasn't just revenge they sought for what they viewed as my betrayal. They feared I would use my skills and knowledge to help other organizations. Framing me was the perfect way to make sure no one ever believed anything I might say to them."

"But you served only 47 months in prison. Not that long if their goal was to keep you out of the way."

Mr. Summers shook his head. "No, I don't think they ever planned to keep me locked up for good. They would've had to frame me for something much worse to make that happen. My sentence was just part of their character assassination. I'm sure you're aware of just how hard life after prison is for ex-convicts. They struggle to meet even their basic needs, like housing and employment. Unfortunately, it's not just Mormons and Adventists who don't like to associate with ex-convicts."

Allison had heard most of the story from him before, but mainly just the basic facts. This was the first time he had opened up about the details behind his incarceration.

"If they assassinated my character, they wouldn't have to worry about locking me up, because no one would support a man believed to be a criminal. Knowing this, Frogburger used members of the LDS Church I'd just become part of, my new family if you will, as a way of driving the final nail."

Her brothers and sisters in the church were involved in prosecuting an innocent man? "But how… why would they?"

Mr. Summers gave her a reassuring smile. "Let me explain. Most of the Mormons involved with my trial were not aware they were being manipulated. Yet, knowing what I know now, it's too astonishing to be mere coincidence. They really wanted to hit me where it hurt the most, by using my new religious family, and as I later discovered, my own relatives to defame me."

"What do you mean?"

"Surprisingly, I'm related to over 40 of the Mormons directly or indirectly involved in my trial and the events leading up to it."

Allison gasped. "What? How do you…" Her voice trailed off as he quirked an eyebrow at her. "Right. Genealogical records."

He nodded. "That and DNA testing. When I first became suspicious of the LDS Church's involvement, I did some research. The more people I investigated, the more I learned just how many of them were related to me." He sighed. "Perhaps Frogburger never thought I would find out, but knowing how important family is to me, he must have gotten a sick satisfaction from watching my own relatives convict and incarcerate me."

A tear slid down Allison's cheek. "How do you not hate us?"

"Oh, my dear. The church cannot be judged based on the corrupt actions of a handful of its members. Besides, as I said, many of them did so unknowingly." He sighed. "But I will admit it's been frustrating. There are certain men within the church who have used me and my family as a stepping-stone for their own gain. Because of their actions, my family is still being denied the right to be sealed together in the temple, even 20 years later." He was silent for a moment, his eyes staring off somewhere beyond the monitor. "There were financial losses as well, money paid for services that were never rendered, but the most hurtful is the church's rejection of our wish to be sealed together for all eternity. What family wouldn't want the assurance they would never be separated? But the church seems to favor only those accepted into their exclusive club." He fell silent, then met Allison's gaze. "I'm sorry."

She shook her head. "No, I understand. I've dealt with that myself." As the only female in her agency, and unmarried to boot, Allison had to pull teeth to even get an interview. She gave a forced laugh. "Funny how being unmarried at 26 is considered so preposterous in the church."

Mr. Summers nodded. "My wife and I weren't even sure we should get married."

"What do you mean?"

"Well, the SDA Church's harassment had escalated. Their most direct and persistent method was using an attorney to demand financial compensation and threaten lawsuits, but some of them turned violent—like the time they broke into my home and murdered my dogs."

Allison gasped. "That's… How horrible."

Mr. Summers nodded. "So, you can understand why I was reluctant to get married and possibly subject someone I love to these attacks. We ultimately decided to get married after a friend introduced us to our stake president at the time, Marcus Tuttle. He encouraged us to get married and start a family. He even recommended we live at a campground within his stake boundary so he could continue to use his authority to help us." He sighed. "I know now that his offer of help was only so he could advance his own position, both politically and within the church. His *help* didn't come in the capacity of his position as stake president. He positioned himself as our agent, claiming he'd be able to use more aggressive measures to protect us. And in the end, we paid him thousands of dollars only to have him turn his back on us."

Mr. Summers ran a hand through his hair. "Ambitious men, driven by ego and in positions of authority within any religious organization, often misuse their power for their own advancement under the guise of helping those with spiritual and physical needs. Marcus Tuttle was no exception. He saw the potential to use me and the information I had to gain influence with the president of the SDA Church, as well as to enter certain political circles in Salt Lake City. He promised to help me build a company so I could support my growing family," he gestured with his hand, "for an additional fee, of course. And he recommended shady investment opportunities. He advised me to consult with attorneys who asked bizarre questions which I later came to realize were attempts to have me investigated by the LDS Church's Strengthening Church Members Committee."

What? While the name of the committee sounded beneficent, she knew it was comprised of retired Mormon federal agents who worked behind the scenes to investigate members suspected of heresy.

Mr. Summers shook his head. "My fault for being so trusting."

"But trusting someone, particularly a presumably respected church official, isn't a crime. But this Marcus Tuttle's actions were. Did you ever file a police report on him?"

"No, he became impossible to find. Every time I called his office, the receptionist just kept telling me he was no longer available. After I was arrested, I tried to get the magistrate to bring Tuttle in for questioning since we paid him so much money to help us with the indictment, but the magistrate insisted he didn't need to speak with Tuttle."

Allison clenched her teeth. She'd heard stories of corruption within religions and political organizations but had never known anyone directly affected by it until meeting Mr. Summers. She couldn't believe the reach of the SDA Church to so thoroughly silence Mr. Summers.

"He did have his man call me after I'd been arrested to ask if I wanted him to use the Presidential estoppel he had secured from the White House. But after careful consideration, I decided it would be more advantageous to allow the indictment process to continue so I could one day resolve the whole issue in a federal court. For that reason, I didn't use the estoppel to prevent a trial."

Summers continued. "You see, the indictment process allowed the federal court to get involved, taking the matter outside the hands of the church. It also helped put a stop to the attacks by the men and women working for the SDA Church. However, the drawback, obviously, is that I ended up losing the case and being sentenced to prison." He shuffled through the papers to the right of the monitor on his desk. "I've uploaded a list of the Mormons involved with my trial, the events leading up to it, and my time in prison onto my database on the Dark Internet. It lists their names, how they are related to me, and each of their roles in my trial. I have a feeling you'll need it soon."

Knowing Mr. Summers' *feelings* always ended up coming true, Allison made a note to gather as much information about the Mormons' involvement with his trial as she could, starting with the list he had uploaded. "So, if these 40 Mormons were manipulated by the SDA Church to walk you through the justice system, why are we now protecting you from the SDA Church? I mean, even if they were manipulated unknowingly, they would still believe you to be guilty and pass off the information you have regarding the SDA Church's movements behind the scenes as simple conspiracy theories."

"Well, your agency isn't so much protecting me or my family as it is protecting the SDA Church. After realizing its members had been used, the Mormons wanted to keep an eye on the SDA Church in case it decided to meddle with its own members again. Keeping tabs on me helps the Mormons keep tabs on the SDA Church. That's why when I suggested you be allowed to get involved with Aldo and his research, your superiors had no reason to object. It also acts as insurance. I'm sure you're aware of the LDS Church's history and how they've covered up certain events that proved damaging to their public image."

"Like the Mountain Meadows Massacre?"

Mr. Summers nodded. "Yes. For one. There have been other scandals and cases of abuse within the church, all of them the fault of individual members and not related to the church as a whole. However, there was the fact that they performed the temple ceremonies to baptize and endow Adolf Hitler, and later seal him to Eva Braun and his parents." He sighed. "Keeping such scandals under wraps is necessary to uphold the church's public image, so of course they'd want to hide the fact their members lied, were bribed, and abused the justice system to put me in prison." He leaned back in his chair. "For now, all I can really do is be patient and try to get the truth into the hands of the people who most need it. You'll help me, won't you?"

Despite her frustration at what he'd been subjected to, she smiled. "Yes, of course. I believe in the genuine good of my brothers and sisters and bringing to justice those who would prey upon that goodness is why I joined the agency."

Chapter Twelve | The PROPHECY

Argentina
April 2013

Aldo sat on the ground beside Benny's dirt bike, stretching the weakness from his muscles. After taking a couple of gulps from the NSA agent's canteen and devouring a smashed yet still edible protein bar, he was finally feeling more awake. Despite the darkness, Benny had thrown a camouflage tarp over the bike after radioing his team for back-up, and then climbed a nearby tree to keep a lookout for Applebee's pursuing men. They had been waiting for his team to show up for over an hour, but as dawn approached, Benny saw no sign of them. Benny's plan would be more effective with the cover of darkness, and they were quickly running out of time.

When he heard a low rumble, Aldo scrambled under the tarp as Benny had directed in case Applebee's men found them. Benny whistled and slid down the tree's trunk, jumping the last few feet to the ground. "They're here." Benny tapped Aldo's shoulder before lifting the tarp. Three dirt bikes identical to Benny's approached, the riders all clad in black from head to toe. "About time you got here, Reeves," Benny said as the first rider cut his engine and pulled off his helmet.

"We hauled ass as fast as we could," Reeves grumbled. "This better be important. There's a good chance that camp knows they were being watched. They could pack up and disappear by the time we get back."

"Probably tipped off."

"By who?" Reeves asked.

Benny turned to point at Aldo. "By the same men who're after him. We don't have a lot of time. We've got to take out their lab before they realize Mr. Lombardi had help."

Aldo listened quietly as Benny, Reeves, and the two other riders who he learned were called Chester and Dogmeat reviewed Benny's plan.

Chester shook his head. "Not gonna work. Surveillance will pick up our movements and we'll be surrounded in seconds."

"No surveillance," Benny replied. "Not that I could see anyway. And I watched them for a good half hour or so. They only mobilized their men when they realized Mr. Lombardi had disappeared." He turned to Aldo. "Nice move by the way, using your wheelchair as a diversion."

Aldo blushed, embarrassed to know he'd had an audience, yet astonished to be praised by such an elite agent.

"Any other objections?" Benny asked. The other three men all shook their heads. "Then let's move out. We only have one hour until first light." They threw camouflage tarps over each of their bikes after loading the pockets of their black cargo pants with various weapons and tools. When they started up the hill, Aldo followed.

"Whoa. Where do you think you're going?" Dogmeat asked, throwing his arm out to stop Aldo in his tracks. "This operation's gonna be tricky enough without civilians getting in the way. Not to mention if you get caught, all this'll be for nothing."

Benny stepped forward. "I already went over this, Dogmeat. Mr. Lombardi's the only one who knows what his notebook looks like. He'll stay hidden beyond the tree line until we give the all clear."

Dogmeat peered down at Aldo, his eyes shining eerily against the matte black face paint. "This notebook of yours really worth risking your life over?"

Aldo nodded. "It's the whole reason I went undercover to begin with. It could be the evidence we need to finally prosecute them."

Dogmeat gave him a satisfied smirk then reached into his pocket and pulled out a small handgun. "Thought you were just a historian." Placing the gun in Aldo's hand, he said, "You might need this."

"Oh, um, but I don't…"

Benny smacked his shoulder. "You never know. Better safe than sorry." He jogged up the hill to lead the way. "Come on. We're short on time."

They trudged up the hill, the four NSA agents quickly leaving Aldo in their wake. When Aldo insisted he return to the laboratory compound with them, Benny warned him he'd have to keep up. Forcing his legs to move faster, Aldo quickly ran out of breath as the blood vessels in his legs struggled to supply his muscles with oxygen. The ascent up the mountain took much longer than the descent, and by the time they could see the compound's flood lights through the trees, dawn was mere minutes away.

Benny signaled Aldo to stay low to the ground as the rest of the team moved closer, spreading out to approach the compound from different directions. Four against ten definitely put Benny and his crew at a disadvantage, but Aldo knew they probably faced these kinds of odds all the time. Crawling through the underbrush on his elbows until he was within a yard of the tree line, Aldo stopped to survey the surroundings. The van still sat where they'd left it on the gravel lot with the body of the dead man lying next to it. Aldo's mangled wheelchair had been tossed to the side, and several of Applebee's men milled about the entrance to the building.

A loud rumble erupted from beside the building, and an ATV with two men emerged, rolling to a stop at the entrance. One of the guards yelled something to them and they roared off down the drive.

How are they going to take out all of the men if they are still scattered? Benny's plan was based on the assumption that after enough time had passed, the men would abandon their search on foot and regroup, waiting until dawn to begin their hunt anew. But this didn't seem to be the case. Aldo counted five men at the entrance. With the two who'd just left on the ATV, that meant there were another three unaccounted for. Who knew how many could be still inside the laboratory—assistants and technicians who wouldn't have assembled in the lot when they first discovered Aldo had disappeared.

Aldo wiped the sweat from his palms and gripped the handle of the gun tighter as his pulse hammered in his ears. He kept his gaze on the front of the building, waiting for a signal as the seconds ticked slowly by. After an eternity, a loud pop echoed around the clearing, and the flood lights went dark. Immediately, several men started shouting, demanding in Spanish to know what was happening.

Aldo blinked repeatedly, trying to adjust his eyes quickly, but he heard the movements of Benny and the others before he could see them. Several thuds vibrated the ground as the bodies of the five guards fell nearby. Silence followed. Reviewing the plan in his head, he knew the team was now making its way into the laboratory. He checked his watch, waiting until three minutes had passed before he crawled slowly toward the van. Praying his notebook was among the bags and luggage he'd seen piled to one side in the back of the van, he pulled himself alongside it. Then peered around the back to make sure the coast was clear before opening the doors. He climbed inside and pulled the doors until they were just barely ajar before turning his attention to the bags. He tucked the gun into his waistband and reached for the small flashlight Benny had given him.

Aldo did not see his suitcase among the bags, but started digging through each one, tossing them aside when he came up empty-handed. He checked the floor of the van where his wheelchair had been secured. Nothing. Moving toward the front, he checked the backseat and then the driver seat. Nothing. He was just about to check the passenger seat and glove box when he heard shouts from across the gravel lot. Peeking through the passenger side window, he saw Applebee running toward him.

Damn it! What now? Ducking behind the backseat, Aldo froze as Applebee ripped the driver's door open and tossed a bag into the backseat before starting the engine. Muttering curses under his breath, Applebee threw the gearshift into drive then peeled out on the gravel as he did a U-turn and headed for the road.

Without hesitating, Aldo grabbed the bag Applebee had thrown into the backseat and dove out the back doors as they swung open from the force. He hit the gravel hard, his body sliding along his left side to a stop as Applebee gunned the van and bolted down the road.

"Shit! Bastard got away," Chester said from across the gravel lot.

"Mr. Lombardi! Are you okay?" Benny ran toward him and gently helped him to his feet. Aldo could feel pebbles imbedded in the skin of his left arm and the burn of road rash along his hip. "What in the hell were you thinking? Didn't I tell you to wait for my signal?"

Dogmeat laughed, a hoarse barking sound, and Aldo wondered if that was the inspiration for his moniker. "You actually thought he'd listen?"

"Sorry," Aldo said quietly, still clutching the bag. "When the men split up, I kinda panicked."

"What? Didn't think we could pull it off?" Reeves asked.

Benny sighed. "Well?" He gestured to Aldo's left arm, the scrapes along his skin just beginning to ooze. "Was it worth it? Did you manage to find your notebook?"

Aldo squatted then set the bag on the ground and unzipped it. On top of a stack of documents was his notebook.

•••

The old cell phone in Tony's pocket buzzed and he fished it out, narrowly avoiding the tree stump at the side of the road. Tossing it to Davis, he asked, "What's it say?"

"*¿Dónde estás?* " Davis read aloud. The phone buzzed again. "*¿Los localizaste?* "

"Tell them *no* and that we're returning to the convoy now," Tony replied. Davis typed the message, and then set the phone on the center console. "Any word from Buster yet?"

Davis shook his head. "Not yet. You know what a slow driver Jones is."

"Well, not everyone is as reckless as you. Still, they better get there soon. The convoy's quickly approaching the rendezvous point. We're running out of time."

The empty soda cans at their feet rattled as Tony hit another pothole. Holding onto the *Oh, Shit* handle above his door, Davis suddenly burst out laughing.

"What? What's so funny?" Tony sure couldn't see anything humorous about their current situation.

"Just, I bet those two in the trunk are getting the crap beat out of them from your driving. I'm just glad I got something to hold onto."

"Yeah, poor bastards," Tony muttered. "Their luck totally went to shit." After slamming them around inside the trunk, Tony's team would haul the men and anyone else they managed to capture alive back to HQ for interrogation. Even if they somehow managed to escape, Tony was certain their mafia boss would never forgive their failure in being captured.

Seeing the glow of headlights in the distance, Tony gunned the engine, pushing the sedan as fast as he dared with the treacherous terrain. Daybreak was quickly approaching, and their covert attack would be blown if Jones didn't get his ass in gear and meet up with Maynard and the others in time. Tony hadn't heard from Benny and his team in several hours, and he could only hope that no news was good news.

•••

Aldo clutched the bag to his chest and slowly stood up. Before he could thank the team for helping him retrieve his notebook, Dogmeat laughed wickedly.

"Now that that's outta the way…" He extended his arm, and Aldo heard a click as Dogmeat pressed a button on the device in his hand. Benny immediately launched himself at Aldo, knocking him backwards into the trees, and their bodies slid down the hill. A moment later, a deafening thud knocked the breath from Aldo's lungs as brilliant light illuminated the forest. Then, just as quickly, the light dissipated, leaving only an eerie ringing echo.

"You asshat!" Benny yelled. "Why the hell would you detonate it without warning? You could've killed us."

"But I didn't," Dogmeat replied, still smiling.

"Doesn't matter, Dumbshit." Chester smacked him upside the head. "There's no do-over for shit like that."

"I'm surprised Jenkins hasn't court-martialed him for that kinda shit yet," Reeves muttered.

"Hey, I was just following the plan," Dogmeat said with a shrug. "You did say to blow up the compound once everyone was out and we made sure the nerd had his notebook."

"Don't try to put this on me," Benny ground out as he pulled himself off the top of Aldo. "And this *nerd* ," he held out a hand and hoisted Aldo to his feet, "just happens to work for the pope."

Dogmeat stared down at Aldo for a moment. "What's he doing out here then?"

"Trying not to become a human guinea pig," Aldo said quietly. "So I appreciate the assistance. Though a warning would be nice next time."

"Ha! Next time, huh? You planning to get caught by these jackasses again?"

"Not if I can help it."

Dogmeat turned to Benny. "See? It's fine." Without waiting for a response, he started down the hill toward the hidden dirt bikes.

Benny watched him leave, and then shook his head with a sigh. "Tony's much better at dealing with his bullshit than I am. Still, he needs to learn a damn lesson." Looking at Chester and Reeves, he said, "I'm putting this incident in my report, so if Jenkins questions you, just be honest."

"Will do," Reeves replied. Chester nodded then started down the hill after Dogmeat.

With another sigh, Benny turned to Aldo. "Sorry about that. Are you okay?"

"Can't lie. I've been better."

Benny chuckled. "Don't doubt that. Come on. Let's get back to base." As he turned to follow his team, Aldo grabbed his arm.

"What about the men on the ATV? And I think there might be a few more unaccounted for."

"Chester sniped them soon after they left the compound. And we didn't see any others before cutting the power." He shrugged. "And thanks to Dogshit over there," he tipped his head down the hill where Aldo could just barely still see the other men's outlines, "if there really are more men out there, they won't be coming back here." He gestured up the hill toward the compound's ruins. "We put tracking devices on all of their vehicles before we took out the guards—just in case—so we'll check for any other active beacons besides that van when we get back to base."

Knowing they would be able to see Applebee's location gave Aldo a small measure of relief, but he couldn't shake the fear that he'd forever be hunted by the SDA Church even if they caught Applebee. Given the amount of money the Comradeship of the Three Woes must have dumped into that research facility, they wouldn't take losing a test subject very well.

With the bag looped over his shoulders, Aldo held onto Benny's waist with his good arm. Benny had field dressed Aldo's injured arm before they left for the NSA's base at Sierra de la Ventana. Aldo had never ridden on a dirt bike before, and Benny's agile control of the bike as they weaved through the trees terrified him.

The sun was already well above the horizon by the time they arrived back at base. Aldo's butt ached from straddling the motorcycle's seat, but he wasn't about to complain. Seeing the hovering drones, armed guards, and camouflaged buildings made him feel truly safe for the first time in months. Following the team inside, he immediately asked Benny to use the phone.

"Hold your horses," Benny replied. "We've got a few things to take care of first."

"Like what?" What could be more important than hearing Allison's voice right now?

"Well, getting your arm properly treated for one. And I can't authorize you to talk to anyone until Jenkins gives the okay. Even though we all made it back safe and sound, the situation's still pretty iffy. We might have to wait a few days for things to die down."

"A few days?" Aldo asked, deflated. "You're kidding."

"Nope. Afraid not. Come on. Let's get you to the medic then we'll call Jenkins."

Aldo followed him through the maze of corridors to a small infirmary where an older woman with horn-rimmed glasses brutally scraped gravel and dirt from the wounds on his left arm and hip with a stiff bristled brush. Benny wished him luck, and then made his escape, only returning once the screaming had stopped. Benny set his laptop on the table beside Aldo's bed and dialed Jenkins.

"Just glad everyone's okay," Jenkins said with a sigh after Benny gave him a rundown of the night's events. "Submit your official report as soon as you can. I'd like to put Douglas on suspension, but I'm afraid we need all the help we can get right now to take out the remaining Fifth Reich camps. But at least with your report, we'll have everything documented so we can deal with it later."

"Yes, sir," Benny replied.

Jenkins turned his attention back to Aldo. "I'm sorry you had to go through that, Aldo. But I'm glad you're okay. It was risky going back for the notebook, and I'm not sure Benny made the right decision in letting you go. Why was it so important?"

"It has all of the information I learned while I was being held captive in Loma Linda. But I'm sorry. Because I let it out of my possession, they now know what I was researching."

Jenkins thought for a moment. "Is this your doodling notebook?"

"It's not doodling," Aldo said defensively. "It's shorthand."

"Whatever." Jenkins smiled. "I don't think you need to be too concerned about them being privy to your research notes. I used to work in the encryption department, and even I couldn't read your shorthand."

"Oh…" Aldo wasn't sure whether to be relieved or offended.

"I'd like to go over the information you collected, but it'll have to wait. I'll have Benny get us on another video call in the next day or two. In the meantime, get some rest. I'll update Allison on your situation as well. Is it all right if she contacts your parents for you? She has a way of getting a hold of them, right? Unfortunately, we'll have to tie up some loose ends before you'll be allowed to return to the States."

Aldo nodded. "That's fine. And Allison has their number." He had a moment of panic that Allison might let slip to his parents where he'd been the last few months, but aside from his father, Aldo hadn't met anyone better at dealing with his mother than Allison.

"Benny will take a full report of your account of the events, but is there anything else I should be aware of now?"

Aldo recalled the events leading up to when Benny scared the crap out of him by peering in the van's window. Most of it was still hazy, but he did remember what Applebee had said. "Well, I'm not sure anything can be done about it now, but while I was still strapped to the wheelchair in the back of the van, I heard Professor Applebee say that he needed to check if the drug he'd given me last month had taken effect yet."

Jenkins stared at him, the silence drawing out to an uncomfortable length. Aldo had already feared the prognosis of Applebee's experiments, but Jenkins' silence wasn't helping.

"Well, shit," Jenkins said with a sigh. "You're right. If the drug was similar to Transpose, there may be nothing we can do about it now. I'll see if there's anyone who might be able to run some tests and see what we're dealing with." He rubbed his temple. "You're gonna become a pin cushion, I'm afraid."

"Beats the alternative," Aldo replied. He would take the battery of tests he knew were coming over the experiments he'd almost been subjected to at Applebee's lab any day.

Jenkins nodded. "True." His gaze shifted to Benny. "Any word from Tony's and Maynard's teams yet?"

"No, sir. Tony requested radio silence about midnight and hasn't reported back in yet."

"I see. And our tracer on the van?"

"Beacon shows it on course for Buenos Aires."

"All right. File a police report with the Buenos Aires authorities so they'll be on the lookout for it as well. I'll get the necessary paperwork together to arrest Applebee for kidnapping and assault the moment we locate him."

•••

"Are you sitting down?" Jenkins asked, his voice scratchier than the last time he'd called.

Allison dropped into the chair at her desk, clutching her blouse at her chest. *Oh, Lord. No.* Swallowing back the tears already beginning to well in her eyes, she whispered into the phone, "Yes."

"Aldo's safe."

Immediately, the tension throbbing in her shoulders dissipated, and she fell back into the back of the chair. "Really?"

He chuckled. "Yes. Benny and his team rescued him early this morning."

"And…and he's okay?"

"Well, a little banged up, but still in one piece. He asked to talk to you the moment he got back to base. Can't risk it though, so you'll have to wait a couple more days before you can apply the advice I gave you last time. Think you can wait that long?" he teased.

She closed her eyes and released the breath she didn't realize she'd been holding. "No, but I'll have to, won't I?" She'd have to wait even longer before he'd be released to come home. Was this anxious uncertainty what Aldo felt the last six years she'd been keeping him waiting?

"I'll try to make it sooner rather than later, but no guarantees," Jenkins said. "Until Applebee is caught, we can't do anything that might be used to locate Aldo."

"I understand. Any leads on Applebee's location?"

Jenkins sighed. "Traced the van he escaped in to Buenos Aires, but the trail ends there. We found the van abandoned in a parking garage and no trace of Applebee. He most likely had help from Fifth Reich members in the city. I'm working on getting a warrant so we can have the Argentinean authorities arrest him if he tries to leave the country. But just in case, I'd keep contact with Mr. Summers to a minimum."

"I will. And thank you."

"Don't thank me. Our little scholar had almost escaped on his own by the time Benny got to him." Jenkins chuckled. "He even demanded to return to the compound to get his research notes. That boy just keeps on surprising me."

"That was how he charmed me."

"And yet you still waited six years to do anything about it." Jenkins sighed again. "Well, I'll do what I can to get him back to the States as soon as possible. Are you in touch with his parents at all?"

Allison reached into her laptop bag and pulled out the phone she'd purchased the day Aldo was taken to Andrew Knight's house. Knowing his cell phone had most likely been confiscated, she reported the cell phone lost with his mobile carrier and had them assign his number to a new phone. She'd been posing as Aldo to his parents ever since. She didn't like lying to them, but what choice did she have? Tell them their son had been kidnapped and was being held captive at the house of a doctor who may be part of a dangerous secret group within the upper echelons of the Seventh-day Adventist Church? If they even believed her, which she doubted, they'd immediately call the police and everything Aldo had worked toward would be wasted. When Aldo was taken from Dr. Knight's house and Jackson and Lawrence lost track of him, she seriously considered calling the police herself.

"Yes, I am. I'll text them so they don't worry."

"Thanks. Well, I have to get to a meeting, but I'll call you later."

Before he could disconnect the call, Allison said, "Jenkins?"

"Yeah?"

"Thanks again."

He chuckled. "Just doing my job."

•••

Amelia Larson followed Paul Holt into the elevator. She had just arrived at the NSA's headquarters in Washington, D.C. to meet with the head of counter-terrorism in person. With the bio-weapons threat still looming, she needed to fill him in on everything she knew about the buyers and their dangerous ideology. She had covered the basics during a video call with the President, sharing only the information she felt was necessary at the time. Now, with the President's approval to take out the convoy at the NSA team's first opportunity, they needed to focus on gathering evidence necessary to identify and arrest the buyers.

She glanced at the man standing in front of her, his right foot impatiently tapping as the elevator made its ascent. Having only seen him through a video monitor before, she got the impression he was rougher around the edges than she had first thought. Definitely a man with extensive field experience and little tolerance for any signs of weakness. His dark suit had been replaced by khakis and a white polo shirt, as though he was preparing to play a round of golf, not discuss the inner workings of one of the wealthiest and most secretive organizations on the planet.

The elevator doors opened, and she followed him down a hallway to his office. He held the door for her as he gestured to one of the black leather chairs opposite his desk. Rounding his desk, he dropped unceremoniously into his chair and leaned forward, resting his elbows on the desktop. "Well?" he asked.

She remained where she was by the door and quirked an eyebrow at him. The man clearly believed he had more important things to do than discuss whatever information she might have. Her own patience wearing thin, she considered calling Judge Jason and requesting they present their investigation findings to other more receptive parties. He'd seemed so attentive during their video conference, but perhaps only because the President was seated across from him. "I can come back another time if you'd rather get back to your golf game," she replied coolly.

He stared at her for a moment then a slow smile crept across his face. "Nah, golf's not my thing. Rather be fishing to be honest."

Before she could reply, a knock sounded on the door behind her. She turned to see a man of similar build and age standing in the doorway. "Am I interrupting?" he asked, a sly smile playing on his lips.

"Ah, Jenkins. Come in," Holt said. "Ms. Larson, this is my subordinate, Dennis Jenkins. He'll be joining us as he's in charge of the team down in Argentina."

Jenkins held out his hand and she took it. "It's a pleasure, Mr. Jenkins."

"Ah, just Jenkins is fine. It's what everyone calls me. *Mr. Jenkins* just sounds like you're talking about my dad." He closed the office door behind him then took the seat closest to the wall.

"Then please, call me Amelia." She took the chair beside him and set her laptop bag on the floor next to it.

Jenkins smiled and tilted his head at Holt who only grunted. "So, how do you feel about fishing, Amelia?"

Is this his way of breaking the ice? She'd been in hundreds of meetings where the men felt it necessary to overindulge in chitchat, regardless of the topic or urgency. "It's something I did every summer with my father when he was still alive. I haven't been in years though. Why?"

Jenkins shrugged. "No reason. Holt just mentioned it right before I came in, so I was curious." He looked at Holt. "I hope it's all right, but I arranged for Aldo Lombardi to join us on a video call from Argentina. He said he has information that's important to the case, but I haven't had a chance to review it with him yet."

"Information he gathered while being held captive?" Holt asked.

Jenkins nodded. "If it ends up being irrelevant to the matter at hand, I'll arrange to speak with him separately."

"That's fine. What's your schedule like for the rest of the day, Amelia? You care if the meeting runs over?"

Amelia? She looked at Holt for a moment and shook her head. "I have no other plans. My whole reason for coming here was to discuss the information my team learned about the Seventh-day Adventist Church during our investigation into the US versus Summers trial."

"Good." Holt turned back to Jenkins. "What time will he be calling in?"

"I can get him on the line now if you want."

"Might as well. Anything we don't cover during the video call we can go over afterwards."

Nodding, Jenkins stood and crossed the room, sliding apart two wall panels which concealed a large television monitor. After turning the unit on, he dialed and waited for the other end to pick up. A moment later, a young man's face appeared on screen.

"Aldo, how are you feeling?" Jenkins asked.

"Better. Still a bit sore though." He held up his left arm which was wrapped in white bandages.

"Good to hear. Aldo, this is my boss, Paul Holt, the head of the Counter Terrorism Unit," Jenkins said, gesturing to Holt. "And this is special agent Amelia Larson. She was, or rather is, involved with the investigation into the SDA Church that began during Mr. Summers' pre-trial. I wasn't sure if the information you had for us was pertinent to the current bio-weapons situation, but I asked them to be on this call just in case."

"Bio-weapons situation?" Mr. Lombardi asked.

All three of them stared at the young man on screen for a moment before Jenkins said, "Right, you've been out of touch for the last few months. I'll give you the short version. About two days ago, a large shipment of bio-weapons left its lab in Argentina. We're pretty sure it's bound for New York thanks to that note you found at the Fifth Reich camp. And we have reason to believe the buyer is a secret group of bigwigs within the SDA Church."

"The Shmita Advent Rite of Freemasonry?" the young man asked.

"What's that?" Holt replied.

"From what I can tell, it's basically like a Freemason fraternity made up of 66 members with positions in the upper echelons of the church. Most of the church's leaders and members aren't even aware it exists. But then there are many things the Rite has kept secret from the church's members."

"How do you know of it?" Amelia asked.

The young man held up a tattered notebook. "When I was being held at Dr. Knight's estate, he allowed me to have free access to his library. I'm still not sure if that was because he was trying to make me feel like he had nothing to hide or if he thought I would be too incapacitated from their sedatives to actually find anything. But I did find something. It was a journal written in the 1920s by a man who at the time was the scribe for the Advent Rite. He recorded all of the group's discussions and rituals, every change they made to the church's doctrine."

"That's the journal?" Amelia asked, scooting to the edge of her seat. If what Mr. Lombardi said was true, it could be the evidence she needed to arrest several prominent figures within the SDA Church.

Mr. Lombardi shook his head and set the notebook back on his lap. "No. The journal's still in Dr. Knight's house. I was able to transcribe most of it into this notebook though. I would've taken it with me if I'd had the chance but..."

"Did the author mention anything about September eleventh?" Amelia asked, undeterred.

Mr. Lombardi flipped through his notebook. "Nothing about the events that took place in 2001, but September eleventh is the date the Advent Rite teaches in their initiation rituals that Jesus was born."

Knowing that tidbit wasn't something the church currently taught its members, she wondered what other secrets the author wrote about. "You mentioned changes to the church's doctrine. Did he write about any prophecies?"

Mr. Lombardi stared at her blankly for a moment. "Uh, yeah. In fact, most of what was said had to do with a prophecy in some way. The Advent Rite often voted to hide prophecies from members, and the scribe detailed their process of erasing all evidence of them, sometimes over the course of years. The most shocking one to me was their transition from following Ellen White's belief in one God to teaching of a Trinity. Kinda seems like by doing so they eliminated one of the major doctrines that set them apart."

"And that's probably why they did it," Amelia replied. "Can you tell me what some of the other prophecies were?"

Mr. Lombardi looked to Jenkins.

"There's a good chance the SDA Church is planning to use the bio-weapons to bring about one of their prophecies, so whatever information you have could prove important," Mr. Holt interjected.

Amelia glanced at him. His cooperation during the call with the President led her to believe they were similarly minded, and she was beginning to see it was true.

"Right. Well, there was one that predicts the fate of our culture."

"What does it say?" she asked.

"Well, it claims that after two Shmitas—uh, that's 14 years—so, after 14 years have passed following the first attack by Islam, our country would become bait for Muslims around the world who already view us as the Great Satan."

"So, in the next two years," Amelia muttered to herself.

"Is this related to the first attack being nine-eleven?" Holt asked.

She nodded. "What else does it say?"

Mr. Lombardi scanned the notebook on his lap then looked up. "Ellen White predicted that our culture would transform into one driven by every kind of sin and debauchery. From tattoos and piercings to pornography, abortion, gays and lesbians openly being united in marriage, atheism, forced vaccination, fornication and adultery, nationalism, polyandry, foul language, alcohol, eating pork, and every kind of greed and criminal action. Seemed a bit pessimistic to me."

"Yeah, none of that is really outside the norm." Holt sat back in his seat and propped one leg on the opposite knee. "I mean tattoos, crime, pornography, adultery—they've all been around for centuries, and it's not like they're exclusive to our country either. Many other nations have an equally sordid culture. Maybe not as much in the public eye as ours, though."

"True, but it seems more prevalent in our country because of the technology we have now," Amelia replied. "And that technology broadcasts all of the nitty-gritty details of our culture to the rest of the world, which attracts waves of Muslims to our shores. It's already begun to happen. Even if your statistics here in the CTU show little change in the rate of terrorism, it still seems like it's more prevalent because of the sensationalism of the media." She looked back at the young man on the screen. "Were there any prophecies regarding the End Times?"

"Actually, most of the prophecies the Advent Rite voted to keep hidden concerned the End Times. There's one about the succession of U.S. Presidents leading to the end of the U.S. Constitution and soon after, the U.S.A." He paused and met her gaze through the monitor.

She nodded. "Go on."

"Well, Ellen White prophesized that there would be a succession of four Presidents, or kings as she called them, leading up to the End Times. The first two kings would begin the fall of our culture into debauchery and immorality, while the third king would open the door to Muslim immigration and oversee the meltdown of morality within the intelligence communities as well as the nation at large. There would be a massive increase in corruption, Satan worship, and body mutilations as well during the third king's reign. The third king would even become known as the first U.S. President to openly try and sabotage the next incoming President by engineering political landmines with the intention of destroying all hope for a successful transition."

Amelia made a note to see what Mr. Summers might know about these leaders. She needed to know if when the Advent Rite believed these leaders would come into office they were going to have any hope of putting a stop to the church's political meddling.

"The fourth king, or President," Mr. Lombardi continued, "she predicted would become a one-man global power and would be far richer than all of the others before him. He'd have the wealthiest advisors as well and would bring distress and concerns to all the nations of the world. She was surprisingly detailed. She predicted his election would come as a surprise as he would not be expected to win the race for the White House because there would be powerful forces trying to stop his ascension. These efforts would be unsuccessful and would result in our nation becoming divided." He looked up from his reading. "Uh, I'm not sure if this will be helpful to you, but the scribe mentions that Ellen White associated this king with the number eight. After his election, his number would become 88, though I haven't figured out the significance of those numbers yet."

"That's fine," Amelia said. "If I've learned anything over my 20-plus years as an agent, it's that you can't overlook even the smallest detail. You just never know what information may prove useful in solving a case. Did he say anything else about Ellen White's prediction of this fourth king?"

"He talks about the decline of our culture during this king's presidency. That women, living in sin, would stand shoulder to shoulder with those who abhor women living in sin as traditional societal boundaries are broken down. She claims martial law would be declared after years of mocking, protesting, and terror attacks that start even before the inauguration of this final king. This will not only bring about the end of the U.S. Constitution, but will also initiate what she called the Sunday Laws, which would make it a crime for anyone other than Jews to worship on Saturday. Our country would be divided into four sections, and at this point, the fourth king, or President, would become known as The World Emperor and his number would then be 888." He paused, his face scrunching up in a look of concern.

"What's the matter?" Jenkins asked.

Mr. Lombardi looked at him suddenly as though startled. "Oh, there was a bit in here that didn't make sense before, but now that I've read it again, I think I know when the Advent Rite believes this last king will be elected."

Amelia rose from her chair and took a step toward the monitor. "When?"

"2016," he replied. "They call it the Sesquicentennial Prophecy, and it's what every new initiate is taught. The prophecy talks about how 150 years after the 1866 appearance of Temple's Comet and the November meteor showers, which they describe as when the *stars fell off the skies*, the last President of the United States of America would be elected. And in that election, there would be signs of a second more powerful leader reminiscent of Napoleon Bonaparte rising to power. It predicts a second civil war and the end of the U.S. Constitution."

"So, we just have to make sure no one inherently evil gets nominated," Holt said.

"Well, not necessarily. Ellen White predicted that the fourth king would start out with good intentions, more so than every other president before him. The problem is that the third king would leave political booby traps meant to disrupt the rule of the fourth king from the moment he's sworn into office. It's the fourth king's discovery of these traps and the growing turmoil during his first few years in office that leads him to declare martial law."

Amelia made more notes before returning her attention to the screen. "Any other prophecies?"

"There was one that concerned the whole of the earth as opposed to just our country. It talked about the existence of a second sun in our solar system."

"You mean Nemesis," Amelia said.

"Yes. I'd never heard of it before finding the journal, so I had to do some research on it. It was only recently that astronomers found evidence of Nemesis, as it only crosses paths with Earth's orbit once every 26 million years. Astronomers are more concerned about the planet they believe orbits around both our sun, Sol, and Nemesis, which they call Nibiru. Some experts believe that Nibiru's last trip past Earth caused the extinction of the dinosaurs. It's supposed to be nine times the size of Earth and believed to be responsible for some of the most catastrophic events in our planet's history. On its way around the sun, it goes through the Oort Cloud, a ring of meteors much larger than the asteroid belt and sends the meteors in its path hurling toward Earth. It's the impact of these meteors that caused the sudden climate changes in our past, such as the extinction of the dinosaurs and the beginning of the last ice age. And then there's the gravitational mass of Nibiru, which is believed to be strong enough to have caused massive flooding at least twice in recorded history, one such time believed to be recorded in the story of Noah and the ark in the Old Testament. When Nibiru passes Earth next time, it's expected to cause the water level around the world to rise over 300 feet. It has a 3,600-year orbit, but astronomers believe it's headed our way right now. That particular prophecy also states that the pope will bring this threat to the world's attention and try to alert everyone to coming dangers." He looked up from his notebook again, his gazed fixed on Jenkins, but before he could say anything else, Jenkins held up a hand.

"Yes, the new pope's been elected. Ordained to the papacy the middle of last month as Pope Francis."

"What's his birth name?" Mr. Lombardi asked.

"Jorge Mario Bergoglio, born in Buenos Aires. He's the first Jesuit Pope."

Mr. Lombardi was quiet for a long time.

Jenkins leaned back and whispered, "His boss was Pope Benedict."

"What exactly was his job?" Amelia asked.

Jenkins smiled. "Well, related to your investigation, but it's probably best to leave the details for another time. It was Pope Benedict who requested he infiltrate the SDA Church, which led to him finding that journal." Jenkins looked back up at the young man on the screen. "You all right there, Aldo?"

Mr. Lombardi's head jerked as though he'd been startled again. "Oh, yeah. Sorry. Uh, then do I report to Pope Francis now?"

"Don't worry about that for now. I've been keeping the Holy See informed during your absence."

"I see."

Another stretch of silence filled the small office until Holt cleared his throat. "Sorry, chief, but time's not really on our side right now. Did you have any other questions, Amelia?"

Trying to not be bothered by this man's casual use of her given name, she ignored him and returned her attention to Mr. Lombardi. "Would it be possible for you to scan your transcription of the journal and email it to me?"

Color tinted the young man's cheeks. "Uh, my notes are encrypted, so…"

Jenkins burst out laughing. "Lucky thing too, it turns out. Kept the Comradeship of the Three Woes from discovering just how much you learned."

Sobering, Jenkins looked up at the monitor. "I'll have Benny set you up with a secure laptop. Mind re-transcribing your notes into English for us?"

Aldo smiled. "No problem."

"I really appreciate it," Amelia said. She mused that the prophecies detailed in the journal would be more beneficial in anticipating the SDA Church's future moves as opposed to offering the evidence she needed to arrest key figures. Still, as Judge Jason used to tell her, even the smallest detail could crack a case.

Paul Holt watched Amelia gather her belongings and shake Jenkins' hand before quietly leaving. He'd never met such a cool-headed woman before, one who didn't let her emotions get in the way of her judgment. She was much taller than he'd expected, too. He smiled at the memory of her excitement when Lombardi told her about the four kings' prophecy. He admired her passion for her work and was frustrated he could not convince her to join the CTU.

Jenkins interrupted Holt's thoughts. "I need you to get in touch with the US Embassy in Argentina. Aldo's going to need a new passport and other identification since the Fifth Reich confiscated the originals."

"Got it," Holt replied, jotting down a reminder on a sticky and adding it to the collection stuck to his computer monitor. "Any word from Tony yet?"

Jenkins pulled his cell phone from his pocket and checked the display. "Still nothing, but satellite images show two vehicles made it to the rendezvous point. The convoy is still moving north and should have reached the point of interception by now. My team of analysts is keeping a close eye on the images as they come in from surveillance, so if anything looks amiss, Benny's team has orders to head that way immediately."

Holt nodded. "I sure will be glad when this is over. We could all use a day off."

"Yeah, I promised Cindy I'd take her out." He gave Holt a look. "You should come, too."

Holt smiled. "Only if Hailey's my date." He wasn't comfortable around little kids, never having had any of his own, but Jenkins' eight-year-old daughter had a mysterious charm that made it impossible not to spoil her.

"That can probably be arranged," Jenkins smiled.

•••

Tony slowed as the convoy neared the interception point. He had finally caught up with the last truck about twenty minutes earlier, keeping as close to its bumper as possible without being suspicious. Their RFV unit would only be able to take out four of the five trucks, and that was a best-case scenario. Maynard's team would have to take out any vehicles not affected by the RFV at the front of the convoy while he and Davis handled the caboose.

Just as they rounded the last curve in the road, their engine died, cutting off the power steering and brakes. Tony wrestled with the steering wheel, keeping it on the road as the sedan coasted to a stop. Before it even stopped moving, Davis jumped out and slid along the driver's side of the cargo truck in front of them. Tony stepped out, keeping his gun trained on the back of the truck. Slipping his thermal imaging goggles over his head, he confirmed there were no heat signatures in the back of the truck. Of the three images in the cab, two sat motionless while the other moved away from the truck further up the road.

Tony ran past the truck, joining Davis as he approached the second truck. Peering around the front of the truck, he signaled Davis to stay low. As if on cue, Tony saw a heat signature leave the driver's side of the second truck while the other crouched below the dashboard. *Damn. They've already realized something's going on.* Tony signaled to Davis again and he nodded, flattening onto his belly and crawling between the truck's rear tires as the driver rounded the side. Tony took out the driver as Davis emerged from beneath the truck and shot the guard through the open window.

As they moved toward the third truck, Tony heard a whistle. Two heat signatures were running toward them.

"It's Jones and Buster," Davis confirmed through is night vision scope.

Removing his thermal imaging goggles, Tony stood to greet his team. "Did you already take out the other three trucks?"

Buster shook his head. "Only two. The lead car and one of the trucks were out of range. Maynard was hoping they'd stop to investigate why the rest of the convoy had stalled, but they didn't. They actually gunned it the moment the other trucks stalled, almost as if they knew what was going on."

"How?" Tony asked.

"Not sure. Maynard's team's in pursuit now, but the lead car and truck had a decent head start since Maynard had to park the Jeep far enough off the road that it wouldn't be seen."

"Shit," Tony bit out, kicking at the gravel beneath his feet. Taking a deep breath, he said, "Send Maynard a message to keep on them like flies on shit. We'll provide back-up if necessary."

Buster nodded.

"Davis, you and Jones round up the convoy's men. I need a casualty count. Secure anyone still breathing and give any necessary first aid so they'll stay alive until we get back to base. I'll suit up and inspect the cargo. Don't come near the back of the trucks without a hazmat suit on. We still have no idea what kind of super virus we're dealing with."

Chapter Thirteen | The AGENT

Washington, D.C.
May 2013

Sitting on the bed in her hotel room, Amelia Larson dialed the number for Allison Gillespie. While the two had never spoken before, Amelia had been in contact with Allison's boss, Robert Benson, numerous times, whenever she needed to get in touch with Mr. Summers regarding her team's ongoing investigation. And every time he responded with vague answers. He didn't seem to be hiding anything. Amelia suspected it was simply due to ignorance, which in turn made her question what information she could safely reveal to him. The fewer people who knew about the true nature of her investigation the more freely her team could act.

Hoping to circumvent Benson this time, Amelia asked Jenkins for Allison's number. Jenkins assured her that Allison would be able to help.

After two rings, a bright voice answered. "Hello?"

"Would this be Ms. Allison Gillespie?" Amelia asked.

"Yes. May I ask who's calling?"

"My name's Amelia Larson. A historian friend of mine recommended you as the best person to interview regarding the history of the LDS Church." It was always awkward speaking in code, but she couldn't trust that the young woman's phone hadn't been bugged. "I was hoping to set up an interview with you sometime soon, preferably in person."

"Certainly," the young woman replied without missing a beat. "Unfortunately, I won't be able to get away for the next few weeks, but if you're able to come to my office I should be able to squeeze you in."

Amelia couldn't help but smile. She already liked the young woman. "Wonderful. I can be there tomorrow. I'll call you once I arrive."

"Sounds good. I look forward to it."

Amelia disconnected the call and opened her laptop to book a red-eye to Los Angeles. Planning to sleep on the flight, she spent the rest of the afternoon reviewing the notes she'd taken during the video call with Mr. Lombardi. He had already messaged her to let her know he'd have the transcription of his notebook downloaded onto the NSA's database on the Dark Internet by the end of the day. That, along with the information she hoped to glean from Mr. Summers, if she was allowed to meet with him, should provide all the evidence she needed.

•••

"And he hasn't shown up at the university either?" Jenkins asked, impatiently tapping his finger on his desk. Frustration gnawed at his ulcer and he popped two antacids into his mouth. How could a professor of medicine be so damn hard to find? Although Jenkins had to admit that if he had a warrant out for his arrest, he'd want to be hard to find, too.

"No," Lawrence said from the other end of the line. "Jackson's been watching the professor's office at the university while I've been keeping eyes on the Knight estate and the professor's house. If Applebee's managed to make it back to Loma Linda, he's being smart about it."

Jenkins rubbed his temple. "What about leads on any other possible hideouts?"

"Not yet. The university staff were surprisingly tight-lipped considering Jackson presented them with the warrant for Applebee's arrest. He said they didn't even seem shocked to learn he'd been involved in a kidnapping."

"So, he has sympathizers there, huh?" Little surprise, considering the NSA's estimate on just how far the Fifth Reich's influence reached. While they had yet to find any Fifth Reich camps in other countries outside Argentina, membership extended from South America to North America and across the Atlantic to Europe.

"It would seem so. Based on the information Jackson gathered posing as a student at the university, the professor seemed well liked. Many of his students expressed concern for him since the university had chalked his absence up to health issues."

Great. Jenkins shook his head. *It's always the fakes who gave my teams the most trouble.* They conned people into believing they were harmless and innocent, and then his subordinates became the bad guys when the time came to arrest them. Witnesses become uncooperative and evasive, sometimes even outright aggressive, when believing someone has been wrongly accused. "Might have to just wait him out then." If they could make Aldo's kidnapping public, Applebee might lose some of his support, but they didn't have that option at the moment.

After hanging up with Lawrence, Jenkins called Benny. "How's the patient doing?"

"Still asking to call the States. I thought you said Allison would contact his parents."

"I did." *It's not his parents he wants to call.* "Set him up on a secure line and limit it to no more than five minutes. That's all I can give him for now. Holt's working on getting him into protective services, so once that's set up and he gets a new passport from the embassy, he should be cleared to go home. Still might take some time though, so don't get his hopes up."

"Will do," Benny replied. "I assigned Chester and Reeves to surveillance on the remaining Fifth Reich camps so I could stay and keep an eye on Aldo and Dogmeat. We won't be able to take any of the camps out until Tony and Maynard's teams get back anyway."

"What's their status?"

"Tony finally reported in about twenty minutes ago. Convoy's been stopped and they're bringing the trucks back to base, but the lead car and one of the trucks managed to escape. Maynard's team pursued, but by the time they caught up, both vehicles had been abandoned. The truck was empty, so we assume they transferred the CBWs to another vehicle."

"And now they know we're onto them," Jenkins muttered. "So they'll likely change the location for the hand-off." Assuming the buyer wanted to follow through with the purchase. With eighty percent of their product now in the NSA's hands, the mafia wouldn't be able to complete their end of the deal. And if Agent Larson's theory was correct and the SDA Church really did want to instigate a third party into starting Armageddon, they no longer had the weapons necessary to do it. Unless the bio-labs had already made more.

Jenkins popped another antacid into his mouth. "Order an analysis of the CBWs the moment the trucks arrive." They needed to know what they were dealing with. If the mafia decided to go through with the transaction, they probably wouldn't bother creating new strains.

"What should we do with the rest of the CBWs once we get a sample?" Benny asked.

"I'll have to contact the embassy for that. We don't have the proper facilities to dispose of them, and if we can't find a location that can, we may have to transport the entire lot back to the States."

•••

"I only get five minutes," Aldo said over the secure line. Silence greeted him, followed by muffled breaths. "Allison?" Panic surged through him. Was someone hurting her? But Benny said they'd called her secure line at the LDS agency.

"I'm here," she said, her voice sounding choked.

Is she crying? Even as his panic abated, his desire to hold her and comfort her grew. What had she been through while he wasn't around? "Is everything all right?"

Her laughter broke on a sob. "I should be asking you that, silly. Is Benny treating you okay?"

Aldo chuckled. "Haven't eaten better meals since the cafés in Rome. He really should consider opening his own restaurant some day." He took a deep breath, preparing for the plunge. "Would you—"

"Yes," she interrupted. "But only if it's a real date this time."

Damn, I love her. "You got it. Just name it and I'm there."

•••

Amelia glanced around at the white marble walls and floor of the LDS agency's foyer, half-expecting to see men and women dressed all in white. While the building wasn't an LDS temple, it had a similar feel of quiet reverence. She'd only been allowed into a temple once during her twenty-year investigation, and even then, it had only been as far as the lobby. Only Mormon men and women who'd participated in a special ceremony to have their endowments taken out were allowed beyond that point. As with most rituals within the LDS Church, the exact details of the ceremonies were shrouded in mystery.

The ring of high heels echoing off the stone broke the silence, and Amelia looked up to see a tall blond woman walking briskly toward her. The young woman extended her hand before coming to a halt in front of her. "Agent Larson?"

"Amelia," she replied, shaking the woman's hand. "Thank you for agreeing to see me. I also apologize for the misleading phone call."

Allison chuckled. "Totally fine. Did you come up with that off the cuff?"

Amelia smiled. "Well, when you've worked for the FBI as long as I have you pick up a few things."

"I'll bet. I—" Allison broke off at the sound of a door opening down the hall. Quickly glancing down at her watch, she slipped her arm through Amelia's. "Let me show you to my office." Pulling her along, Ms. Gillespie led her down another hallway and a flight of stairs to the basement. Only when the door to the small office was closed behind them did she release Amelia's arm. "Sorry about that. Brother Benson doesn't know you're here, and I would've had to lie if he saw you."

"Well, technically not telling him to begin with is a kind of lie, but I appreciate your discretion."

Allison smiled. "You're a by-the-book person, huh? You remind me of Aldo." She gestured to the pair of armchairs sandwiching a small round table at the end of the room. With a desk and office chair occupying the other end, the furniture felt too big for the space and Amelia wondered if the armchairs had been brought in just for this meeting.

"Mr. Lombardi, you mean?" Amelia took a seat and set her laptop bag on the small table between them. "He's the reason I requested a meeting with you. I've dealt with your boss in the past, but… Let's just say it proved unproductive. I was actually hoping to speak with Mr. Summers, but I've been warned that won't be possible for the time being."

Allison shook her head. "I'm afraid not. Even I've been ordered to limit all communications for a while. Brother Benson is concerned that with Applebee still at large, the Comradeship of the Three Woes will try harder than ever to find any leads to Mr. Summers' whereabouts."

"I see." Amelia opened her laptop and retrieved her case file from the bag. Since confirming the facts she'd gathered with Mr. Summers wouldn't be possible, she'd have to settle for verifying the information with Allison. But first, she needed to see what the young woman knew. Giving out information could jeopardize all of the hard work her team had put into the investigation. "How much do you know about the US versus Summers trial, Ms. Gillespie?"

"Please, call me Allison." When Amelia nodded, she tilted her head in thought. "Well, not as much as you do, I'm sure, but having been his liaison for the last six years, I probably know more than most of the people in my agency."

Hopeful, Amelia smiled. "As part of your contract agreement with the NSA, I ask that what I'm about to tell you not leave this room." When Allison nodded, Amelia said, "My team is preparing to arrest a few key figures within the Seventh-day Adventist Church, but in order to do so, I need to confirm some details with you."

"I can't give you any information that might put Mr. Summers in jeopardy, but outside of that, however I can help. Personally, I can't wait to see those jerks finally get what's coming to them."

"Don't get too excited just yet," Amelia said. "It may still take some time. Arresting elite members of any religious organization requires the same planning and preparation as would the arrest of a foreign dignitary. Because many religions have branches in other countries, those countries' governments often become involved. Religions also often settle matters outside of court, as with Roger Frogburger's case. Even with criminal allegations, Frogburger was only removed from the office of president of the World Church and ordered to pay a fine. That's why we've spent the last twenty years gathering evidence, to make sure the leaders of the SDA Church aren't able to buy their way out this time."

"I understand. What is it you need to confirm?"

"Part of the arrest warrant will be for obstruction of justice. I need to confirm that those involved in Mr. Summers' trial were indeed manipulated by the president of the SDA Church. Thanks to his Stuttering Brief, we've known from the get-go that something had been going on behind the scenes, but we're still not sure what connected each of the people involved."

Allison stood up and walked around her desk. Unlocking one of the lower drawers, she pulled out a file and handed it to Amelia. "After receiving your call yesterday, I had a feeling you'd want to see this. Mr. Summers put together a list of the 40 Mormons who were involved in his trial and the events that led up to it. He also detailed how each of those 40 men and women are related to him."

"What?" Amelia flipped open the file and quickly scanned the list of names. The list provided each person's title and occupation at the time of the trial, their actions taken during the trial, and how they were related to Mr. Summers.

"I don't have any proof," Allison continued, "but Mr. Summers believes these 40 Mormons were intentionally selected to participate in his trial. The SDA

Church used and manipulated them to walk Mr. Summers through the court system."

"Why Mormons specifically?" Amelia knew the LDS Church had been involved with Mr. Summers' safety after his incarceration, but this was the first time she'd been able to link each of these people through a commonality—their religion.

"Mr. Summers had joined the LDS Church prior to his indictment. He feels the choice of using Mormons in his trial, specifically ones related to him, was an attempt to hurt him mentally and spiritually. It also discredited him to his new brothers and sisters, forcing him into isolation even after his release from prison."

"Yes, they were quite thorough in their character assassination. With their money and influence, the SDA Church managed to indict, convict, and incarcerate Mr. Summers in a matter of three years, yet it's taken my team nearly 20 to gather enough evidence to bring them to justice. Even with the testimonies of James Blanc, among others."

"Who's that?" Allison asked.

"He was a medical doctor with the SDA Church. After Frogburger was removed from office, he and a few others cameforward and submitted testimonies that they hadlied, made false allegations, and stolen or destroyed evidence in order to support Frogburger's prophecy that Mr. Summers would end up in prison. Through their confessions, we were able to expose others who played a role in falsifying Mr. Summers' indictment." Amelia shook her head. "One physician ended up being arrested for sexual assault on minors. Another for grand theft, elder abuse by embezzlement, and destruction of evidence." A horrified look spread across Allison's face, and Amelia reached over to touch Allison's hand. "It's unfortunate that not even religious organizations are exempt from such crimes."

Flipping through the printouts that Allison had given her, Amelia noticed a name that had come up repeatedly over the course of her investigation: Marcus Tuttle. She had her suspicions the retired Mormon politician had played a direct role in helping the SDA Church walk Mr. Summers through the court system, thereby acting as an accomplice to their obstruction of justice, but she had yet to find solid evidence. She assumed Tuttle had been compensated, but without probable cause, getting his financial records proved a challenge. But now with Mr. Summers' statement, she could finally get a warrant to request the financial records.

Amelia's frustration grew as she read further. She had tried for years to interview Mr. Summers directly to get his statement. During his trial, the prosecution was given over three weeks to make their case, while the defense was allowed merely nine hours. The defendant wasn't even allowed to testify. The only statement Mr. Summers was allowed to submit was the Stuttering Brief which he submitted of his own accord prior to the start of the trial. Since then, Mr. Summers' Mormon watch dogs made it impossible for her to interview him. Amelia looked up at Allison. "Do you think there might be another reason the SDA Church specifically chose to use the Mormon Church to fulfill Frogburger's prophecy?"

"What do you mean?"

How could Amelia say what she was about to without offending Allison? "I've been in contact with your boss, Mr. Benson, multiple times over the years, and while he's done an excellent job of keeping Mr. Summers safe, I have the impression he doesn't fully understand why he's even guarding Mr. Summers."

Allison sighed. "Yes. Mr. Summers mentioned the same thing. There is a kind of *do as you're told and don't ask questions* mentality within the LDS Church."

"Do you think this could be another reason so many Mormons were involved in Mr. Summers' trial?" Amelia flipped back through the list. "Some of the names listed are people not directly involved with his indictment or conviction. Why would they make sure he was sentenced to a prison with a Mormon warden or given a Mormon prison guard if their goal had already been achieved? Perhaps they chose the Mormon Church because they knew its members were loyal and bound by ritual to follow the wills and commands of their priesthood."

"It's possible," Allison said.

"But then that begs the question: Why would the Mormon Church be acting as his guards?"

"It might have to do with his genealogy." Allison flipped through the printouts in front of Amelia and pointed to a graph. "Mr. Summers was able to trace his ancestors all the way back to a son of Mary and Joseph of Nazareth, Christ's half-brother. Lineage is extremely important to our church, so when the church caught wind of what was going on, they felt the need to protect Mr. Summers and his family because of his ancestry." Allison's expression turned puzzled. "But I still don't understand why they wouldn't have just stopped the whole thing if they knew the truth."

"Well, if you think about it, it kind of makes sense. I doubt the SDA Church would have just let everything go if it came to light that the allegations against Mr. Summers were false. I understand them to be fiercely protective of their public image, so there's no way they wouldn't have done everything possible to ensure Frogburger's prophecy came true and keep their image clean at the same time. If the leaders of the Mormon church made any accusations, it could have been seen as slander. So, all they could really do was lessen Mr. Summers' sentence and keep him safe after his time had been served. By making him a ward of the state, the Mormon church made sure the SDA Church could no longer be involved in his life."

"You said they lessened his sentence, but isn't the sentence he was given typical for the type of crime he'd been accused of?"

Amelia shook her head. "No. A typical sentence for falsifying accounting records is up to 30 years, with the option of early parole depending on the severity of the crime. I think the SDA Church had originally planned for Mr. Summers to be locked away for that long, but when it began to look like things weren't going their way, they executed other plans. If they couldn't silence him by imprisonment, they decided to assassinate his character, so that even after he'd been released from prison, they wouldn't have to worry about anyone believing what he said." Amelia uncrossed her legs and leaned forward, resting her elbows on the small table. "Honestly, the whole trial was a mess. I wouldn't be surprised if Mr. Summers opens a fraud against the court case once the threat on his safety is removed."

"How was it a mess?" Allison asked.

"Well, it became pretty obvious once the trial actually started that the prosecution was grasping at straws and using underhanded methods to ensure they won. The jury selection alone was a sham. For larger trials like his, they gather around 500 people from which to select the jurors. The defense maintains the right to disqualify up to six people from the venire, but they ended up having to use three of those to disqualify the wives of three separate prosecutors, all of whom had been appointed by the presiding judge."

"That sounds like more than just a coincidence," Allison said.

Amelia nodded. "They also used distraction methods by planting people among the potential jurors to cause disruptions and confusion. The defense team also told Mr. Summers' close associates that their testimonies would be a vital part of Mr. Summers' defense. They spent hours preparing to be cross-examined only to be threatened with indictment by the prosecution if they testified. After starting my investigation, I learned that Mr. Summers had also been threatened—by his own attorney—if he chose to testify."

"With how one-sided everything played out, did Mr. Summers ever file an appeal?"

"Of course, while he was in prison. But the Ninth Circuit Court of Appeals wrote that they couldn't give a ruling on Mr. Summers' defense during the trial because they couldn't find any credible information offered by his attorney. Mr. Summers' court-appointed attorney had based his defense case around the paternity of the bookkeeper's twins."

Allison quirked an eyebrow at her. "What do twins have to do with Mr. Summers' trial, other than it was the bookkeeper who falsified the accounting records which led to Mr. Summers' indictment?"

"The attorney was trying to bring to light the material perjury of the bookkeeper and a dentist during the cross-examinations. If he could prove that the dentist was the father of the bookkeeper's twins, it would prove they had both lied under oath. Since the Appeals Court felt Mr. Summers' attorney had not presented an appropriate defense, they denied his appeal. The judge who presided over his trial did grant Mr. Summers a rare writ of *habeas corpus* while he was in prison, but since it was granted so close to his release date, Mr. Summers didn't pursue it." Amelia leaned back against the chair. "Mr. Summers may have lost his case and been overruled in his appeals, but with the information my team's uncovered, he shouldn't have any problem winning a fraud against the court case should he choose to pursue it. Once we make our arrests, I'll be able to provide you with all of the information that's currently under seal."

Allison nodded. "I'm sure he'd appreciate that. I think it'll make him happy just knowing someone out there cares enough to uncover the truth."

"Well, part of the reason I took this case was because I can't abide injustice. There's so much of it in our world already that it shouldn't be allowed in our justice system. Mr. Summers and his family were backed into a corner and hurt, and not just during the trial, but I would imagine every day since. Yet, none of the truly guilty people involved behind the scenes have been made to suffer. Frogburger may have claimed his prophecy came true, but there was no divine power at work. He used money to manipulate people, something that's all too common in our society. But given enough time, the truth usually comes out."

•••

Aldo never felt so nervous in his life. Benny and Tony both assured him there was nothing to worry about but riding in the front of a truck loaded with biological weapons wasn't exactly a common occurrence for him. Jenkins had arranged for the bio-weapons Tony's team had seized from the convoy to be destroyed at the US Embassy in Buenos Aires. Since Aldo needed to get new travel documents, they allowed him to tag along. Now he wished he had declined their offer. Hitchhiking might actually have been safer.

At least he wasn't driving. Being under that kind of pressure would crush him. But Benny kept his speed slow, taking every precaution not to disturb their dangerous cargo as he followed the other three trucks out of the mountains and down into the city. Aldo held his breath over each bump and pothole even though he knew the mild turbulence couldn't rupture the canisters.

When they finally arrived at the embassy, they drove the trucks around the back of the building to a sunken loading area. As the truck rolled to a stop, Aldo unfastened his seatbelt and was about to open his door when Benny grabbed his arm.

"Not yet. Tony has to clear us first."

"What do you mean?"

Letting Aldo go, Benny returned his hand to the steering wheel. "Even though the embassy is expecting us, we still have to be cautious. The chances of anyone knowing what's actually in these trucks is low but we still can't run the risk of even one canister falling into the wrong hands."

"Right." All the more reason to dispose of them quickly. "What about the truck that got away?"

"Don't worry. We'll track it down. And we have the evidence we need to get the Argentine government to shut down the mafia's bio-labs for good."

Aldo only nodded. Somehow he didn't share Benny's optimism. He wanted to, but he couldn't help feeling the SDA Church would find another way to achieve its goal. They were known to go to great lengths to fulfill even the smallest prophecy, and Aldo doubted this would stop them.

One by one, the NSA's men backed the trucks into a loading bay. The driver of each truck stayed behind the wheel while his partner got out to supervise the unloading and disposal of each canister. Finally it was their turn. When Benny nodded, Aldo climbed out and walked around to the end of the truck where Tony stood, his arms folded over his chest. Workers in hazmat suits opened the truck's rolling door and carefully passed the canisters one by one out of the truck.

Should we be wearing those? Aldo wondered as he observed the methodical process.

"Nervous?" Tony asked.

Aldo nodded.

"It's fine. The embassy brought in scientists specifically for this." Tony turned to look out beyond the loading bay. "I'm more concerned about you. You won't be assigned a permanent guard until you return to the States, so one of our guys will be with you from the moment you leave the embassy until you arrive at the NSA's headquarters in DC."

"Who?" Aldo asked. Since the explosion of Applebee's lab, he hadn't had any other run-ins with Dogmeat, but the idea of spending a twelve-hour flight with him was not appealing.

"Douglas," Tony said. "He's under suspension anyway, so he has to go back to DC since Jenkins isn't able to come here. So, two birds one stone. You know how it is."

Seriously? He was beginning to feel like his ordeal would never be over.

"He's not too bad once you get to know him," Tony continued. "Just make sure you don't feed him after midnight."

"Ha, Ha. Very funny," Aldo said.

Chuckling, Tony smacked his shoulder. "Come on. Let's go get your new passport before Allison has my head."

Aldo followed Tony up a back staircase to the ground floor of the embassy building. Bypassing the front reception area where armed guards performed body searches and people formed lines, Tony led him down a hallway lined with small offices. The men stopped at the door of *Stephanie Lopez, Embassy Clerk.* Tony knocked once and opened the door.

An older woman sat behind a desk piled high with file folders. She glanced at them over the top of her glasses as they stepped inside the small room and closed the door behind them.

"We're here for Mr. Aldo Lombardi's new identification documents," Tony said.

The woman stared at them for a long moment then stood and rounded the desk. "So, the surgery was a success, was it?"

"What?"

"Oh, apparently Applebee presented documents stating you had suffered a traumatic spinal injury to get you through customs at the airport," Tony answered. "He claimed he was bringing you down here to try an experimental new surgery. After we found out, Jenkins had Gladys submit your full medical records to the embassy."

"I see."

"It's created quite the headache, let me tell you," Ms. Lopez said. "Trying to convince the Argentine government to tighten their customs protocols has been no picnic." She retrieved a large envelope from her desk. "Would've helped if I could've used Mr. Lombardi as an example."

"Sorry," Tony replied. "The fewer people who know he was even here, the better."

"Which is why Jenkins asked for me directly, right?" She sighed and handed Tony the envelope. "Tell him he owes me one."

Tony smiled. "Will do."

•••

Allison paced back and forth, only stopping to check the reader board again. Aldo's flight from DC landed ten minutes ago, so where was he? *It's fine* . Allison tried to reassure herself knowing Jenkins had assigned him a permanent bodyguard while he was in DC sorting out everything that had happened. Allison wasn't sure how she felt about a bodyguard encroaching on her time with Aldo now that she finally got to see him, but she had to admit it was better than the alternative.

The buzzer for the baggage carousel beside her sounded and she jumped. A voice overhead announced the flight number and slowly bags began appearing on the circular conveyor belt. She glanced around at the gathering crowd for Aldo.

"Looking for me?"

She whipped around to find Aldo standing behind her. Hesitating only long enough to ensure with her own eyes he was all in one piece, she launched herself into his arms. "How dare you keep a lady waiting."

"Sorry," he breathed into her ear. His body felt tense and she worried she'd hurt him but a second later, he wrapped his arms around her. "I missed you, too." Too soon, he released her then looked down at her face. "Decide where you want me to take you yet?"

She smiled. "Of course. But I have somewhere I want to take you first." She glanced at the tall man standing beside a pillar silently watching them. "I suppose your guard dog will have to come, too."

She took his hand, not releasing it until they got to her car. Aldo's bodyguard, Kaito, loaded their luggage into the trunk as she climbed behind the steering wheel.

"You sure you don't want me to drive?" Aldo asked.

"Do you even know how to drive in LA?"

"Can't be much different than driving in Rome."

She gave him a skeptical look.

"What?"

"You never drove in Rome. You always took the Metro." She shifted into gear. "You're not afraid of my driving, are you?"

He forced a smile. "Of course not."

She laughed. "Well, get used to it." She drove away from the airport toward her agency's headquarters. Aldo filled her in on everything that had happened while he was being held at the Knight estate and then in Argentina. Her hands clenched the steering wheel every time he mentioned Applebee's name. Knowing the evil man was still at large and most likely targeting Aldo turned her stomach.

"Thanks for keeping in touch with my mom."

She shook her head. "I just hope she doesn't hate me when she finds out I've been pretending to be you this whole time."

"I think she'll understand. I'm going to have to tell her and Dad all about it someday."

"Wait until after we get married. It'll be harder for her to get rid of me."
Silence filled the car, weakening her confidence, and she glanced over at Aldo. He
stared at her. Returning her attention to the road, she caught a glimpse of Kaito
in the rearview mirror, smirking from the backseat. "What?" she asked.

"Uh, nothing," Aldo replied.

The silence continued all the way to her agency's headquarters. As Aldo
climbed out of the passenger's seat, Kaito leaned forward and whispered, "Am I
invited to the wedding?"

"If it doesn't take the groom another six years to give me an answer."

Kaito chuckled and followed them into the building.

Allison led the way down to her office. "Would you mind waiting here,
Kaito?" Allison asked, gesturing to the white concrete corridor outside her office.
"I'm just going to borrow Mr. Lombardi for a moment so we can make a phone
call." Kaito nodded, standing at attention against the wall as she closed the office
door behind them.

"Who are we calling?" Aldo asked.

"Mr. Summers." She opened her laptop and dialed into the secure line. As the
call connected, she gently maneuvered Aldo into her chair, resting her hand on
his shoulder. A moment later, Mr. Summers' face appeared on the screen. "Hello,
Mr. Summers. This is—"

"Aldo! So good to see you, my boy. We were all so worried about you."

When Aldo continued to silently stare at the screen, she squeezed his
shoulder. "Uh, hello. Good to finally meet you face to face, sir."

"Jenkins told me about the journal you found at Andrew Knight's estate,"
Allison explained, "and gave us access to the transcription file you uploaded for
Agent Larson. After reading it, Mr. Summers wanted to talk to you in person, but
we can't risk it with Applebee still on the loose."

"I see."

Allison frowned. She thought he'd be more excited to finally meet Mr.
Summers. "You okay?"

"Huh?" He glanced up at her, his cheeks blushing. "Oh, yeah. Sorry. I was just
surprised."

"Aldo, I can't thank you enough for bringing this information out into the
open. With your help, the members of the SDA Church will finally know the
truth."

"Is this regarding that premonition you had?" Allison asked.

"Yes. The SDA Church has hidden or changed so many of their doctrines over the years, while their members have been ignorant to the type of church Ellen White had intended from the start. And the leaders of the church are continuing to make changes even now." Mr. Summers looked from her to Aldo. "They plan to change their teachings about the Sabbath."

"What do you mean?" Aldo asked.

"Over the next sixteen years, they will slowly convince their members that the Sabbath is for Jews and not non-Jews. I plan to put together a video explaining how they will be going about doing this and what explanations they might give, but I'll need your help getting the video out to viewers."

"Why a video?" Allison asked.

"More likely to reach a wider audience," Aldo replied.

Mr. Summers nodded. "Yes, I want to document my predictions so that when they come to pass, there will be no question of their truth."

"Certainly," Allison said. "Whatever we can do to help."

Mr. Summers nodded again. "Now, what can I do to help you?"

"What—" Allison began before she noticed Mr. Summers' gaze was locked on Aldo.

Aldo's right knee bounced, a sure sign he was nervous about something. "When I was with Applebee in Argentina, I overheard him say that he needed to see if the drug he'd injected me with a month prior had taken effect yet."

What? Why hadn't he told her something so important? Seeing the look on Mr. Summers' face, Allison bit back the urge to demand answers.

"I never learned what drug he used and there was nothing written about it in the notes I stole when I retrieved my notebook. The lab was destroyed before we could search it for clues, too. And the typical battery of tests Jenkins had his associates run haven't come up with anything. So, I was hoping you might have some thoughts."

The silence drew out until Mr. Summers slowly shook his head. "No, I'm afraid not. It could be the newest version of Transpose or something completely unrelated. Knowing the Comradeship of the Three Woes' desire to make life extension possible, I would assume it's some type of anti-aging drug. Have you had any symptoms so far?"

"No, but I'm not sure if they might have been masked by the sedatives."

"Very possible. Sedatives slow down the body's processes, so it could take more time for symptoms to appear. If Jenkins will allow it, I think it'd be a good idea to pay a visit to my nurse, Alexandra Simpson."

"Your nurse?"

"Yes, she's been monitoring my health for over 20 years now."

"Wouldn't a doctor handle that?" Aldo asked.

"Well, I would see my doctor as symptoms arose, but Mrs. Simpson's in charge of monitoring my daily health and informing my doctor of any notable changes. She's well aware of my particular situation and has kept meticulous records. I think she would have a better idea of what we're looking for than a doctor would."

"Where can we find her?" Allison asked. When Aldo looked up at her, she said, "You didn't forget we're in this together now, did you?"

"I thought you were joking."

"Man, Aldo. A woman asks you to marry her and you think she's joking?"

"But we've never even gone on a date before."

"You're worried about details this late in the game? Besides, I already have our first date arranged. We're going on a trip."

"Where?" Aldo asked.

"Colorado." She watched his eyes grow wide and chuckled. "I think it's about time I met your parents in person, don't you think?"

Mr. Summers chuckled. "Sounds like you've got your hands full, Aldo. I'll send you Mrs. Simpson's contact information. Good luck and congratulations." A moment later, the screen went dark.

Allison reached around Aldo to disconnect the call from her end then turned his chair and knelt down in front of him. "We're in this together, right?" she asked softly.

He stared down at her for a moment then leaned forward to cup her face with his hand. "Definitely."

To Be Continued

About the Author

Samuel David Steiner was raised as a Seventh-day Adventist but left the church when he could no longer support its teachings. In 1983, Adventist leaders initiated a vindictive campaign to punish Steiner—someone they had been grooming for leadership—for leaving the church. In 1989, he adopted the Jewish surname of his mother's ancestors as a way to make a formal break from the Seventh-day Adventist Church. He embraced his Jewish roots and found a home in the ancient faith.

Bipolar Winter is a fictionalized account of his story.

CPSIA information can be obtained
at www.ICGtesting.com
Printed in the USA
BVHW071516200122
626624BV00007B/1404